"*Light Bread,* a first novel by Cordell Adams, weaves a lovely story around the tumultuous 1960s in his creation of Veola Cook--a brave, Black earth mother of wisdom, warmth and wit. But Veola has the strength of goodness and godliness to offer love and comfort to those in need, regardless of the danger she faces, regardless of the unrest in America...and regardless of the color of the many who depend on her."
--Billie Letts, author of Where the Heart Is (an Oprah Book Club selection), and MADE IN THE USA

"We all know her. That go-to person for all our troubles. And in his debut novel, *Light Bread*, Cordell Adams gives readers that person in the form of Veola Cook, who just about everyone in Parkerville, Texas, comes to count on when they need a little homespun wisdom and propping up. Adams has created a warm, caring, colorful and insightful character who will be a delight for readers. A woman with the wisdom to avoid trouble and the insight to handle it, if it rears its ugly head."
--Robert Greer, author of seven novels in the CJ Floyd mystery series (the latest two, The Mongoose Deception and Blackbird, Farewell), two medical thrillers, and a short story collection.

"Cordell Adams' wonderful debut novel, *Light Bread,* took me back to my youth in East Texas. He describes the times, the people and their circumstances with stunning accuracy. Ms. Veola is a true character and I found myself cheering for her through her tribulations to the satisfying ending."
–Evelyn Palfrey, author of The Price of Passion

"A good book happens when a good story is told or when a story is told well. Cordell Adams' *Light Bread* does both. I went back to my own childhood and opened the door to characters who were coming in anyway. The breath and wisdom of *Light Bread* leaves you wanting more."
--Bertice Berry, author of Redemption Song, When Love Calls, You Better Answer, and The Ties that Bind, A Memoir of Race Memory and Redemption

"Engaging and engrossing...filled with heartfelt characters and achingly realistic portrayals of a time passed but not forgotten. Miss Veola, Miss Loretta, and Fayetta Dewberry reminded me of women that I have known, loved, and celebrated. *Light Bread* will make you laugh out loud and praise your ancestors. Hallelujah."
--Gabrielle Pina, author of Bliss, Chasing Sophea, and Children of Grace

Light
Bread

PUBLISHED BY SWEET TATER PIE PUBLISHING

This story is a work of fiction. The characters, places, and incidents are a product of the author's imagination.

Copyright © 2007
Sweet Tater Pie Publishing,
3600 Gaston Ave, LB 64,
Dallas, TX 75246

Library of Congress Card Catalog Number: 2008904097

ISBN: 978-0-9816805-0-7

PRINTED AND BOUND IN THE UNITED STATES OF AMERICA
FIRST EDITION: 2008

Light Bread

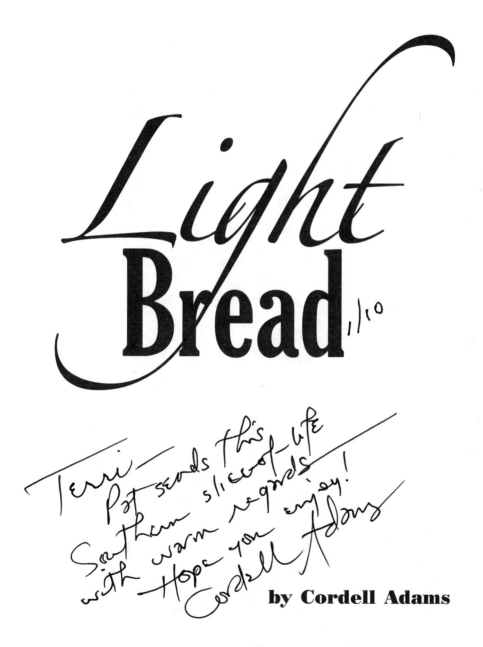

Terri —
Pat sends this
Southern slice-of-life
with warm regards!
Hope you enjoy!
Cordell Adams

by Cordell Adams

IV

For Leola Cox

LIGHT BREAD

Cordell Adams with the inspiration
behind this novel, his grandmother, Leola Cox.

(photo dated c. 1965-1966)

ACKNOWLEDGMENTS

For this project, my debts are substantial, and I must pass out these light-bread sandwiches of appreciation.

Thanks to my sister Claudette and brother Rickey for making sure I treated the spirit of our beloved grandmother, Leola Cox, with tenderness.

To Uncle Sang, my only surviving maternal uncle, for showing me support as I fictionalized the mother he so desperately loved.

To my first cousins for not expecting this to be their story, but for knowing I just wanted to share our "Mama" with others.

To nephews, nieces, and the rest of my family, knowing they will continue to love our ancestors who continue to watch over us from above.

To my writing consultant and coach, Pamela Renner, who labored over this manuscript so lovingly, I'd attempt to describe my gratitude in words, but then she'd have to edit them, and she's worked too hard already.

To Galen Hays, Pam's husband, for understanding all the early and late phone calls and for feeding me throughout all the writing sessions.

To Emma Rodgers for her guidance and introduction to those I needed to know in the writing business.

To the entire Letts family, especially the matriarch Billie who inspired and guided me.

To my book club, Michael Allison, Mike Anglin, Mike Birrer, Dean Carter, Bill Kolb, Red Starks, and Kay Wilkinson for their helpful suggestions and pushes from behind.

To Parker Shade for his architectural expertise with the map legend.

To my readers Xenobia Brown, Graham Cauthorn, Floyd

Cotham, Yolanda Crear, Kim Fennell, Carol Fletcher, George Harris, Lois Lilly, Tim and Robin Newberg, Dr. Nancy Parks, Constance Riles, Ken Row, Bernestine Singley, Gene Schulle, and Nona Walker who constantly propelled me to have this dream completed.

To Elaine Hightower for all the prints and reprints.

To my office personnel, Lori Salazar and Danny Chavez, for taking control of my schedule, and to my patients for making sure I know my purpose in life.

To Baylor Surgicare and its affiliates for unending trust.

To my first-grade classmates who are still in my life and the class of 1979 for votes of confidence after all these years.

To Opal Jones, one of my grandmother's dearest, for keeping our parents' home a welcomed place.

To godparents OM and OD (other mother and daddy, Dr. Mary Bone and J. Robert Adamson) for continuous guidance away from home.

To Ron and Matrice Kirk, extended family, who can't get rid of me.

To North Bolton Street Christian Church, Brentwood Baptist Church, and St. Luke "Community" United Methodist Church for making sure I knew and continue to know WHOSE I am.

To my neighborhood and lifelong friends in Jacksonville, Tyler, Dallas, Houston, DC, Atlanta, Los Angeles, Long Beach, New Orleans, and NYC.....for just being in my life.

To Gene Danser for his patience in knowing that my countless hours in front of the computer did not go in vain.

And finally, to my mother and father, Claude and Cordelia, my angels who guide me from on high. Oh, how I love and miss you.

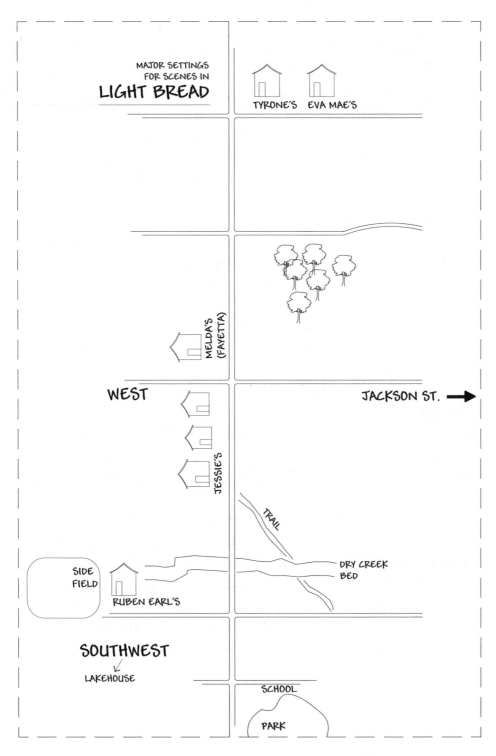

MAJOR SETTINGS
FOR SCENES IN
LIGHT BREAD

TYRONE'S   EVA MAE'S

MELDA'S
(FAYETTA)

WEST

JACKSON ST. ➡

JESSIE'S

TRAIL

DRY CREEK
BED

SIDE
FIELD

RUBEN EARL'S

SOUTHWEST

LAKEHOUSE

SCHOOL

PARK

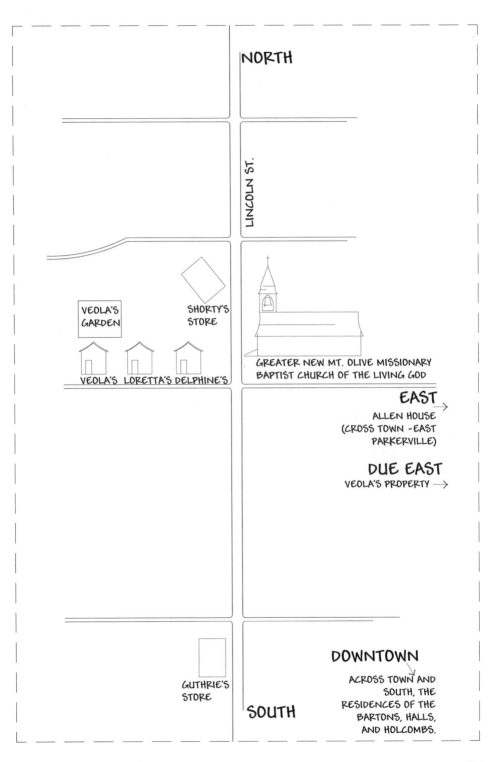

NORTH

LINCOLN ST.

VEOLA'S GARDEN

SHORTY'S STORE

VEOLA'S   LORETTA'S   DELPHINE'S

GREATER NEW MT. OLIVE MISSIONARY BAPTIST CHURCH OF THE LIVING GOD

EAST
ALLEN HOUSE
(CROSS TOWN - EAST PARKERVILLE)

DUE EAST
VEOLA'S PROPERTY →

GUTHRIE'S STORE

SOUTH

DOWNTOWN
ACROSS TOWN AND SOUTH, THE RESIDENCES OF THE BARTONS, HALLS, AND HOLCOMBS.

Chapter One

Veola Cook kept her basics on her nightstand— her cat-eyed bifocals, a framed picture of her three children, another of her seven grandchildren, a sharpened pencil (her favorite writing instrument), a nineteen-cent Bic as back up, and on top of the electric radio lay her worn-out Bible. She seldom turned on the lamp since she preferred reading under the light attached with iron prongs to her wooden bed frame. Her wind-up alarm clock got little use. She often awakened naturally before dawn, but this Easter Sunday she was startled awake by a tapping noise coming from the front of her house. She opened an eye; the other remained buried in her pillow. The tap, tap, tap remained soft, rapid.

Next, she heard: Bam! Clank-a-lank! Whop!

The knock sounded as if it were right outside her bedroom window, but the clank-a-lank, like a pan hitting the kitchen floor, seemingly originated out front. Now, she had to investigate.

Rolling over, she noticed a beam of light shining from the next room, her dining area. By stretching to the corner of the bed, she realized the light came from her neighbor Loretta's window.

The day was to be filled with the Holy Spirit, but she wondered whether or not the devil had anything to do with the disruption.

What in the world was going on at Loretta Mayfield's?

Veola became concerned for her friend, so she retrieved her eyeglasses and caught sight of the hour—4:31 a.m. Good God A'mighty, it truly was early, even for her.

She whirled herself into a sitting position, slid into her pink slippers, and donned the matching housecoat from the foot of her heavily covered bed.

Tip-toeing through the dark dining room, she peeked through the blind facing Loretta's lighted house. She saw nothing unusual—no human shadows or broken glass. Next, she moved quietly to the living room windows, but all appeared normal. She had no intention of opening the front or back doors, even though her doors were locked. If someone was out there, the invitation to come in need not be extended.

That tap, tap, tap? Was she asleep when she heard it? Was she dreaming?

On her way back to bed, Veola thought she heard a loud rattling toward the back of her house. She turned off the reading lamp then made her way to the kitchen window and peeked through the blind.

Nothing caught her attention, so she squinted to sharpen her vision. She saw three dogs pacing back and forth, but not barking, tied to their chains in their backyards.

She was certain that tapping noise had begun at Loretta's house. Sitting on the edge of her bed, she dialed her neighbor. "Loretta, did I wake you?"

"Naw."

Veola heard huffing and puffing through the receiver. "Well, your light was on, and—"

"I can have my own light on in my own house any time I want to, can't I?" Loretta shouted.

"Why sho' you can, but I heard this noise. Sounded like it came from your—"

"Won't you," Loretta paused between each word, "get out of my business?"

"Baby, I was just concerned about you," Veola said calmly. Never had anyone twenty years her junior talked to her this way and gotten away with it.

"Don't waste your time 'cause I'm fine. I can take care of

myself. Now, I gots to go."

"I'm sorry I disturbed—"

"What if I was asleep?"

"Like I said, I heard something."

"You 'bout the nosiest woman I know. Seem like every time something happened to folk, you are all up in their damn business. You just can't stay out of folks' lives, can you? I'm through talking to you."

"I'm gon' keep the day holy, Loretta, since it is the Lord's day."

At the mention of the word Lord, Loretta hung up.

"Well, ain't that something, you ungrateful little—" Veola slammed her receiver. Here she was being neighborly by checking on Loretta, and the woman had cussed her out. In twenty years living beside Loretta, she had never been so mean and disrespectful. Why just last week, Veola lent her a cup of flour. Now she wanted it back.

Irritated and hurt, she wanted to go next door, grab Loretta by her nappy hair, and drag her until she got some sense, but that wouldn't be very Christian-like. So she redirected her thoughts. She had a list of chores to complete and stewing over Loretta's rudeness was unproductive.

"Hallelujah, Lord, hallelujah, hallelujah," she cried out, lifting her hands in the air with balled fists, expressing her gratitude to her Maker as she did each morning.

"Thank you, Lord, for your glorious day. I don't know where I would be without you—especially right now." Usually, her morning message of thanks was stated in a soft, composed, and reflective tone of voice, but today she shouted. She knew Jesus was listening, and that's all that mattered.

She grabbed her Bible from the nightstand. As a black woman Southern born and Southern bred in 1905 in a tiny community called Beaver Flat, in rural East Texas outside of Tyler, her Bible had been her mainstay throughout her most perilous and most triumphant of times.

The outside disturbances still concerned her. Clutching the good book, she stepped over to the bedroom window again.

She flipped to one of her favorite passages and read out loud Joshua 1:9. "Have I not commandeth thee? Be strong and of good courage; be not afraid, neither be thou dismayed: for the Lord thy God is with thee whithersoever thou goest." She placed her Bible back on the radio.

Past the trees and the dogs between her house and her nearest neighbor opposite Loretta, the rumbling seemed to come from somewhere close to the street. What was it? People talking. Yeah, that's it. Were they moving something? Not able to tell, her eyes squinted as if that would improve her hearing. Abruptly, the talking stopped. The clock read 4:45 a.m. Lord, she had no time to waste. Whoever it was appeared to be gone now.

But for reassurance, she called Cuddin' Jessie since the people she'd heard talking seemed near Jessie's house. "You up?"

"Yeah, I'm up, but I ain't moved much," answered her cousin.

"Girl, did you hear something this morning?"

"Yeah, I was trying to see what it was, but I didn't see nothing."

"At first I thought I heard something coming from Loretta's. Her light was on way 'fo I had planned to even move, and that's a whole 'nother matter we'll talk about later. But then, I heard something coming from your way, over near Melda's house. Chile, I don't know where it was."

"I ain't gon' lie and say it woke me up, 'cause I was already stirring," Jessie said.

"What was it?"

"I don't know. I didn't see nothing from my windows."

"Me neither, but it shole sounded like people talking. Then it sounded like a car door slamming."

"Yeah, and once I started looking for it, I didn't hear it no more. Probably dogs turning over trash cans. We got too much to do to worry about that now."

"You're right. We must get rid of fear and anxiety from our minds. I'm gon' let that alone, so I'll see you later."

"See you in a bit."

Veola had a lot to do before sunrise service at six o'clock, and this did not include preparing breakfast. Breakfast was going to be at church this morning; it was the assigned job for the men folk. Veola hoped that Deacon Ruben Earl Mosley would wash his hands before he scrambled eggs or buttered toast.

She headed to the kitchen, passing the dozen eggs she'd dyed the day before for the Easter egg hunt. They had to be packed in her box along with her fresh sweet potato pie and chocolate cake. She had retrieved an old cardboard box with handles from the corner store, Shawty's (the sign read Shorty's), located caddy-cornered across the street from the church.

Now, she had two dishes to make—her well-known fresh green beans with new potatoes and some hot-water cornbread. She'd resigned herself to buying her fresh snap beans and potatoes, as her garden had yet to be planted. The night before she'd snapped the beans and measured out the dry ingredients for the cornbread. In fifteen minutes, her front two burners glowed under these Southern delicacies.

Veola had forgotten to ask Jessie what she was making for dinner. Her mind was centered on those noises.

Eva Mae Walker, a dear friend for forty years, always brought the same potato salad, but the ingredients weren't quite right. According to Veola, "Eva Mae must have got too much salt in her blood" because her potato salad never had enough of it. The lack of salt and too little mayonnaise was definitely the problem. "Something was sho nuff missing," Veola muttered to herself.

She tried to bring it up to Eva Mae one time, but feared hurting her feelings. Her children should have told her, but Veola guessed they didn't know any better. Veola was just picky about what she did and didn't eat from Eva Mae's kitchen.

While the food simmered, she now had to think about herself. Her attire for the day required one last inspection, so she headed toward her guest bedroom.

Traipsing through the dining room, instinctively, she glanced out the windows, but all was quiet. She threw her hands on top of her head and felt her headrag. Despite her tossing and turning during the night, it remained in place. Headrags were made out of old, worn-out nylon stockings or a silk scarf. Both had their share of holes from uncontrolled hairpins and were never meant for the public eye. On the off chance it might become loose, she had placed a little extra Vaseline on her scalp the night before just to give her graying hair the added smoothness she claimed from her American Indian heritage.

Lord, she took time with her looks, for she was proud of her appearance and rightfully so. That's how she'd grabbed her husband in the first place.

"You da prettiest thing I ever seen," said the man who had swept her off her feet at age sixteen. She'd worn her best cotton dress to the creek gathering that Sunday after church which made him take notice. That man, Ervin Cook, became her husband that same year. "Some folks say I married you for your looks, Veola," she remembered him saying. "I told them they only halfway right. I told them I married you 'cause of the way you looks *and* cooks."

Veola smiled at the memory, yet on that day, she had laughed out loud along with Ervin. Even before they married, she remembered the first time she grabbed him and almost squeezed him to death. They were walking in the wooded area of the land his family had when he took out his pocketknife and carved their names in a tree.

"Nobody ever put my name in a tree before," she told him.

"Well, it's already written in my heart, so I might as well put it somewhere for the squirrels and the birds to see, too."

Even with the wonderful memories of her husband doting over her, times were not always as wonderful as these recollections. Her husband had died almost forty years ago from consumption shortly after the birth of their third child. She had raised her kids with some help from his family initially, yet when the age spread of her children spanned between six and ten years old, she felt confident to go out on her own. Veola's determination to make a life for her and her three children made her stronger than ever. She had done it without depending on anyone, and the only keepsake of his she kept to this day was his pocketknife. Whenever she wanted to re-live that vivid moment of her past, she'd pull that old, rusty knife out of her jewelry box.

She thanked Ervin for her three wonderful children. Her oldest, Carneda, and her family lived across town. She taught English at the black high school, Booker T. Washington, on the north side of town. The older son was in the army, stationed in Germany; the younger one was an airplane mechanic on a naval ship in the Mediterranean. She was proud of both of them and she paused, thanking God that the older one had survived his assignment in Vietnam.

Veola caught herself daydreaming, and now at almost sixty-one years of age, she was still concerned about looking just perfect—this time, though, not for Ervin.

Sunday, the social outing for the week, was the day for black women to show themselves off—to look their very best. But Easter Sunday was special, second in importance only to Mother's Day.

As a woman of color, church was not only her refuge, but also a place where she sought her direction, asked for guidance, renewed her strength, and affirmed her faith. Black folks knew what church was for, and this March 26, 1967, Easter Sunday morning was no exception.

The new pastel print dress of yellow and green linen had been ironed the night before and laid out on the high bed with her matching purse, gloves and feathered hat nearby. Ironing was a sin on Sunday in Veola Cook's house or any other house she had to be in on the Sabbath. She had no problem telling all of her children and grandchildren or anybody else about how this was the Lord's day.

Her white patent leather square-toed heels sat on the floor. These would raise her about three inches from her mere four-feet, eleven-inch frame, giving her added confidence. They were a far cry from her usual white uniform flats. If she had to wear white to work during the week, what would make her want to wear white on the weekend? Nothing but Easter. She had even bought her some new stockings the day before at Luke & Lane's, the closest five and dime store within walking distance to her house.

She had caught Carneda, her only daughter, using words like hosiery, pantyhose, and even nylons, but to Veola they would always be stockings.

She got out her white flats just in case her low heels hurt her feet. She would find room for them in the bag she would carry, which would hold her plastic rain scarf and umbrella. East Texas weather was unpredictable, and she hoped the children's egg hunt wouldn't get rained out.

The words of the song, "woke up this morning with my mind stayed on Jesus," ran through her mind as she scurried about. Veola wanted to sing those words to Loretta right about now.

What's yo mind on this morning, Miss Loretta Mayfield? On Jesus or something else?

Once she got to the kitchen, she glanced under the old Melmac plate covering the hot-water cornbread. That old plate had functioned as her skillet cover for as long as she could remember, and when she wanted to, she flipped the plate over and used it to sample her fixings. The green beans and potatoes still simmered, seasoned with plenty of chopped onions, black pepper, and other carefully selected spices. Veola's stomach grumbled. Instinctively, she reached into the bread compartment of the metal three-tiered canister on the countertop and after undoing the wire twist, retrieved a thin-sliced piece of light bread (white bread to northerners). The brand was always the same: Sunbeam.

From her icebox Veola pulled out a tomato and the mayonnaise from one of the door compartments. She cut two slices and slapped a little mayonnaise on the bread. Finally, she folded the single slice of bread into a half-sandwich for her pre-breakfast treat. If Veola was out of mayonnaise, tomatoes, and fresh light bread, then in her opinion, she was out of groceries.

As she left the kitchen, the phone rang.

"You 'bout done?" Jessie asked.

"I was on my way to the bathroom. My beans is just about ready, Girl."

"Well, I was thinking," Jessie shot back, "that I'd just bring what I have to take to da churchhouse over to yo house so when Carneda come down to get yo food after church, she could pick up both our boxes. Then I wouldn't have to come back home."

"I'm sure that'll be fine, but is you gon' try to walk over here with that box this morning?"

"Yeah. It ain't heavy. It's only barbecue chicken and a buttermilk pie. See you in a minute," Jessie answered.

"All right then. Call me when you're leaving so I can make sure you get here in one piece."

"I'm gon' keep my eyes open myself when I head yo way."

"You do that. We both be looking." She snuck one more look through her bedroom blinds. Still nothing.

As Veola fixed her face, she thought how full of folk the churchhouse would be this morning. She and Jessie, ten years her senior, were head ushers. Seating all these folk would keep them busy.

Most of the regular membership attended sunrise service, Sunday school, and morning worship. Many visitors came along with the so-called "CME" members of her Christian faith, not to be confused

8

with the C.M.E. denomination. This "CME" stood for the days that folk would crawl out of the woodwork to go to church—Christmas, Mother's Day, and Easter. To each his own, but Veola Cook had attended every Sunday since she was a tiny girl.

After more primping, Veola stood back from her dresser mirror and eyed herself from head to toe. Lord, I look cute today, she thought, and hoped her church folk knew it, too. On a schedule, she was off to the kitchen to finish packing her box.

Jessie Davis lived one block west and a half a block south of Veola. Veola tried to watch out for her in case the box was too heavy for an old woman. Jessie would question her in a minute if she knew Veola's thoughts. "Who you calling old?" Jessie would say.

When Veola opened the storm door as Jessie approached, her heart raced. One of her clay pots had been shattered, and a pile of trash had been dumped all over her front porch. Veola didn't know what to think.

"Who done that?" Jessie asked.

"Chile, I don't know. But I've got to clean up this mess 'fo I go. I can't leave my front porch with all this trash on it."

She swept the pile into the garbage can she had retrieved, and Jessie held it in place, so none of it would fall into her flowerbed.

Lugging the can on her way to the back of her house, she got another shock. The bushes around back, the ones close to her bedroom window, had been trampled on, like someone had run through them.

Reaching her back porch, she noticed a closed paper sack full of cigarette butts. She put the sack inside the trash can and secured the lid. She would investigate later.

Veola and Jessie descended the front steps together, and as soon as they got into the street, a car in the distance shone its headlights right at them. They turned in the direction of the car, and immediately, the lights went out. Veola and Jessie frowned at one another for it didn't appear to have a driver. No shadows.

"Shhh," Veola ordered.

"Why?" Jessie whispered.

"See if we can hear something."

Jessie obeyed.

"I don't hear nothing," Veola said, within seconds.

"Me neither."

"Let's get to the churchhouse."

"We wasting time out here listenin' for Lord knows what."
They nodded at one another.

The dogs barked and Veola and Jessie could see them moving about, held close by their chains. They must have been a part of some of the ruckus, for near them were overturned trash cans.

The church was about fifty yards east of Veola's house, on the opposite side of the street. Those arriving on foot were unprotected by a stop sign or stoplight and had to watch for occasional speed racers going and coming down North Lincoln Street.

As Veola crossed the intersection, she knew she had to take her mind off what she had just seen and turn it over to God. Besides, He was the focus of this holy day. Because of Him, a big day of excitement was planned at Greater New Mount Olive Missionary Baptist Church of the Living God, and as difficult as it was, she willed her heart to be in the right place. She knew she wasn't crazy, for she was right. The noises, that trash, and her trampled bushes were proof.

Chapter Two

After Tyrone Walker and Jeremy Barton conducted their business, Tyrone asked Jeremy for a ride to his friend's, Fayetta's house, not wanting to take his own car. As they pulled to a stop, they spotted two old ladies walking toward the church or dressed for it anyway on this Easter Sunday. Jeremy and Tyrone ducked down, hoping they wouldn't be seen.

When the coast was clear, Tyrone exited immediately. Jeremy sped off using the back way in the opposite direction of the church.

When Tyrone heard Fayetta was in town, he had to see the woman he had cared about for so many years. Surprising a woman at this hour was a gamble, but because she was special, he was certain she'd understand. The purpose for his early visit was to catch her before she busied herself with Easter plans. Something told him she might leave town without seeing him, and he couldn't let that happen.

He knocked a couple of times before she answered the door.

"I need to see you," Tyrone said, smiling as he requested a bit of her time.

"Right now?" Fayetta frowned.

"I heard you were here, and I wanted to see you 'fo you got away."

"Why you have to come over here waking everyone up this early in the morning?" Fayetta whispered loudly.

"'Cause I didn't know if you was gon' leave and head back today or what." Tyrone stared at the ground and fidgeted with nail clippers in his pants pocket.

"And wake everybody up at this hour?"

"You don't understand."

"Understand what?"

"That I still care 'bout you."

"That was a lifetime ago, and you know it."

"No, I don't know it. It ain't never stopped for me."

"After all these years, it should have. Being stuck in the past is your problem." Fayetta rolled her eyes.

"No, it's not just mine. It's a problem for everybody. Leonard. Me. You."

"We have been through this, Tyrone, but you won't let go." She turned, then backed away, but he grabbed both of her shoulders and swung her to face him.

Tyrone maintained his grip, making sure he wasn't hurting her. Right now, he had to take control, yet he didn't want to scare her. "Why you want to shut me out?" he asked.

She jerked away and freed herself. "I am not going to talk to you about this right now. You don't get it, and you never have."

"I don't believe you. I think you have feelings for me."

"What are you talking about?"

"Why you love Leonard so? He ain't got no job, no car, and I damn shole look better than him."

"This is not about you."

He softened his tone of voice. "But I care about you, always will. What I feel ain't never gon' go away, and I don't want it to."

"Coming over here disrupting the whole neighborhood don't impress me one bit. You've got to get over this," Fayetta warned, and hurried into the house, catching the screen door before it slammed.

Tyrone realized he had forgotten to ask how long she would be here, and maybe he had made a mistake by being too honest. He always seemed to say the wrong thing to her. His heart was on the line, and he didn't know any other way to approach it. He walked home.

❦❦

Positive her neighbors were watching from their windows, Fayetta wondered who had seen the ridiculous encounter. She hoped they would not get to meddling into the situation, and how she wished she could excuse herself from it. But, she couldn't. She'd come to Parkerville for a purpose, unwilling to let anyone stop her.

Tyrone was living in the past, but she had moved on. She knew Tyrone had feelings for her then, but he should have gotten over her by now.

Emotionally, she was a wreck. She made a cup of instant coffee and went around to her mother's back porch. She sat, trying to put some semblance of order to her life. Her day was not supposed to start this way, and the fact that it was Easter made it that much more difficult.

❦❦

On the other side of town, Veola's six year-old grandson, Cameron Allen, had used two alarms this Sunday morning. His mother, Carneda, stepped into his doorway to tell him to get up, but he was already awake from the peal of the church bell at First Presbyterian Church at 9:00 sharp. Cameron assumed it was a white folks' church since he didn't know any black churches in downtown Parkerville, which was located across the railroad track and southwest of his family's neighborhood of KIBI Hill.

KIBI was the local radio station, and he lived right near the tower. The residential community surrounding the tower was likewise elevated on this hill, thus the peal of the infamous church bell carried into Cameron's bedroom.

Anticipating this Easter Sunday, he had recited his Easter speech to his older brother, Kenny, one more time before he'd gone to bed the night before. Cameron rattled off Psalm 121 for the umpteenth time to Kenny, his fifteen-year old elder sibling, who appeared bored. Cameron cared less about Kenny's boredom for he thought that was part of the job of being an older brother.

It was going to be a long day—Sunday school, worship service followed by dinner, the Easter program, and the Easter egg hunt. Easter Sunday meant a new suit, new shoes, new shirt and tie, a fresh haircut, the works.

Cameron beat Kenny to the breakfast table, and they quickly ate the bacon, scrambled eggs, and jellied toast. Their mother spared them sunrise service at 6:00 this morning since the Easter program would require them to be awake and alert, not somewhere on the back row stretched out while the other children were reciting their speeches. They needed their time of preparation, and sleep was definitely a requirement for their best performances.

The breakfast was hurried so they could jet off to Sunday school, and even waking up at 9:00 would be pushing it to get there by 9:45. Their father, Charles, was absent at breakfast. Carneda, affectionately called 'Dear' by her children, told the boys that their father had eaten earlier then gone back to bed.

"He's coming to the eleven o'clock service." Carneda reassured the boys that he would be there to see them perform. The Easter eggs were packed, and the banana pudding and mustard greens were secured in her carrying basket.

After the boys had inhaled their breakfast, and Cameron had polished off his chocolate Nestle's Quik, Carneda came down the hall in her newly made Easter dress. Both boys stood slack-jawed as if they had just seen Jesus get up out of the grave. Carneda shared Veola's high cheekbones and skin as smooth as a rose petal. She had found a light-green chiffon fabric to capture her spirit, and the floral shawl and matching shoes were exquisite accessories. Quite a seamstress and designer, she'd made her dress and shawl, and her finished products were usually stunning. Knowing fashion was part of her background in home economics, so finding material to match shoes, hats, gloves, and all the other accessories was not considered a challenge but a necessity.

Her light caramel complexion was even more so highlighted on this picture of pastel perfection. She hoped Charles would notice later when he got his behind out of bed and to morning worship service on time.

Charles worked out of town during the week, so sleeping in his own bed on weekends was a luxury. She let him sleep this Sunday morning as long as he could, but come eleven o'clock, she expected him to be at church.

Carneda spread cocoa butter lotion onto the boys' hands. They weren't ashy, but now the grooming was finished.

"Okay, boys. Let's go." She then walked to the end of the hall and called toward her and Charles' bedroom, "Charles, we're gone. See you there."

Charles' snoring drowned her out, but she had done her best to be heard.

Kenny carried all the food to the trunk of the car, a sparkling baby blue 1966 four-door Buick Skylark. He had cleaned it inside and out the day before in preparation for a chance to drive it around the block. Carneda occasionally gave in to his begging and pleading and let him drive to the Piggly Wiggly grocery store that was down the hill on the other side of the railroad tracks. This Sunday morning, she drove and Kenny rode shotgun.

At 9:40 they were off to Greater New Mount Olive Missionary Baptist Church of the Living God. Mama would be there, waiting.

Tyrone checked to see if his mother, Eva Mae, was spying out of her window when he heard Leonard knock at the front door. "Did you know Fayetta's down at her mama's house?" he asked, watching Leonard barge in.

"How you know?"

"'Cause I know, that's how. What do you think she's here for?"

"Hell, it's Easter. A lot of people come home at Easter—see they family, visit folk." Leonard patted his empty pocket. "Give me one of your cigarettes. I done run out."

Tyrone obliged, used to Leonard mooching smokes. Tyrone squinted. "When was the last time you talked to her?"

"This week."

"This week?" Tyrone froze.

"Yeah, she called and said she was coming in town early to see her people. I didn't know she'd be here for the weekend."

"Well, hell. She got to be here for something."

"Probably is."

"Why you didn't tell me she was coming?" Tyrone's interest piqued, and he studied the floor.

"What the hell you got to know that for?"

"Shit, I'm just asking. Why you all uptight just 'cause I asked about Fayetta?"

Leonard stared at him.

Tyrone realized he had too many things to do today other than to get into it with Leonard, besides, he knew him well enough to know he'd clam up. "Look, man, I got to go take care of some business. I'll holler at you." Tyrone stood up.

"All right. Later."

Leonard left, on foot, not having a car to his name, and Tyrone thought that whatever Leonard had come for was quickly forgotten.

୭ᘜᔎ

Sunday school at Greater New Mount Olive Missionary Baptist Church of the Living God was supposed to start at 9:45 a.m. But most black folks' churches start when they start, and they end when the preacher gets hungry.

Kenny and Cameron entered the main sanctuary from the back of the church after dropping off their mother's food box in the dining hall. They avoided Mrs. Eva Mae trying to steal some "sugar" from them. Once they rounded the corner by the choir stand, they were in full view of their grandmother. The love in Veola's smile after catching sight of her grandchildren was infectious. With everyone dressed to the tee, and they knew it, too, they bee-lined for her embrace.

"Hey, Mama," shouted the boys. Carneda's children knew Veola as "Mama" because they called their mother "Dear." Not MaDear or Mother, just Dear. Since Veola had the title of "Mama" from her own children, including Carneda, then Carneda's bunch joined her in referring to Veola simply as "Mama." Big Mama, Nana, and even MaDear were left to anyone else who wanted those labels. The choice of these terms of endearment was common in black families.

16

"Hey, babies. Y'all look so nice. You're so dressed up." She inspected them simultaneously: their ties, their sparkling white shirts, their coats and pants, their shoes, and finally their faces.

"What's that on you?" Veola asked Cameron. "Come here. Let me get that off." With one quick lick of her finger, she rubbed Cameron's cheek. Whether it was dry skin or a piece of lint, it disappeared.

"You look good, Mama," Kenny said, and Cameron nodded. The hugs and kisses were cut short for the time had come to end socializing and be in the pews.

Veola took her place at the head of the table as secretary of the Sunday school. Her note-taking came later.

Once the congregation sang "Jesus Keep Me Near the Cross," and Deacon Ruben Earl Mosley prayed, the people separated into their individual areas, grouped according to age.

Sunday school was more interesting since there were more people than usual. Once everyone congregated back in the main sanctuary after their individual classes, they gave their reports. The official headcount, according to Veola's tally was sixty-three; last Sunday's count was thirty-two. As Veola looked over the attendees, she noticed the abundance of new hats and patent leather shoes. Loretta Mayfield was nowhere to be found.

The pianist chose "He Arose" for closing, and after Reverend Johnson gave the benediction, everyone immediately began to anticipate who else would arrive for the 11:00 worship. Who was coming? What would they be wearing? Who was in from out of town?

Veola asked Carneda to drive over and get the boxes of food since they had a little time in between services. Veola rode with Carneda to have the opportunity to tell her daughter about her morning surprise. "You're dressed up today, and you look good in that color." She complimented Carneda on her exquisite outfit purposefully before she eased into her news. "Oh, I just wanted to tell you when I opened my door this morning, someone had dumped their trash on my front porch."

"What?" Carneda glanced at her. Her expression showed deep concern.

"I opened the door watching for Jessie, and it was all over the front porch. My clay pot was in pieces." Veola knew her compliment to Carneda was long gone.

"Did you hear anything?"

"Yeah, I heard some noises, but I didn't open the front door yet. I looked outside a few times, but I didn't see anything."

"I'm worried about you."

"Why?"

"'Cause this is serious. You don't know if someone was trying to get to you. It's too dangerous for you to be here by yourself."

"I've been here all these years, and I'm not going to get all up in arms over some garbage."

"Mama, someone was on your front porch in the middle of the night, so you can't tell me that I wouldn't see that as dangerous."

"I'm not saying I'm not concerned, but I'll deal with that later." She wanted to stop the conversation now; it was ruining Easter.

Veola decided not to mention the trampled bushes. That would send Carneda into a hissy fit since she had had this kind of reaction just to the trash. Besides, the hour for morning worship was close, and she didn't want to get her riled up before the Easter program.

"You know we're going to talk about this later," Carneda warned.

"I know." Veola wished she'd kept her mouth shut.

Carneda waited in the driver's seat of the car as Veola locked her front door. An unfamiliar face glanced up as she exited her porch. The lady was dressed for church, and she walked in the direction of Greater New Mount Olive.

"Good morning," she greeted Veola.

"Good morning, Sister." Though Veola didn't know her, calling her "sister" further personalized her greeting. In the car, Carneda glanced over, and the women exchanged nods.

Veola was nosey when she wanted to be, but she didn't ponder over the woman's identity or destination long. Sooner or later, if the stranger lived nearby, she'd see her again.

"Mama, who was that? Does she live around here?"

"I don't know her, Carneda."

They drove around to the back of the church and unloaded the boxes, but Veola saw no sign of the stranger.

Morning worship had its share of Easter rituals, including the songs. "He Lives" was the choir's processional number, and Kenny stood on the back row, next to his friends. The boys replaced their suit coats with choir robes, but they would re-appear in their chic ensembles afterward.

Cameron sat close to the back of the church with his buddies. His daddy arrived and sat next to Carneda down front. Veola guarded the side Cameron was sitting on as she ushered, keeping an eye on him in case his little bunch acted up. She knew they were eager for the Easter program to be over so they could get to the Easter egg hunt.

At that second, the stranger caught Veola's eye. She realized the woman was the lady she had spoken to earlier. The lady sat on the pew in front of the first graders. She knew the woman was dressed for church when she saw her earlier, but now upon close examination, her outfit was nothing short of plain. Usually on Easter, folks dressed up for bringing Jesus back to life. But this woman's attire seemed peculiar: no special hat, no new shoes. Veola stepped forward, astonished to see the woman wasn't even carrying a purse, much less a new one!

She knew the sisters would find time to pull each other back in a corner of the dining hall and attempt to figure out who this woman was, where she lived, what she was doing at Greater New Mount Olive. The sisters thrived on gathering that kind of information.

After everyone had been blessed or scorned by the pastor's sermon, they stood and sang the recessional hymn, "God Be With You 'Til We Meet Again." With the final amen, the parishioners scattered.

Out of nowhere, Veola called, "Cameron, now don't you be running around and getting dirty while we're getting ready for dinner."

She spoke as if she were the spokesperson for all mothers and grandmothers of the church. The children heard her warn Cameron, and if the warning was good enough for him, it was good enough for them, too. Cameron played it safe by going up to his six-foot, four-inch daddy and giving his leg a hug.

The women gathered in the kitchen to sort their boxes and baskets, and the men planned their strategy of hiding the Easter eggs during the Easter program. Some children read over their speeches, and others rehearsed moving their lips while facing the walls or windows. The teenagers talked about make-up, new love interests, and the latest LPs being played on the radio.

Dinner was almost ready to be served, and Veola's food box was not yet set out. The box could wait, she decided. She had to meet this strange woman.

Chapter Three

Veola extended a hand to the stranger. "My name is Veola Cook, and I saw you walking up Jackson Street. I didn't know you were on your way here."

"I know who you are, Miss Veola, but you probably don't remember me, do you?" The woman maintained Veola's handshake.

"I noticed you didn't stand up as a visitor. I just don't remember you being here before."

"Well, it's been a long time. I'm Fayetta Dewberry, Melda's youngest daughter."

Veola's smile broadened. The two women embraced as if they were long lost cousins at a family reunion. "Lordy, lordy, lordy. No, it ain't. Little Fayetta who went off to Dallas? Now that I look at you, I can see you favor your daddy with those cheekbones and eyes. When was the last time you was in Parkerville?"

"You knew my daddy?"

"'Course I knew your daddy. After he left Parkerville, he headed for Houston, I believe. Now, I knew your mother much better. We were surely sorry to hear about her passing. Y'all had the funeral there in Dallas, didn't you?"

"Yes, ma'am. We moved there almost fifteen years ago when

I was sixteen. I've come back to Parkerville a few times to visit my auntie and cousins, but that's just been in the last few years."

"Now did y'all ever sell your mama's house?" Veola asked. She was curious about what everyone was doing. Other folks' business was not off limits.

"No, the family kept the house, because we never knew if Mama would want to come back to Parkerville again. My cousins rent it out, but with all of us, don't much come to me," Fayetta explained.

"So glad you could make it today. Well, are you here for a while?"

"Well, at least for a few days. Hopefully not too long, though." She forced a smile and blinked rapidly.

Veola knew there was more to this story, but now was not the time. She had her food to tend to in the kitchen.

Just then, Carneda came to the back door of the sanctuary. "Mama, do you want me to start putting your food on the table?"

"Come here a minute, Carneda. This here is Fayetta, Melda's daughter. You remember her, don't you?"

"Fayetta? Oh yeah, you were just a teenager when I saw you last. I think Kenny had just been born when you left here," Carneda said.

"That's probably right," Fayetta said.

Veola interrupted the reunion. "Now Fayetta, we're going to talk some more, but I've got to get my dinner ready. You're planning on staying, aren't you?"

"No, I'm sorry. I've got to go myself. It was good seeing you this morning. I didn't stop you earlier when I saw you on your porch, but I still remember you in that swing. I knew you were probably in a hurry since I was almost late myself. I'll see you next time, Miss Veola." Fayetta turned and exited the church.

"Good seeing you too, Baby," Veola added as she watched her leave.

Veola thought about her old friend, Melda Dewberry, and how she regretted not seeing her before she passed away. The word on the street was that she got a bad case of pneumonia and her heart couldn't handle all that extra fluid that developed in her lungs. They said she almost "drowned herself in her own liquids" without ever even touching water. Veola knew she had that story right because it was hot gossip when it happened. Well, God knows best, and it was good to see Fayetta. She wondered what had brought her back into town, but right now, her box was calling her.

❧

Tyrone made a week to a month's pay in five minutes stealing. He was with and without a job so often that he had to keep up an image with his mother that he always had an income. The goods he obtained sometimes more than satisfied his bookies, and dealing weed on the side was his added cushion. All his mother cared about was that he left the house every morning and she got her rent money on time.

An ideal robbery for him usually involved three particulars— good if he were high, better if he found loose cash, and best if some real jewelry was mixed in with the costume stuff.

A good thief should always do his homework, and he had been watching this house for a while. The target of his quest was the Simpsons. He was in real estate, and his wife's picture frequented the newspaper at social events. Tyrone called Mr. Simpson's office earlier this week and according to the secretary, he would not return until Tuesday morning.

The neighbors had not been home the last couple of Sundays, so he assumed everyone around here went to church, simplifying this job even more so. Good Christians, he guessed. While he still felt his high, it was time to move.

He parked his car at the nearby apartment complex. He strolled around to the back, scanning for any watchers before quietly scaling the fence. He headed down the alley behind the realtor's house.

Darting off the main path, he started toward the garage door of the next door neighbor. The brick was still where he had placed it last week. His target—the room next to the master bedroom.

After putting on his gloves, he removed the outside screen and broke the glass with little noise right at the latch. He slipped in and strode into the master bedroom.

The purses were easy to find. The chest of drawers. The

dresser. The nightstands. He found the jewelry box full of cheap stuff. Nothing anywhere. No cash. Shit. Now frantic, he dashed off to the other rooms.

In the spare bedroom closet, he was surrounded by a ton of dresses. Obviously her domain, he ransacked the drawers. Extra underwear, but not a goddam thing he wanted. Time to go. This had taken him longer than he thought.

He slipped back out the same window, still noticing no one and angry that this job was a screw-up. As soon as he reached his car, he sped home.

Because of his frustration, his high had worn off. Damn, he needed a joint—badly. Easter Sunday was supposed to have been as lucky for him as it was blessed for Christians. Instead, he was scammed.

He would work on another plan later, but not with these Simpson folk. They didn't have nothing he wanted, but he was certain he'd try again. Odds were on his side for scoring well the next round. Surely bad luck wouldn't doom him twice.

❧❧

When the Easter program began, the youth of the church had assembled in the sanctuary. The adults finished up their chores.

At 2:35 p.m., Cameron was flanked by a couple of his friends. The boys were ready to say their speeches and showcase their talents so they could beat the girls to the eggs. They could outrun all the kids their age, and today it was a matter of being quick on the draw. They had seen all the eggs beforehand, and they were concentrating on filling their own Easter baskets. Their minds raced, jumping the gun, of course. One more hour of being dressed up and then the coats and ties would fly off. In spite of the all the differences between the frilly-hairdo'd girls and tie-clad boys, everyone got hand claps of praise.

One boy's speech was "Why I Love Jesus." Another gave his rendition of "What Easter Means to Me," and Cameron completed his recitation of Psalm 121. Veola always stuck out her chest in maternal approval of her children in all of their accomplishments and endeavors. Once again, she sat proudly on "her" pew and shouted

"Amen, Amen" louder than anyone when each child finished his or her presentation.

Kenny was in the choir for young adults, and they sang Veola's favorite song, "How Great Thou Art." Oh, Lord, how she loved that song. The opening lines touched her soul intimately.

'Oh, Lord, my God, when I in awesome wonder
Consider all the world Thy hands have made.'

Every time she heard them, she immediately raised one hand in the air as if to thank God personally or bow her head as if she were about to use the line and break out in her own personal prayer. A good song will do that for a soul if the heart is open to receive it.

After the second benediction of the day, everyone exchanged hugs and proud moments. Veola realized most of the men were missing. They had sneaked out during one of the choir selections to hide the eggs. All the fathers heard their own children though, for missing their child's performance at Easter was not an option.

At 3:45 p.m., everyone gathered in the dining hall, and the children were set loose for the hunt.

Parents of the younger children helped their infants find the eggs close by while Cameron and his crew tore out to the far ends of the grounds in hopes of finding the ones that the girls surely wouldn't go after. Everyone had a reason for hunting eggs, and Veola saw it as a day to bring harmony to the church family. The members basked in the children's excitement—everybody except Loretta Mayfield. Veola had yet to lay eyes on her neighbor.

The Easter egg hunt was executed without a glitch, but now, Cameron and his friends knew they had twenty minutes to get their parents packed up, head home, and get undressed for the second main event of the day. Every child, and even some of the teenagers, knew what was about to occur. On television, starting at 5:00, on Channel 7 would be—*The Wizard of Oz!*

After a round of goodbyes, Charles took Veola and Cuddin' Jessie home. As Veola dropped her box containing its empty containers on the dining room table, the phone rang.

"Hello, Veola?"

"Yeah, Eva Mae."

"Who was that woman you was talking to after church?"

"Let me call you back. I just walked in and a couple of things I need to do 'fo I get comfortable and sit down."

"Call me back."

"I will."

Veola exited her front door and saw her porch was clean. She didn't miss a scrap when she swept before going to church, but now it was due for a full inspection. She wondered who would do something like this.

Still clad in her church clothes, she made her way to the trampled bushes outside her bedroom window. From where she stood, she wondered if Jessie could see what she was doing. Her hedge branches were bent out of order, yet none were broken. Her space had been violated. Someone had been close to her window. Was this the tapping she'd heard?

A clue to her dilemma could be within the trash. She opened the lid and saw that it did not deserve to be re-dumped and sorted through, but from the empty containers, she knew that it was her own trash.

Why would anyone dump her garbage? What were they looking for?

Lord, help me get through this, she prayed. Something wasn't right. She'd have to be more careful in her daily activities, for she didn't know who was watching her. She stared at her neighbor's back door, wondering whether or not Loretta had anything to do with this. Surely not, since their disagreement occurred after she heard the noises. Veola entertained all possibilities. Where was Loretta anyway? She hadn't seen her all day.

After returning inside and still with her church clothes on, she returned Eva Mae's call and explained who Fayetta was. They shared stories about Melda, yet most importantly, they talked about how shabby Fayetta's clothes were and concluded she couldn't even afford a purse.

Passing judgment was much too late and enough to end the conversation. After hanging up, Carneda buzzed right in. "Mama, I'm checking on you. Are you all right?"

"Yeah, I'm fine. I started not to tell you anything, because I know how you worry."

"I can't believe you wouldn't tell me. You know we are not finished talking about you living over there by yourself."

Veola felt Carneda about to get huffy. "Well, I'm not going to let you talk too long about it, because I like being over here by myself. Quit worrying about me. I'm fine."

"That's easier said than done, but I know I can't tell you anything anyhow."

"So leave it alone, then. You know I'm not going anywhere. Go take care of those boys."

"I'll talk to you tomorrow because it's obvious you don't want to talk right now."

"You're going to worry about this more than I am, I know, and I can't help that."

"I promised my brothers I would keep an eye on you while they were gone, and they expect me to do just that. They're going to think I can't do my job. Bye, Mama."

"You tell them I'm fine. That's what you do."

By the time Veola went to bed, she knew Easter Sunday had been for the most part a glorious day. Realizing Carneda wanted her to be more careful since she was getting older, Veola was certain the time had yet to come for her children to tell her what to do and how to live. She'd continue to keep her safety in her prayers, and now she had something new to give God—the unwanted visitor outside her house.

God had to handle this matter, but she was determined to help Him out anyway she could. Surely He wouldn't be mad about that.

Facing Leonard in court was not something Fayetta had wanted to go through, but she knew it was her only choice. Not knowing his state of mind with the court date drawing near, she wanted to get a feel for where he was mentally. Perhaps it didn't matter, but she felt like they could have a conversation outside of the courtroom, and hopefully before the big day. Leaving messages for him was useless, so she thought she'd try to find him at his usual hangouts, starting with Tyrone, his best buddy. After her encounter with Tyrone early this morning, she thought twice about heading over to his house. But one thing was for sure, Leonard will eventually show up.

Fayetta knocked on Tyrone's door. "Leonard, here?" Fayetta asked Tyrone.

Tyrone answered. "Yeah, he's—"

Leonard interrupted him. "I'm here."

Fayetta leaned around Tyrone since he stood in her way. She didn't expect hospitality after their previous encounter anyway. "Can I talk to you?" she directed to Leonard. She was right about where to find him.

"We can go out back."

Fayetta followed Leonard's lead and she felt Tyrone's eyes as they walked through his house. She had no desire to even address what Tyrone was probably feeling, already uncomfortable in his house.

"You know I've been looking for you?" she asked Leonard after they closed Tyrone's back door.

"What makes you think I want to see you when I know what you're here for?"

"Leonard, it didn't have to come to this."

"Naw, it damn shole didn't. But it did."

"Am I asking for too much by trying to get some help from you?" She watched him squirm, not saying a word. "Huh?" She wondered if Leonard felt her desperation for answers, direction, but she had to stay determined.

"You know I do what I can."

She felt his tension and abruptness. "How am I supposed to know that? I haven't seen you or any money from you in God knows when. I can't even get you to call and check on them. They're your kids just as much as they're mine. I feel you do what you want when you want to. And that's not enough for them or for me."

He cut her off. "We've talked about this over and over—"

"And it hasn't done a bit of good. Nothing has changed." She felt her voice escalating, even though she promised herself that she would remain calm.

"Fayetta, I work everyday just so I can provide for *me*."

"Well why is it that you can't offer to provide for anyone else? You don't give me half of what I need. I want our kids to have a chance, and they need new clothes and new shoes more often than you think. If I'm working two jobs and you're nowhere to be found, they will get into trouble. They deserve better than that."

"You know what I make and what I can do. Ain't nothing left."

"I don't believe that."

"I don't give a shit what you believe. Hell, I know what I bring home every week, and I have to stretch that out as it is."

"Leonard, you tell me this now, and the next thing I know, it'll be another mini-Leonard around here I hear about." Fayetta was steaming, and she finally shouted, "and that's what I'm sick and tired of. Hearing about your other little ones you got and you can't take care of those you already have."

"I ain't got to listen to this shit from you. I'm out of here." He opened the back door and headed through the house.

Fayetta followed him, but she knew trying to apologize for her temperament would be a waste of time. Exiting the front door, Leonard headed north, and she hurried back to her mama's house.

✲

Monday morning, Veola woke up at dawn, anticipating a full day of work. But first, she decided to make sure her trash can was outside her back door, untouched. She wanted no more early morning surprises. She opened the door but shut it immediately when she glimpsed two people arguing in the back field of her neighbor's house. To get a better view, she moved to her dining room window. The only light on in her house was a lamp in her bedroom, so she doubted she could be seen. Peeking through the blinds once again, she caught sight of a man and a woman scuffling.

The woman had a big shopping bag with handles that she shoved at the man. Her arms flailed and Veola thought she must be calling him this and that. She wished the sun would come up so that maybe she could identify them.

Who were these people? She wondered if the reason she couldn't tell who it was out there was because her glasses were not up to par.

The woman pushed him a few times, but he didn't push her back. She pointed her finger over and over. Now one of the man's hands held the bag, the other pointed back at her. It was an argument all right, and Veola was relieved it hadn't gotten violent.

Finally, the woman appeared to have had enough. She picked up a large stick and waved it in his face. Please, Lord, no, Veola said to herself; she didn't want to see nobody get hurt. If she were to start beating him, Veola would call the police. Meanwhile, she stood poised for action.

Then, the man threw the bag at her. Clothing fell out everywhere on the ground. Suddenly, the woman dropped the stick. The man gathered up the clothes, stuffed them in the bag and stomped off. The woman turned in the opposite direction and ran. Veola's mouth gaped as the woman seemed to be aiming for Veola's back door. She dropped the blind, thinking she had been spotted. But Veola had to look out once more, curiosity getting the better of her.

Oh, my gosh, it was Loretta headed right to her own porch. What in the devil was she into now? Who was that man? What in the world was that about? Veola frowned.

She thanked God they hadn't come to blows. Even though Veola was mad at her neighbor, she didn't know if she could stand to witness any violent exchange—fist-fighting or with sticks. She hated to see a man and woman resort to violence to work out their differences, and it brought up unwanted memories Veola didn't want to think about.

Veola became uneasy. Was she safe living alone? She'd always thought her neighborhood was safe, but she wondered now. She realized that no matter what, these days someone was out there doing bad stuff. And that some of the bad stuff was too close lately. With the overturned trash, the trampled bushes, and the noises she heard the other night, she was beginning to feel in jeopardy.

Veola made up her mind that something had to be done about this and quickly before it got worse. She vowed to find out who that man was. He may be the one responsible for her trash, but she couldn't ask that sassy Loretta about it. That was all right, though. She would do her own investigating for she saw what the man was shaped like. He wasn't fat, skinny either, and probably lived somewhere in the direction where he walked—to the north. Hopefully, she'd recognize something about the way he appeared once she got on the prowl. She'd get on this immediately before things got bad enough to get the police involved.

She'd begin right after she got home from work. She mustn't dilly-dally too much longer, for she had a lot to do before Mrs. Barton picked her up.

What was the world coming to? Nobody was safe anymore. Something had to be done, and as God was her witness, she was the one to get to the bottom of it.

Chapter Four

Veola was the housekeeper for three different families. To hear her job classified as someone's maid didn't bother her. Instead, she knew the real meaning. Keeping the house was easy, but managing the members of the household was far more challenging.

This gift came naturally—nothing she'd asked for. She had the Bartons on Mondays and Thursdays, the Halls on Tuesdays and Fridays, and the Holcombs on Wednesdays. Mrs. Holcomb wanted an extra day during the week for her family, but Veola told her she would have to find somebody else. Veola refused to work on Saturdays, her only day free. She knew how to do her job well, training and spoiling her families at the same time.

The family members felt comfortable discussing anything with Veola. She was that extra mother to the children, the decision-maker about what was for dinner, the voice of reason between the spouses, and even the referee for most of the sibling rivalries.

When secretly approached by one spouse as to what gift to buy for the other, Veola knew. On the day the gift was received, quite naturally the spouse had been warned to act surprised.

Veola was not a stranger to work, and she looked forward to time at each of the households. She normally finished between one and two o'clock in the afternoon, and depending upon the family, that would include having dinner almost completed. She didn't mind having a three-course meal planned since her families valued her cooking as worth their begging and definitely worth the wait. However, Veola had no problem suggesting to them to have a bologna sandwich for dinner if her day had not gone according to her plan. Extra chores or other complications in her day made dinner the lowest priority.

Veola and her families possessed chemistry. They knew how she felt that day according to what was on the stove or in the oven when they arrived home. "Veola must be mad" was not an uncommon statement to be heard if nothing was found.

At the Bartons, Veola suspected there would be more to do following Easter. A few extra clothes from the boys, maybe a little extra kitchen duty if Mrs. Barton had entertained guests for brunch or dinner, and more laundry from Dr. Barton's golf bag would not be a surprise. Knowing him, a holiday weekend always brought about more towels, shirts, and shorts. He got restless in all the hoopla, and he'd have his own private messiness. He was not known to find his way to the dirty clothes hamper. Veola told him her job was to wash the dirty clothes, not go find them.

Veola had a relationship with Dr. Barton similar to the television series with Hazel and Mr. Baxter. Veola knew he was the best family doctor in Parkerville, the community thought so, too, and in spite of his good standing and prestige, she had no problem telling him what to do. In the Barton household, she spoke her mind—the maid with clout.

Mrs. Barton made the boys keep their respective rooms as neat as possible. Getting Dr. Barton to comply was another matter. Jeremy was the oldest, a senior in high school this year, and Veola watched him mature into a handsome young man. He shared his father's height, over six feet, and dirty blonde hair, yet his mother endowed him with her olive complexion and captivating smile.

Veola's approach with Bobby was one of a third grandmother. She tried not to play favorites, but with Bobby, whatever she said was gospel.

Bobby had gone to kindergarten unwillingly, preferring to be home all day with Veola. A year later, about to finish first grade, he saw her only when she worked for his mother on special occasions. Whenever he could, he would ask his brother or his parents to drive him over to see Veola either after school or on a weekend.

Veola, dressed in her starched white uniform, waved at Mrs. Barton when she pulled up at eight o'clock sharp in her navy blue Ford Fairlane. Veola didn't know the year of the car. To her, it was just new. She glanced down at her porch. Thankfully, there was no trash.

Once she was outside, she secured the bottom lock and the top deadbolt of her front door. The storm door closed automatically.

Mrs. Barton normally reached across the seat to open the door for Veola. Today, she didn't.

"Good morning, Mrs. Barton," Veola said, opening the car door. "How are you this morning?"

"Good morning, Veola. How was your Easter? Did you prepare all that wonderful food you were telling me about?"

"Yes, I did. Now I asked how you were doing," Veola inquired. She tried to assess her employer's state of mind.

"Oh, I'm all right, Veola," replied Mrs. Barton without conviction.

"Well, you sure don't look all right," declared Veola, prodding for more.

"What makes you say that?"

"For one thing, I give you credit for speaking before you started asking me about how my weekend went when usually, you start telling me about everything you did first," Veola pointed out.

"Do I do that?"

"Most of the time, but let's not talk about that right now." Veola was determined to learn what was troubling Mrs. Barton. "I know you too well. What's bothering you?"

"Jeremy didn't come home Friday night until almost six in the morning."

"Well, you might as well say he didn't come home that night at all. Six o'clock in the morning is the next day. I've never known Jeremy to do anything like that. What did he have to say for himself?"

Before Mrs. Barton answered, Veola had a revelation. "No, don't answer that yet. Better yet, what did Dr. Barton say?"

All kinds of thoughts raced through Veola's mind. Dr. Barton was not the type of man known for listening to an explanation of a truant teenage son before reacting.

"He and his daddy were at each other's throats all day Saturday, so it put a damper on the Easter spirit. Jeremy said he spent the night at the lake house, and because he said he and the boys had had a few beers, he didn't want to risk driving. I'm sure he made the right decision, and since Roy and I had fallen asleep the night before, we would not have heard him come in anyway. We just wished he would have called. This has never happened before."

"Your child is experimenting, Mrs. Barton." Veola grasped for the right words to say to a worried mother. "You know he thinks he's some big-shot senior, graduating from high school this year, so he's out with the boys. I'm not saying it's right, but I bet that's what is on his mind."

Veola spoke her point of view as if she could read into Jeremy's thoughts, for she had had children who had acted similarly. This was not their usual behavior, or Jeremy's. She consoled Mrs. Barton the best way she could by understanding Jeremy's side of the story, no matter how inappropriate or wrong his behavior was. Right now, she vowed to keep listening, not quite understanding why Mrs. Barton couldn't see this for herself. Upon occasion when Mrs. Barton didn't understand what was really going on, it drove Veola crazy. Veola hoped this one wouldn't get to that point. She'd make it a priority to hear Jeremy's explanation.

Mrs. Barton added, "He said he was coming home for lunch today, so you might see him. I have to run out to Montgomery Ward's to pick up those rugs I ordered and probably won't be home by lunch time."

It seemed to Veola that Mrs. Barton ordered merchandise all the time. If not from Montgomery Ward's, just as many pages were turned down in the Sears & Roebuck catalog. What for? Absolutely nothing. She occupied her time by spending money. Some folks do that, Veola thought, believing they needed something more productive to do.

"It will be good to see him." Veola smiled. She knew she'd take that opportunity to pry into Jeremy's business. He might not want to talk much, but she thought she'd work her magic to see what he would be willing to admit.

Mrs. Barton drove to their house, and Veola was in deep thought about Jeremy's night out. The Bartons went out to the lake for a little relaxation on the weekends since they were all fond of water sports. Roy and Ann Barton had invited her several times since it was only ten minutes from the house, but in the ten years she had worked for them, Veola had yet to set foot on the banks of Lake Parkerville. Even the boys were unsuccessful in getting Veola to go.

Any water deeper than bath water was off limits to Veola, and she was content to let this fear remain. Why go changing things now? She didn't need to see the boys water skiing, for she had heard about it firsthand when they returned. Bobby couldn't wait to tell Veola the first time he'd gotten up on skis, but she worried about her little Bobby out there in all that water. Veola would come up with some kind of excuse each and every time she was asked to journey to the lake, and after several refusals, she finally admitted her fear of deep water. They convinced her she would be safe on the bank and after her many refusals—"no,""not today," or "maybe next time"—they finally quit asking.

On his way to work, Tyrone drove by Mrs. Veola's house. It had been a prospective target for a while, and he wanted to do this when she was at home. She had valuables, but more importantly, she had money. He didn't know how much, but working for a bunch of rich white folk meant somewhere in that house, she had a stash. She wouldn't give him any trouble once he got inside for her good church lady attitude meant she'd put up little resistance.

He couldn't be recognized. His old, winter black cap with the eyes barely cut out would assure him of that, so he promised himself to search for it after work.

Approaching the house, he slowed down. Why hadn't he noticed this before? The top of the storm door was all glass. From his previous jobs, he'd become an expert with glass. He'd break it quickly right at the door handle and get inside before she'd get to the phone. Easy enough.

Her front door was closed, and since no cars were behind

him, he stopped right in front. Now, he concentrated on when to do this break-in. The details he would work out while he was at work, because nothing, absolutely nothing must go wrong. He was desperate for cash to keep his operation afloat.

***

As Mrs. Barton and Veola entered the driveway, they noticed Dr. Barton's car still in the garage. Veola saw Mrs. Barton's brow furrow as she glanced down at her watch. Veola knew he'd be late to work. Mrs. Barton threw the car into park with such force that they sprung forward. They hurried in.

"He was getting up when I left," Mrs. Barton told Veola. "Roy?"

Mrs. Barton left the door open and Veola watched her scurry down the hall to their bedroom.

"Roy?" Mrs. Barton called again.

"I'm still in bed," Dr. Barton replied.

Veola heard his muffled tone, and she knew he was halfway under the cover. Veola stood within earshot as Mrs. Barton entered her bedroom.

"What's wrong, Roy? You're going to be late for work."

"I don't feel well."

"You were getting up when I left."

"Yeah, but my head is making my stomach sick."

"That doesn't make sense."

"Well, my head hurts, and my stomach's upset. I called work and told them to cancel my morning appointments. I told them I would try to make it in by this afternoon."

"I'll leave that to you, but do you need me to get you anything? I think there is some Pepto Bismol in the kitchen." She sat on the bed next to him and felt his forehead. "You don't feel like you've got a fever."

"I've got a dull ache right behind my eyes, and my stomach gurgles on and off. Maybe it's something I ate. But I don't think I need to take anything. I'll lie here for a while. I'll be all right."

"Are you hungry? Do you want something to eat?"

"Not yet."

"I'll check on you later." Mrs. Barton headed toward the kitchen.

Veola had snuck back to the kitchen as soon as she heard Mrs. Barton leaving the bedroom and immediately went outside. She tiptoed onto the front lawn and picked up the Parkerville Daily Progress. She retrieved it quickly, for she didn't want to get her stockings wet—not a great way to start a workday. She told the paperboy nicely one morning to throw the paper on the sidewalk, so people wouldn't muddy their shoes trying to get the news, but they had been wasted words.

With the paper still outside, and Dr. Barton's car still in the garage, Veola knew something was wrong with him. Dr. Barton usually retrieved the paper, fully dressed, before he left for work, with a cup of black coffee in tow.

Mrs. Barton met Veola in the kitchen. "Roy doesn't feel well—a bug, I guess. He's not going to work this morning," Mrs. Barton stated.

"What's wrong with him?" Veola had lots of work to do without extra trouble with these Bartons today, young or old.

"I don't know. He says it's his head and stomach."

Veola picked up the jug of Mogen David wine on the bar in the dining room. She shook it and heard nothing. "Was he drunk?" Veola didn't bat an eye, wishing the problem was something else.

"Why no, Veola, he's never drunk. What made you ask that?"

"That jug over there is empty, and I know you yo'self usually have no more than one glass. Otherwise, you'd been falling over, asleep before you know it. You should never enter a contest for drinkers, Mrs. Barton, for you would surely lose. So, you say he drank all of that?"

"I guess so. I'll tell you what happened. Saturday, I kept busy. I handled Jeremy not coming home as well as I could, but I had to be a mediator between him and Roy. Keeping them on opposite ends of the house was best. Roy left early after the big blow up, darted in and out all day, and had a couple of beers here and there. A late round of golf helped calm his nerves, and Jeremy spent most of the day catching up on sleep. He didn't want to talk much about what happened after he explained himself earlier. I tried not to let the mood of the household affect the fact that it was Easter for God's sake. It may have been a

Good Friday for Jeremy, but it surely put a damper on Saturday for everyone else."

"Well, I'm glad you put God somewhere in the weekend. He'd have been mad otherwise." Veola decided not to go any further—for now. "What happened next?"

"Sunday was better for everyone—church, brunch, and dinner last night. What a difference a day made. We were on our best behavior. I just don't remember Roy drinking all this wine last night."

Veola sat back and formulated her own assessment of all she had seen and observed. Out of habit, she tried to slip into Mrs. Barton's mind.

Here it is Monday morning, and her husband is in bed—sick, Veola thought. Mrs. Barton will handle this as she usually does. She'd grin and play as if nothing is wrong. Soon, Mrs. Barton would leave, starting on her list of errands, praying she wouldn't have to alter her schedule too drastically with her husband being home.

Thank God for Veola. That's what Veola told herself, anticipating what Mrs. Barton must be thinking.

Veola was on target because she had seen similar denial from Mrs. Barton many times before. She knew her worth in taking care of the house and the household, and she was glad she was here. God guided her feet, steering her in this direction.

Reading Mrs. Barton's mind was easy now, but today, Veola didn't relish babysitting grown-ups. Some of what she so easily recognized seemed oblivious to Dr. and Mrs. Barton. Veola was riled sometimes with what seemed to be a lack of common sense in some folks.

But before any words were uttered, Veola spoke under her breath, "Mrs. Barton, just so you know it, for me being here, you're quite welcome."

Sensing Dr. Barton needed a second opinion from Dr. Veola, she made her way to their bedroom. "Dr. Barton?" She got close enough to see his face. "You sleeping?"

"No." He barely opened his eyes.

"Good morning."

"Yeah," was all he could muster.

"I think you said good morning to me, too, didn't you?" she asked light-heartedly.

"Humph."

"You sick?"

"A little."

"Stomach?"

"Yeah," he replied in a childish whine. "My head, too."

"Well, are you hungry?" Now she would know just how sick Dr. Barton was.

"I don't think so."

She tried another angle. "Well, whatever is wrong with you, I'm not going to let you get in my way today. For now, you be just as sick as you want, but when I get ready for this room, I'll give you plenty of time to get yo'self cleaned up. That bed needs to be aired out since you've been in it all night long. You're messing up my schedule, and if you need something, holler loud, 'cause won't anyone be here but me. Mrs. Barton said she had a few errands to run. Going downtown, I think. Shopping. In a minute, I'll see if you can eat something." She left the room. No response needed.

Veola would make him a good, country breakfast. When she was through, those smells would either make him turn over and bury himself further in the sheets or make him hop in the shower and be at the table drooling. In case her food didn't make him stir, the thought of his wife shopping while he was home sick should make him quiver. Veola worked miracles over a stove. An iron skillet and some grease was all she needed. With Dr. Barton out of the house, she'd have private time with Jeremy.

When Veola returned to the kitchen, Mrs. Barton was working on her list. Why would she go and add more errands when her husband might need her? "Where all do you have to go today?"

"I thought I'd run to the cleaners and Montgomery Ward's. I want to be there when it opens at 9 o'clock. I heard there was a sale at Bea's shoe store, and I'll swing back by the grocery store on my way home. I'll only be gone for a couple of hours."

"You gon' leave your husband here—sick?"

"What does he want me to do?"

"Nothing, I suppose. But I don't want him to need anything from me with what all I have to do. I'm gon' make him some breakfast. That should get him moving and out of my way."

"Roy can take care of himself, Veola. He shouldn't need me."

"You know how some men folks are. They think they can't do anything on their own when they're sick, and I'm hoping we can get him well enough to get out of the house as soon as possible. I figure after breakfast, I'd start running the vacuum, and just the noise alone should make him want to be at the office rather than here with me."

"He's not going to mess up my plans. I will be back shortly, and I don't expect you to take care of him. You may be right about him being tipsy from last night."

Veola realized Mrs. Barton was trained to be lady-like and not classify her husband as drunk unless she was mad at him. True Southern ladies choose their words wisely, and to use the word "drunk" was appropriate for someone else's husband, not your own.

Veola was convinced Dr. Barton wouldn't die soon according to his wife, so her breakfast feast needed to be underway. The grits simmered, the biscuits baked, the ham steak sizzled, and the eggs waited for the ham grease. Now, in complete control of her meal, Veola saw the desire in Mrs. Barton's eyes for a taste, as always. So, she put two more eggs on the counter. She'd fry his first and pass them on to Mrs. Barton in case he wasn't up for eating. Good greasy food after or during a hangover was a remedy. Dr. Veola banked on her diagnosis. She heard bedroom commotion.

"Honey?" he screamed.

"See, I told you he was gon' need you." She raised her eyebrows. Veola didn't hide her smirk. Usually she didn't gloat in her successful predictions, but she was on a mission today.

"Yes, Honey," Mrs. Barton sang out. "I'll be right there." She traipsed back to their bedroom.

Veola noticed his favorite, Pabst Blue Ribbon beer, was missing from the icebox, usually never touched until company came over. She suspected most of the beer was kept at the lake, but she didn't make it a point to keep a tally on its consumption. The empty jug of wine was enough. Dr. Barton was drinking because of Jeremy. He's sick physically and mentally. She felt certain Dr. Barton didn't know how to handle this situation with Jeremy.

No sooner than she had taken the butter and a jar of her own homemade pear preserves out of the icebox that Dr. Barton came scooting down the hall in his pajamas and housecoat.

"Sit down, Dr. Barton. That is, if you're hungry. Otherwise, Mrs. Barton and I are going to have to handle this breakfast on our own, and we still can't eat all of this. I'd be too full to get my work done, and you might as well take me home after that."

Veola drew a smile from them both, as she played hostess. "Juice? Coffee? Breakfast for you, Mrs. Barton?"

"I'm going to get me a biscuit with a piece of ham. I didn't know you made biscuits."

Dr. Barton was treated like a king. This didn't happen often. Veola brought him his plate, grapefruit juice, and black coffee. The aspirin was forgotten.

As he was about to dig into the butter, Veola shrewdly and noticeably cleared her throat, her way of telling him he needed to say grace. He kept his eye on his plate as he offered the blessing.

Dr. Barton began devouring his meal, barely taking a breath between bites. With one less Barton to worry about, Veola resumed her morning duties.

That same ham would make good sandwiches for Jeremy. She hoped for time alone with him, intending to find out exactly what was going on with her extended family.

By the time Dr. Barton left for the office, Mrs. Barton had her list of errands on paper. "If I leave now, Veola, I might be back in time to see Jeremy. When he first told me he was coming home for lunch, I thought he might want to talk to me about the weekend, you know, away from his dad, but he had all day Saturday for that."

"I think he's coming home because he knows I'm here," Veola laughed.

"That could be, but Veola, sometimes I feel lost when it comes to him."

"Why is that?"

"This may be typical adolescent behavior for boys, but I have to convince myself that there was nothing Roy or I did to warrant him acting this way. Then again, Jeremy is so much like Roy—so stubborn. They're set in their own ways, which is why they can't talk to each other sometimes."

Veola nodded, taking it all in. She refused to comment; yet she suspected Mrs. Barton wanted her to.

"I'd better get out of here. Otherwise, I'd still be here talking about this, and it'll be lunchtime. I'm gone, Veola. Be back as soon as I can."

"All right, see you later."

Veola went back to her chores, since preparing Dr. Barton's breakfast was not in her original plan. She had never heard of a doctor playing hooky, but it was only for a few hours. Eating must have soaked up the alcohol and settled his stomach.

Of all weekends to have too much to drink, why did he pick Easter when we're trying to raise Jesus from the dead—not trying to drown Him in liquor. A gospel number would come in handy right about now.

Veola's thoughts moved from the Bartons briefly.

Fayetta Dewberry. Now what was she doing in town? As she straightened the room, she wondered how that trash got on her front porch. Did that man with Loretta have anything to do with it, even though he was nowhere near Veola's back door?

That Loretta Mayfield. No wonder she didn't show her face at church. Whatever she's got going on over there in her household don't appear to be quite right. Lord, I hope she ain't in danger.

She jumped back to the Bartons. This family was in disarray. Mrs. Barton was acting funny. Jeremy was staying out all night. She needed to see little Bobby to make sure he wasn't affected.

Trouble don't last always for joy comes in the morning. Oh glory, Hallelujah! Just that quickly, she diverted to a little inspirational uplifting without losing a stroke in her dusting.

Veola decided no one was off limits for providing answers into why the Barton family was having such pain. Typically, she'd start with the woman of the household. Despite Veola's line of questioning, Mrs. Barton had been no help.

Bobby's room required the least amount of work, so she was off to Jeremy's domain. As soon as she entered his room, she had a revelation. The time had come to call on the Higher Being. She spoke to the walls and furniture as if they were her congregation.

"Oh most Gracious and merciful God, you know I don't know who else to turn to. I've brought you everything I've ever had when I've been troubled. Anything I've ever needed or asked you for, you've provided. Dear God, you know what this family needs, so just come on into this household and touch them. Guide them in the right direction. I love them dearly, Lord, as if they were my own. If you need me to be a

vessel, then use me like you told me you would. And I'd be willing to do whatever I can, Dear God, for their particular need and purpose. (She paused and opened her eyes.) All right, I'll get back to you later, Lord. I'm telling you bye for now, but you know I'll be back shortly."

Veola glanced over the room to see where she would start, yet her mind continued to wander. Those dogs yesterday morning were not just barking for nothing. Over by Melda's house, someone was in that car when those lights went off. She wondered if Fayetta'd heard anything.

Cleaning and thinking had taken a lot of time. According to Jeremy's clock radio, it was 11:38 A.M. He would be home in the next ten to fifteen minutes, so she headed for the kitchen.

The last load of clothes was washing, and Mrs. Barton had yet to return. Lord, that woman shole could shop.

Jeremy's desk and his clothes on the floor were the last chores in his room. As she rounded the door of his room and headed toward the kitchen, she met him in the hall. She screamed, dropped her spray bottle and cloth and clapped her hand over her heart—monitoring its accelerated heartbeat. "Boy, you scared me."

Jeremy reached to give Veola a hug. "Veola, I'm sorry. I didn't mean to scare you. Are you all right?"

"Yes, I'm fine." She braced herself against the wall. Gasping for a few breaths, she finally calmed herself.

"I forgot it was your day here, and Mom's car is gone."

She moved toward the kitchen, walking past him, and lightly tapped him on his chest. "Boy, don't you scare me like that again. This old woman can't handle it." Veola had been tapping and swatting on Jeremy for years, and once again, she had him pinned.

He laughed and followed her to the kitchen.

"You're home early, aren't you?" Veola asked.

"Well, we got out a few minutes early."

Veola opened the icebox. "I assume you're hungry. I could make you a ham sandwich, and I saw some chips in the pantry. What about that?"

"You know me. Anything you make, I'll eat."

❧❧

Jeremy headed back down the hall to see if Veola had moved anything. He should have cleaned up his room before he left this morning.

He reached into the pants pocket on the floor, emptying its contents. He put the money from the old jeans into his present ones and grabbed some scribbled notes on his desk. To make sure the coast was clear, he came back to the door and glanced down the hall. He heard Veola in the kitchen.

"Almost ready, Veola?" Jeremy asked, straddling his door's entrance.

"I'll let you know when I'm ready. Don't you go rushing me."

Jeremy immediately jumped across the bed and hit the floor in one swoop. He raised the bedspread and moved a stack of magazines out of the way. Between the stacks was a wooden box; inside the wooden box was a brown paper bag. He grabbed the crumpled sack, and shoved the box back under the bed.

With combined breaths of excitement and secrecy, he stuffed the bag in his pocket. Based upon his stash, he would have to see Tyrone tomorrow to get more. But he had to remember the last time he was in Veola's neighborhood, he almost got caught. This time he'd go right after school while Veola was still at work. He headed for his sandwich.

❧❧

"What do you want to drink?" Veola asked Jeremy. She held the icebox open.

"Any lemon-lime?"

"I see a cream soda."

"That's good." Jeremy sat at the kitchen bar and started with the chips. He didn't say grace, and she decided not to chance a change of mood by correcting his table etiquette.

"Veola, I'll need another sandwich. Any more ham?"

"With the chips, I thought one would be enough. I'll make you another. And what happened to 'please'?"

"Please," Jeremy begged with a smile.

She was ready to fish for clues, and slicing and dicing would give her time to pick Jeremy's brain. The alternative was to sit directly in front of him while he ate, staring into his eyes and point blank asking *what is wrong with you and what is going on in this house?* She opted to be more subtle.

"You know, Jeremy, your father needed a little breakfast this morning."

"Oh, really." Jeremy chomped on sandwich number one.

"He wasn't feeling well, so I had to get him started the best way I could," Veola explained.

Jeremy said nothing.

Veola brought out the fixings once again and glanced at Jeremy periodically. "Your mother told me about Friday night."

"What did she say?" He slowed his chewing and eyed Veola.

"Well, she was worried about you—thinking maybe you were upset with them so you stayed out all night without calling."

"Why would she think that?" Jeremy let go of his sandwich.

"You tell me. School going all right?"

"I'm okay. Nothing's wrong with me. We were out late, and I ended up staying all night at the lake house. I didn't want to drive all the way home."

"I know you tried to do what was safe, but that didn't keep your mama and daddy from worrying since they didn't hear from you."

"Veola, now you're sounding like them."

"You should have called, and you know it. This was the first thing out of your mama's mouth when she picked me up this morning."

"What else did she say?"

"Nothing more than what I just told you. She seems kind of down."

"Well, I'm sure Dad has something to do with that."

"What do you mean?" She stopped slicing the tomato.

"Dad was kind of out of it this past weekend."

"Was he sick? He wasn't feeling well this morning, but—"

"He stayed away a lot after we fought on Saturday. When I woke up that afternoon, he was gone."

"Afternoon? Jeremy, you have to be the most *sleepin'est*

teenager I know on the face of this earth."

"He left after we talked, and I went back to bed for most of the day. The next thing I remember, it was late afternoon when he came home from the golf course."

"Was he still upset with you when he left?"

"I guess. He kind of blew up at me at first. Then, I heard him and Mom arguing in the other room. After that, he left."

"What were they arguing about?"

"I don't know."

Veola didn't believe him. "And all of that got better by yesterday?"

"Yeah, kind of. After church, we came back home and had breakfast. Everyone fended for themselves. Dinner was late, and a couple of their friends stopped by. Dad was drinking. It was a holiday."

"Was he drinking a lot?"

"I didn't see him drink anymore than anybody else. Dad wasn't yelling or nothing. Since then, I just stayed out of his way."

Veola realized Jeremy gave no indication that anything was bothering him; however, information about Dr. Barton flowed freely.

Jeremy had almost finished, and Veola had stopped everything to listen to him.

"You know, Jeremy, before the weekend, I saw Dr. Barton on Thursday. He was okay then. You saw him Friday when you got home from school, right?"

"It was Good Friday. We didn't have school."

"So you're saying the last time you saw him was Thursday night before you came home on Saturday morning?"

"Yeah, I guess. Maybe Mom knows what's bugging him. Look I gotta go." Jeremy sprinted out the door.

Veola sat in Jeremy's chair at the bar, trying to piece the puzzle together.

To Veola, Jeremy appeared not to have a care in the world. Mrs. Barton didn't know her husband was drinking too much, a habit so out of character for him. Now she wished Mrs. Barton would walk through the door.

Jeremy backed out of the driveway quickly. He didn't understand why everyone was trying to run his life. Old enough to make decisions for himself, he didn't need any help from anybody, even Veola. How dare his parents go and get her involved and now he worried that Veola would believe their side of the story. When he was close to Bobby's age, Jeremy felt Veola was there to make things better. Now, he felt he was being cornered, even by her.

When he neared the school entrance, he emptied his pocket and placed the brown paper bag underneath his seat.

Chapter Five

Veola noticed Jeremy had attempted to straighten his room. The clothes were now on the bed, and the desktop was clutter-free. She missed his jeans for the first load of laundry, now wondering why teenage boys wore blue jeans over and over again. She'd ask Kenny later.

The front pockets were empty. Right back pocket—clean. Left back pocket—matches. Veola was puzzled. What was Jeremy doing with matches? Was he smoking? Good at detecting odors, she had never smelled smoke from his clothes. She took a whiff of his blue jeans. No smoke there, but Lord knows they need washing.

Should she keep the matches and ask Jeremy about them later? She convinced herself this was an innocent occurrence. Chile, those kids could have been lighting candles at the lake house or picked them up at some eating place. Surely he had checked his back pocket since then.

Normally she didn't pry, always respected her family's privacy, but their out-of-character behavior warranted some investigating. She glanced around the room for anything out of the ordinary. She saw his books about cars, college information, sports books and magazines. His bookshelves contained the rest. Nothing seemed unusual, not really knowing what she was looking for.

Let it go, Veola, let it go. But she couldn't. This had already been a Monday to remember.

She prided herself in knowing Jeremy considered her someone who understood him. Maybe it was time for her to be observant and inquisitive, but how could she when she was only here twice per week?

She stacked his papers, arranged his books, hoping something would jump out at her. She waved her magic wand over Jeremy's room, leaving her trademark spotless touch, and moved on to the rest of the house. Little Bobby had halfway cleaned his room; his toys were put up. Her two o'clock day was easily going to turn into three.

About the time Veola had washed, dried, and folded all the clothes, Mrs. Barton opened the back door with bags in tow. Veola had expected many more sacks considering the length of time Mrs. Barton had been gone.

Veola poured herself a second glass of iced tea, having one earlier with a ham sandwich and a sample of Mrs. Barton's potato salad. Something was missing from it, too, just like Eva Mae's—too many potatoes and not enough onions and pimentos.

"Veola, I'm home," she announced as she tossed the bags on the kitchen counter. "I decided to pick up a few more items."

"I see. Well, you truly went shopping."

"I have a few more bags in the car."

Veola nodded.

"I know. Once I thought about what I really had to get, it reminded me of something I had been putting off."

"Putting off? With you coming in here with all these bags, what could you be putting off?" Veola was bewildered. Chores get put off, cleaning out the closet gets put off, paying bills gets put off—not shopping.

"No, Veola, I wanted to pick up something special for the boys. I saw this shirt at the Sport Store that I thought Jeremy would like. Went by Discount Palace for that new Spirograph for Bobby. A little surprise for them."

Veola didn't get it. Mrs. Barton tried to convince herself she really needed to do all these "errands." Had these bags contained essentials for the house, she would have asked Veola to help her unload them. What Mrs. Barton considered special was really a peace offering for Jeremy and she couldn't leave Bobby out. Veola asked if she could help unload the additional bags but Mrs. Barton politely declined.

Veola sat at the kitchen table, finishing up her iced tea. She had more than she could handle from the Bartons for the day, and it was almost time to pick up Bobby. "Since I'm here this long, I'd like to see Bobby. I don't get to see him much anymore, so would you mind picking him up before you drop me off at home?"

"Why no, Veola. He would love to see you, too. He's going to be so surprised. Give me a minute to unload the bags, and I'll be ready."

"All right. I'm ready when you are."

Mrs. Barton hauled the non-kitchen bags down the hall to her bedroom.

"I fixed Jeremy lunch today, and it was good to see him."

"Oh I know he loved that," Mrs. Barton said, unloading kitchen towels from one of the remaining bags.

"Yeah, I wanted to see him eat. He still eats like two fresh pigs. Probably always will. He didn't seem too upset by anything. I thought maybe you would be here when he came home." Once again, Veola fished for more information.

"Well, did he wonder where I was?" Mrs. Barton asked.

"He scared me when he came in, thinking no one was here when he didn't see your car."

"Was he looking for me?"

"I can't say that, Mrs. Barton. I thought maybe you two would have had time for just the two of you before everyone else got home this evening. This weekend may have been rough on everybody. You know what I'm saying?"

Mrs. Barton stopped unpacking. "What did he say?"

"About what?"

"Did he say what's bothering him?" Mrs. Barton's tone changed.

"Not really. But he talked about you and Dr. Barton." Veola realized she opened up a can of worms, but she wanted to.

"About me and Roy?"

"Yeah."

"Like what?"

"He noticed Dr. Barton stayed away a lot this weekend."

"What does that have to do with me?"

"Jeremy said even though he and his father had their tiff, he thought his father staying away had more to do with you and Dr. Barton, and not his coming home the next morning."

Mrs. Barton caught her breath and sat down across the table from Veola.

Veola didn't feel like she'd betrayed Jeremy by telling her this, but to her, Mrs. Barton appeared desperate in her need to know more information. "He says you two had a heated discussion after his talk with his daddy. Now, Mrs. Barton, I'm only prying because something is wrong. Dr. Barton drinking. Jeremy staying out all night. And you, shopping more."

"Roy went to Jeremy's room when he came home. When they got loud, you could hear them outside the door. When I could, I tried to listen, but I couldn't take it. Roy was handling the matter, and I knew he'd tell me later. Roy came to our room afterwards, and I asked him what Jeremy said. He gave me some excuse of 'well, Jeremy said it was too late and they had been drinking,' but I heard more. That was not good enough for me, and I let Roy know it. Jeremy needed to explain why he didn't call. Roy then tells me 'you wanted me to handle it, so let me.' For the rest of the weekend, I got nothing from either of them."

Mrs. Barton's sunken eyes showed her emotion, and it was felt in her speech. Perhaps, this had been eating away at her, and she needed to express it. A tear trickled down her reddened cheek, and she wiped it with the back of her hand. "Why do they do that to me, Veola? I feel as if they are of the same mold, hiding secrets from me I feel I have a right to know. For God's sake, they are too much alike for their own good, and sometimes, it just kills me."

"That was all Dr. Barton said?" Veola interrupted her.

"I got nothing. Absolutely nothing. Then, Roy and I had a fight because he wouldn't open up to me. I felt like such an outsider in my own house. Jeremy wasn't talking, Roy was gone, and it was Easter." She paused.

Veola stood up, made her way to Mrs. Barton, and embraced her across the shoulder. "Sometimes, Mrs. Barton, when you have two family members that are so much alike, you can't help but to have these kinds of problems. They are both stubborn in their own right, and you ought to be thankful you at least recognize it. You've said a whole lot, and I'm not sure what all of this means. But it's going to work out; it's just going to require you to be strong enough to get through it." Veola squeezed Mrs. Barton's shoulder. "Now let's go get Bobby."

Before Veola could ask any more questions or understand any more of the behavior from a family she thought she knew so well, she needed her own time to process it all. Definitely more than one problem existed, obviously, and Mrs. Barton and Jeremy only provided bits and pieces. But at least now, Mrs. Barton no longer looked tense. Perhaps her emotional load had been eased by opening up to Veola, and intentionally mentioning Bobby's name surely helped.

The women exited hurriedly, both needing a change from the present mood. Veola vowed to take this whole matter up with God later.

🦋

After school, Bobby usually waited at the curb for his mother's Ford Fairlane, but not today. Mrs. Barton and Veola scanned the crowd for him.

"Do you see him?" Mrs. Barton asked.

"There they are," Veola said.

"Where?" Mrs. Barton asked. "Who is 'they'?"

"There's Cameron and Bobby over there," Veola answered, pointing in their direction. "Let me get out for a minute."

Mrs. Barton pulled over and stopped. Veola walked across the school yard in their direction. They were in deep conversation, lunchboxes and windbreakers in hand.

Spotting Veola, they raced toward her screaming.

"Mama!" Cameron yelled.

"Veola!" Bobby shouted.

Reaching her at the same time, their belongings plummeted to the ground. Bobby and Cameron wrapped her up from both sides with full arm extensions. She basked in this special moment, a first, and she saw that Mrs. Barton had rolled down the passenger window. Veola was sure Mrs. Barton heard the boys' screams of excitement, and surely she could see Veola's approving smile.

"Cameron, your mama on her way?" Veola asked.

"Yes, ma'am," he replied.

"Bobby, your mother is right over there." Veola pointed in the direction of Mrs. Barton's car. Mrs. Barton waved, and they returned the gesture. "We were waiting on you, yet you two were just too busy to even look our way," she joked.

"I didn't see Mom," Bobby explained.

"Well, she's waiting for both of us now, so go let her know I'm on my way. By the way, I think she could use one of those hugs you gave me."

"Okay," Bobby agreed, and he picked up his belongings and ran for his mother. Abruptly, he stopped and turned back. "Bye, Cameron. I'll see you tomorrow."

"Bye, Bobby. Don't forget the hot wheels car," Cameron said, reminding Bobby of their previous conversation.

"I won't," Bobby yelled, running for the Ford Fairlane.

Veola turned to her grandchild. "What time does Carneda usually pick you up?"

"Between 3:30 and 3:45."

Veola checked to see how much longer her grandson would be waiting, 3:40 already.

Carneda taught English at Booker T. Washington High School, on the north side of town. She drove south to pick up Cameron who was one of only two black children in this elementary school of grades one through six, almost seven hundred kids. Veola knew her children and grandchildren could adapt to any environment, yet she was taken aback for a minute by taking a census of the playground. She and Cameron were the only two black people on this entire schoolyard. Mrs. Barton was taking her home, and she was about to leave Cameron out here all by himself.

Was her baby safe? Was he afraid of an environment where he was so outnumbered? She'd known this from the beginning, but to be standing in the middle of it shed a whole new light on the situation. She knew there was a reason for all these civil rights demonstrations. Black people were trying to get to the point where Cameron was right now. Lord, have mercy. How blessed he was, she thought. At least that's what she hoped.

Just then, a little blond-haired girl ran up to Cameron, grabbed his hand, and asked him to come and play on the merry-go-round.

"Mama, Dear will be here in a minute," Cameron said.

"Well, I've got to go anyway. They're waiting on me," Veola said, trying not to appear that she wanted to stand guard just a little while longer. "You tell your mother to call me when y'all get home."

"Yes, ma'am. Bye, Mama."

Veola barely heard those last words, for he had run off with that little blond-haired girl just as fast as he could. Ain't that a sight, Veola thought.

Once she got to the car, she glanced back in the direction of the merry-go-round, and Cameron wasn't there. She spotted him hanging upside down on the monkey bars, showing his belly. He was having fun, but he looked a mess.

'Lord, I'm blessed,' Veola quietly acknowledged. Seeing her grandson had been a treat, yet she had felt more racial tension just by standing on his playground than he had even thought about.

She put her thoughts in perspective, particularly reflecting on Dr. Martin Luther King's speech about four years ago in Washington, DC. This big march got everybody together in one place for one purpose. He talked a lot about equal rights, but she remembered how he specifically targeted schools for giving everybody access to get a better education. Because of such unrest, she knew President Johnson was doing everything he could to protect black people when he signed that law that next year.

She looked at her grandson and the white folk she worked for in the same place—playing together. It wasn't like this for her growing up, and she knew it wasn't like this for everybody even now. With only one other black child at this school besides Cameron, Veola took notice.

Was her grandson better than other little black kids? No. Was her family so privileged that they deserved to be at an all-white school? No. Was Carneda so brave as to want the exact same possibilities for her own children as white kids had had for so long that she stuck her neck out to enroll Cameron here rather across town in a black school? Without a doubt, yes.

The march two years ago from Selma to Montgomery had a lot to do with what black folks were doing and feeling. Why just a couple of weeks ago, even the Parkerville newspaper had pictures of

Selma, Alabama, since it was the two-year anniversary of "Bloody Sunday." Folks wanted equality for everybody. Racism wasn't right. As unfair as it was, it was here, there, everywhere. No two drinking fountains, no two entrances to food places, no two lines to the grocery stores, no two different times for folks to be able to shop. Maybe Veola was finally seeing some of these efforts coming into play. Veola knew change wouldn't happen overnight, but what she'd just witnessed on that playground was a start. Tonight, she promised herself to read the bulletin she got from the Southern Christian Leadership Conference, the organization Dr. King helped found. Maybe there was something she could do, for she knew that everyone in her situation wasn't quite as blessed, and she would even go as far as to say even not quite as lucky. With the white folks she knew, it was a whole lot of both.

She was daydreaming when Mrs. Barton reminded her to get in the car. Bobby had thrown his belongings in the back seat and had scooted himself as close to his mother as possible. He wanted to ride in the front seat with both of them.

A car horn was blowing from across the schoolyard. Before Veola planted herself in the passenger seat, she glanced in its direction. Carneda was blowing for Cameron, but Veola thought it was for her.

"Hey, there!" Veola answered and waved, as if Carneda could hear her.

Once again, Mrs. Barton appeared confused. "Who are you talking to, Veola?"

"That's Carneda over there picking up Cameron."

"Does she see you?"

"Probably not, but I waved at her anyway."

"You want me to drive over there?"

"No, she'll call me later."

Veola watched as Cameron upended himself from his playground activities and ran toward his mother's car. She could see Cameron's arm and index finger pointing from the passenger side of their car in her direction, and she assumed he was telling his mother where to find his grandmother. Veola imagined the dialogue. She heard the car horn again. Cameron waved, so Veola waved back.

The passenger door was still open, and Mrs. Barton spoke up.

"Veola, let's go."

"I'm ready," then added in a whisper, "Thank you, Jesus."

Veola and Bobby talked about everything from frogs to stick figures while Mrs. Barton listened. He was truly animated, and Veola enjoyed his many stories. His energy, Veola thought, mirrored Cameron's.

She heard Cameron speak of Bobby and vice versa, but today was the first time she had seen them together at school. They met long before first grade and who would have thought they would end up at the same school, South Side Elementary.

Veola noticed that Mrs. Barton did not take her usual route to Veola's house. She drove downtown, passing by the Sweet Potato Bowl where the Parkerville Panthers played their high school football games. Jeremy's team only won half of their games, but he concentrated on baseball. He had yet to decide on colleges, hoping for a baseball scholarship. The University of Texas at Austin was a hopeful option, and Mrs. Barton's alma mater, Austin College in Sherman, was also a possibility.

Downtown, the main bank was at the corner of Commerce and Main, and a stop sign brought all of them to silence. Veola glanced out the window and noticed the eye doctor's office next door to the Rexall Drugstore. Seeing the eyeglasses in the window reminded Veola to schedule an exam—the quicker the better.

Mrs. Barton turned onto Jackson Street and parked next to Veola's curb. Veola reached for the door handle, but Mrs. Barton touched Veola's arm closest to her.

"Thank you, Veola, for listening to me today."

"You know you can always talk to me."

"No, today, you did more than that."

"You needed somebody to talk to or better yet, somebody to listen."

Bobby remained frozen between the two women.

"I'm not sure what's going on, but I'm sure it will work out," Mrs. Barton continued, still clutching and jiggling Veola's forearm in appreciation. Veola felt Mrs. Barton's emotion. The sentiment was deep, powerful.

"Of course it will." Veola attempted to reassure Mrs. Barton that whatever she was going through would not last forever. "You know, Mrs. Barton, there is a song we sing at church. It's called 'Trouble Don't Last Always,' and you have to believe that."

Mrs. Barton smiled, and Veola watched Bobby stare at them. She wondered what he was thinking. She told him goodbye, but he didn't answer.

"I said goodbye, Bobby." Veola extended her hand through the passenger window to him.

"Bye, Veola," Bobby said.

She broke his stare. "Maybe we'll get you over here with Cameron one weekend. Would you like that?"

"Yeah," he exclaimed. He turned to his mother. "Can I, Mom?"

"We'll have to work that out with Cameron's mother and Veola," Mrs. Barton said. From the look Mrs. Barton gave her, Veola felt she was being summoned to help calm Bobby's excitement. "You just leave that to me, Mister." Veola nodded to Bobby, assuring him she would make it happen.

Bobby stuck his whole arm out to wave goodbye to Veola, who stood on her sidewalk. Mrs. Barton turned around at the corner, and when she drove back by, he had crawled over his mother's lap, still waving. The women shook their heads and laughed at Bobby.

Veola ascended her steps and stared at Miss Loretta Mayfield's front door. Loretta was hiding something because she was avoiding the world. She only showed herself in the early morning hours, and Veola began to take it personally. Maybe Loretta was purposefully avoiding her only, but that won't last forever. Eventually, Veola would finally see her, and when she did, Veola'd have some questions for her. She'd start with the dumped trash.

Veola eyed the peephole in her mailbox. She had mail, and at the foot of her storm door, there sat another envelope. She picked it up and saw handwritten, "Miss Veola." No return address. No stamp. Somebody had hand-delivered the letter. But who?

Chapter Six

The other envelopes could wait. The handwritten one took priority. Veola tossed her handbag and scarf into a living room chair as she proceeded to her dining room table, where she read her serious mail. Her pleasure reading was reserved for when she crawled into bed at night.

She opened the letter and read out loud.

Dear Miss Veola,

I'm writing this after seeing you at church to see if you could find the time to sit and talk with me. I walked by your house today, hoping to see you then. There are some things that are going on in my life, and you seem like the closest person here who I can talk with about them. I'm leaving you my cousin's number, where I am staying, and you can just ask for me. Marvella's number is LA5-1798. In case I'm not here, leave me a message with someone, and I will call you back. I hope you will call.

Sincerely,
Fayetta Dewberry

Veola re-read the letter. She wanted to make sure she didn't miss anything other than Fayetta's request for a phone call. She's got a nice handwriting, Veola told herself. She continued to unwind in her bedroom as she peeled off her work attire. She had spent a lot of time in the Barton's kitchen today, so she had no desire to cook. She had made a plate to take home from church on Sunday, and she could make do with some of that leftover fried chicken from Jessie and a few collard greens. At four/ o'clock in the afternoon, she wasn't hungry—not yet, anyway.

She replaced her uniform with one of her favorite housedresses. Getting out of the stockings was a relief, and she wanted to rinse and hang them over the bathtub to dry for tomorrow. A pair of stockings was good for at least two or three day's worth of wear. Tuesday with the Halls would be easy; she'd be home by one o'clock.

She called Fayetta. No one answered. She put the receiver down, and called again, making sure she'd dialed the right number. No one was home.

Whatever Fayetta wanted to talk about wouldn't be discussed right now. Veola grabbed her large Mason jar full of more ice than water from the icebox, her mail from the dining room table, and headed outside to her swing.

Before opening the envelopes, she rocked for a minute. This average day for Veola would have been a little too overwhelming for some. She silently reminisced and paced herself in her swing.

Mrs. Barton wasn't one to handle stress and family problems well, so she'd passed her family troubles onto Veola as soon as she got in the car this morning. She'd always come to Veola for a listening ear and sometimes for advice. Veola didn't touch alcohol, but she knew a hangover when she saw one. The only kind of high she wanted was to be high on Jesus. Hallelujah.

Staying out all night long was a college thing to do from what she had heard. Sometimes white folks got lenient with their children when they got to this stage in life, nothing Veola hadn't seen before.

She wondered what Carneda would do if Kenny did that. He'd never leave home again after he got his behind beaten by Carneda and then again by his daddy that weekend. He'd be in trouble with the whole family because Veola would have had a few words of advice herself.

Veola's concentration was broken. The neighbor, two houses up the street, Delphine, came out of her front door.

"Hey, Veola," she hollered through the porches in between them.

"How you doing, Delphine?"

Before Delphine could answer, she had gone back into her house. Had Delphine answered, a conversation would have followed. This time, she just wanted to say hello. No social custom was violated.

Veola and Delphine didn't have to yell at each other because their houses were so close. Presumably, Loretta Mayfield was still at work. Had she been home, Loretta would have heard the entire conversation between Veola and Delphine, absorbing every single word, and she had the nerve to call Veola nosey. Veola thought Loretta was too young to be in folks' business like that, always keeping some mess stirred up. Loretta lived her life through other folk, so Veola learned to be careful about what she said around her.

Veola returned to her earlier thoughts of the Bartons, becoming aware of how much time she had let them occupy. She had cleaned their house, washed their clothes, fed their bellies, and here she was on her own time still thinking about them. Enough was enough. She wondered what time Fayetta would be home so she could call again. Then she got an idea. She decided to walk over to Jessie's and in the process, she'd see if there were any cars parked at Fayetta's house.

She grabbed her keys and locked her door. As she approached Jessie's, Fayetta's house appeared to be void of human souls.

Veola banged on Jessie's door. Finally, Jessie came around the side of her house, covered in dirt. "That's what took you so long to get to the door. You was out back."

"Girl, I'm out here moving some of those pots around on the back porch. I think I need to re-pot my ferns. They ain't doing too well."

"Well, what are you doing tomorrow?" Veola didn't move from the front. She wanted to keep an eye on two houses, her own and Fayetta's.

"When tomorrow?"

"Tomorrow afternoon."

"Nothing, I guess. What you thinking 'bout?"

Veola was on a mission, recruiting her running buddy for her plan. "How old are your eyeglasses?"

"You is asking me some crazy things, Veola. I don't know how old my glasses is. They still work. I can see." Jessie wiggled them on her face.

"I was with Mrs. Barton today, and I saw a sign down at Dr. Sweeney's office. You know, that eye doctor next to the bank. He's having a sale on eyeglasses, and I've been wanting some new ones. Come and go with me. You could get you some, too. Besides, you ain't got nothing else to do." Veola spiced up her invitation.

"How you know I ain't got nothing else to do? I don't need no new glasses."

"I figured we'd go tomorrow, avoid that Saturday rush. I bet he's gonna have all kinds of peoples in there then."

"What time?"

"I'll get home around one, and it won't take me long to change."

"I'll go wit cha. Call me when you're ready." Jessie started off toward the back of her house.

"What you rushing off for?"

"I told you I was busy. Now what else you got to tell me? You find out who put that trash on your porch?"

"I ain't thought about that no more." Veola lied. "That wasn't what I was talking about. When I got home from work today, I had a note in my door from Fayetta, you know, Melda's daughter who was at church yesterday." Veola volunteered only a small amount of enticement.

After glancing at Melda's house, Jessie hurried closer to Veola. "Oh yeah?"

"Yeah," Veola answered. "She came by and left her number. She's staying there at Melda's with her cousin. In fact, the number she wrote down looks like Melda's old number."

"Well, what she leave her number for? What she want?"

"She didn't say much. She just asked me to give her a call." Veola attempted to remain elusive, tried not to relay any more information than what was necessary, yet she remembered she'd started this. She fed Jessie just enough to tease her, made her want more, so now it was time to go.

For those two, gossip ain't good if it ain't got all the details in between—why, when, who done it, why come this, why come that, and even what happened next. All they needed now was Eva Mae to complete the sistahhood. With a Bible in one hand, finger pointing was done with the other.

Veola continued. "I'll let you know what she says when I call her. I don't think she knows too many people here other than her family."

"Girl, you ain't heard? I should have told you earlier. Fayetta used to go with Delphine's stepson, Leonard Johnson."

Jessie just turned the table. Veola was on the inquiring end now, shocked by what she just heard.

"What?" Veola was completely surprised. "How you know that?"

"I got this from Eva Mae this here mornin'. Now you know that son of hers, Tyrone, is right next door, so after church yesterday, Tyrone told Eva Mae that girl been up to his house visiting that Leonard boy."

"Hush yo mouth. So Tyrone and Leonard is friends?"

"Now wait. Let me finish. Real good friends, I think. They both 'bout the same age, but anyway, he told Eva Mae he saw Fayetta yesterday when she came over to his house. She came looking for Leonard and wasn't nobody there but him and Tyrone. According to Eva Mae, Tyrone told her that Leonard and Fayetta walked to the back of Tyrone's house and got into a little disagreement. It didn't get to the point of an argument 'cause Eva Mae said that Tyrone would have told her that."

"Girl, naw!" Veola stared at Jessie's face, watching every word flow from her mouth.

"Now that's what I heard. I don't know how much of that is true, but supposedly she left church and went to Tyrone's."

Veola's curiosity reached a second peak. "Well, how Fayetta know where Leonard was? Would she have been going just to visit Tyrone?"

"What makes you think I know that? We gon' have to get that from Eva Mae."

Again, Jessie had the upper hand with Veola, piquing her interest with only a teaspoonful of gossip. Veola wanted more.

"What else you know, Jessie?"

"That's all she told me."

"Talk to you tomorrow, if not before." Veola knew she wasn't going to get anything else from Jessie. Any further details would come directly from Jessie's source, Eva Mae. Veola thought fast on her walk back to her house. What Eva Mae didn't know would probably come directly from Fayetta. Now, she didn't want to rush getting Fayetta on the phone. By the time she called her, she wanted to have as many details as she could manage to obtain on her own to be able to ask the right questions. Before the night was over, phone calls would be made.

The contents of the letter replayed in Veola's mind: *There are some things that are going on in my life, and you seem like the closest person in this town that I can talk to.*

What did Fayetta want to talk to her about? What did she want to tell Veola and didn't want to tell anybody else? Veola knew there was only one way to get the answer, but after deciding to wait before she called Fayetta was going to kill her.

Eva Mae would give her the inside scoop on Fayetta's purpose of being at Tyrone's, visiting her old boyfriend, Leonard. The common bond appeared to be Fayetta and Leonard, not Fayetta and Tyrone. Otherwise, Eva Mae would have told Jessie. Of course, good friends don't tell all their business to their closest sistahs, but something like this didn't seem like a big secret for Eva Mae to keep from them. Surely not, so she decided to call Eva Mae and get the information firsthand.

Later, Veola sat in her bedroom chair, and before she picked up the receiver to call Eva Mae, she heard a car door slam. Cameron was at her front door, and Carneda was close behind.

"Hey, Mama." Cameron entered the house after Veola unlocked the screen door.

"Hey, Baby." Veola sighed with relief, not having to talk to Fayetta, Eva Mae, or even Jessie with more gossip. She relaxed for her grandson.

"What are you doing?" he asked.

"Nothing. What are y'all doing?"

"We were on our way home. Dear and I went to the post office and Piggly Wiggly after school. Was that your first time at my school?"

"I think it was, but do you remember when we drove by there so you could show me where you'd be in first grade?"

"Oh, yeah." Cameron followed Veola to the kitchen. Carneda

slipped off into the bathroom.

"You like going to your school?" Veola asked. She thought about her moment of reflection she experienced on the playground earlier. She was asking if he felt safe, but now she could tell something was on his mind.

"It's fun. You got to see both Bobby and me, huh. But you know what?"

"What, Baby?" Veola didn't know what he would say next.

"Bobby acted like you were _his_ grandmother."

What a statement this child had made. Veola had to plan her response, but not yet. Cameron had more.

"Mama, when we were running to you, do you remember he was calling you 'Veola! Veola!'? Why didn't he call you Miss Veola or Miss Cook? I didn't know he called you by your first name."

What a delicate situation for Veola to handle. She knew Carneda had been hit with the same observation, but Cameron needed to hear from his grandmother directly. Once he had something on his mind, he wouldn't let go. She knew where this particular trait came from; it was in his blood. Veola began as if she were on trial with Carneda nowhere in sight. She wasn't sure if Cameron was mad or jealous of Bobby for the way he felt, but she needed his undivided attention for her reply.

"Cameron, there are certain people that Mama has to take care of everyday, and you know that I have been with the Bartons for a long time. You see, I knew Bobby's mama and daddy long before I even knew Kenny or you. They have been a part of my life, and they have needed me to love them as much as I possibly could. Sometimes, other people need other folk to take care of them. I always knew that even though that is where I worked, they tried to make me feel like I was a part of their family. Mama has always had enough love in her heart for all her children and grandchildren, and you know how much I love you."

They reached for each other, and Veola knew Cameron didn't have to share the hug with Bobby this time. She was all his at this point and his alone.

"Bobby needed me to show him just a little of that love you get from me, and so, he gets hugs just like you get. He only knows me as Veola since that is what he hears from his mama and daddy. That doesn't mean he doesn't know how to address grown-ups, but he calls me what he hears in his house. If I ever thought Dr. Barton or Mrs. Barton didn't care for me or respect me in the manner I deserve or the way I deserve to be treated, then, I might have had to ask them to call me Miss Cook or Miss Veola. Now they are good friends on top of paying me to do what I do. I make a living, and I get to love them at the same time. I don't feel anything less than their friend as well as their housekeeper. Why, you call me just what you hear and know, too. That's Mama—not Grandmama like I really am. That may be a lot for you to understand, but I know I can depend on you to try to see Mama's point. I want you to try to see Bobby's side, too. Does all that make sense?"

"Yes, ma'am." Cameron nodded.

Veola sensed him trying to put all of that into perspective. For a moment, there was silence. She was doing her best to put it on his terms, and he would not have been satisfied with a one sentence answer. Veola knew he always needed explanations, ones that stimulated his thought process. She hoped what she had said would do for now.

"I'll tell you what," Veola continued. "This weekend, how about I ask Mrs. Barton if Bobby could come and spend Saturday night over here with you? We could go to the park that evening and then to church Sunday morning. How does that sound?"

"We played with our G.I. Joes today, and maybe he can bring his over on Saturday," Cameron said.

From his response, Veola realized he was satisfied with her explanation. Her suggestion of the sleepover was icing on the cake, and the idea of having company made it that much sweeter.

Carneda appeared in Veola's dining room. What timing.

Cameron began to tell Carneda the plans for Saturday. His enthusiasm was obvious, and Veola already planted the bug with Mrs. Barton and Bobby. Cameron flipped the channel on Veola's TV.

"Mama," Carneda began, "he asked me how old do you have to be to call a grown-up by their first name and he asked me if Bobby had a grandmother. He wouldn't let that rest, so we just made a little detour to let him come by and talk to you himself."

"And I'm glad you did. I think there are some things I'd rather explain to my grandchildren myself. Y'all might get it wrong."

Veola and Carneda shared a laugh.

"Well, let me get to the house," Carneda said. "Got to think about what I'm going to fix these boys for dinner since they don't want leftovers."

"I can't blame them. I don't want turkey and dressing myself."

"Yeah, and they don't want that anyway. Mama, are you sure you're going to be safe here with these kids Saturday night?"

Veola knew what worry looked like on her daughter's face. She'd seen it before. "I'll be ready for these boys and anybody else for that matter. Besides, this will be fun for them. I saw them playing today, and I can't wait for Saturday so we can have some more fun. Then, we're all going to church Sunday morning—together."

With Veola's experience on the playground, Bobby's observation in the car, and Cameron's line of questions, she anticipated the dynamics of what this weekend could mean for everyone. Veola knew children of all races possessed one commonality—innocence. What was important was to get the boys together, outside of school, where she could place a small amount of her wisdom on the minds of her young ones. She considered them both her offspring, and she had something to contribute to their upbringing. After all, she had spent the last ten years trying to keep Jeremy on the right path, too.

The reason she sat down in the first place was to call Eva Mae. She had been on one mission and was briefly sidetracked with another. Dispensing love came naturally for Veola, especially to her own family. But now, the investigation was back on course.

Everybody shared more goodbye hugs, and Carneda and Cameron were off to the other side of town. For Veola, the investigation was back on course, so she was back to her chair by the phone before they drove off. Veola knew her daughter would sense she was up to something, and she'd give Carneda details later. Maybe, maybe not.

Veola dialed Eva Mae's number and got a busy signal. Eva Mae was still running her mouth, Veola thought.

She dialed Mrs. Barton and made plans for Saturday and Sunday. She managed to finish quickly for more pressing business was at hand.

She re-dialed Eva Mae.

"I told you I'd go get him in a minute," Eva Mae screamed.

"You has to give me time!"

"Eva Mae? This is Veola."

"Oh, Girl, I thought you was somebody else," Eva Mae explained, sounding embarrassed.

"Who was you expecting?"

"I just hung up with that Fayetta girl, and she wanted to talk to Tyrone. You know, his phone ain't working right now, and she asked me if I wouldn't mind telling him to call her. I don't know why that damn boy don't keep his phone turned on. That's just lazy. You have to remind him to pay his own bills."

"You was talking to Fayetta?" Veola was surprised the two of them were acquaintances. She had no reason to assume otherwise.

"Yeah, she was up here yesterday and she done called here three or four times today. I'm tired of her. In fact, I ain't gon' be here when she call again. I'm on my way to yo house. Meet me in your garden."

According to Veola, Eva Mae didn't know she was making Veola's fact-finding mission much easier. Eva Mae could talk until the cows came home, and now she wanted to rattle her chops in person. Veola would let her.

Within minutes, Eva Mae came through the back way to Veola's garden. "Veola, you know that girl been here for a few days, and if you asked me, she's on a mission."

"What kind of mission?"

"She been trying to get close to Leonard, you know Delphine's husband's boy, who be with Tyrone all the time. Seem like everywhere she think Leonard is, that's where she wanna be."

"What for?" Veola didn't want to miss a bit of this.

"That I don't know. At least, not yet. Tyrone told me yesterday when I got home from church that Fayetta came up to his house looking for Leonard. She and Leonard got into some kind of argument. Now, Tyrone didn't tell me what the argument was about, but you know Tyrone. Sometimes I can't trust my own youngun' to get the facts right. I didn't think nothing of it 'til she started calling my house today looking for Tyrone. She know his phone ain't working, and she's worrying the shit out of me. Hell, I ain't the damn operator. He'll get the message when I feel like it. I ain't trying to be no delivery gal and haul his lazy ass to the phone."

"Why is she calling Tyrone?" Veola asked, perplexed about the matter.

"I told you it's got something to do with Leonard. You know Leonard Johnson's been treacherous all his natural born life, and what she sees in him, I'll never know," Eva Mae stated.

"Where is Leonard now?"

"Hell if I know. I guess she thinks Tyrone knows Leonard's every move or that he be over there all the time. I told her I didn't know who be over there, and if I did, it wasn't my place to tell her."

"Then what'd she say?" Veola egged Eva Mae on for more.

"She was nice about it, but you could tell she was kind of desperate in finding that Leonard boy."

"There's something fishy about all this. I thought she was in town to handle some of her mama's business, but seem like she got more business of her own." Veola openly discussed the matter, hoping Eva Mae would share more.

"In a minute, I'm gon' git Tyrone, and if he walks back to my house to call her back, so be it. I'm shole gon' be somewhere close so I can hear what they saying. Tyrone don't know what I be doing in my own house sometimes, so he ain't gon' have a clue I'll be listening."

"Don't get caught," Veola warned. "Don't nothing get past you, but if they know you listening, they might not say nothing."

"Chile, Tyrone can't hold water. If I hear anything, I'll call ya."

"Bye."

"Talk to you after a while. When you gon' plant your garden?" Eva Mae asked as she headed back toward her domain.

"Soon as it be ready." When she was talking with her good sistahs, she spoke as they did. Good Southern black women didn't have to master good English; they mastered good conversation.

Veola tried to put all of what she just heard together but nothing made any sense. Eva Mae didn't know about the letter Fayetta left in Veola's front door, so Veola kept her ace in the hole until she knew more from Fayetta.

Veola sat back to catch her breath once she went back inside. How the parties involved were connected made this too interesting. The letter on the bed required re-reading one more time. Now she realized when she called Fayetta, she wanted to be ready with her own questions. Then again, what Fayetta wanted to talk to her about

71

might not have anything at all to do with what she was thinking. Fayetta might have just wanted to unwind, maybe talk about her mother. Veola did not want to take that chance. She wanted to be prepared for whatever was in store.

Normally, Veola didn't visit Delphine, but she wondered what she knew. They were back porch or speak-when-I-see-you kind of neighbors, meeting somewhere between the two houses and talked about nothing in particular. To hold a conversation with Delphine meant accepting one particular trait Veola found deplorable. She dipped snuff.

Delphine Turner, Veola's neighbor for years, displayed the brownest teeth on the block. Most of their exchanges occurred outside so Delphine could spit. Veola never understood what would make a woman want to dip snuff, so unbecoming and unattractive. Delphine needed all the help she could in that category. Veola thought Delphine let herself go as far as appearance was concerned. To where was the question. Come back to God, she reminded herself, trying not to continue these thoughts. The divine master loves us all, even the nasty snuff dippers.

Veola planned the meeting with Delphine. She would go to the back porch, act as if she was sorting potted plants, and strike up a conversation with Delphine if she came outside. She would work the conversation toward Eli and then on to his children, particularly Leonard.

All Veola wanted was to know about Delphine's stepson's relationship with Fayetta. At least she would try, for she had nothing to lose.

From the back screen door, Veola could see there was no evidence of existence at Loretta's. Eventually she would show her face, and Veola would be ready for her when that happened. Her back porch was devoid of life—no potted plants, no worn out mops or brooms, no old galoshes or mud-soaked shoes. In contrast, Delphine and Eli's was covered from top to bottom with potted plants, an old foot tub, washrags hanging over the railings, a basket of clothespins, and lots of Eli's and her old shoes and boots for outside work.

All of a sudden Veola noticed something. Loretta normally had a trash can somewhere out back, but it wasn't there. Where was it? Was she dumping trash somewhere and had yet to put it back?

Veola needed to be strategically placed for her chit-chat with Delphine. She'd bet Delphine knew more about Leonard's welfare than his real daddy.

She retrieved her Mason water jar from the icebox, filled it with more ice, and headed outside. Ruben Earl would be here before she knew it to plow for another crop of fresh vegetables. She enjoyed gardening, and this was a perfect pastime for her love of growing things—flowers and plants alike. Since she loved good food, why not grow it? Walking across the untilled ground, she spied on Delphine's back door, thinking if Delphine saw her alone, she would come outside.

She lulled around the area, kicking at the few weeds and hard soil. Delphine was not catching the bait. Her unnecessary movements and fake tasks went unnoticed.

No one paid Veola any attention, so she made her way back inside. She couldn't just come right out and call Delphine. She couldn't borrow a cup of sugar from her. That would have been too obvious. Veola, the premiere cook of the block, kept her kitchen stocked.

Now she would have to rely on Eva Mae to find out what she could, yet she'd see what Fayetta had to say. Surely Fayetta had made it home by now. Veola picked up the phone.

🐚🐚

Right after work, Ruben Earl stopped and picked up a surprise for Veola. He just knew she'd like it. Once he got home, he realized he was covered in sawdust. While he was already dirty, he could change into more work clothes, grab his mule, and head over to Veola's backyard to start on her garden. Every year, this was his routine. Today, though, he felt differently. He wanted to go over there, but not looking like he did, and especially with his recent purchase.

Veola's garden had been something he'd enjoyed plowing for at least ten years, but maybe the reason he wanted to keep doing it was not only because of fresh, country vegetables. Instead of starting to plow right off the bat, he'd give her a chance to iron out details of what she wanted where and any special requests—maybe smaller rows. Besides, he knew that to assume a woman wanted one thing was a huge mistake when actually she preferred another.

So, he quickly took a bath and put on clothes usually reserved for the weekend. He wanted her to see him in another way, another light. Just because he was her official yardman didn't mean he had to look and smell like one.

Chapter Seven

When Veola picked up the receiver to call Eva Mae again, the doorbell rang. Ruben Earl was standing on her porch, probably on his way home from the box factory. She mostly appreciated his promise to till her garden this week. Too much was happening, and she was going to have to keep it all sorted out in her mind. Is this going to be the pace of her week? After all, it was just Monday.

Veola saw Ruben Earl twiddling his hat, when she peered around the side of the icebox. At first glance, he didn't look like he just came from work. "I'm coming," Veola hollered, walking to the front door. She opened the storm door and saw Ruben Earl's shadow moving on the side of her house as he headed out back. She met him in the garden. He was unusually clean for this time of day. "You don't look like you went to work today."

"Well, I got off early and wanted to give you time to get home before I dropped by. Wanted to see when I can get started on your garden."

"As a matter of fact, I just came in from out here. I'm wondering how much to plow up this year."

"What? You ain't gon' plant the whole garden?"

"It's such a big garden, and I don't know if I feel like trying to

75

keep up with all the weeds. Last year, I was out here two to three times a week pulling up this and that, busy. I'm not even sure what all I want to plant besides the usual."

Veola wondered if Ruben Earl saw the trampled bushes as he made his way to the garden. She noticed he didn't bring it up, so neither would she.

"Well, I'm gon' plow up what I did last year. If I got half that land ready, you'd call me right back over here to plow up the other. I'm gon' get it all done at once."

"If I don't feel like planting the whole garden, the rest gon' go to waste."

"Veola, you gots more people to help you plant anything you want. Everybody on this street helped you last year 'cause they like seeing your garden just as much as you like having it."

Last year, Veola remembered Leonard helped her move some cow manure. Said he planned to taste her tomatoes when they got ready, but he never did.

Veola took her compliment from Ruben Earl and didn't let him see her smile. "You think so?"

"Think what?"

"That people like looking at my garden."

"Why sho they do. You ought to know that. The best turnips, turnip greens, poke sally, snap beans, and new potatoes always come from your garden and your kitchen."

"I guess that settles it. Plow up this whole garden one more time, and let's see what we can raise out here." All she needed was inspiration from someone she admired and respected.

"Now you've been over here many a time right after work, and you didn't have to clean up to ask me about this garden."

"We had more dust today, so I had to freshen up for the both of us."

Veola was lost for words. The slight pause seemed awkward for them both, yet not uncomfortable. Veola redirected her feelings. "So, when you gon' get started?"

"That's why I came over, to make sure it's all right to start either tomorrow or Wednesday since I may be tied up this weekend. My sister ain't doing too well down in Alto, and I wants to go see her."

"That's fine. I'll try to get what I need so I can start planting this weekend."

"Oh, I forgot something." Ruben Earl walked toward his truck out front.

"Forgot what?" Veola followed him past the bushes, still unnoticed by Ruben Earl.

"I brought you something." He leaned over the side of his truck and hurled over a bushel of peas, filled to the rim. "Look what I got."

Veola's face lit up. They looked like purple hull or cream peas from the color of the pods. "Where did you get those peas this early in the year?"

"Now, these here is cream peas, an early batch I got from a man on the highway. He had an early harvest, and knowing he's gone have plenty more, he selling 'em already."

"Before you set them down, would you mind bringing them to the back porch? I'll move 'em later."

"Why sho. This bushel is kind of heavy for you anyway."

Veola knew what it meant to have a strong friend around. Grinning from ear to ear, she led the way this time on the side of the house facing Loretta's, moving crepe myrtle branches out of the way so they wouldn't hit him in the head. "You seen Loretta?" she asked, making sure she wasn't the only one Loretta was dodging.

"Naw, not even at church, but I bet you'll see her once she find out you got these peas sitting over here."

Veola thought to herself if Loretta even thought about coming over asking for peas the way she treated her on the phone, she'd send her right back home empty-handed. "Now how much do I owe you?"

"You know you don't owe me nothing."

"Peas ain't free."

"Cooking for me all these years ain't been free either."

"You sure I can't pay you something?" She refused to be a freeloader.

"I'll tell you what. When you get these peas ready, I'll be here to eat some. That's a fair trade."

"Now you know when I have food on the table, you're more than welcome," she politely replied, but careful not to pinpoint a day. When was the key. Some men, even in her own church, got downright ornery and wanted to push their way right under her dining room table.

"That's fine by me."

"Thank you for these, Ruben Earl." She grabbed one of the pods and opened it. Inspection was mandatory. "They look good. I wonder how he gets his peas this early in the year."

"Probably planted them 'fo time, not worried about any more cold weather."

"I guess not."

Peas were planted when there was no more indication of a late frost. In northeast Texas, the weather was still unpredictable in April.

"Well, I've got to be going." He turned in the direction of his truck. A voice behind them approached.

"Hey, y'all," Delphine interrupted.

"Hey, there," Veola acknowledged.

"How ya doing?" Ruben Earl returned Delphine's greeting.

Veola and Ruben Earl spoke simultaneously.

"I'm gon' let y'all talk," Ruben Earl said, walking away.

"Hold on, Delphine, be right back." Veola escorted Ruben Earl to the front, seeing him off. He waved, and she saw him watching her through his rearview mirror.

The relationship between Veola and Ruben Earl was one of understanding. She didn't hug him when she greeted him, and she didn't shake his hand for this business deal. The peas for the free meal were traded on trust.

≈≋≋≈

Ruben Earl knew Veola appreciated everything he did for her. That's why he didn't think twice about bringing her the peas. She was such a good woman, and sometimes he sat and wondered just how good of a woman she was. Maybe too good, but he tried not to think about that too often. Upon occasion, he caught himself thinking about Veola in another way, but he tried to dismiss those feelings and thoughts. Convinced he made the right decision by cleaning up before he went over to Veola's, he wouldn't dare jeopardize their friendship. Leave that alone, Ruben Earl, he told himself. He drove on to his house.

Veola made her way back to Delphine. Veola felt the only reason Delphine was in Veola's backyard was because of peas.

Good Lord of Jesus, what was this woman wearing?

Veola evaluated Delphine's attire from top to bottom. The hair gave a whole new definition to 'combined curling.' The bulk of it was in pink foam rollers, and from the edges to the back, pin curls. What kind of hairdo would this make? From the way she usually looked, it was a waste of time.

The housecoat, light green nylon with a heavy white topstitch, was barely tied in the front and covered a dingy-blue cotton nightgown. The back hemline couldn't be seen, probably because Delphine had a big booty and everybody knew it. She wore tube socks, burgundy-striped at the top, and pulled halfway up her leg— downright country. Look at dem house shoes—bought as a matching pair, but one now darker than the other. Delphine had no business in public looking like this, and to think she crossed over a backyard without being arrested.

"Girl, is them peas?" Delphine asked, making her way to the porch.

"Cream peas."

"So early in the year?"

"I thought the same thang, but Ruben Earl said the man who planted them didn't think there was gon' be no more bad weather."

"Well, he damn shole got lucky. I ain't never seed peas look this good in March."

"That's what I told Ruben Earl." Veola anxiously waited for Delphine to ask her for some peas, unshelled or not.

Walking through the garden, Veola showed Delphine where she was going to put her crops this year even though she had probably been looking out of the window anyway at her and Ruben Earl. She wondered if she'd seen her and Eva Mae, too. Delphine was nosey like that, but Veola would never admit she was the same way. "Delphine, it's not too cool for you out here with that housecoat on?" she asked.

Delphine answered, but Veola didn't hear a word Delphine said. Veola looked in her eyes, yet Veola's peripheral vision worked overtime, stealing one more look at Delphine's attire. Delphine must have been ready for bed, yet Veola and Ruben Earl's presence had summoned her for a garden tour and chit-chat.

On the garden walk-through, Delphine had heard how many rows would be in collards, turnips, and mustard greens. They made their way back to the peas.

"I still got some black-eyed and purple hulls in my deep freeze from last year. Leonard brought them to me from Athens. You know, they got their good share of black-eyed peas," Delphine said.

Veola heard her mention the man of the hour, Leonard. At least he was good for something, Veola thought, bringing home black-eyed peas and helping her move cow manure. "Speaking of Leonard, how's he doing?" Veola decided to pick Delphine's mind. She turned completely away from the garden, staring directly at Delphine.

"Truth be told, Veola, we ain't seen much of him lately, and you know when we don't see him, he done got himself into more mess. Forty-five years old, and he ain't grown up yet."

"He in trouble?" Veola asked.

"He stay in trouble. Hell, everybody in Parkerville know that—always somewhere with the wrong people at the wrong time. That was one of his excuses. Then, he'd be chasing after some new gal who got three or four kids to start with, and the next thing you know, he shackin' up with 'em. First of all, who'd want a woman with three or four kids? They husband, if they had one, already gon', and they be the type Leonard move in with. Don't make sense to me, but me and Eli done decided he just lost."

Without interrupting Delphine, Veola nodded, sighed, and acted interested when she was supposed to. She waited for the right time to bring up Fayetta.

"Well, I just got off the phone with Eva Mae a while ago, and she said that he was up visiting Tyrone yesterday."

"Yesterday?" Delphine asked in disbelief.

"Yeah, after the Easter program."

"He done told us that he had to go out of town."

"That's what Eva Mae said, and I—" Veola began, but she was cut off.

"That fool come over here last Friday, but he asked me for money. Said he had to go out of town to take care of some papers. Neither one of us is crazy 'bout giving him another dime, and I didn't want to get his daddy all worked up. I didn't ask what papers, but we knew this last girl been trying to contact him about some money he owed her. He wanted twenty dollars."

Veola saw Delphine become more frustrated the more she kept going.

Delphine continued. "I thought if he could get himself right by twenty dollars, which I ain't got laying around, then it would be worth it. Lord knows that boy can worry the shit out of us. Now I wonder if he even left town. Veola, I gots to go. Talk to you later." She stormed off.

"Before you go, did you hear anything strange outside your house early Sunday morning?"

"Naw, I ain't heard nothing."

"Did you see anything?" Veola searched for clues, regretting she didn't get to ask if Loretta had her own trash can or if she saw anyone near hers.

Delphine didn't answer. Her beat-up house shoes were flopping, barely staying on her feet. The stripes on the tube socks were nowhere close to being even, comparing her right and left legs. Before she even reached the back door, she hollered for her husband to get up.

Veola heard Delphine yelling after she entered the house, and Veola didn't make a sound. When Delphine's back door slammed, Veola remained as quiet as she could as she tip-toed closer to their house, trying to hear as much of Delphine's screaming as possible from outside. There was no doubt in Veola's mind that Leonard was in trouble. Veola wondered if Delphine would tell Eli only about Leonard not going out of town or would she include the part about the borrowed money. Desperately, Veola wanted to hear the conversation. Once she realized she had creeped too far, she stopped.

How was Fayetta tied up in all of this? Nothing made sense. Maybe Fayetta didn't have anything to do with the new information Delphine shared, but Veola couldn't chase that notion away. She knew if her suspicions couldn't be squashed, it must have some validity and more often than not, she was right.

As Veola turned and headed for her own back door, she stared at Loretta's back window. Veola knew Loretta was probably peeking out the window right now, trying to see everything she could.

Knowing her, she's probably been watching my house and saw those peas being delivered. The nerve of Loretta calling her nosey, telling her she was up in everybody's business.

When Veola reached the steps of her porch, the curtain of Loretta's back window moved. Veola stood still and watched. At the bottom of the curtain, Veola spotted a finger, though the curtain was motionless. Loretta was in there snooping.

With all this drama, Veola worked up an appetite. She heard the phone ring over her own TV noise. Rushing into the house, she caught it. "Hello? Hello?" she answered. No one was there. She wondered if she had just missed Fayetta. She turned the TV off, knowing she was wearing her TV tube out when she wasn't watching it. She had heard and believed that an unwatched TV tube would burn out if it was left on too long.

Once Veola finished one meal, she prepared for the next. She took a chicken out of the freezer and put it in the sink. When she rang the dinner bell, she knew Jessie and Eva Mae would be front and center, ready to eat. Eva Mae told her one day, "Girl, you shole can cook," and Jessie followed right behind her with "shole can."

Veola joined their dialect when she was in their presence, yet she corrected herself in front of Mrs. Barton or the insurance man. Even the Watkins man, who sold household potions and cooking ingredients out of the back of his station wagon, heard her most correct English. She stocked up on his black pepper and witch hazel.

Nobody corrected Veola's speech. She said what she wanted and when she wanted to say it, but the key was that she flowed from one dialect to the other. She didn't waste time thinking about what she should say and how to say it. Sometimes, southern drawl and dialect came out worse in white folks than it did in blacks.

Fumbling in her kitchen, she caught herself laughing. She imagined what Jessie and Eva Mae would say if someone corrected them.

Eva Mae didn't care. She was so comfortable saying anything she wanted to that it "wasn't nothing" for her to use a four-letter word every now and then, never extending beyond hell, damn, shit, and ass. That pretty much got them all, now that Veola thought about it. She was a good Bible-carrying, funeral home fan-toting, sick and shut in-visiting Christian woman of the church, but she would cuss everybody out if they crossed her path. 'Curse' was not even in her vocabulary.

Jessie told Eva Mae one time, "I ain't talking to you 'cause you is too busy list'ning to how I'm talking rather than what I'm trying to tell ya." Veola rolled in laughter.

Moments like this kept Veola at peace. She lived alone, and one day some prowler outside would hear the excitement inside where no one lived but one woman. Undeniably, she'd be declared looney.

These bits of nostalgia propelled Veola. They gave her inspiration, and it was good for her to know and appreciate from where she had come. Cameron's reciting of Psalm 121 at church yesterday came into mind.

I will look unto the hills from whence cometh my help.
My help cometh from the Lord.........

Fayetta was still on her mind as she ran her bath water. She wasn't quite sure if Delphine helped or added more pieces to the puzzle. Veola went to retrieve the letter from the dresser, and as soon as she sat in her chair, the phone rang again. Maybe it was who she had missed earlier.

Veola answered after the first ring.

"Miss Veola? This is Fayetta. Fayetta Dewberry."

"Oh, how are you doing, Chile?" Veola smiled as if Fayetta saw her through the receiver.

"Well, I wish I could say I was fine, but I'll make it."

Veola detected the change in Fayetta's high spirits from the day before. Before Fayetta continued, Veola cleared her conscience. "I got your letter when I got home and was just sitting down to give you a call. One thing led to another, and I'm sure you understand when you work everyday."

"Oh yes, ma'am, I understand. I came back by your house earlier on the way to the store. That's when I left the note. I didn't know what time you got in, guessing it would be sometime tonight before I heard from you. I jumped the gun and called you first. Is this a bad time?"

"Not at all, Baby. Now what's going on?"

"I didn't want to alarm you, Miss Veola, but I wanted to come and sit and talk with you in person, not over the phone. You were always someone my mama admired. Calling down to Parkerville so many times and talking to people about my mama and her business stuff, it would be nice to be right in front of the person for a change. Does that make sense? The swing on your porch would be good for that."

Veola knew exactly what Fayetta was saying, a southern kind of hospitality between folk. "Why, you're more than welcome to come to my house. That would be nice. What are you doing tomorrow evening?" Veola asked, not giving her time to answer. "I'm coming back from downtown late tomorrow afternoon, and we can talk while I make dinner. Come on by. I might ask a couple of my good friends over for supper, but that won't be until about six or six thirty. How does that sound? Stay for dinner if you'd like."

"I don't want to impose on you with supper, but it would be kind of hard to refuse a meal like yours. If I remember right, you always cooked. Somebody from the neighborhood was always sampling something from your kitchen."

Veola realized Fayetta wanted to talk with her alone and not with Veola's good sistahs. "I'll give you a call once I get in from downtown. Come over a little early before my friends get here, and that way, we can have a little time for ourselves. These friends are just neighbors, folk from the church."

"Oh that would be fine. I'll see you tomorrow."

"'Night, 'night, Baby." Veola hung up. She knew she had not gotten anywhere with the conversation. Maybe there was no need to jump to suspicions or conclusions about Fayetta's letter. She called it a note, but to Veola, anything more than three or four lines constituted a letter.

Veola felt special knowing Fayetta wanted to confide in her—a welcomed feeling from someone she barely knew, yet the letter added a personal touch.

In spite of it being her bath time, Veola called Eva Mae and Jessie. Eva Mae was a late owl. She stayed up all night piddling. The ladies agreed on six thirty the following evening and didn't offer to bring a thing. Why would they? Veola had it all.

After her bath, Veola sat on the bed, grabbed her glasses, and watched the news at ten o'clock. Even with the voices on the TV, she played others in her head. The entire Barton family. Carneda and Cameron. Ruben Earl. Jessie and Eva Mae. Fayetta.

She got up, turned off the TV and quieted the room. She even turned off the people involved in her day. Upon crawling in between the sheets, the two blankets, and the one quilt, something hit the floor. The envelopes were displaced by her foot. She got out of bed one more time and surveyed the return addresses of her mail.

Montgomery Ward's. A bill. Sears & Roebuck. A bill. The Christian Women's Fellowship. Probably a newsletter. Lloyd's Furniture Store. Her two new lamps were almost paid off, looking perfect in her living room. One final letter caught her attention. It was from Esso, the gasoline people, so she opened it.

Squinting in her glasses, she sat up and read the letter carefully.

March 22, 1967

Veola Cook Estate
116 West Jackson St.
Parkerville, Texas 75799

Dear Mrs. Cook:

We have determined that you are the owner of the property listed in the tax office of Cherokee County, Texas approximately 3.67 miles east of New Winterfield on Highway 79 and 4.25 miles north on Farm to Market Road 1917.

As the owner of this property, we would like to discuss your mineral rights along with a separate contract involving a local company in the area to remove timber. These timber rights would allow the tree company to cut the timber and remove it from your property for the manufacture of wood materials and paper products.

As you are aware, coal is one of the natural resources found in our country that can be used for heating and cooling systems, solar energy, and other systems for the production of energy.

Our records indicate that the area east of New Winterfield is rich in this vast resource, and our fuel-based division of Esso Corporation is pleased that we do not have to travel outside the state of Texas to achieve our goal of obtaining resources for the products we are able to provide.

We would like to discuss this with you further if you are willing to call our headquarters, for we are arranging private interviews with you and your neighbors to better give you the benefits of what we would like to accomplish with the land you so rightfully own.

We have opened an associate office in the area for your convenience, and the contact person for your area is Richard Edelson. He can be reached at the affiliate office, area code 214, phone number Jupiter 8-4929.

Once you have contacted Mr. Edelson, his secretary will arrange to meet you at the property or at your home to discuss our desire to pay you for the rights to obtain these natural resources from your property.

Thank you for your time and cooperation, and we hope to hear from you soon.

Sincerely,

David Brooks

W. David Brooks
Vice President of Operations
Esso Corporation
2515 W. 3rd St., Ste. 100
La Marque, Texas   77986

Veola thought she understood what she read, but she knew she would re-read it one more time tomorrow. What was going on with her property? That land was special. Besides the part she acquired from Ervin, the additional land was the first thing she had bought flat out from her hard work and savings. She managed this in spite of taking care of her kids. The letter suggested her prized possession was in danger and posed a threat to her history. That property was a part of her upbringing, and she couldn't bear the thought of something happening to her and Ervin's tree.

Chapter Eight

After an early day with the Halls, at 12:30 p.m., Veola dialed her traveling buddy. "Jessie, I'm home. I'll be ready once I grab a quick bite."

"I could walk out the door in five minutes. All I need to do is put on my girdle and grab my purse."

"By the time you get that girdle on, I'll be out of this uniform and at the front door." Telling Jessie she was going to make a quick sandwich would delay her further, and from years of experience, Veola knew she had a little extra time.

"I'll be there in a few." Jessie hung up.

"Well, come on." Veola realized Jessie had already disconnected. Veola hurried herself since Jessie could have had that girdle on the bed, ready to throw it on and go.

Veola had a quick chicken salad sandwich at the Halls, but it was not the best. She was polite to eat Mrs. Hall's cooking, yet she used some no-name light bread. Of all of life's requirements that could be sacrificed, fresh Sunbeam bread was not one of them.

The Halls were warm, good-natured employers, but Veola didn't devote the time to their family dynamics as she did with the Bartons. The children were grown and out of the house. Mrs. Hall needed some help with the chores, allowing her devotion to her hobbies. What made a woman want to play golf three or four times per week truly puzzled Veola. She considered it wasting time chasing a little white ball. If it went in the bushes and trees, Veola suggested leaving it there. Get another, move on, that made sense. Veola put golf for Mrs. Hall and water-skiing for the Bartons in the same category.

Veola had been with the Halls for less than three years compared to the ten plus years with the Bartons, so to some extent, she shared a mother and daughter relationship with Mrs. Barton. With Veola's pointers, Mrs. Barton had almost mastered Veola's chicken salad recipe because she had a willingness to be nurtured. Veola suggested using dill relish instead of sweet relish, yet Mrs. Barton continued the sweet relish anyway. Veola left it alone, but she tasted the difference. She concluded that white people preferred sweet pickles and blacks preferred dills. She wondered why, believing it even if she couldn't prove it. For Eva Mae, it would have been one more difference between white and black folks rather than white and black people.

Mrs. Hall had never asked for any help in the kitchen. Whether it was sweet or dill relish, her food was bland, prepared without love.

Veola threw a dab of mayonnaise and a piece of salami on a slice of Sunbeam. While smacking, she planned her evening with Fayetta. She would have much of the food prepared before she arrived. That was basic southern hospitality. Besides, Veola was on a fact-finding mission and all parties involved had to concentrate. How could someone be serious with fried corn, onions and green peppers frying? Discussing important matters and the cook leaving the conversation to cut the fire down under a pot of cabbage was distracting.

Veola had thawed a chicken and some chicken wings that morning to make room in her freezer for those peas on her back porch. Smothered chicken with a bunch of onions, rice with chicken gravy, and a green salad were on the menu. A few pickled beets were in the icebox somewhere. That was it—a light meal. She had no time to make a pound cake, besides everyone had had sweets this past Sunday.

Veola chose a pastel green sundress and a pair of ivory shoes that didn't scream like bright white. She grabbed her scarf and sweater since it was windy, and because the sky was clear, she left her umbrella behind.

Even though the front door was open, Jessie banged on the top of the locked storm door. "Hey there! You ready?"

"I'm coming." Veola grabbed her purse and double-locked the front door.

Before they exited the porch, Jessie asked, "What is you gonna cook?"

"Don't you worry about that. You just be here," Veola answered. "If I was gon' cook an inner tube from a tire and if seasoned right, you'd eat it like it was your last meal. You eat everything I put in front of you, and you know it."

Sharing a laugh, they chatted about neighbors who got out of line, church ladies wearing inappropriate clothing, and milk prices going up.

"Have you seen Loretta recently?" Veola asked.

"Naw. Last week maybe."

They talked for the entire one and a half mile walk to the office of Dr. Harold Sweeney, Parkerville's notable optometrist.

Veola greeted the middle-aged, bouffant brunette, ever-so-plump white woman receptionist. Since she didn't have an appointment, she smiled. Sweet-talking may be required to get her eyes checked today.

The woman asked Veola and Jessie to have a seat, and she glanced over her appointment book. "We'll be with you shortly."

Pleased at the news, Veola began to survey the inventory. She spotted a pair of frames from across the room, and the silver-lined beauties seem to stare back at her. Rising to inspect them, she was summoned to the back.

"Mrs. Cook, we're ready for you," the receptionist announced, gesturing at Veola.

"Come on, Jessie," Veola said.

"Girl, I'm right behind you. You gon' git your new glasses soon enough."

A chair in the corner of the exam room was designated for guests: spouses, parents, best friends, boyfriends, co-dependents, or good sistahs. Jessie took that seat, and Veola sat in the exam chair.

Dr. Sweeney entered the room and after a pleasant greeting, he scanned her chart and got right to the point. "Let's see, Mrs. Cook. It seems you were last here," pausing, "three years ago. 116 West Jackson, West Jackson." For some reason, he mumbled Veola's address out loud—twice. "Well, what brings you in today?"

"Now, Doctor, you said it best. It's been three years, and I think I need some new glasses."

"Are you having any trouble with your old ones?"

"Maybe. I can still read my Bible, though it's getting difficult to thread my needle. But I was trying to see somebody far in the distance the other morning, and I couldn't tell who it was." She didn't tell him it was still dark outside.

The doctor whirled around on his stool, and he swung all sorts of gadgets toward Veola. "Well, let's just see what you can see now." He grabbed his fancy tools. He put her head behind some contraption and shone a light at her.

"Ooh, that light shole is bright."

Unfazed, he kept right on with his clicking and shining flashlights. "Mrs. Cook, can you see those letters?"

She leaned out from behind the contraption. "Those letters down there?" she asked, pointing to them.

"Yes, those letters."

"Let's see now. That's an F. Could be a Z. Well, it looks like a Z. And that's a B. And a D. The last one is an E."

Jessie got up and stood beside Veola. She left her purse in her chair, while Veola clutched hers.

Dr. Sweeney scrolled down the eye chart and after three more lines of reading the letters perfectly, Veola stumbled on the last letter. "That's a 7, I think. It looks like a 7."

"No it ain't," Jessie blurted out.

Veola passed Jessie her purse to shut her up, not moving from behind the contraption.

Dr. Sweeney looked up from his desk. "What did you say that last one was?"

"A seven."

"Well, it ain't," Jessie continued.

"Hold on. Don't move a thing. Oh, that's a T," Veola said.

"It shole is," Jessie declared.

Veola sensed Dr. Sweeney wanted to laugh as he cleared his throat and then flipped some lenses, asking Veola if she liked lens number one (click), versus lens number two (click).

Veola made her decision and the exam was off to the next part, reading up close. After Dr. Sweeney dialed some wheels in front of her, Veola cruised down the reading chart with ease.

"That's it, Mrs. Cook, the 20/20 line," he said, scribbling something on her chart.

"20/20," Veola said, remembering the ideal vision from her previous eye exams.

"Now, let's look at your eyes," he said. As he swung another machine in front of Veola, Jessie finally took her seat with the purses.

Veola leaned abruptly around the machine.

"Doctor, do I have cataracts? Are you checking me for the glaucomas?"

"Let me take a look." He directed her head back into proper position within the machine.

"You know, Veola, I thinks that Eva Mae gots the glucoma. She said she had catarats, too," Jessie said.

Veola watched Dr. Sweeney almost burst out laughing as he swung the machine away from her. She guessed he was trying to remain professional, but a mere chuckle escaped from his lips. His face turned red, and he had a little sweat across his forehead. He couldn't stop. Veola and Jessie looked at him, then at each other, and then back at him.

"I think I have heard it all, ladies. I'm going to give you a handout on GLAUCOMA and CATARACTS, so you can know what they are."

Veola didn't see what set the doctor into his laughing spell. She knew it had something to do with what Jessie said, but she hadn't registered the true pronunciations of the words in question. If it was the glucoma and catarats Jessie was telling her about, then she still didn't get it. What was funny about that? Jessie, always loaded with funny and odd expressions, had set off Veola's poor eye doctor. Veola wished she understood the joke.

Dr. Sweeney informed Veola she was free of the big bad cataracts and glaucoma she dreaded. He led the ladies to the reception desk to check out. "Oh, I know now why your address sounded familiar. I just saw a patient yesterday who lives on West Jackson. A Miss Mayfield. Miss Loretta Mayfield. She had a bad fall and broke her glasses this past weekend."

Veola and Jessie exchanged glances as soon as 'Mayfield' exited Dr. Sweeney's lips.

"Oh, really?" Veola asked.

"I believe that was her name," he said.

After Veola chose the frames she had eyed earlier, the silver beauties, she and Jessie were on their way home.

Veola attempted to make sense of Loretta's broken glasses. Because it wasn't light enough outside the other morning, Veola didn't know if Loretta was wearing them or not when she saw her run into her house. If she had fallen, she wasn't broken up or limping from the way she was moving about.

"Jessie, I didn't know Loretta broke her glasses. Maybe that's why we haven't seen her, 'cause she's as blind as a bat without them."

"I ain't never seen her without her glasses—church or nowhere else."

"I wonder how she broke them."

"The doctor just told you she fell."

"He don't know everything."

"Leave that alone, would you?"

"For now anyway."

No sooner had they gotten into their stride as she approached the corner, she noticed a familiar car, Dr. Barton's. Nearing the corner, Veola glanced inside Rexall Drugstore and spotted Dr. Barton in one of the booths. What was he doing downtown, having lunch, at the sandwich shop of the downtown drugstore? But he wasn't by himself. Some woman was sitting across from him whom Veola didn't recognize.

Veola pretended to be waiting for the red light to change, so she instructed Jessie to hold on. In spite of the green light permitting them to cross the street, she didn't move.

Cleverly, Veola shaded her eyes as she stared through the drugstore window. The woman would occasionally write something, and Dr. Barton was engrossed in the papers near his side of the table. Veola felt safe from his view since she was slightly to his back. If he turned around, she would surely be spotted. He'd recognize her anywhere. Oh Lord, what was going on? The woman was attractive, though casually dressed. She doubted this had anything to do with business. Veola wished she could hear what they were saying.

Jessie spoke to people on the street while Veola stared into the drugstore window. Jessie recognized everyone. "How ya durrin'? How yo mamanem? How all yo chirrens?" She greeted them all.

The stoplight had turned again. Finally, Veola was ready to cross. "Come on Jessie, let's go," Veola said as she almost jumped off the curb to get into the intersection. She'd seen enough.

These church buddies and true cousins were well into their walk home. The chit-chat picked up where they left off before. Veola promised to find out about Loretta's fall. What she kept to herself was that she'd also find out about Loretta's early morning skirmish with that man, why her trash can was missing, and why Dr. Barton was downtown at lunchtime with a strange woman.

Veola and Jessie headed toward Jessie's house to see her newly potted plants. As they neared the long stretch prior to Jessie's street, Veola noticed a truck go by that looked like Jeremy's.

Having just seen Dr. Barton in the drugstore, here she was thinking Jeremy's truck had just driven by. Maybe it was too much concentration on the Bartons, usually reserved for Mondays and Thursdays, not on Tuesdays. As much as she tried to discard the idea, she couldn't. That was Jeremy's truck, and she'd bet on it.

What was he doing over here in this part of town? She checked her watch to make sure he should be out of school. The truck turned on the old Frankston highway in the direction of Eva Mae's. Where was he going?

She wondered if he saw her and Jessie. He would have stopped, asked if they wanted a ride, or at least said something. Now she doubted herself. Maybe it wasn't him.

Veola picked up the pace, obviously on a mission. "Come on, Jessie, I want to see something. I thought I recognized that truck that went by." Veola bypassed Jessie's turn. "We'll see your plants later."

"Where we goin'?"

"Just follow me. You ain't got nothing to do until you come to my house and eat." Veola quieted Jessie and kept her close on her trail.

Her hunch paid off. Jeremy's Fightin' Panthers decal for his high school mascot was in the back window of the truck, parked in front of Tyrone's house. She saw that with her old glasses. Veola's thoughts raced. How did her Jeremy know Eva Mae's Tyrone?

"Jessie, I know that truck in front of Tyrone's," Veola whispered, as if the truck could hear her. Veola wanted Jessie to share her intrigue and curiosity to know more.

"How you know it?" Jessie asked.

"That's who I work for, Girl."

"Naw, Chile?" Jessie asked, putting her hand over her mouth and stopping dead in her tracks. She appeared shocked.

"Oh yes it is, too," Veola exclaimed, looking Jessie dead in her eyes with no smile.

Veola wasn't sure of her next move. There was no need to go to Eva Mae's. She'd see her later. She knew Jessie, her accomplice, awaited her direction.

All eyes were on Tyrone's front door. She thought she saw movement through the window, so they hid behind Eva Mae's tall bushes.

Jeremy opened the door, and Tyrone followed. Jeremy got into his truck and drove off. Tyrone went back inside and closed the door.

Veola couldn't hear a word, but she saw everything. Jessie, Veola's extra pair of eyes, caught it all.

Suddenly, Eva Mae came out her front door. "What is y'alls old asses doing behind them bushes?"

Scared to death, Veola's facial expression couldn't hide her guilt. Once she got over her initial reaction over Eva Mae's accusation, she and Jessie bolted for Eva Mae's front porch.

Tyrone looked out his front window.

Eva Mae stood with her hands on her hips, obviously waiting for one of them to answer the question.

Veola moved right past Eva Mae. "Come on and get in yo own house. I got something to ask you."

Eva Mae followed Veola as she was ordered, and Jessie stopped the screen door from slamming.

Normally, Veola would tell Eva Mae to quit cussing since she was a so-called woman of the church, a good and faithful soldier in the army of God, but right now, Veola was not interested in keeping

Eva Mae on the path to the Promised Land. The pleasantries were avoided.

Detective Veola Cook had arrived on the scene, and she went over what she had witnessed, bringing Eva Mae up to date. "Eva Mae, you know whose truck that was parked at Tyrone's?"

"I've seen it over there before," Eva Mae answered.

"You've seen it before? A whole lot?" Veola dug for information.

"Well, it's been up to Tyrone's a few times," Eva Mae explained.

"Do you know who that is?" Veola asked.

"Who? That white boy?" Eva Mae interjected.

"Yeah, him," Veola answered.

"Now how would I know who that is? Veola, if you got something to say, say it. Spit it out. Quit playing this guessing game. Tell us all, dammit."

"That's who I work for, Chile!" Veola exclaimed.

Jessie didn't even bother to put her purse down. She stood in between Veola and Eva Mae and Veola was glad for the separation.

"Well, Leonard be with him when he drive up here sometimes," Eva Mae added.

"My Jeremy knows Leonard? How in the world does he know Leonard? Oh, my Lord!" Veola's heart rate increased, and she didn't want Eva Mae to clam up now.

Veola held court as the lawyer, Eva Mae, the witness, and Jessie, the expressive lone juror with a few yeahs and naws being heard periodically. No judge would declare contempt on anyone.

Eva Mae fed Veola information, and neither one of them knew what it all meant.

"I don't know nothing about nothing, and y'all ain't helped," Jessie said. "I listened to y'all and y'all still ain't put the pieces together for me."

That was not unusual for Jessie, and Veola knew it. Eva Mae bid them farewell as Veola and Jessie headed home. The session ended with nothing solved.

Veola batted questions to Jessie, and Jessie had no answers for her. Veola tried to connect Jeremy to Tyrone. Jessie had no answers for her. What was that friendship about? And then, Leonard.

What could these black men have in common with a white teenager whose daddy was one of the town's most respected doctors?

Jeremy had plenty of friends—black, white, Mexican, never limited by race or color. He had been raised right, at least in Veola's mind. He loved all people, and Veola helped see to that. But what did he need from a grown black man who hadn't amounted to much? Delphine and his lazy daddy, Eli, could vouch for that.

Veola didn't know what all this meant, and if she were to make her mind up on speculation, she might be mistaken. She'd keep her mind open and think about it later.

Jessie branched off at her corner, and they agreed to see her backyard later.

❧

Tyrone picked the perfect time to be at his window. He caught Miss Veola and Miss Jessie turning the corner as he continued to chew on his cookie. He'd just gotten home from work, and he wondered what they were doing at his mama's house this time of day. Ain't no telling, stupid old women. All they have to do all day is watch stories and go to prayer meeting.

However, that didn't concern him right now, since he had enough on his mind already. Watching Leonard and Fayetta together on Sunday was bad enough. Why she continued to chase that man was a mystery to him, and it was obvious that he didn't want her with all the other damn women he got 'round town. Fayetta must not have told Leonard about the early Sunday morning visit he paid her. Otherwise, Leonard would have been in his face with some bullshit. Tyrone hoped she still had feelings for him after all these years and just didn't want to share them yet. He'll deal with that later.

Jeremy was throwing off Tyrone's concentration, so the key was to get this young white boy out of his house. He made the deal quickly and Jeremy was gone. Now that his house was empty, he thought about tonight. He'd ironed out every detail and seeing Miss Veola made him more committed to proceeding with his plans.

❧

Veola thoughts continued to run amuck. With guests on their

way shortly, she headed for her kitchen. Sometimes she did her best thinking while rattling pans and stirring pots.

In a matter of time, the chicken was savoring, smothered in just the right amount of onions, green bell peppers, lemon pepper, and garlic salt. The doorbell rang and Veola saw Fayetta through the storm door glass. She knew Fayetta could smell every bit of its succulence as she ascended Veola's steps.

Once inside, Fayetta followed Veola back to the kitchen table where Veola poured her a glass of sweetened iced tea.

"What's going on, Fayetta?"

"I told you I was here trying to handle some things for my mother, but actually, I'm here to take care of some matters for myself. Before I left here going to Dallas, I was pregnant. My oldest child is here with me at my cousin's house. He's on his spring break, and my daughter will be here tonight with some more cousins on their way to Henderson. They'll drop her off here. Tomorrow, we're in court."

"Court?"

"That's why I'm here. Do you know Leonard Johnson? His mama and daddy live a few houses up from you."

"Why, sho I know Leonard."

"Leonard's older than me, but he's my children's daddy."

"Both of them?"

"Yes, ma'am. My children were born in Dallas, and for a while, Leonard moved there with us. We thought we were going to get married, so one thing led to another. We had a girl eight years later."

Fayetta's facial expression immediately changed. Her back straightened, her solemn face became hard, and her voice turned from sweet innocence to rigidity. "Now I know what he did. He used me. He told me he wanted to be with me and to be a part of his children's lives, and I thought that he was going to help me raise them. To me, that meant being there for them and to help me out financially. That didn't last long. He came right back to Parkerville, and now, I can't get a thing from him. I've written letters asking for help, called down here to his probation officer to see if he would pay anything, on top of everything else I could do. It hasn't been fair to me or the children. We never married, and I ended up marrying someone else. That didn't last too long, because I think I was still angry with Leonard. Part of it may have been anger, and the other part was that since he was older than me, I trusted him more than I would have trusted someone my own age. That's why it was hard to let him go. The children and I have made it up to now, but it's getting harder and harder, Miss Veola."

Veola remembered her food on the stove. Keeping her eyes on Fayetta, she turned off the burners. This girl bared her heart and soul, so the meal preparation had to wait.

Fayetta stated her case, and Veola absorbed every detail.

"After Leonard came back home, he was always up to no good. I didn't want my kids to be a part of this, and that's why it was easier for me to stay in Dallas rather than here with him. My life, their lives, too, would have been miserable. Leonard didn't even want us here, always saying he never had any money. I knew he worked, but we never saw any of it. Even as their mama, I'm tired of doing all I can for my children by myself. I need his help, and too bad I have to go to court to get it. They set me up with a lawyer here, and that's where I've been going all week getting ready for tomorrow."

Veola was speechless. Fayetta verified once again how Leonard was no good. Veola tried to give him credit for helping her in the garden once, but that was the only lifeline she could muster for him. What stuck out mostly was knowing he had been in and out of jail. He'd had odd jobs on and off. She recalled hearing some folks at church talk about how he'd shown up for work drunk a few times. Once he almost threw up right in front of his boss.

Veola knew Delphine knew her stepson was not the most model citizen of the community. Veola would bet that Delphine also knew that Leonard was the father of many children around here in town and Veola would stake a claim that Delphine knew about these children of his in Dallas. Never did this come up in any conversation she'd had with her neighbor—something Delphine probably avoided discussing.

Fayetta blinked back tears of pent-up frustration and asked Veola for a Kleenex.

Veola returned from the bathroom with a box of tissues and embraced Fayetta. "It's gon' be all right, Baby. It's gon' work out. You think you're in this all by yourself, but you're not. Right now, you've got me here with you, but better yet, you've got God with you all the time. Let Him know exactly what you need, and He'll help you."

"I know, Miss Veola," Fayetta said between the sobs, "but I just want him to help me out with my children. I want them to have things in life, go places, do things other kids do. For me to get a new man in my life to do that for them is wrong, and unfair to him. Leonard should be the one doing more for them. Those are his kids."

"You're right, Baby, we know you're right. I know what you're trying to get from him, but are you sure he has the money to help support your children?"

Veola knew the answer to this question before she asked it. She tried to see what could become of this court proceeding. He hadn't been responsible before now, and no judge would make him change.

"Every time Leonard gets a job, he is always taking care of some new woman in his life. Lord knows, there have been a few others. Some of these have been good jobs, and I just want it to be on record that part of what he makes needs to be for my children, his children."

"You mean a part of his paycheck should go to you for your children?" Veola needed clarification.

"Right, not for me, but for my kids. We weren't ever married, and maybe we were together long enough to be common law. And it's probably some more women in that same situation with him. I know he has some more kids out there, somewhere. Lord, what was I thinking? I was young, young and in love. At least that's what I thought."

"Baby, don't beat yourself up. You've suffered enough. I'm sure questioning why you did what you did is just adding more salt to the wound. But now you have to do what you think is right. In doing what's right for them, you'll be doing what's right for you, too, and that doesn't matter whether you're married or not. You see, Fayetta, even when you're married, you have the same doubts of whether or not you are doing the right thing. There will be problems, but you have to get through them. Just because my husband carved my name in a tree trunk once didn't mean I didn't think about chopping that tree down when I got frustrated with him. You've heard this before, so there is no need of me rambling about it."

"I've tried to reason with him since I've been here. You've seen me walking up and down your street. I've tried to catch him at his mama and daddy's house, and he's never there. I called his best friend's house, had to go through his mama, Miss Eva Mae, for that, though, and Tyrone protected him forever. He would say, 'he was here earlier, but he ain't here now'. Finally, I just showed up at Tyrone's and that didn't do a bit of good. We just got into it even more. I know why they hang out together because the two of them together are nothing but trouble—selling dope, chasing women, you name it, they're doing it."

"Leonard? Selling dope? Tyrone, too?" Veola hated to hear such bad news. She could not downplay what was just thrown in her lap. If Leonard and Tyrone were such good friends, then they could be partners in a lot of other activities, obviously up to no good.

Selling dope was terrible, and what would make them want to do that? The womanizing was not a shock, but selling dope was against the law. Was that why Leonard had been in and out of jail? She even remembered Tyrone having to go there for some violation. Lord knows how many times that happened, but she only recalled one time Eva Mae told her about. Eva Mae said it was related to some speeding tickets. Now Veola wondered if that was all it was.

Veola wanted answers. She couldn't wait for her sistahs to get there for dinner. Eva Mae would have to put more pieces of this puzzle together with a few more questions. Yes, God, she shole would.

"Jeremy," Veola said. She couldn't contain her outburst.

"Jeremy?" Fayetta asked, sounding surprised. "Who is that?" She dried her tears.

"Oh, you don't know him. Something you said about Leonard and Tyrone made me think of him, but I'm talking to myself."

Veola realized she was off the subject of Leonard and Tyrone, but she couldn't go into any further detail, not just yet. It seemed to Veola that Fayetta didn't care about who Leonard hung around. Her mission was to get some financial help.

Veola smelled her food, and she knew Fayetta did, too. Veola returned to her kitchen and changed subjects, attempting to lighten the somber mood. She noticed Fayetta had a blank stare.

Abruptly, Fayetta arose from her chair. "Miss Veola, I'd better be going now."

"You mean you don't want a bite to eat?"

"No ma'am, I'd better get home to make sure I'm ready for

tomorrow." Fayetta made her way toward the front door.

"You know, I was planning on you staying for dinner," Veola offered, knowing her last plea was in vain after witnessing Fayetta's desperate look.

"I thought I could, but I can't. Your food smells mighty good, but I wanted to tell you what was going on."

Veola accepted Fayetta's change of heart over dinner, and she believed the woman's reason for departing was sincere. Jessie and Eva Mae would arrive in a few minutes, and maybe Fayetta didn't feel comfortable in this present state of mind being with other company. Veola knew even though Fayetta opened up about her present matter, she still may have been uncomfortable divulging such personal matters. If she was reserved in discussing it with Veola, then she knew she was going to be even more guarded when Jessie and Eva Mae arrived.

"Can I get you a plate to take with you, Fayetta?"

Veola wanted to make sure she hadn't been the reason Fayetta had such a change of heart, and she wanted to take care of her end of the invitation of breaking bread together with a plate for the road.

"No, that's okay. You're too kind, Mrs. Cook. Just think about me tomorrow, and keep me in your prayers," Fayetta said, descending Veola's steps and waving goodbye.

Veola noticed that Fayetta went in the opposite direction of her mama's house.

No sooner than Veola was about to go back inside that she spotted Jessie coming up the street from the direction she thought Fayetta would have headed. Eva Mae couldn't be that far behind, so Veola decided to save her story for the both of them. Not wanting to repeat it, they both needed to know the real reason Fayetta was back in town.

Good gossip was about to be served.

Chapter Nine

Jeremy had one of those shitty days at school, so immediately afterward, he drove to Tyrone's to get his fix. His baseball coach had been riding him and had nerve enough today to tell him he'd have to fight for his starting position at first base. He'd played first base for three years, and he was not about to let some newcomer take his place.

He got word from his buddy that the girl he'd thought about asking out sent him a message to not even waste his time because she'd gotten wind of his presumed "bad habits." Some nerve of that goody two-shoes, a stick-in-the-mud like her.

Jeremy cared little about his coach or this girl. For right now, he was feeling good in his own world lying on the pier. Last Friday night he may have gone too far by falling asleep out here. When he told his mom and dad he decided to stay at the lake, he withheld how he'd slept out on the pier because he was too high to get up and go inside the lake house. This time, a weeknight, he couldn't make the same mistake.

As he drifted, he thought about why his coach was picking on him, what was happening between his parents and the suspicion that maybe his dad was fooling around, and how he can go after any girl he wanted. He didn't need any one of them right now—his coach, his parents, Veola, absolutely no one, except Tyrone.

Tyrone always had some good stuff, and it was worth every bit of the ten dollars he paid per bag. As he relaxed, he floated somewhere far away.

❧

The sistahs gathered once again outside the churchhouse. Eva Mae, two minutes behind Jessie, entered Veola's house gabbing. "I just passed that girl, Fayetta, on the street. I wonder where she was going."

"She just left here," Veola added.

"For what?"

Instead of giving Eva Mae a disapproving look for asking about Veola's business with other people, Veola kept right on talking. Then, she moved her pots on the stove to make a space for the hot biscuits coming out of the oven.

Veola appeased Eva Mae. "She just stopped by for a second. Said she had some places to go."

Eva Mae chimed in. "She could be going anywhere, maybe back up to Tyrone's. I'm gon' talk to him about the company he keeps."

Veola knew Eva Mae was a meddling mama, protective and overbearing. Sometimes, though, she was too controlling. A little for Eva Mae was way too much by most standards. Besides, she was the one who bailed him out of his misfortunes. Where were his so-called friends when Tyrone really needed them?

Jessie came for one reason—to eat. "It shole do smell good in here. Girl, you must have started cooking as soon as you got home." She left to wash her hands.

Putting the food on the table kept people out of her kitchen, including her good sistahs from Greater New Mount Olive Missionary Baptist Church of the Living God. Veola surveyed the presentation— smothered chicken and rice with extra gravy, French and Thousand Island dressing for the freshly tossed salad, and a pan of hot biscuits coated in dripping butter. She used the glass salt and pepper shakers from the china cabinet behind her, rather than the aluminum ones with dents and grease spots she kept over the stove.

"We're ready to eat. Time for grace," Veola announced.

Eva Mae dabbed the few spots of sweat on her forehead with a Kleenex she'd snatched as she came out of the bathroom. For women, tissues were staples for the hand and for the purse. She seated herself on the opposite end of the table from Veola, who remained close to the kitchen. Jessie sat between them, ideally positioned for the conversation between Eva Mae and Veola.

"I'll say grace," Veola said. They bowed their heads and closed their eyes.

"Oh, most gracious and mighty Father, we come today with bowed heads and humble hearts giving you all the praises and honor you so deserve for watching over us, guiding us in your footsteps, keeping us on the right path, and we just want to say thank you, Lord. Just thank you for what you've done for each and every one of us here today. We catch ourselves in critical times, dear Master, for you know your children's needs. Be here with us, right now, and everyday of our lives."

Jessie and Eva Mae had their respectable moans and grunts and amens in the middle of Veola's blessing. Their heads raised. They glanced in Veola's direction. They immediately closed again when Deaconness Veola Cook continued.

"Dear God, some of your children are hurting, needing you to touch them in a special way to let them know you're still the only One who rules, sees, hears, and knows all things. Lord, you know what is best for each and everyone of us. You're the doctor when we're sick, the lawyer when we've been abused, and the comforter for those in pain."

A few "yes, Gods," head nods, and amens came from Sistah Eva Mae and Sistah Jessie. Finally, Veola rounded the prayer corner.

"We want to bless the food we're about to receive for the nourishment of our bodies, bless the hands that prepared it, and bless those that partake that we may use it for our strength and the wellness of our bodies. In Christ's name, we pray. Amen."

"Veola, that shole was a long blessing," Eva Mae stated.

"Sometimes you got to say a little more than usual over the food," Veola replied.

"That's right," Jessie said, reaching for the salad.

Veola knew that prayer over a weeknight dinner was typically not that detailed, so she wondered if her dear sistahs would suspect anything. Her prayer meant something more than blessing the food.

"Well, I know we gon' talk about that later," Eva Mae said, "but for now, Jessie, hand me that salad."

"Eva Mae, pass me them biscuits and while you're at it, give me some of that butter," Jessie ordered, interrupting Veola's serious thoughts.

Obviously, they were content for now enjoying the food set before them. Mouths chomped and lips smacked. These ladies knew each other well enough that if they licked their fingers, so unlady-like, in front of each other, their secret would stay right there at that table.

After the dishes were moved to the kitchen, Eva Mae found her a spot on the living room sofa. Veola and Jessie joined her after iced tea refills were poured.

"Veola, I know I've seen Fayetta up to Tyrone's. I usually knows what goes on during the day on my street, but I don't always know what goes on at night," Eva Mae began.

Veola and Jessie glanced at each other.

Eva Mae continued. "Fayetta came to church on Sunday, and from what I hear, she been in town a few days. Folks say she here tending to her mama's business. You said she stopped by here a while ago, and I want to know what you know. I think you're holding out on us." She raised an eyebrow.

"Now y'all," Veola said, happy to convey what she knew as she crossed her legs and her hands idly fingered the ruffle thrills of her apron. She paused. "I know that girl has a good heart. She was raised right, but she got herself mixed up with Leonard. He ain't right for nobody. We all heard the same thing about what he's done, who he been with, and all that mess. Right now, she has some things to work out with him. As children of God, we need to pray for them and ask God to make her strong with whatever she going through."

"I'll pray for them, all right, but I needs to know what I'm praying for," Eva Mae blurted out.

Jessie threw herself back in her chair. "Amen, Sistah Eva Mae, I know that's right."

Veola crossed her arms. "It doesn't matter what she's going through. They both need prayer."

"Now, Veola, we all needs prayer, mind you, but what was she here for? I bet she didn't come here with a bowed head. She here for something, whether it's got anything to do with her mama's thangs or anything else. Is she moving back? I heard she got one child down here, and I don't know nothing about another kid they say she got in Dallas. Tyrone told me she had two, and—"

"Yeah, she here for her children," Veola interrupted Eva Mae scowling. "To go to court in the morning to get money from her children's daddy, Leonard." Veola lifted an index finger. "It's all about getting help. I don't know if she ever received any, if the money done stopped, or whether she trying to get him to pay up for lost time. Now that much I know." Veola saw them staring at her.

"Girl, hush yo mouth!" exclaimed Jessie.

"Chile, if I'd knowed that, I'd have cussed Leonard out for her everytime I see his no-good ass up to Tyrone's," Eva Mae vowed.

Perhaps now Veola felt Eva Mae understood why Fayetta came up to Tyrone's looking for Leonard. Because they were running buddies, she wondered if Tyrone protected Leonard since she just happened to find him at Tyrone's place that day.

"Do you think Tyrone know about this, Eva Mae?" Veola asked.

"Hell, I don't know," Eva Mae answered. "That poor chile."

"Who?" asked Jessie.

"Who else, Jessie? Fayetta. Keep up, Girl," Eva Mae snapped.

Only now did Fayetta become that poor little girl. She used to be a nosey little thang who needed to head right back to Dallas where she belonged. What a bit of knowledge can do to bring about a change of heart.

Eva Mae continued, "Well, if she going to court, surely she gon' see him there. What she looking for him on the streets for? He got to show up there, don't he?"

"Well, if he don't show up, they shole nuff gon' lock him up." Jessie said, wide-eyed.

A man and a woman fighting over money was nothing new, but

to air it out in court was a last resort. Their speculation turned into gossip. They'd pray about it later.

"Veola, was they ever married?" Eva Mae asked.

"Now that I don't know. From what I gather, she didn't mention nothing about no alimony or anything for herself. She just wants what's right for her children."

"She should take every rotten nickel he got. That fool ain't worth a damn and never will be," Eva Mae said. "If he can't give her nothing on his own, then let her do what she gotta do to get what she need. It's a shame she have to go to court."

"Yes, it is. Now how many children you say they got?" Jessie asked.

"Two," Veola answered.

"Well, he damn shole got more around here," Eva Mae said.

"He shole do. I know of at least five or six more kids right here in Parkerville. That is too many chirren for anybody that can't support 'em. Minerva's grandkids is by him, Dollean's grandchirren by her middle daughter is his, and I can't think of that girl's name out in Shady Grove. But one of them kids is his, too," Jessie declared.

"You see what she's going through?" Veola asked. "She is a brave soul going after him with so much on her already. I'm hoping and praying it works out for her. It ain't right to have to beg the daddy to help take care of his own children."

The discussion moved on, and Eva Mae asked Veola about her neighbor, Loretta. Veola reported that she hadn't seen her but informed Eva Mae about Loretta's visit to the eye doctor after she'd broken her glasses. Veola decided then that enough gossip had already been on the table. The ladies called it an evening before it got too late.

Walking in the dark was commonplace for the sistahs, and anyone in their right mind would have been too scared to attack them. They seldom walked at night, but for the couple of blocks that separated them, they were as comfortable as if it were mid-afternoon. Only in their own little residential area were they not worried about getting caught by nightfall, yet they didn't branch outside of this comfort zone.

Veola stood on her front porch and watched the women part in the middle of her street and head to their respective homes.

"Y'all call me when you get home," Veola ordered.

"I'll call you before you get back into that house," Jessie said. She laughed at her own joke as she picked up her pace.

"All right, Veola. I'll buzz you in a minute. I'll be in the bed after that," Eva Mae shouted back, heading the back way through the garden.

After watching them turn their corners, Veola wished she could have lounged on her front porch for a minute. A slight breeze fueled the smell of her flowers and plants. The air was addictive, conducive to relaxing. Instead, she returned to the kitchen.

Her clean-up was essentially done for she tidied up as she cooked. Those sistahs ate everything, so there was no food to place in the icebox.

About the time she left the kitchen to prepare for her evening bath, Jessie and Eva Mae both called, one right after the other. She hadn't worried about them, but she was assured they were home. The thank-yous for the meal, prayers and concerns for Fayetta, and wishes for a good night were passed on.

Veola sympathized with Fayetta and thought about how she, too, was a single mother raising kids on her own forty years ago. She had a choice. Maybe her circumstances would have been different had she accepted the invitations of the men who came her way. But she didn't need them, and she didn't want them telling her what to do. She'd gone through that once. Never again.

But she made it. God never stops looking out for His children. Oh, what a mighty, mighty, God we serve. He is so good to each and every one of us. She wanted God to look out for Fayetta tomorrow when she went down and fought for what is right. Even look out for Leonard, Lord, to show him the light. Your children get lost, Lord, and we stray. Not a single one of us is perfect. Far from it. That's why you have to stay on us. The devil is busy, and she knew she didn't have to remind God of that. She stopped walking for the rest of her silent prayer.

God, guide over my baby, Jeremy. You and only you, Lord, knows whatever purpose he plays in this matter, but if it ain't what you want, shield him from harm so he won't get hurt. I couldn't bear it, and I know his mama and daddy couldn't take it either. Mrs. Barton

*is over there crying, and Dr. Barton is drinking everything in sight. I
don't know what he's up to, but Lord, you and only you can make it
right. Tell me what I can do to help.*

Adding all the emollients she found on her bathtub—something
green from one bottle, something lilac from another one, and some
perfumed salts, she climbed into the concoction she had created. Her
mind at ease, she took time for herself. Once she'd given her concerns
to God, that was all she could do.

She crawled into bed and reached for her old glasses. Her day
had been full. Glad she didn't put her new glasses on layaway, she'd
have her new ones this Sunday. They should be ready by Friday, Dr.
Sweeney said.

As soon as she read two pages of her Bible study, her eyes were
closed. Too tired to dream, she roused briefly to take off her specs and
turn off the light. The hot bath full of potions and lotions worked its
magic. This night, God blessed her with rest.

Sleep, my Child, and peace attend thee. All through the night.

❦

In spite of God's plans for Veola, the devil had some of his own.

Tyrone made his way through the brush surrounding Veola's
garden, watching for any lights in her house. If she went to bed like
most old ladies, he counted on her being asleep for at least an hour.
The lights in all the houses in the neighborhood were out.

Surely nobody was looking out of their windows at midnight.
Just in case, he pulled his black cap from his pocket and put it on.

With three houses on this row, he kept an eye on each of them
as he made his way around to Veola's front door, treading lightly on
the side of the house opposite her bedroom. He encountered a few
barking dogs close to his own house when he ventured off the main
street, but he began to get a little energy knowing none of Veola's
neighbors had dogs. All he heard was his own footsteps and his
pulsating heartbeat. His adrenaline peaked as he held the rock he
found and carried, specifically for this purpose.

He'd done his homework. Going through one of the high
windows would take too long; she would have too much time to call the

police. He wanted to go through the front door while she was home. Folks hid their money, so he needed help. Going through shoe and hat boxes, he'd often found a stash. The mattress and under the corners of rug mats were big hiding places. He was sure of her cooperation.

Inspecting her storm door one last time, the top third was double glass-paned, the bottom panel aluminum. He breathed deeply then exhaled through his mouth. He hurled the big rock.

The glass shattering made less noise than he'd thought. He thrust his hand and arm through and fidgeted with the lock on the storm door. All he had to do was unlatch it and he could kick in the front door. He hurried. Assuming Veola was in her bedroom, he hoped that by the time she realized what had happened, she'd have little time to react. He counted on it.

But the storm door latch wouldn't budge. The glass was broken unevenly and only in the center on the front door. He leaned in farther to grab and yank the door knob. He became confused and rattled, and his forearm caught on the glass. The pain shot up into his neck.

❦

The noise of the glass breaking woke Veola. She wasted no time wondering what was going on. Snatching up her glasses, she reacted quickly with purpose, rushing to the front door.

Veola saw glass scattered on her living room floor. The glass from both of her doors was broken, and a burglar was breaking into her house. His arm dangled through a jagged hole in the glass, while his hand rattled her deadbolt. She knew she had to react quickly; she couldn't afford to freeze or panic.

Veola flew to her bed and grabbed the gun between her mattress and box springs. She ran back to face her predator. This monster must be stopped!

"What is you trying to do?" she screamed. "If you don't get out of here, I'm gon' shoot you dead."

The man did not answer but continued to wrestle with the door, rattling the doorknob. She realized she might have to use her gun if he managed to break through. Lord knows, she didn't want to, so she begged and pleaded with her Lord to keep her finger off the trigger.

The top broken glass slipped from its edge and came down right across the man's forearm. Suddenly the man's arm was caught. He cried out in a muffled voice, "Aw, shit."

Veola was on the verge of panic. Was he large enough to crash through the door, get his arm free, and attack her? "You'd better get out of here and get out of my door. This is my house. Help me Lord!" She spotted her broom from its silhouette the streetlight provided by shining through her front bedroom window.

Thank you, Lord.

Still holding her gun in one hand, the other hand grabbed her broom handle just above the bristles. She began batting the intruder's hand and arm, hammering him like she was swatting flies. Finally, he extracted his arm from the broken glass, letting out a muffled scream. He jumped off the porch and ran straight out through the open lots across the street.

Veola quickly dialed the police. "Somebody just tried to break in my house, and I need y'all now."

Then she called Carneda.

"Mama, are you hurt?" Carneda asked.

"I'm all right," Veola answered, "Just a little shaken up."

"We're on our way," Carneda promised and hung up the phone.

Veola called Ruben Earl as if by instinct and gave him a blow-by-blow account. The police arrived first, shortly before Ruben Earl, and Veola repeated every detail. By the time Carneda and the boys arrived, she'd already recanted the story twice. Ruben Earl embraced her across the shoulders. Veola knew he'd do whatever he could to make sure she felt safe and secure.

Ruben Earl stared at the front door. Veola sensed his mind was hard at work already. The aluminum and wood frames of the doors were intact other than the broken glass. Promising he'd be back shortly, he left.

Veola got her nerves together. Amazingly, she was much more relaxed than her family. The police went about their normal routine checking around the property with flashlights. Their search for clues was hampered by the dark.

Carneda appeared worried once Veola admitted she'd pulled out her gun.

"You needed your gun, Mama?" Carneda asked.

"I didn't use it, but it shole felt good to have it in my hand."

The police asked questions and took notes. "Mrs. Cook, do you think you might have known what he was after?"

"What difference does it make?" Veola snapped sharply. "Whatever it was, it was mine. Not his."

"What I'm asking is do you have some valuables anyone might have known about here at the house?" he asked.

"Everything I have in this house is valuable, Officer, and I'm gon' keep it that way," Veola added calmly.

"Do you have any idea who might do something like this to you?" Commanding everyone's attention, the officer stopped writing.

"Sir, if I knew the answer to that question, me and you wouldn't be having such a long conversation. I would have given you the name a long time ago, and then you'd be out there banging on his door while I'm trying to fix mine. I know it was a man from the size of those gloves. Ain't no woman got hands that big. He was kind of tall, even though most of him was bent over trying to reach in and open my doors."

"Could you tell if he was black or white, ma'am?" he asked.

"I don't know. It was too dark and he was all covered up."

"Well, ma'am, could you make out—"

"What makes folks wanna steal—be a crook?"

"I don't know, ma'am—"

"Well, they either looking for money or something to sell for money, that's why," Veola said with conviction. "People do things now-a-days for no good reason. I told you earlier, I had trash dumped on my porch this past Sunday mornin' and now, a break-in."

"Do you think—"

"The trash was mine," Veola interrupted, "and I don't know what they was looking for. I just feel like somebody's watching me."

"We're going to do our best to locate him, Mrs. Cook," the policeman said.

"You do that, Officer," Veola said, planning to hold him to his word.

Ruben Earl returned with plywood he had at his house, and he boarded up the area between the storm and front doors. The plywood fit perfectly for a temporary fix. Lord knows, Ruben Earl was worth more to her than she realized.

Reassuring everyone she was fine, Veola refused to go home with Carneda for the night. She just needed some sleep, and she'd deal with what all that happened in the morning. No one could convince her to leave her house that night, so she made everyone go home.

Ruben Earl told her he'd see her when the sun came up. All she had to buy was the glass for her doors and he'd take care of everything else.

Saying good-bye to Ruben Earl, she glanced at her neighbor's house. Where was that heifer, Loretta? With all this commotion, she didn't even have a light on. Now she wondered if she was even home, or was she peeking out the window again? Veola wondered if the man Loretta had thrown the clothes at been put up to do this? Had she made Loretta that mad?

As they left, the policemen told Veola she was very lucky.

Veola knew otherwise. She was blessed, and she thanked God for it. She had God on her mind when she finally dozed off, but as usual, the devil was somewhere nearby. Her gun remained under her spare pillow on her bed, at least for tonight. She was so thankful she didn't have to move the latch from its safety position.

❧❦

Ruben Earl wished he could get his hands on the man who tried to break in Veola's house. Why would anyone want to hurt such a sweet person, a dear, dear friend of his, and a woman he cared so much for? Even though she didn't have to, he was glad he was one of the first persons she called—made him feel mighty special. As soon as he got the call, he headed right over just in case it still might not be safe for her? He barely remembered to brush his teeth so he could get to her as fast as he could. What he wanted to do was to protect her from any harm and danger, but he knew that was out of the question. Beating that man with a broom handle took the cake. It was not a laughing matter, so he told himself that seeing Veola beat him the way she described was not funny. He was glad she knew how to protect herself, but in the back of his mind, he thought about the remote possibility of something happening to her. That he couldn't take.

Veola got a gun, and she didn't even tell him. He wasn't privy to all her information and maybe she wasn't supposed to tell him what she got and where she got it. Step back, Ruben Earl, he told himself. He was moving just a little too fast. Now, if she would have had to shoot somebody in self-defense, then he was glad she had a back-up plan. That broom would only keep 'em off so far and for so long.

At least he had her safe for the night with that plywood. He had not checked the back door to make sure it was secure. Luckily, there were no windows, so he felt safer about whoever it was entering that way. Surely she wouldn't be bothered again on the same night.

Watch yourself, Veola, watch yourself. I just couldn't bear anything happening to you.

🕊️🕊️

Tyrone's gash had finally stopped bleeding and it needed ointment. All he had in the house was Vaseline. An old ace bandage without clamps was under the bathroom sink, so he doctored on himself the best way he knew how, using duct tape to secure it. When he moved his arm in certain directions, the pain showed on his face, letting him know just what he'd done. She's supposed to be a Christian, but something told him that that bitch would have shot him.

Tyrone anticipated the next day already, knowing he had to go to work. For sure, he'd wear a long-sleeve tee shirt. He expected some comments from his co-workers since he was sure to get hot with his extra covering. He'd tell them he was feeling chilly, like he was catching a cold or the flu. Looking at his bandaged arm, he determined this was way more than he had bargained for.

Tomorrow, he'd see how he felt. If need be, he'd get help. He'd come to the aid of his friends many times in the past, and he knew they'd do the same for him. Dammit, his arm was killing him.

Chapter Ten

"Mama, am I waking you up?" Carneda asked. "I'm making sure you made it through the night."

Veola answered on the first ring. "I did fine. I went to bed right after y'all left. Slept pretty good."

"This may not be the time, but you know we're going to talk about this later, right?"

"Talk about what?"

"You over there by yourself. That's what."

"Here we go again. We just had this talk, and nothing has changed since then."

"What do you mean, nothing has changed. Someone tried to break into your house last night, and you had to use your gun. The trash stuff you told me already had me on the edge, but this time, you need to face the fact that it's not safe for you over there."

"Carneda, there you go. People break into folks' houses all the time."

"It's not just anybody I'm worried about. It's you. I can't believe you don't see this as dangerous. You're not safe there, Mama, and it's time we all talk about you living alone."

"This is not going to be a fight you're gonna win, Carneda. I am not moving, and you or none of the rest of y'all are going to tell me otherwise."

"You are so hardheaded. Why are you so stubborn?"

"I can take care of myself. I always have. If for one minute I didn't feel safe over here, you'd be the first one to know. Somebody may be trying to tell me something, but I got news for 'em. I've got something to tell them right back. Better yet, last night, I had something to show them. Nobody is going to run me out of my own house, and that includes you."

"I'm through talking. I can't do this anymore. I'll call and check on you later."

From Carneda's tone, Veola knew Carneda appeared disgusted. "You tell those boys of yours that Mama's going to be all right. You'll go and get them all worried, just like you, and then I'll have to hear it from them, too."

"We'll talk about this later, Mama."

"You can talk until you're blue in the face, but I have said what I have to say. I'm not going anywhere."

"It's time for me to get the boys moving. Bye, Mama."

"Bye, Baby." Veola suspected Carneda didn't appreciate being called that, especially not after this conversation.

As Veola made breakfast, she reminded herself that her daughter was being her usual protective self, and Veola anticipated more of this discussion later. It wouldn't be the first time, undoubtedly, not the last. She felt Carneda had a point with two occurrences back to back, but Veola didn't want to give in to that. She meant what she said that no one was going to run her out of her house. That's one of the reasons a gun was in the house to begin with.

With the front boarded up, Veola greeted Ruben Earl at the back door.

"Veola, I came by early in case you were going to work. I need to measure the glass and order it on my way in. I'll work through lunch to make sure I'm back by two or so with everything I need."

Veola realized he was just what the doctor ordered, putting

her mind at peace. A break-in was difficult on anybody, and doing this for her was above his call of duty, even from her good friend. She gave him her spare key and work number. He left after he had his dimensions.

Expecting to be a wreck, she felt better than she would have guessed. Her culprit got what he deserved, and she was thankful it was no worse than it was.

She felt like the women on the TV westerns carrying pocket pistols. Her automatic 38 was a gift from her father-in-law since she'd lived alone. She'd killed many chicken hawks in her hen houses through the years, but never pulled it on a human.

Last night she was tested. She was furious with her intruder. She felt violated. Her own space had been compromised, and the fact that she was that close to him to be able to beat him off with her broom made her shake from realizing her own peril. Veola felt he didn't care about her house or her possessions and that made her even angrier. Nothing in that house was more important than her life, and she did what she had to do to protect herself. She shimmered as she thought about what could have happened had she pulled that trigger. Then again, _better them dead than me._

Silently, she prayed over two matters—thanking God for what Ruben Earl was doing and her doors to be repaired without delay. Prayer changes everything, but always on God's time, at His will. All Veola's responsibility was making the request, angry or not.

And we just hope Ruben Earl be swift about his business today, O Lord. Watch over him and don't let nothing get in his way.

She had no intention of staying home, mulling around the house, sulking over this misfortune. She had already turned it over to God and Ruben Earl, so why not·go to work. It would take her mind off this mess.

She'd call Jessie and Eva Mae later since she knew they heard the police siren. Besides, they might see her front door before Ruben Earl got to it. Before she explained what happened, Jessie would worry herself to death. Eva Mae would be ready to fight, cussing everybody out. Veola didn't want that for either of them or anybody else.

Later when Mrs. Holcomb picked her up, Veola told her she was having new glass installed on her storm door. That was enough information for her.

Not quite sure of herself, she went about her usual chores. She usually didn't forget anything she had to do, but just in case, she made herself a list to clear her mind of other non-household matters.

Mr. Holcomb, a retired attorney, barely sixty-five, and Mrs. Holcomb, a former assistant in an insurance office, in her mid-fifties, quit her job to be home with him. Sometimes they acted older.

Tending to her many plants in her greenhouse was Mrs. Holcomb's daily ritual. She'd grown African violets year-round, had some of the biggest philodendron plants ever seen, and craved the smell of roses. She often exchanged tips for growing roses with Carneda since she found out Carneda's rose and rock garden was spectacular. One downside to Mrs. Holcomb's green thumb was how she tracked dirt back into the house.

Mr. Holcomb added to Veola's duties by leaving his goods all over the house. Then he'd go somewhere, returning in ten minutes asking where he was supposed to be going. Veola had never heard of such. Most of the time, Veola was empathetic with him when these memory lapses occurred, but sometimes she'd sneak down the hall and get in a quick laugh. He was in and out of the house, and when he remained at home, he went from one room to the next, forgetting what he was supposed to do.

So for her, these two required being picked up after constantly. She joked with them about the difference between a housekeeper and a slave. In spite of their amusement, nothing changed. She liked the Holcombs because she liked keeping her old folk in line just as much as the young ones.

She pulled out her list.

That man. Her intruder had been hurt, and that may help her find his identity. If he knew her, then she'd keep her eyes open for somebody with a cut forearm, wearing either a long-sleeve shirt or a bandage to hide his wound. As rude as it would be, she'd look at his arms before she'd make eye contact. She didn't want to think about it, much less discuss it.

Fayetta. Undoubtedly, God would watch over the judge's decision, but Veola anxiously wanted to know the results of the hearing. She had Fayetta's note with her phone number in her purse, but when the time came for Veola to be informed, she decided not to push it and let Fayetta call her.

Jeremy, Dr. B. She'd be back at the Bartons' tomorrow, but she desperately wanted to talk to them—individually, if she could. She didn't like what she was hearing about Jeremy and the company he was keeping. Now, she wanted to talk to Vickie, the Holcomb's youngest daughter, and Veola anticipated Vickie's arrival from school. Since Kenny and Vickie first started attending the same school with Vickie being in the tenth grade and Kenny in the ninth, Vickie and Veola had shared stories about Kenny and even talked about Jeremy and his popularity. Veola knew Vickie kept up with Jeremy, so she might know something. It wouldn't hurt to ask.

What about Dr. Barton's company in the drugstore? Veola knew she couldn't touch that, but Lord knows she wanted to. This was just as important as her own investigation into her burglary.

The letter. She needed to call this man from Esso Oil Company in Henderson to arrange a meeting, and she needed to call the Cherokee County Tax Office in Rusk to verify the status of her taxes. She wanted clarification.

Veola didn't bother to put Carneda on her list, but Veola banked on Carneda dropping by to talk to her about moving, but she'd have Carneda read the letter then. Carneda was good at reading white folks' letters and making sense of them.

Veola felt she had a right to perceive a certain amount of distrust because of all the people she heard about losing their land and houses to taxes, they were all black.

She'd put the letter in her purse on Tuesday morning to show it to Mrs. Hall, who knew about taxes, land, and property, but she decided to let Carneda see it first. There was no doubt Carneda or Charles, that smart husband of hers, would know exactly what needed to be done.

Lord, have mercy, she thought after her quick assessment of the house. She knew why Mrs. Holcomb wanted her more than one day a week. Too much junk—old heirlooms, unpolished silver, and trinkets by the dozens.

The rooms were full of dolls from all over the world: cloth, paper, wooden, Russian, Eskimo, African, even Aunt Jemima dolls. Never in her life had she seen a grown woman with so many and placed everywhere—the beds, the walls, end tables, on every chest of drawers. No matter where they were from, she referred to them all as dust magnets. Even though it was easy work, she knew why she was hired.

In spite of her mental complaints on a day she did not want to be at work, she moved through the chores rather quickly. She'd rather be home so she could start her investigation.

Kitchen duty was minimal with the Holcombs. They stocked sandwich meat and preferred fruit and raw vegetables for side dishes, giving Veola a break from the stove. With such different daily interests, coming together for their meals was a top priority.

Determining she'd done enough, she retrieved her purse, scarf, and sweater hidden in the hall closet. Before Veola rounded up Mr. Holcomb, the side door opened, and never had she been so happy to see Vickie. If Vickie was coming home, it had to be way past three o'clock. Veola glanced at her watch—3:17 p.m. Where had the day gone?

With dusty blonde hair, a medium frame, and the bluest of eyes, Vickie was very attractive. Her mother's homeliness set them apart.

"Hello, Vickie," Veola greeted a welcomed, fresh face. "How was your day at school?"

"Hi, Veola." Vickie opened the icebox door. "My day was fine. And how was yours?"

"Busy as usual. Trying to take care of your mama and your daddy is enough for anybody."

"I know. Tell me about it. I've almost given up."

"Have you really ever tried to take care of them?"

"Sometimes on weekends. That's enough for me and more work than I can bear. They drive me absolutely crazy."

Veola understood the physical and mental work required. "You've got them seven days a week, and I've got them one. I love them to death, but my day is done."

"What's there to eat around here?" Vickie asked, moving things around on the shelves in the icebox.

"I made lunch for them, but they ate everything in sight. You know your daddy. He's had something in his mouth all day long, and everywhere you look, there's crumbs."

"Next time you make lunch, think of me," Vickie pleaded. Her puppy-dog expression tickled Veola.

"I'll save you something next Wednesday," Veola promised. "Vickie, I want to ask you something, and you know we've shared things like this in the past."

Vickie reached for the crackers in the cabinet. "Wait, Veola, me first. I've got something to tell you—about Jeremy."

"What about him?" Veola was happy Vickie brought up the subject she wanted to discuss.

"He almost got in trouble today."

"In trouble? For what?"

"I think he was outside with some friends, and some teacher almost caught him smoking pot."

"Smoking pot? At school?"

"Well, he wasn't like smoking it, but he was passing it to this other guy, and I heard the teacher saw him."

Veola's expressions evolved with Vickie's every word. "How do you know this?"

"A friend of mine told me. I never saw him smoking, but the scoop on campus is that he has access to it."

"How do you know about pot? Isn't that dope? You don't need to be messing with that stuff." Veola thought, *save as many children as possible. Start wherever you can, even in other folks' households.*

"I wasn't. I was telling you because we've talked about this kind of stuff before. I think he should be careful. You're not going to tell him I told you this, right?"

"I would never do that. But why are you telling me this? Has he been doing this long?"

"I don't know if or how long he's been smoking pot, but he needs to avoid trouble. Everybody thinks he's cool, but he needs to keep that stuff away from school. If I'm hearing about it, I'm sure the teachers will, too."

"You're right." Veola thought he should not only keep it away from school but get rid of it all together. "I know you care about him, and I'll see what I can find out—secretly, that is. Well, let me get out of here, but you call me if I need to know something."

"I will. Promise." Vickie continued eating dill pickles and cheese and crackers.

Veola had yet to finish. "Do you like Jeremy, Vickie?"

"What do you mean?"

"Like—"

"No, not like that. He's a senior. They don't have time for sophomore girls."

Teenagers don't realize how they shock grown-ups with the statements they make. Deep down, Veola wanted to throw her purse down and run around the house. Be reasonable and mature, she reminded herself.

Veola stood in a complete state of immobility, in shell shock without the bullets. Daggers pierced her heart as she heard about Jeremy, and she was never going to make sense of the Barton puzzle by staying at the Holcombs.

Mr. Holcomb came down the hall jiggling his car keys.

"Ready, Mr. Holcomb?" Veola didn't give him time to answer. "I've been waiting on you." Veola passed next to Vickie on her way out. "Bye, Vickie, and please tell your mother I'll see her next week."

"Between us, right?" Vickie asked.

"Between us." Veola assured Vickie and hurried toward the Holcombs' Studebaker.

"What are you two up to?" Mr. Holcomb asked as he climbed into the car.

Veola shrugged. "Just us girls talking."

"Even I know to stay out of that."

Veola remembered that she wanted to pick Mr. Holcomb's brain. "Sir, in your expertise as a lawyer, you know very much about robberies?"

"It's against the law." He smiled.

"I know that much. What does the law say about an attempted robbery?"

"What do you want to know, Veola?"

"How long is jail time for someone who breaks in somebody's house?"

"That varies. Anybody hurt? Anything stolen? Any prior violations or convictions. Why do you want to know?"

"I was just curious. A friend of mine wanted to know, and I forgot to ask you earlier." She hoped he didn't sense her lying.

"I'd be more than happy to help your friend. Be sure to tell her."

"Thank you." Veola knew she had not told Mr. Holcomb it was a female she was asking for, but she left it alone. She was already treading on thin ice trying to keep herself out of it.

When Mr. Holcomb pulled up to Veola's house, she thanked him, told him she'd see them next Wednesday.

She stood on her curb and looked at her entrance, and it was as if nothing happened. No scrap of wood or glass was anywhere. Even the porch had been swept. God heard her prayer—even the part about Ruben Earl being quick, too.

"Ruben Earl," she began on the phone, "I don't know what to say."

"Then don't say nothing. I was just doing what I said I would do."

"Yeah, but you made it perfect. I owe you more than I could ever repay, but you let me know what my bill is, you hear?"

"Oh, we'll get around to that later."

"Well, give me to the end of the week when I have a chance to go to the bank, all right?"

"Like I said," he paused, "we'll worry about that later."

"Thank you again, Ruben Earl." Veola fought back her emotions. "I don't know what I would have done without you."

"Don't worry about that either. I ain't going nowhere."

They laughed and hung up the phone.

Veola raised her eyes up and threw her hand in the air. She knew to Whom she was giving praise. She could not hold back her tears any longer.

Thank you, Jesus, for looking out for me. For Ruben Earl, I thank you, and I hope he didn't hear me crying just then on the phone.

※

No sooner than she had realized she had taken a cat nap in her rocking chair that Carneda and Cameron knocked at her front door. Veola was still in her uniform.

"Hey, Mama." Cameron burst through the doors as soon as Veola unlocked them. "I have something to show you."

Carneda and Veola exchanged their hellos, hugs and kisses, and Carneda followed her mother into the dining room. Cameron led the way speeding past Veola after his quick initial hug to get to the TV.

"I was going to call you about the time you got home, because I wanted you to come over," Veola began.

"I was going to come over anyway. I see you have already got your doors fixed. What would you do without Ruben Earl?" Carneda asked.

"I don't even want to think about what I'd do without Ruben Earl, but before you get started, you know I can't worry about what happened last night. It's on my mind, but I can't let it get me down. Since I don't have any control over it, I have to trust that it's going to take care of itself." *Work this out, God, work this out.*

"But you could have been killed, Mama," Carneda said.

"Not before I kill them first. I'm gon' be in this house 'til I get ready to move, and I'm not near 'bout ready to go anywhere."

"You keep us all worried to death when *you* can't see the big picture of you living by yourself. We can't help it."

"Jessie lives by herself. Eva Mae lives by herself. And a whole bunch of more people. You can't hem me up somewhere other than my own house. What am I gon' do? Where I'm gon' go?" Veola put her hands on her hips.

"Come and live with us."

"What for? I'm not sick yet. I can still do for myself. There's no need of me packing up my house just 'cause y'all don't want me to be alone. This is my *house*, Carneda. I can't leave it yet. Y'all need to be worried about that man last night. He's the one in danger."

"Arguing with you over this gets me nowhere. Nowhere at all. It's like talking to a wall."

"Well, this wall talks back, and I'm done with it. Until it comes up again, which I'm sure it will."

"Okay, okay. I'm done." Carneda held up a hand.

Veola was glad Carneda had surrendered. It was a never-ending story that crept up upon occasion, and Veola won every time. One of these days, she was going to get to the point of not being able to take care of herself, and when that time came, she'd relent, unwillingly, no less, but she'd do what she had to do. The time had yet to come.

After the tone changed, Veola asked, "What is this world

coming to?" Veola suspected Carneda knew to be quiet when grown folks ask this question, for usually, they're about to answer it.

"What are you talking about, Mama?"

"Wait a minute." Veola checked to find Cameron engrossed in Dick Dastardly. Satisfied, she filled Carneda in on her many concerns—Fayetta's court case, the Barton household, and Jeremy's questionable extracurricular activities.

Veola recalled the state of shock she felt when she'd left the Holcombs. Now, she tried to think clearly giving Carneda an earful. Maybe Vickie's friend thought she saw dope, when it was really a cigarette? That would explain the matches. What she didn't want to believe was that Leonard had been supplying Jeremy with this terrible drug.

Carneda appeared dumbfounded as Veola unraveled the lives of others. "Mama, you know you get so wrapped up in these people that they start to take control of you and how you feel."

"Nobody is in control of me, Carneda. This is life. You get involved and concerned about people you love, and you want the best for them. Do I have to remind you of the students you've taken under your wing? I don't want to see these folks in trouble, in danger, and when they need help, I'm going to do my part."

"And what do you think I'm trying to do with you?"

"What you're trying to do is different. You're trying to take away my independence, my control over my own being."

"No, I'm not."

"What I want to control I can't do. I want to go off on that trash-dumping Loretta. A fine neighbor she is, and did I tell you what she said to me on the phone the other day?"

"What did she say?"

"Told me I should stay out of other folks' business."

"Well, it's true. So preoccupied with the matters of others, you haven't taken time for yourself. Here you are still in your uniform."

"She doesn't know a thing about these other people and how I am involved. But I'll find out eventually. Mark my word."

"Leave that alone, Mama."

"I'm going to find out everything. Give me some time. Now that isn't why I wanted you to come over, though." Veola went to retrieve her purse from under the bed. "I have a letter I want you to read."

"A letter?"

"Yeah, a letter from a man at some oil company, drilling for coal, clearing some timber, and some more things about some taxes on the New Winterfield property."

"Doing what, Mama?" Carneda asked, blank-faced.

Veola realized her main points didn't work for an explanation by the look on Carneda's face when she returned to the dining room. "Here it is. Read it and tell me what you think." She passed the letter to Carneda and went back to her bedroom to check on Cameron. He was still watching TV.

"What did you have to show me, Sugar?"

"Huh?" Cameron stared at his television show.

"What did you say?"

"I mean, yes ma'am." He looked at this grandmother, ungluing his eyes from the TV.

Veola knew Cameron knew how to respect his elders. Besides that, 'huh' was not a word. He wasn't allowed bad manners, especially not with her. "Now that's better. What is it you had to show me?"

"I'll show you this weekend when I come over."

Veola suspected he didn't want to depart from the TV. "What is it?"

"I'm going to surprise you."

"Then why did you tell me you had something to show me as soon as you hit my front door, and then try to get out of it by telling me you'll show me later? What makes you think I can wait that long?" She tried to coax him into giving her a hint, wanting him to feel guilty about teasing her.

"I need to bring it on Saturday," Cameron said.

"Now, you got me wondering what you're up to," Veola said. "Don't you come over here with no frogs and dead bugs." Veola warned, remembering the worm and ant farm he brought into her house last year in a shoebox.

Cameron laughed. "I'm not going to bring that. Besides, it's not live."

Veola felt relieved. "Let me check on your mama. I've got her reading some papers. Then, you can get back to your show. The people on there are crazy. They're trying to kill each other if you ask me."

She caught Cameron smiling when she left the room. She watched Dick Dasterdly, Muttley, and Penelope Pitstop for two minutes, and she had already figured out their desire to sabotage each other to get to the finish line. She even knew who Speed Racer was, but she didn't let all of her cartoon knowledge out of the bag.

"What does that letter say to you?" Veola asked Carneda. She sat down for her explanation.

"Mama, is this the first letter you've gotten?"

"As far as I know."

"It sounds like they are digging for some coal in the area around the property, and people around you are participating. Companies usually send some general letter to let you know the possibility of finding something before they really go out and set up shop. They're out of Houston, but they're already in Henderson." Carneda summed up the key points.

Veola understood most of it. "Now what was they saying about the taxes?"

"I think they secured the records from the tax office and made sure you owned the property and your taxes were current. If somebody's taxes weren't paid, then they might have started digging on land the state could already claim if the owner was delinquent."

"You got me wondering what they're doing out there. The letter said something about some man contacting me about the timber on the property, and I haven't heard from him yet. How do they know I got some timber I want cut down?" Veola briefly thought about her husband's carving in the tree—a tree no one could touch.

"I don't know. They probably wrote that in general for everybody."

"I'll give him a call soon." Veola placed the letter back in her purse, closing the matter for the moment. Quietly, she had already started to devise a plan. She'd tell Carneda about it later.

"I need to go out to Gibson's and run by Beall's before they close. Do you need anything while I'm out?" Carneda's day wasn't finished.

"Nothing I can think of."

"Are you going to prayer meeting tonight?"

"I don't think so. I'm going to shell those peas Ruben Earl

brought yesterday. Eva Mae and Jessie could have helped me last night. It would have served them right to pay for the meal they got for free."

"You need help? Cameron doesn't want to run around with me, so I'll zip back by and pick him up."

"He might want to stay anyway."

"I'll check," Carneda answered as she made her way into Veola's bedroom. Cameron sat mindlessly, watching his TV show.

"He might not want to shell any peas, though." Veola didn't want her to force Cameron to stay for that purpose.

"You know as well as I do that he'd rather be here than running around with me. If you're sitting in here shelling peas, then he'd want to do the same thing."

Veola didn't say she would be inside shelling peas. The pea-shelling spot was the front porch with old newspaper spread out for the empty shucks. Veola greeted people passing by, and Cameron had been right there with her too many times in the past.

Last night's break-in ran across Veola's mind. What if she were out front and she was being watched? Would she be putting Cameron in danger, too? Should she avoid being outside and spread the newspaper on her dining room floor this time?

If last night was to make her afraid of continuing with her usual outside chores, it wasn't working. She refused to give in to any demands of trying to second guess what she should and shouldn't be doing in public. She convinced herself that going on with her normal activities she had always enjoyed was definitely the way to go. Even if she were being watched, that person would see she wouldn't dare let him win by having her resort to being cooped up in her own house, afraid to be seen. She'd be shelling peas on her front porch, like she always had, but she wouldn't take the peas out front until after Carneda left.

Cameron told Veola he'd help at the end of his program, ten minutes.

Veola changed into a sundress suitable for front porch pea-shelling. Some of her good sistahs shelled peas in pink foam rollers, cigarettes in their mouths, ashy knees and torn up tennis shoes that had become outside house shoes—a sight to see, no less. Refusing to look country and tired simultaneously, she had a reputation to uphold.

Plenty of onlookers eyed Veola and Cameron shelling peas. They spoke, waved, and kept their buckets full of hulls—a team in action. Had these peas arrived on Friday, then Bobby Barton would have been introduced to the art of a pea-shelling in case he was a first-timer.

She saved the pile of scraps for fattening a church member's hogs. Last year in return, he gave her a couple of packages of pork chops when the hog was slaughtered. One good deed got her well-fed.

They retrieved some empty buckets from underneath the storage house, and while stuffing the hulls into them back out front, Delphine stepped outside.

"How y'all doing?" Delphine hollered.

"Hey, there," Veola yelled back and turned to Cameron to whisper. "She got a mouth full of snuff. I can tell by the way she said 'how y'all doing', all bunched up, she tried not to let the spit run out before she got her words out." Snuff wasn't lady-like at all.

Veola was certain Cameron heard what she said, but he put his peas down and ran to Delphine's. Veola assumed he did it for curiosity sake.

As soon as Cameron got close enough for a rub on the head, sure enough, Mrs. Delphine spat. In the direction of Cameron's feet, out poured brown, nasty gook.

"Oooh-eee," Cameron screamed, and he scrambled back to Veola's porch.

Veola dropped her bucket of shucks, not knowing what happened. "What's wrong?"

"She just spit. That was nasty," he said, his face contorted and catching his breath.

"I told you. That makes a woman look a mess." She couldn't blame his reaction since her grandmother had dipped snuff, too.

"Come on, let's move these hulls before your mother gets back." Veola led Cameron to the back again. She anticipated the boys' helping to plant the vegetables on Saturday. Ruben Earl had already done enough for her already in one week, and she didn't want the favors to pile up.

Carneda wasn't gone long. At the sink, rinsing the peas, Veola heard the car horn.

"Cameron, your mama's here," Veola announced and found him

back in front of the TV. Carneda banged on the storm door.

Cameron quick-kissed and hugged Veola before he jumped off the porch. "Bye, Mama," he said, and ran to his mother's car.

Carneda and Veola exchanged goodbyes.

As soon as she raised up, her attention was drawn to Delphine's house. A man wearing a long-sleeved shirt entered Delphine's front door. She could have sworn it was Leonard. Her mind raced. Leonard was in court today with Fayetta and was in the same vehicle with Jeremy at some point. Was he hiding a gash on his arm? Identifying her intruder was always on her mind. Now, she had to investigate.

Veola sprinted off her porch to Delphine's. Think, Veola, she told herself, for some reason for visiting Delphine. She sweated without a definite plan, her breathing labored. She knocked on Delphine's door.

"Why, hey, Veola," Delphine answered.

"I was about to baste my peas, and I remembered you have my big pot. Can I get it from you?" Veola was glad she came up with a good excuse.

"Chile, I forgot about that pot. Let me find it. I didn't realize I still had it." Delphine went into her kitchen.

"Here, I'll come in with you." Veola let herself in, a few steps behind Delphine. Veola didn't care about that pot for she had plenty to spare, but she had to eyeball that visitor.

As soon as they entered the kitchen, Veola heard voices from the back bedroom. The visitor must be in the back with Eli.

On her knees, Delphine rumbled through her bottom cabinets.

"What are y'all doing in here?" Leonard entered the kitchen.

"I think I got Veola's pot somewhere." Delphine could barely be understood as she directed her answer into the cabinet.

"How are you, Leonard?" Veola asked. She briefly made eye contact, for she was more interested in his arms. And they were covered by a long-sleeved shirt. Is he the one? She wondered.

"Doin' fine, Miss Veola. Hope y'all find it." He went back into the room with his daddy.

Veola wanted to see if he was uncomfortable in her presence, but he didn't give her a chance.

Delphine arose. "I can't find it." She pointed to the cabinet. "If

I had it, it would be under here."

"Well, let me go search one more time. I probably put it somewhere and forgot about it. I'll check the storage room." The ladies walked to the door.

"Thank you for trying to help me find it." Veola didn't care about that pot. Her mission was accomplished, and she realized that she wanted a conversation with Leonard, but it appeared he could have cared less about her in the room. That made her mad. She wanted to inform him that they shared a mutual acquaintance, Jeremy, and to leave that boy alone. Not getting to see his arm frustrated her, too.

Veola made her way back to her house, slowly. She didn't go in. While she was investigating and before she knew it, she stood on Loretta's front porch. Veola knocked. Loretta's absence was killing Veola. Why was she hiding? Why was she peeking through the curtain? Who was she fighting with so early on Monday?

Veola had an idea and Loretta needed to know. Answer the door, Loretta. Veola knew she was in there, and Veola vowed to beat on this door until Loretta showed her face.

Finally, Loretta cracked open her door and said through the screen, "What do you want?"

"I need to talk to you. Did you know my house got broken into the other night?"

"I don't know nothing about that."

"Who was that man you were fighting with Monday morning?"

"Well, I'll be damned. I knew you was nosey, but I didn't know you were that bad. That man ain't got nothing to do with you."

"Oh, yes, it does." Veola wished she could see more than just the right side of Loretta's face.

"How you figure?"

"I think you're lying about him and some more stuff."

"I ain't lying."

"Yes, you are, I know you are, 'cause you been acting funny for the last four days. I don't know what's got into you, but I don't believe for one quick minute you don't know something." Veola pointed her finger. "You didn't even turn on your lights when the police got here. Tell me the name of that man you was wrestling with out back with that stick. That's what I want to know. He got something to do with this, don't he?"

"I'll have you know the folk I 'sociate with ain't the type to be breaking in nobody's houses."

"How you know that? He ain't got no place to live with his clothes all in a bag, slung around in the dirt."

"That's a lie."

"Tell me this then. Do he have a broke up arm?"

"What choo talking 'bout?"

"Is his arm all cut up?"

"How the hell am I supposed to know if his arm is cut up?"

"That's what I'm asking you for."

"I ain't seen him since that morning."

"Well, you need to find him so I'll know if he da one that broke in my house. I'm trying to help you out, too, by getting that no count vagabond out of our neighborhood. He can't be good for you either since you done threw him out. You need to be careful 'bout the company you be keeping."

"I can keep any kind of company I want, and like I said, that ain't got nothing to do with you. Now, I done told you I don't know nothing about somebody trying to break into yo house, and as far as that man is concerned, it's none of your business, woman."

"If he the one that tried to get up in my house, then it is my business."

"I'm through talking to you."

"I'm gon' get to the bottom of this, and Lord knows, I hope you ain't got nothing to do with it, 'cause if you do, I'm gon' come—"

Loretta slammed her door. The screen door rattled.

"This ain't over, Loretta," Veola yelled. "I want you to know that." Veola had been shut out, but she needed to get that last bit in anyway.

Fuming, Veola stomped back to her house. Loretta had cussed at her on Easter Sunday, had hung up on her, and had slammed the door in her face. Veola thought that was soon to be her last straw because her nerves were now as thin as onion skin.

I'm gon' get you, Loretta, if it's the last thing I do. You got something to do with this. I just know you do.

Chapter Eleven

After she calmed down, Veola wanted answers from Leonard and Loretta. Was Fayetta going to get some help from him? Did he have a job? What was his connection to Jeremy? How did they meet? When would Fayetta call? What did Loretta know? Why was she hiding? One question followed another.

Jeremy invaded her thought process. He was the pride and joy of his parents, doing well in his endeavors, a good teenager. What did he see in Leonard, a man who had God knows how many children, known to be a skirt-chaser, irresponsible, with his work and family? After Vickie dropped her tidbit of information, Veola could make no excuses for Jeremy's matches.

Dr. Barton was still on the hook. What if Mrs. Barton had been downtown yesterday and spotted her husband with another woman? What would she have done? Mrs. Barton was too fragile for that, and that might send her over the edge. After all, she almost lost it when she realized her husband got drunk on Easter Sunday.

Then again, Mrs. Barton might have known her husband had a late meeting with this woman, and he was not trying to hide anything. Keep it Christian-like, she reminded herself. Don't let the devil in this. Lord, this was difficult to do.

No matter how she tried to convince herself that there were logical and reasonable explanations for all of this, she wanted all these answers yesterday. She had enough in her own world to keep track of, but now the concerns of others weighted heavily on her.

Just when she needed it, a song popped into her head. She hummed the tune, "Just a Closer Walk with Thee." The lyrics, *'Grant it, Jesus, if you please'* and *'I am weak, but thou art strong'* gave her the strength to see her through this crossroad. What better therapy and consolation than to let go and let God.

She hummed louder. Not able to carry a tune, but she still sounded well enough for her soul to be happy. What a difference a few minutes made, for just a few seconds ago, she was about to jump down Loretta's throat. Truth be told, she wanted to jump on Leonard, too.

Into each life, rain must fall. It fell on Fayetta, Leonard, Jeremy, Mrs. Barton, and probably on Dr. Barton. Afterward, the sun would shine—God's promise. Veola wanted the sunshine now.

Dinner had escaped her. She had no leftovers from dinner with her good sistahs, so she'd have to make do with something as long as it went in between two slices of light bread.

Her good sistahs? She had an idea.

Veola dialed Jessie, then Eva Mae, and told them to hurry over. Eva Mae took a long time to get to the phone. Where was she?

Within ten minutes, Veola had her sistahs in her living room once again. "Did you hear that siren last night?"

"It shole did sound close, but not like next door," Jessie said.

"I was the one who called the police. Somebody tried to break into my house, and they broke the glass in my storm door and the front door, too." Veola heard Jessie gasp, watched Eva Mae show no reaction, so she kept on with her story. "He didn't get in, and I had to scare him away with my gun. Ruben Earl fixed my glass today, and you can't even tell nothing happened." Veola caught her breath.

"Girl, is you all right?" Jessie asked.

"I'm fine," Veola said. "At least I think I am. I meant to call y'all when I got home, but—"

"Don't you worry about that. What's most important is that you're okay and you didn't kill him. But do you know who it was?" Jessie asked.

"I got an idea, but I can't prove a thing yet."

"Who?" Jessie asked.

"Somebody with a broke up arm that I done beat to death. That's who did it. And the only person I've seen with his arm covered is Leonard. But I ain't got enough proof yet to say he's the one since he didn't look like his arm was in pain. Now, I wanted y'all to hear about the break-in from me, not from the street. Y'all would have been worried out of y'all's minds."

"I'd have been mad if I heard it from somebody other than you," Jessie said.

"Eva Mae, you haven't said a word," Veola said.

"Chile, I'm just sitting here thinking," Eva Mae said. "If it ain't one thing, it's another. Scared you to death, didn't it?"

"You know it did."

"You said you didn't kill him, but did you have to shoot him?" Eva Mae asked.

"Naw. I used it to run him off. Thank God, it didn't come to that. But I beat the living fire out of his arm and hand with my broom handle," Veola said.

"You're better than me, Veola," Eva Mae said, "'cause I'd have shot the bastard and got upset about it later."

"Don't say that, Eva Mae. I don't wish that on nobody," Veola vowed.

"I ain't doing nothing but telling the truth. Jessie know what I'm saying." Eva Mae explained.

"Humph," Jessie uttered.

"The main thang is that you and your house is back in order. I didn't even notice that when I came," Eva Mae said.

"Me either," Jessie agreed.

"Have y'all seen a man with a broke up arm?" Veola asked.

Eva Mae and Jessie shook their heads.

"Be on the lookout for somebody with an injured arm, probably wearing a long-sleeved shirt to cover it up." Veola suspicioned that Eva Mae knew more than she was telling.

"We'll notice that fuh sho in this warm weather," Jessie said.

"Shole will," Eva Mae agreed, "but he might be long gone after such a beating."

"Could be, Eva Mae. You know, I meant to ask you when you first stepped in my door, what took you so long to get to the phone when I called? I let it ring five times," Veola said. "You must have been in the bathroom."

"I wasn't in no bathroom. I was at the back door wondering what is going on over at Tyrone's," Eva Mae answered.

"Were you spying on your own son?" Veola asked.

"I sho' as hell was not," Eva Mae stated feistily. "Of all people, how you gon' ask me if I was spying?"

"Then what was you doing?"

Eva Mae shared her story. "Just a short while ago, Leonard came up to Tyrone's in somebody's car. At first, he and Tyrone was talking real loud outside, and I thought I was going to hear what happened in court today. I figured Tyrone would be the first person he'd want to talk to. I couldn't just go right over there and ask, since he don't know that I know what's going on between him and Fayetta. Something's up, ya'll. I can tell by the look on his face after he stood there for a while that maybe things didn't turn out the way he wanted. He started explaining some things to Tyrone, and I guess he realized how loud he was talking, so he took Tyrone in the house."

Jessie interrupted. "I was gon' ask you, Veola, if you've heard from Fayetta."

"No, I haven't, but I assume everything's all right. It's early, and she is probably working through what all was said in court. I might not hear from her tonight, but I just saw Leonard a while ago up to Delphine's."

"Is you two cacklers gon' let me finish my story?" Eva Mae asked.

Both mouths shut.

Eva Mae continued. "Something ain't right. I hope Leonard ain't trying to get Tyrone involved in nothing. Y'all know that boy of mine don't need no more trouble. That's what I know, but the day ain't over. If I was to go to Tyrone's when I get back, he might not tell me nothing. I gots to get my information from listening in on thangs. You know what I'm saying?"

"Yeah, we know what you're saying," Veola began, "but wait a minute. After Leonard left Tyrone's he must have come this way, 'cause I just saw him with his daddy at Delphine's."

"What did he say?" Jessie asked.

"All he did was speak. Unlike you, Eva Mae, I was not about to pry right then and there in front of other people." Veola looked toward Eva Mae. "You know you can't be prying into Leonard's business by way of Tyrone. He's gon' always protect his buddy, especially from you. Us mamas is always the last to know anything when it comes to finding out stuff like this from our children."

"You right about that, Girl," Jessie said.

"How you know, Jessie, you ain't no mama?" Eva Mae asked.

"Yeah, but I'm the last one to know so you just as well say I get treated like one," Jessie surmised.

"Well, if I hear from Fayetta, I'll let y'all know. I'm hoping everything went well for her 'cause judging from Leonard earlier, he didn't look too happy. That might be good news for Fayetta, but we'll wait and see what she says 'fo we gets to jumping to conclusions."

"I ain't jumping to conclusions," Eva Mae declared. "As loud as he was talking to Tyrone, I know he can't be pleased with whatever happened today. Ain't no celebrating going on with him, Baby."

"I want you two out of my house so I can grab me something to eat," Veola announced and stood up. She followed her guests to the door.

"Veola, let us know if you hear something about Fayetta," Jessie said.

"Oh, I will," Veola answered. At this point, Fayetta's personal life was everyone's business.

On the porch, Veola noticed Ruben Earl's truck on the side of the house. She was certain her sistahs saw it, too.

"So, Veola, you gon' fix Ruben Earl something to eat, too? You making dinner two nights in a row, huh?" Evil Eva Mae asked with a smirk on her face.

Veola knew Eva Mae was being catty. "No, he's coming over to start plowing, but I wanted to be through with my dinner 'fo he got here."

"This shole is late to be starting to plow, ain't it, Jessie?" Eva Mae asked. "You know, I've been trying to tell y'all for years that Ruben Earl's old ass is ignant, and I think y'all 'bout to realize that."

"It ain't even six o'clock, Eva Mae. I'm sure he'll quit if he can't see how deep his till be going," Jessie said.

"He's not ignant; he just does things on his own time, the way his mind sees fit. I told him I wanted to plant this weekend." Veola rushed to Ruben Earl's defense.

"Well, good luck with that fool, Veola. He ain't wrapped too tight when it comes to common sense, but that's a cross you gon' have to bear yo-self."

"He's not gon' bother me doing what he do whenever he wants to do it. He'll get paid one price for the job, whenever that is."

"You might want to wait 'fo you eat, Veola, so then y'all can eat together." Eva Mae laughed, winked at Veola and simultaneously, nudged Jessie with her elbow.

Jessie fired back. "Eva Mae, you got about as much sense as a dead rat. You ain't right and you ain't never gon' be right."

"Both of y'all need to get out of here. I'll holler later," Veola promised.

"Do that," Jessie said. "Come on, Eva Mae, let's get to the house." She tapped Eva Mae with her purse.

Veola heard Jessie mumbling and Eva Mae laughing. She was certain they were mocking the notion of Ruben Earl being more than just a friend, but this was not the first time she'd heard these rumblings. Undoubtedly, it wouldn't be the last.

She decided that the only people who knew anything about what happened today with Fayetta and Leonard were Tyrone and maybe Eli. She found something to eat, and after the dishes were washed, she spotted Ruben Earl out back. With a few rows finished, she wouldn't dare interrupt him.

She straightened out the wrinkles of her uniform for the next day, and as usual, her mind never rested. How was her own family? Is Carneda all right? Anything wrong with Kenny? He's out there with the rest of those boys, and she wondered if he was mixed up in the wrong crowd. Surely Carneda could tell her if he was. She thanked God for watching over Kenny. Who knows what teenagers have access to these days.

What she really wanted to do at this point was to don her nightgown and ready herself for bed. But rather than be surprised later, she took Ruben Earl a tall glass of iced water.

"Thank you, Veola." Ruben Earl grabbed the napkin-wrapped glass.

"Thought maybe you could use this. It's almost dark, and I was about to call it a day."

"I sho do 'preciate it." He turned up the glass.

"You know you're welcome." She watched him almost choke. "I didn't even hear you drive up. Take your time, but don't be out here too long."

"Oh no, I'm gon' be through in a minute. Got to work tomorrow. I might be back some of these evenings since you're planning on getting yo planting done by this weekend. Don't feel much like going to Alto to see my sister anyhow."

"I told you that I'd like to get started by this weekend, but I know I won't finish it. Besides, you've already done more than enough for me. I don't know if I'm going to plant the whole garden as fast as I did last year. Working with my two little ones will slow me down, but that will give them something to do. I guess I'll see you when you get back over here, then." She took the empty glass and paused. "You don't know how much I appreciate you, Ruben Earl."

"Why sho I do."

"I thank God for watching over me, and I thank Him for you, too."

"Just keep on thanking Him, then."

Veola knew his intent was to lighten the seriousness of what she said, and it was difficult for her to show her deep gratitude in front of him. She headed toward her back door, and out of the corner of one eye, she noticed that Ruben Earl was staring at her.

She turned and waved goodbye. Ruben Earl was frozen, yet he waved back. Once she was inside, he and the mule resumed their duties.

Veola wondered what that was all about—looking at her like that. Maybe she turned around at the wrong time. Watching someone walk away was all right, but other matters come to mind when the person gets caught doing it. Don't read into that, Veola, she told herself.

She quickly needed to remove herself from this particular feeling. So, she retrieved the letter from the Esso Corporation in her purse, next to her bills, and headed for the phone in the guest room.

She dialed the number on the Esso letter, not expecting anyone to answer. She didn't want them to cheat her, so she made sure this was a real phone number. Some companies took advantage of women, especially black women.

That feeling came back. *Why was Ruben Earl looking at her? Was he interested in her? I don't want this relationship to change because if something went wrong, who would she get to plow her garden? Ain't nobody else got a mule in their backyard.*

Veola tapped her foot nervously. After three rings, someone answered. Her foot stopped.

"This is Dick Edelson. Can I help you?" A deep male voice sounded white.

"Sir, I received—"

"I bet you're calling about a letter from the Esso company."

"Yes, sir, I am." Veola regained confidence. "My name is Veola Cook, and I live here in Parkerville. I'm calling to find out exactly what it is y'all want to do with my land. I want to make sure I understand it."

"Mrs. Cook, I know what you're asking. Of course, we're interested in your property, which means we want you comfortable with anything we're proposing."

"Y'all are looking to do some business with me by leasing it, right?"

"You're right, and I'd be more than happy to meet with you about the letter."

"That's what I want."

"I'll be in Parkerville tomorrow, sometime late afternoon. I could come by and show you our proposal, answer any of your questions. In that way, you'd be more informed before proceeding."

It was just what Veola wanted to hear. She had wanted to put a face with this man Edelson. Good business practices involved knowing whom you were dealing with on matters of this kind. Meeting someone from the company made it better for her, and she'd put this whole proposal into perspective. The only place she'd seen the name Esso was at the service station where Carneda bought her gas. What did she have to lose? The property was idle, and for a brief second, she thought she'd get lucky. Lord, she might get some big money.

"Okay, then," Veola agreed. "I'll be home around five o'clock or so, and if I miss you, I could be home a little earlier on Friday." Friday afternoons were usually empty for her, and Mr. Hall would bring her straight home if she needed to meet this oil and gas man.

"I pulled the letter from your file, and let's see, I have the address. All I need now is the phone number."

Veola caught the gentlemanly-like nature of his asking.

"Your phone number, Mrs. Cook?" he asked again.

"Oh, I'm sorry," Veola said, still thinking about his persuasiveness. "It's Lakewood - 5, 4-1-1-7."

Mr. Edelson repeated the number. "I appreciate you calling. I'll look forward to meeting you tomorrow. Good night."

"Thank you, and good night." She hung up the phone knowing she had handled her own business. She'd arranged to get the ball rolling. "Thank you, Jesus."

Ruben Earl banged on the back door, and he spoke through it. "I'm gone, Veola."

Veola unlocked the screen. Ruben Earl had made his way off the porch. "Okay." She turned to come back inside, but hollered back at him. "And thank you." She didn't forget her manners.

From her bedroom window, she watched him get into his truck with the mule tied to the back of it.

Veola knew it was time to go to bed, but before she did, she sat down at her dresser. She opened the top drawer and brought out the tiny jewelry box she had bought when she first arrived in Parkerville. She kept her baubles and long necklaces in the chest of drawers, but this ornate box was special. It was missing so many rhinestones and colored glass, but never, ever would she throw it away. The small felt flap on the inside gave way to her secret compartment where she had two items—a hundred dollar bill, and her husband's old knife.

After listening to Mr. Edelson talk about timber today and cutting down trees, she pulled out Ervin's old knife that she had treasured all these years. If she decided to proceed with Mr. Edelson's request, or rather the Esso company's, then she didn't have to sell all the timber. Maybe just a portion of it; she would tell them which trees to cut down. She couldn't let them chop down that tree where her name was engraved; it was much too special. She kissed her rusted keepsake and slipped it back into its secret hiding place.

She was glad the day was over, and as promised earlier, she'd finish her conversation with God. Her daily prayers kept her going. They always did.

Not knowing what to expect from the court system, Fayetta had prepared herself mentally for a bitter fight. Sunday afternoon taught her a lesson that Leonard was unwilling to cooperate with lawyers. His mind was on himself. According to him, his money was so tight, he could barely survive, much less support a bunch of kids.

This day involved a lot of paper work. She had brought birth certificates for the children, and all the other required documents. The half-day afternoon session was loaded with a lot of yes and no questions, but what made Fayetta uncomfortable was they had to answer them all in front of other people. Why couldn't they have hashed out these details long before they came to the courthouse? She obeyed the system and did her best to be cordial about it.

After the session, Leonard ignored her. They parted ways, each going to their lawyers' offices to prepare for the following day.

That night while she was at her mama's house, Leonard came by.

"You still want to talk?" He stood on her porch.

"Isn't it a little late for that?" She didn't unlock the screen door.

"Not for me. There's got to be a better way than this."

"I always thought so."

"But I got to get out of here. Away from this front porch."

"Why? Don't want to see your oldest son?"

"No, it's not that. I just don't want to wake anybody by being out here. Just do me a favor. Come go with me and let's see if we can handle this better than what them damn lawyers is doing. I know we can work something better than the shit they coming up with."

"I've been telling you that all along." Fayetta was torn. She saw that Leonard was driving a vehicle for a change. Did it belong to one of his many women? "Who's car is that?"

"My daddy's. I borrowed it for a few hours. What difference do it make?"

"Peace of mind. That's what difference it makes." Fayetta felt better. She could only imagine what the word on the street would be had she been seen in the car of one of Leonard's women.

After she informed her cousin of her leaving for a few minutes, she got in the car with Leonard. He burned rubber as he sped off, and Fayetta began to think she'd made a mistake. "Where are we headed?"

"Let's ride first. He got enough gas for a while."

"How are you going to talk and concentrate on driving at the same time."

"Okay, then. Let's go to the school yard downtown. We can sit outside."

"Fine by me. We won't get in trouble?

"Ain't nobody gon' see us out there."

Fayetta didn't know what made Leonard want to be cooperative, but she didn't want to ruin the mood when he was willing to sit down. Maybe he didn't want this to get more ugly than it appeared it was going. Maybe he was used to that type of ridicule, but deep down, she couldn't stand the way it was making her feel. So, she felt she had nothing to lose by seeing what he had to say.

When Leonard parked, they walked almost to the opposite end of the playground and sat down on the merry-go-round.

"Why are you doing this?" he began, and he pulled out a joint and lit it.

This is not the way she wanted the conversation to begin. "Why are you asking me this?"

"I have told you that I will do what I can to help with the kids, but I can't promise you no certain amount every month."

"Leonard, you've promised time and time again, but after a couple of months of you sending twenty dollars here and there, you just quit. You die off. Then you don't answer the phone when I call. You move around to different houses, so I can't track you down. How do you think that makes me feel?"

She waited for an answer.

"You're making me look like a fool. I ain't told nobody I'm having to do this."

"This has nothing to do with anybody except us. Tyrone doesn't even know?"

"Especially not Tyrone. I don't want him in my business."

"I thought y'all were close like that."

"I ain't gon' tell him this when it makes me feel like shit. Just drop this, would you?"

"Drop it? Are you crazy?"

"Tell the lawyers we worked it out."

"We haven't worked it out. Besides, I didn't come this far to get nothing."

"That's it. It's all about you."

"No, it isn't. It's about the kids, and you know it.

"This is killing me, goddammit. Just killing me, and you ain't got to do this."

"Yes, I do." Fayetta noticed Leonard was becoming agitated, but she vowed to remain calm.

"No, you don't." He jumped up, leaned over, and shoved her hard.

Her head banged against the metal bars of the merry-go-round. She was out cold.

"Fayetta? Fayetta?" he screamed. He shook her, but she did not respond. He picked her up and carried her to the car.

After driving around for a few minutes, Fayetta awoke with a pounding headache. "What happened?"

"You hit your head."

"How? Did you hit me?"

"No, I didn't hit you."

"Then why is my head hurting?" She didn't believe him. She became extremely afraid, wondering what he might do next.

"Let me out of here. I want to get out of this car right now. Stop the car!" Fayetta yelled. "Stop the car!" She reached for the steering wheel to pull the car over.

"Let me drive. I'm taking you home."

"No, pull over. Let me out now."

Leonard backhanded her.

Fayetta noticed blood on her hand, and she grabbed the door handle. She had to get away from this maniac. "Leonard, stop the car!"

"Well, get out, goddammit," Leonard screamed as the car halted.

Fayetta slammed the car door, and through tears, watched Leonard burn rubber as he sped away. Now, she realized she had gone from one danger to another. It was pitch dark, and she began to walk ahead in the direction of the intersection where she saw

146

lights. She had no idea where she was, realizing she had been stupid to get out of that car. Now, she was terrified. She silently prayed for her safety, but she had to get to that corner. Maybe she'd find a gas station.

When she saw car lights coming from behind, she glanced over her shoulder and saw an old sedan slowing down. She quickly re-focused and stepped up her pace. She heard the motor purring. The car was following her. Her heart raced.

Finally, the car pulled beside her, and the window rolled down. She saw the head of what appeared to be a black teen.

"What choo up to, Sistah? Wanna have some fun?"

Fayetta stopped abruptly and glared at the two teens. "You don't want to mess with me, 'cause I'm whupping bad boys like you these days. I've had one fight already tonight." She balled her fists.

"Man, she crazy," the driver shouted, and he floored the accelerator.

Fayetta felt relieved to have gotten rid of those hoodlums, but she kept moving forward toward the light, hoping not to encounter any more passersby. She sprinted across the street and saw a phone booth by the street sign. Her head pounded, and her stomach seemed queasy as she pushed the door open and reached for the phone. She quickly dialed zero. She knew she had to get to the hospital. "Please send an ambulance to Border and Clayton Streets, by the school. Please hurry, please," she pleaded. She sat down in the cramped booth, praying help would come soon.

Within seconds, Fayetta felt dizzy. She dropped the receiver and it swayed in mid-air. She was sprawled out, her head hanging out the door.

"Ma'am? Ma'am? Are you there?"

❧❧

When Eva Mae went to bed that Wednesday night, she noticed the car Leonard drove to Tyrone's was still parked out front. Tyrone and his friends were up all hours of the night during the week, so she didn't think twice about it until she heard the car leave at 2:30 the following morning and return about four a.m. What made Eva Mae roll over in her warm, comfortable bed was that Leonard, or whoever was driving the car, had the nerve to rev up the engine when he left and when he returned.

Her instinctive reactions were trigger-happy when it came to Leonard, but four o'clock in the morning was too early to march over to Tyrone's and let him know his company was disturbing her sleep, dammit. Tyrone should be ashamed of himself, carrying on like that when he knew he had to get up and be down at the factory by eight o'clock sharp. He'd been in trouble with his foreman, and Eva Mae knew his job was on the line already. Her sleep was most important and she'd deal with Tyrone's foolishness and his ignant friends in the morning.

When Eva Mae got up, it was a quarter past nine. She was beside herself for sleeping so late. Her good judgment told her not to call Tyrone on his job and give him a piece of her mind about the shenanigans in the wee hours. If he was going to have company during that time, then he should be responsible for keeping their asses quiet and respect other folks trying to sleep.

Tyrone and Leonard should know better since they were grown-ass men. She was convinced the one revving the engine was Leonard, and he was probably drunk. Tyrone will one day learn about the company he keeps. That's why he hadn't amounted to much—he ain't responsible.

Once Eva Mae picked up her morning paper, Leonard's car was still there. Now, she worried that Tyrone had gotten so drunk he didn't make it to work. Her rent money from her son was too important for her to sit by idly. It was time to make a phone call.

She didn't walk next door because of her dress—hair in pin curls, housecoat, and worn-out slippers, for she wasn't meeting Veola in the back of her garden this time. So, she eased back inside and before she put in her dentures, she dialed her son's number.

Leonard answered the phone on the first ring. "What'd you find out?"

"Who is this?" Eva Mae shot back. Her blood pressure soared twenty points at the sound of Leonard's voice.

"Who you looking for?" Leonard retaliated.

"I'm looking for my son, and what the hell you doing answering his phone? Let me speak to Tyrone," Eva Mae demanded. Her hand was on her hip as she tried to keep her composure. It was wrong to wake up cussing folks this early in the morning, but if Leonard took her there, she was ready. She didn't give a shit.

"He's gone to work," Leonard said.

"Then what are you doing there?" Eva Mae asked.

"Excuse me? I believe this is Tyrone's house."

"Hell, that's my house. Tyrone pays me rent, and I want to know what yo ass is doing over there when he's at work. What's going on with you two?"

"I'm 'bout to leave, Mrs. Walker. I thought Tyrone was calling."

"You 'bout ignant, Leonard. Do I sound like Tyrone? I know you thought this was him on the phone. Why else would anybody answer, 'what'd you find out'? But I'm fixin' to call Tyrone right now and get some answers real quick," Eva Mae promised.

As soon as she slammed the phone in Leonard's ear, she dug through her address book, searching for Tyrone's work number at the mobile home plant. Tyrone changed jobs so fast that she got tired of putting the number in pen and scratching it out. She remembered the number was penciled on a scratch pad in a kitchen drawer.

"Good morning," she greeted the secretary. "Tyrone Walker, please."

"Just a minute, ma'am," the receptionist stated. Shortly, she returned to the phone. "I'm sorry, but Mr. Walker has not made it in today."

"He ain't at work?" Eva Mae questioned.

"No, ma'am, not yet," the secretary answered.

"Well, I 'preciate you looking for him," Eva Mae said and hung up.

She didn't know what to do next. Tyrone was somewhere other than where he was supposed to be. Leonard was in and out of Tyrone's house at all hours of the night. A phone call from Tyrone was supposed to tell Leonard something before he made his next move. This was a mess.

The time had come for her to march right next door while Leonard was still there. She was determined to get an explanation for these unusual events. She took the pins out of her hair and brushed her dentures like she was mad at them.

Chapter Twelve

Thursday morning, Veola laid her purse and sweater in the living room in anticipation of Mrs. Barton's pick-up. She checked her purse for her billfold. She had had it out last night searching for a layaway ticket. There it was—wrapped in a handkerchief, tied twice for good measure, and then secured with a rubber band around its greatest width.

Though usually calm, collected, eager to get her day under way, Veola felt agitated. Her morning prayer had been a continuation of the night before. In essence, she had begged God to guide her feet in the right direction for the days ahead and to keep Ruben Earl's mind on plowing. God was her closest friend and confidant. Her friends and family wanted the job, but rightfully, she gave that position to the Master.

Jessie and Eva Mae had wondered about Ruben Earl's intentions with Veola for a while, but Veola never let any part of her conversations with Ruben Earl veer in any other direction. No more thoughts about Ruben Earl, she promised as Mrs. Barton tapped her horn.

As Mrs. Barton pulled into her driveway, she braked to keep from hitting Jeremy.

"Oh, mercy!" Veola exclaimed.

Jeremy had managed to grab his jacket with one hand and clutch a pop tart with the other as he raced toward his truck.

"Don't drive too fast," Mrs. Barton screamed. "Better to get there safely than to not get there at all." Under her breath, she added, "I don't need any more bad news today."

"What are you talking about?" Veola asked.

"Well, Roy told me that a friend of ours, Joe Simpson, had his house vandalized while they were gone for Easter. Nothing was taken, but they just felt violated. It makes me so uneasy."

Jeremy's tires squealed as he backed out.

"You locked your door this morning, didn't you, Veola?"

"Yes, I did. I always do." She had no intention at this point of telling Mrs. Barton that her house had been broken into this week, too.

Jeremy burned rubber, and he sped off in the direction of Parkerville High.

"Jeremy's been a handful already this week, Veola." Mrs. Barton sighed. "He has so much going on right now, and even though it's the end of the school year, he's going a mile a minute to everything."

"I don't think you can expect him to be any other way, can you?"

"He's sleeping at odd hours, tossing and turning no doubt, just unusual behavior for him. I can't explain it, but I think he was up for most of the night. Or at least I saw the light on under his door."

"Maybe he was studying," Veola offered as consolation. "It appears it may be wearing more on you than on him. Did you ask him if anything was wrong?"

"Why, of course I did."

"What did he say?"

"Says he's fine. He never admits to anything these days—at least not to me."

"That's probably 'cause he's a senior now. You may be a little too worried for your own good." Veola patted Mrs. Barton's shoulder. "We'll see."

Veola recognized that Mrs. Barton didn't want to talk about this subject anymore. Veola was content leaving it alone. She felt if she were to press the issue, she might bring Mrs. Barton to tears. Upsetting the poor woman was not on Veola's agenda any day.

Mrs. Barton went to her bedroom, and Veola headed straight for Jeremy's room. Veola was no expert on what effect smoking dope had on someone, but it must be bad. In conversations with her know-it-all good sistahs, Jessie and Eva Mae, Veola remembered them describing someone as "looking like they're on dope." Neither of them described exactly what that look was, but obviously, the behavior was atypical, socially unacceptable.

She did know what 'look like he been dranking' meant. She only guessed about the dope, but the 'dranking' one, she witnessed firsthand. When neighbors drank too much, she avoided them. But when her own family got tipsy, she told them exactly how she felt. As her mind wandered through this analysis, her cleaning produced no clues.

Snapping her back to reality, the Barton phone rang. Veola waited for Mrs. Barton to pick up. After the fourth ring, Veola made her way to answer it. The ringing stopped before she got there.

Mrs. Barton called down the hall, informing Veola that the phone was for her.

Veola was surprised. A call at work for her could be bearing bad news. Veola trusted her instincts. Her stomach gurgled—a sure sign she wouldn't like what she was about to hear. "Hello?" Veola answered with trepidation in her voice.

"Veola, it's Jessie, and I got to tell you about Fayetta."

"What is it?"

"She is in the emergency room at Evan Memorial. She look like she got beat up last night."

"Oh, Lord, no!" Veola exclaimed. She swung around and sat on Dr. and Mrs. Barton's unmade bed. "What happened?"

"Well, May Pearl relieved the nurse this morning who took care of Fayetta last night. When May Pearl got there around seven o'clock this mawnin', she called me to see if I knew a Fayetta Dewberry from Dallas. When I said yes, she said Fayetta came in the middle of the night by amberlance. They picked her up at some pay phone near downtown. Her family went to visit her this morning. Everybody is wondering where Leonard is."

"Did he do this?"

"Don't know yet."

"Is she gon' be all right?" Veola's heart raced.

"May Pearl say Fayetta got a few bruises, even some on her face, and other than Fayetta complaining about being sore and her head hurting, she say she gon' be all right."

"How long is she going to be in the emergency room?"

"They gon' watch her for a while."

"She won't be admitted?"

"Naw, ain't nothing broken. She got a slight headache from hitting her head, so they gon' see how she do."

"Well, that's a blessing."

"She shole is lucky."

"She's blessed, Jessie. When I get through, I'm probably gon' go down there. I'll see if Mrs. Barton will drop me off at the hospital. Let me get busy so I can get through. Do Eva Mae know?"

"I'm gon' call her next."

"She probably don't or she'd have called you by now."

"You're right about that. Now, get this. May Pearl also said the people down there taking the information from Fayetta is having a hard time getting her to talk about thangs. She said she talking in spurts, giving them bits and pieces about this whole matter."

"How May Pearl get all this information?"

"From the nurse taking care of her last night. May Pearl be the only black nurse down there today. The doctor probably thought May Pearl could help the woman feel more comfortable if Fayetta see one of her own caring for her. Besides, you know how them nurses can be at both of them horsepitals. If they don't know nothing about someone coming in there like this, they gon' get on the phone for sho and find out, somehow, some way."

"Lord, how mercy. That's a crying shame. I got to go, Girl. I'll call you when I get ready to see what else you done found out."

They hung up.

Veola's 'Lord, how mercy' meant 'Lord, have mercy', but church-going black women didn't know any better. As long as the

Lord was called, it didn't matter.

Shocked by the news she'd received, Veola went to the kitchen to find her boss lady. "Mrs. Barton, I'm going to try to get through a little early today, and on the way home, would you drop me off at Evan Memorial? I've got to see a friend."

Veola's intent was for Mrs. Barton to be mindful of the time she had allotted herself to run errands, yet she was certain Mrs. Barton suspected something since Veola routinely didn't receive phone calls at work.

"Is everything all right, Veola?" Mrs. Barton stopped reading the newspaper.

"I hope so," Veola answered. "A friend of mine is in the emergency observation section. I certainly hope everything's all right." _What did Leonard do to that poor girl? I'm about tired of him messing over the people I be caring about._

҂Ж҂

Tyrone had tried for two days to handle his bandage himself. He couldn't move his arm in certain directions without writhing in pain. It was getting much more difficult to conceal his anguish. However, even though he didn't cry out or moan too loudly, it showed on his face. He avoided as many people as possible, and he made excuses all day at work on Wednesday. Last night was unbearable, so he had come to get help this Thursday morning. There was no way he could go through such pain another day or night.

He knew exactly where the Medical Center emergency room was in Tyler, and he wanted to get there about the time the shift changed at seven in the morning. Therefore, he could get a shot or some stitches and be back at work by mid-morning. He just had to get some relief.

He told the nurse that he'd cut himself on a mirror; it fell and one of the shattered pieces came right across his forearm. He didn't care if they believed him or not. After he gave them his real name but a fake address in Parkerville, he was asked why he'd driven thirty miles to get his wound attended to. So he lied and told them that he just happened to be in the area and all of a sudden, it started to throb and hurt. He wanted to make sure he wasn't getting an infection.

Tyrone received an antibiotic shot along with stitches for his deep cut, for he was told there was no way the wound would have healed on its own. He was so glad the doctor had to inject numbing medicine to sew it up, because once he was pain-free, he felt he could function again. Besides, he knew if the pain came back this time, then his weed along with a good drink and a mouthful of aspirin would do the trick. It wasn't doing shit before.

Now that he'd been operated on, he felt like he could go to work and be normal. The arm felt good, and he would make it a point to let everybody at work know he was fine. Once he got a better night of sleep, that would help him at work anyway, and maybe them damn folk would quit asking him what was wrong. He couldn't wait to get them goddam people at work off of his back.

❧❧

The usual procedure for passing information along the grapevine was that the one who knew the scoop called all interested parties. Jessie had briefed Veola about the ungodly crime involving Fayetta, and next she called Eva Mae to relay the headlines on the Parkerville Gossip Gazette. Then, Jessie went into all the details she heard from May Pearl with Eva Mae.

"Girl, shut cho mouth. What time did the poor girl get in there?" Eva Mae asked.

"I don't know, but it had to be sometime late last night or early this morning during the graveyard shift. I find it funny that they call it the graveyard shift everywhere else except in the horsepital 'cause that's the time that most of them peoples in there be dying. That's right. They put more folks in the morgue from eleven o'clock at night to seven o'clock the next morning than any other time."

Eva Mae listened out of respect as if Jessie proclaimed gospel, proven facts. "How you know that?"

"'Cause I know, that's how. Think about it. Don't you always get a phone call in the mawnins about somebody dying last night when they is in the horsepital? You hardly ever hear about somebody dying in the morning or afternoon. Folk tell you about death in the morning 'cause they done found out about it in the middle of the night."

Eva Mae never challenged Jessie. "Girl, we was talking about Fayetta. How long she gon' be in there?"

"Well, they say she just in observation in the emergency room. She might be coming home today. Speaking of which, I wonder how her trial came out. I suspect her ending up in the emergency room meant it went better for her than for Leonard."

"I just talked to that ignant ass Leonard next door, and he was on his way somewhere. He must have borrowed a car from some fool 'cause he's always riding with somebody when I see him at Tyrone's. He ain't got enough sense to keep a car for himself."

Eva Mae didn't divulge that Leonard was waiting on a phone call from Tyrone. She hoped Tyrone wasn't involved in this in any way. She checked outside for Leonard's car as she talked about him. She hadn't seen squat going on over there. He was gone, must have left right after he hung up with her. She was surprised she didn't hear that loud ass car, but she'd had the TV on.

"May Pearl said Fayetta's family is looking for him," Jessie said.

"Well, they ain't looking too hard," Eva Mae volunteered. "This car he been in was up here on and off all last night."

"Fayetta got to the emergency room after midnight, Chile."

"What're you trying to say, Jessie?"

"Sounds like they just started looking for him this morning, not last night. You say he's in somebody's car?"

"Okay, then, so he was hiding out up here, huh?"

"Could be. Don't know for sure, but it's possible, ain't it?"

"I guess."

"Folks that know Leonard know he's everywhere. He got so many places to go, especially with all them chillens he got."

"Yeah, Jessie, but all these places you think he can go to may not be that many after all. I bet all them women is probably tired of his ass. He ain't gon' be hanging out at these women's houses where he got a bunch of chirren. What about the police? They after him?"

"Chile, I don't know, but I bet you the clothes off of my back that thangs didn't go his way in court if she wound up like this."

"This is a damn shame, Jessie. Just a damn shame. It's just pitiful that the girl has to come to town to get the money that was owed her in the first place from a tired ass, no count, trifling fool, and see how she ends up."

"She gon' need some help to get herself together 'fo she can even go back home. I don't know all the family she got here, but she told Veola she was staying with her cousins there at Melda's. She might not even be through in court."

"Was it a trial she was there for or was it just a hearing?"

"Honey, I don't know the difference. If you ask me, Leonard was being tried by some lawyers to find out if he any good. Now that's a trial to me. Anybody listening to him trying to explain his way out of this is hearing him just the same. Trial, hearing—it don't matter."

"Sounds like you done got it worked out, Jessie."

"Only thing missing is that if he guilty, he don't have to go to jail. He's just got to pay some money."

"What did Veola say?"

"'Bout what?"

"About Fayetta getting beat up and all."

"Oh, just that she was gon' try to visit Fayetta when she got off work."

"What for?"

"To check on her."

"Will they let her have visitors in the emergency room?"

"I'm sure they'll let her see her if she say she family."

"She ain't family...is she?"

"Well, you tell her that. I ain't. You know how Veola is. She gon' find a way to see that gal. When I hear from Veola, I'll call you. She might want us to meet her at the horsepital."

"Until then, honey, I'mmo keep a watch over here and find out where Tyrone is. You know he can't keep a job. I'm ashamed to say it, but that boy of mine ain't worth two quarters when it comes down to being stable. You know everybody as old as he is ain't necessarily grown-up—if you know what I mean."

"Well, I'm gon' pray for him, Eva Mae."

"Jessie, that's always a good idea. Don't you ever stop praying for my boy. I pray for him, too, but I wish I could whup his ass sometimes. I done got too old for that, but take away thirty years from both of us, I'd git me a good switch."

"Eva Mae, leave that alone. You can't whup that boy, so don't

158

even think about it. We just gon' have to pray for him."

"He needs prayer all right. Hell, we all do, but every now and then, I want a good brick in my hand to bust him upside his head."

"You is a mess, Girl. We'll talk later."

⤚⫷⫸⤙

In Jeremy's room, Veola wanted obvious clues without checking in between the mattress and the box springs. Her conscience couldn't defend this intrusion. Her need to find something overwhelmed her. As lead detective and prosecutor, she'd undercover the goods, solve the case, and put this whole predicament behind her. Case closed.

Maybe this wasn't fair to Jeremy. She had no intention of getting him into trouble. She set her heart on finding what troubled him and squash the culprit before it squashed him. But Jeremy didn't make it that easy. She found nothing suspicious among his dirty clothes in the floor nor anything unusual hidden under his bed.

After Jessie's phone call, Veola wanted to hurry and finish her duties. She kept moving. In the master bedroom, the first thing Veola thought about was Dr. Barton's late lunch with some woman a couple of days ago. Nothing was out-in-out wrong with it, but Veola thought it was suspicious.

Oh, Lord, no, she thought. Was Dr. Barton having an affair? Quit it, Veola. She shook her head to clear the absurd idea.

Who would want that man? She loved him, and of course, he was a doctor. But he can't cook. He helped a little around the house, but he rarely picked up his dirty underwear off the floor. But then again, when someone is having an affair, it usually ain't the underwear being picked up that they're looking for. Forget those thoughts.

Veola gave her extended family the benefit of the doubt. In spite of whatever was going on, they should be assumed innocent until proven otherwise. The devil was busy, and Veola knew it. _Get thee behind me, Satan._

Bathrooms—spotless. Floors—shiny. Windows—sparkling. Clothes—freshly folded. The boys would put their own clothes away today. Veola told them they needed responsibility. Mrs. Barton okayed it.

Veola made one last walk-through to make sure everything was done. She trusted herself, but today she classified herself as a little off kilter. When she summoned Mrs. Barton, she had made sure she was ready to go.

"Mrs. Barton?" Veola called from the kitchen, draping her sweater across her shoulders. She listened for an answer. "Mrs. Barton?" Veola repeated.

"Yes?" came the distant, barely audible reply.

Veola approached the master bedroom.

"I'm in the closet," Mrs. Barton added. She sounded upside down, buried in clothes.

That's exactly where Veola found her. In the middle of her husband's suits, she was deciding which ones to take to the cleaners, an errand she'd forgotten earlier.

Veola didn't understand how a woman ran all over town running errands, forgot to do what she was supposed to do, and returned with shopping bags. That was her routine on Mondays and Thursdays. Who knows what the other days did for their bank account. That wasn't her business, and she knew it, but penny-pincher was her middle name.

"I'm ready to go, Mrs. Barton, when you are," Veola stated.

Mrs. Barton tossed suits on the floor, checking the pockets of the coats and pants. "Okay, let's go," Mrs. Barton replied, yet she kept piling clothes.

Veola got the impression Mrs. Barton wanted to finish her self-appointed task and drop the clothes off when she took Veola to the hospital. She said she was ready, yet she dug through more pockets. Lo and behold, she held up a receipt. "What's this?" Mrs. Barton asked rhetorically.

Veola edged forward to see what Mrs. Barton held in her hand.

"Oh, it's a receipt from the floral shop I found in Roy's pants pocket. I wonder if they're for me?"

"Could be."

"Maybe someone died from the office and he ordered them himself?"

"Could be that, too." Veola hoped the flowers were for Mrs. Barton. *Chile, surely he didn't send them to that other woman.*

"I'd better save it for Roy just in case he needs it."

Veola froze. If Dr. Barton tried to hide something, then he wouldn't be so negligent to leave incriminating evidence where his wife could find it. No, he was not that forgetful nor that stupid.

Whatever went on in the dark was bound to come to the light, but now was not the time for her to get involved. Dr. Barton could save himself on this one, and once again, Veola reminded herself there was some logical explanation for all she saw on Tuesday when she left her eye doctor's office and for the receipt Mrs. Barton found. The two may be unrelated.

"Are you ready, Mrs. Barton?" Veola exited the room.

"I'm right behind you, Veola. I'll put this in Roy's office, and tend to those clothes tomorrow."

While Veola stood at the back door, and Mrs. Barton gathered her purse and car keys, Veola called Jessie. "I know I was supposed to call you earlier, Jessie, just in case you were going to try to meet me at the hospital, but I got busy and forgot. We're leaving now, and I'll call you once I know what's going on."

"That'll be fine. I can't leave now anyway," Jessie explained. "I'm in the middle of my flowerbed covered with dirt."

"No, Girl, you can't go anywhere then."

"Well, if you're going to the hospital straight from work, them peoples down there gon' think you one of the nurses with your uniform on." Jessie giggled.

"You may be right, Chile," Veola said, surveying her white uniform, white stockings, and white shoes. "I hope Fayetta's still down there. You haven't heard anymore, have you?"

"No, but I know she down there, 'cause May Pearl said they was gon' keep her in observation for a while."

"I'll call you later."

On the way to the hospital, Mrs. Barton anticipated some explanation from Veola as to the phone call she received this morning. No such exchange occurred. They talked of a sale on full-length skirts at Ethylene's department store, chuck roasts on sale at Piggly Wiggly, Jeremy's upcoming graduation, and other routine subjects at hand. To Mrs. Barton, Veola appeared to be a bit preoccupied.

Mrs. Barton dropped Veola off at the front entrance of the hospital, and Veola showed her appreciation. Something troubled Veola, and Mrs. Barton wanted to make sure she was doing everything in her realm to take care of her trusted employee. After this long, Veola was family. "If you'd like, Veola, I'll come back by after picking up Bobby, and we'll take you home."

"Oh, that's too much trouble," Veola said. "I'll be fine, but if I need someone to get me, I'll call Carneda."

"How long are you planning to stay?" Mrs. Barton fished for anything she could.

"I don't know. I'm not sure what I'll find. My friend may or may not still be here."

"Do you want me to wait while you check?"

"No, you've done enough. In case my friend is not here, another church member may need a visit to cheer her up. You go get Bobby. Give him a hug for me. I'll be fine." Veola closed the car door.

Mrs. Barton knew she was being dismissed, so she waved goodbye and watched Veola march to the hospital entrance.

Veola headed for the nurses station in the emergency room, and she spotted May Pearl Lewis. "Maybe you can help me, May Pearl," she began, directing her entire conversation to the whites of May Pearl's eyes. "Is Fayetta Dewberry still here? You know her mama just recently passed, and I'm here to check on her. How is she doing?"

Veola knew that declaring herself as the surrogate mother added some validity to her plan. She not only let May Pearl know her true compassion for the patient in question, but she also tried to get some indication of Fayetta's physical and mental state. She wasted no time since some other nurse could be making her way to the front desk the longer she delayed.

May Pearl stood up with a chart in her hand and directed Veola to the back.

When a patient comes to the emergency in this physical state, it is customary to find out all the particulars of what might have happened and what could have happened. There is always the truth involved in any assault case, but often that is not the first history taken.

According to May Pearl, Fayetta fit the first scenario. May Pearl knew that Fayetta had not been raped, and all her tests and x-rays had turned out normal. From what May Pearl said, Fayetta had not divulged her attacker.

May Pearl led Veola to a closed curtain toward the back of the emergency room. As they approached, Veola's heart beat a little faster. Her coming to the hospital would shock Fayetta anyway, and now the surprise factor affected her, too. May Pearl motioned for her to stop outside the door.

"Miss Dewberry," May Pearl began as she tapped on the curtain surrounding Fayetta's bed. "I brought someone to see you."

When Fayetta saw Veola coming toward her, she covered her face and cried. Veola wanted to fix her beaten and troubled heart; she had to work her magic. She outstretched her hands to Fayetta, hoping to give her the hug she needed, but Fayetta didn't uncover her face. As a mother would do, Veola laid her hands on Fayetta's head and stroked her slightly disheveled hair.

"It's gon' be all right, Baby," Veola said. "We gon' get through this."

Fayetta sobbed and held tight to Veola.

Chapter Thirteen

Eva Mae glanced up and saw Leonard get out of a different car from the one he was in this morning. She ran back to fetch her broom—time to sweep off her sidewalk.

"Leonard, you not working today?" she hollered from her porch.

"No, ma'am, not today."

Eva Mae didn't think the sorry bastard worked any day, and she couldn't figure out why he was back up to Tyrone's this early afternoon.

"You know Tyrone is at work, don't you?"

"Yes, ma'am." He walked to Tyrone's front door.

"Oh, I see, must be important that you couldn't wait until he got home."

"Yes, ma'am, it is." He put a piece of paper in Tyrone's mailbox and started toward the car.

"Well, I'm looking out for my son's house, you know, folks breaking in and out of houses these days."

"Say they is?" He kept walking.

"They shole is. That's why I got concerned when I heard that loud ass car over here in the middle of the night. I have to be careful these days. Don't know who's trying to get in my house. Somebody tried to break in Veola's house the other night. You heard about it, didn't you?"

"No, ma'am, I didn't."

"Wonder if she'll think you might have done it since you be up all times of the night."

Eva Mae had yet to make one stroke with her broom. She realized she had accused Leonard of a crime, but she didn't care.

"I don't break in folks' houses, Miss Walker." He stared at Eva Mae.

Eva Mae decided to give him a reason to rev up his engine one more time. "Matter of fact, Miss Veola went to check on Fayetta today. Heard she in the emergency room. Know anything about that?"

Leonard piled in the car and slammed the door. He started the engine and sped off.

Eva Mae leaned on her broom and laughed. She hoped she had riled his nerves the same as he'd done to hers.

❧ ❧

Veola released Fayetta's hand long enough to open a full box of tissues on the bedside. Fayetta had poured out her story about everything that had happened in court the day before and that night with Leonard. Veola was glad to help Fayetta get that off her chest.

"What hurts you the most?" Veola asked, her face concerned. Fayetta remained silent, so Veola continued. "I think you're hurting in more places than one. Your heart is beat up because you had to be in court to get something done you'd think would come natural to any parent. But for some folk, it doesn't work that way. Your body hurts because you're dealing with somebody who wants to hurt the one he thinks is trying to hurt him. You might want to think about which hurt you can live with and which one you can't."

Fayetta swallowed and frowned.

Veola sensed Fayetta was perplexed. She heard what Veola had said, yet it hadn't quite digested. Veola had to break it down some more, so she grabbed Fayetta's hands. "Do you love him?"

Fayetta closed her eyes. "Not all of this is Leonard's fault."

"What do you mean?"

"Because of the way I was acting to get out of the car, maybe he did what he had to do so we wouldn't have a wreck. I think he would have acted worse had he wrecked his daddy's car."

"But you don't slap people to calm them down."

"I know, I know."

Veola continued. "Listen, Baby, and listen to me good. It's impossible to live with a person who has never grown up. These outbursts of violence are a result of him not getting his way as an adult. You don't want to feel cornered or pushed against the wall by any man. You deserve better. One day y'all get along, and the next, you're protecting your life. Just get what you need from him, Baby, and get away."

"But, Miss Veola, I feel if I cooperate and be nice, then it would be easier for my children to get what they need. I tried to put it on his terms, thinking he would be more willing to do it."

"Think about it, Baby," Veola interrupted. "If he wanted to do this willingly without a fight or struggle, then why are you even here?"

Fayetta stared at the ceiling, and Veola sensed she'd hit a nerve. Then Fayetta's head dropped, and she dabbed at her eyes. "Lying here in this bed with my mind wandering is not doing me any good. I have to get out of here."

"When can you leave?"

"I think I can go home now, but I'm not sure if that's where I want to be. I don't want my children to see me like this, and I'm in no position to talk to them. They know I can't get any support from their daddy, and they have their own opinion of him. But he is still their father. I will be so glad when all of this is over and I can get back to Dallas."

"Fayetta, I have to ask you one more question. Were you trying to make Leonard feel guilty by surrounding him with his children?"

"I've tried that in the past, but since we've been here, not once has he laid his eyes on our son. Not once."

"You know what I'm saying, right?"

"That's why he moved to Dallas in the first place. I figured if we worked things out between us, then he'd want to do more for the kids."

Veola now knew that Fayetta didn't need Leonard for anything but money. Apparently, feelings she'd had for Leonard were gone.

Veola was relieved that she'd come to Parkerville solely for her children.

"Then, let's work this out," Veola offered. "I have an idea."

"What?"

Veola's heart raced with anticipation. "How long is this hearing supposed to last?"

"We were supposed to finish today, but we had to cancel. My lawyer said tomorrow, at the latest, and he told me he was going to file charges against him. I told him no 'cause that would delay this whole thing a few more days or even weeks if he got locked up. And I can't go through that. Leonard will do nobody any good if he's in jail."

"Makes sense to me, but what I was getting at is this. Why don't you come stay with me the next couple of days? You would be right down the street from your cousin's house, and you might have some peace of mind. Nobody's gon' bother you there."

As soon as the words poured from Veola's mouth, she had a revelation. Leonard was her culprit. She was convinced he was the one who'd broken into her house. She wanted desperately to say something to Fayetta, but now was no time to trouble her further.

"Oh, I couldn't do that, Miss Veola. I'm dreading facing my children, but they need to know that I'm all right. My daughter is supposed to be here today, and I don't think my family will understand me being away again."

"I just want you to be comfortable. You have to feel safe."

"Oh, I won't see Leonard until the hearing, but like I said, I don't think he'd intentionally hurt me."

"That's a chance you'll have to take, Sugar, and he may not even show up there."

"Let me think about. Right now, my cousin is coming to pick me up. You would think that lying up here in this room, I could clear my head, but I'm more confused than ever since part of the blame I'm putting on myself."

Veola prepared to leave, feeling Fayetta needed to be alone. Veola felt as if she'd done all she could. According to her watch, she had some time before that Esso man arrived.

"I'm going to the main waiting room and wait for my ride. Let May Pearl know if you need anything. Me and her go way back. She'll take good care of you. Think about my offer. My extra room is yours if you want it." She touched the back of Fayetta's hand and headed for the hospital lobby.

Veola had no intention of calling Carneda, but she wanted to update Jessie. At the information desk, she spotted two women with two little boys tagging along. She recognized her treasures from behind, Cameron and Bobby. They had pulled out their pant pockets, probably trading marbles or toy cars. Veola suspected her daughter and her employer were trying to find her, questioning the desk volunteer.

Veola observed something magical, almost surreal as her mind escaped her whereabouts for a moment. Everyday, she caught herself thinking about the injustices encountered by her people. She was in the Deep South where in some places, white people and black people still couldn't use the same hospital. She had thought about this earlier and even this year Dr. King had been on the radio and the TV talking about this over and over again. Now, she felt even more blessed.

Lord, watch over my people. We need You. Thank you for where I am today for not having to look at separation based upon the color of skin in the face in everything I do. But I am not crazy. It's all around me. Lord, don't ever forget about us.

By the time she finished her prayer, the boys spied her, and she snapped backed to reality. They raced, full-force, toward her, catching the attention of their mothers.

"Mama!" Cameron shouted.

"Veola!" Bobby exclaimed.

Veola embraced the boys, grabbing them around their heads and pulling them to her hips. Their arms overlapped, hugging Veola from both sides.

Carneda and Mrs. Barton had surrounded Veola, their expressions filled with concern.

"Mama, are things all right?" Carneda began.

"Yes," Veola answered.

"Mrs. Barton called me at work, so I called Cousin Jessie to see what she knew. She told me about Fayetta Dewberry. How is she?" Carneda asked.

"Her injuries checked out okay, but in the mind, she's shaky."

169

"And I was worried about you," Mrs. Barton said. "You were so quiet after your phone call. Didn't seem like yourself. Maybe I overreacted by calling Mrs. Allen, but you know me. I'm known for that."

Mrs. Barton spoke the truth, and Veola didn't hold that against her. Veola watched them glance at each other, and after they'd given their explanations, she noticed they awaited her response. Even the boys' eyes were fixed on her. "I appreciate your concern, but you don't need to be worried. I'm here to check on my friend. Both of y'alls houses got plenty love, and sometimes, we take that for granted. Some of us don't have that, and Fayetta needed a dose of that kind of love today."

Veola grabbed the boys again, bringing them close for pats on the head. "Give me a minute, Mrs. Barton. I'd like to borrow Bobby. Cameron, too, Carneda. I want them to see something, so do me a favor. Call Jessie and tell her I'll be home after a while."

Veola noticed Carneda and Mrs. Barton glanced at each other, then each nodded at her. The boys followed.

"Where are we going, Veola?" Bobby asked.

"Is someone sick?" Cameron inquired.

"I want you to meet someone," Veola answered.

She thought about what she'd say. Were six-year olds allowed to see someone in this condition? She prepared herself for whatever their little minds would throw at her. She'd tell May Pearl whatever she needed to hear to get the boys to see Fayetta. With her purse over her forearm and before they reached the swinging doors, she stopped and turned to them.

"Put your pockets back in, please. You're going to look presentable. I'm gon' introduce you to a friend of mine. She could use a dose of love from the likes of you two."

Veola grabbed their hands and resumed her walk.

"Don't nobody love her?" Cameron asked.

Veola let his grammar go this time; his concern was more important. "I'm sure her family loves her, but today, she needs more love than usual. I saw her earlier, and I know you two will brighten her day. She's cried a lot; let's see if you can make her smile."

Aware that this may be unchartered territory for the boys, Veola held their hands.

The nurse's station was empty, so Veola sped up, straight toward Fayetta. Fayetta sat on the side of the bed, having changed back into her clothes.

"Fayetta, I want you to meet my little ones." Veola let go of their hands. "This is Bobby, one of my special children." She winked at Fayetta. "And this is Cameron, Carneda's youngest."

The moment Veola had called out each name, she'd placed a hand on top of each head. Veola could feel them trying to look up at her, but she kept them staring ahead.

"Boys, this is Miss Fayetta, and she's the one I was telling you about. She has a son of her own, and she hasn't seen him today."

"Mama said you could use some love," Cameron said, inching his way toward Fayetta with outstretched arms.

Fayetta dabbed at her eyes.

Bobby followed him, grabbing Fayetta's other side. "Veola said this will make you feel better."

Veola watched the Fayetta sandwich. When Bobby leaned against her, Fayetta was overcome with emotion, releasing a full cry, still holding the boys. Veola noticed the boys eyed each other, but they kept their grip on Fayetta.

Veola let the boys work their magic. Finally, Fayetta controlled her sobs.

"I know now why I did what I did. I doubted myself this morning, Miss Veola, wondering if I did the right thing by bringing Leonard to court. I love my children. I really do."

Veola put her purse on the hospital bed, and motioned the boys to her side, giving Fayetta room to breathe.

"Your children, Miss Veola, have been the best medicine. I thought about not appearing in court in the morning, but I know I must for my children's sake. God is going to get me through this, and I have to let Him do just that."

"Fayetta, sometimes the best way is not the easiest. Court gives you the ways and means to help provide for your children. God gon' direct your path if you let Him, for the devil is busy, always will be."

Fayetta nodded. "Thank you for being here with me."

"My offer still stands; call me. Let me try to ease some of your pain. That's all I'm saying."

171

"I look into the eyes of these children, Miss Veola, and I know they're happy. I want to see that look in the eyes of my children, too."

"I don't know this for a fact, but I'd bet what you're seeing in the eyes of your children is not their own feelings. It may be the reflection of yourself that you see in them—your desire, your wants, your needs. Not necessarily theirs, but yours. You can't make their daddy love them, but you can make him be a provider for them."

Fayetta said nothing, and the boys stood still. She smiled at them. "Thank you, Cameron and Bobby. I needed your hugs, and I hope to see you again. I can't wait to tell my children about you."

"How old is your son?" Bobby asked.

"He's sixteen, in high school, and my daughter is eight."

"Do they live here?" Cameron inquired.

"No, we live in Dallas. Maybe we can get together sometimes when we're visiting."

Cameron and Bobby grinned. First impressions for six-year olds were unforgettable and often unchanging. She used every opportunity to give her children the proper training. Their hearts needed to be in the right place.

"Fayetta, we're gon' leave you," Veola said, but not before the chorus of a song popped into her head, "Safe in His Arms." *'Safe in the arms of the Lord, oh, I'm safe in the arms of the Lord.'* There was no better place to be.

Fayetta and the boys exchanged goodbye hugs.

"Come on now, your mothers are probably wondering what happened to you." Veola grabbed her purse.

"Miss Veola?"

"Yes?" Veola and the boys glanced back.

"My mama used to talk about you all the time. You are one special lady, and you've helped me in more ways than you know."

"Baby, it was a pleasure. You just take care of yourself."

"No, I'm serious. I know what she was talking about now."

"I don't need any credit for anything I do, Fayetta. Give that glory to the Lord." Veola's mission was accomplished.

That no good Leonard was back on her mind as she walked with the boys to the lobby.

"Here are your little ones." Veola hurried toward where Carneda and Mrs. Barton sat, engaged in deep conversation.

"We met a lady named Fayetta," Cameron informed his mother.

"Yeah, and she was really nice," Bobby added. "Was she sick?"

"Her doctor's in Dallas, so she came here to have a few things checked out," Veola explained. Bobby had suppressed his curiosity earlier, but now his inquisitive nature burst forth. It was bound to come from one of them. With her answer, she set the tone for any more questions Mrs. Barton or Carneda may encounter later.

"My daddy could be her doctor," Bobby said.

Everyone smiled.

"Mama, are you ready to go?" Carneda asked.

"It's nearly 4:30, and we all need to get home." Veola turned toward her employer. "Mrs. Barton, I appreciate you more than you know. Thanks for bringing Carneda and the boys here."

Mrs. Barton grabbed Veola's hand. "I know you're a strong woman, but that doesn't mean I don't get concerned when you're in a difficult situation." The two embraced.

Veola thought she had truly hugged a lot of folk today. God's work, no doubt. When they separated, Veola grabbed Mrs. Barton's hands. "We'll talk before Saturday to see what time is good for Bobby to come over. Y'all ready to go?"

꧁꧂

Carneda wanted more of an explanation of what was going on with Fayetta than what she received from her mother in the hospital foyer. "Seriously, Mama, is Fayetta going to be all right?"

"That girl is going through some tough times. She's doubting if she's doing the right thing," Veola explained.

"You had everybody worried, as usual, but then again, you're just being you," Carneda said. She knew that physical abuse was the reason for Fayetta's emergency room visit.

"Let's talk about that later." Veola raised her brows in the direction of Cameron. "That oil and gas man is coming over, and I don't want to miss him. Ruben Earl may be at the house already plowing, so if the oil and gas man is there, Ruben Earl will keep him occupied 'til I get there."

Carneda remained quiet and drove as her mother changed

the subject. Carneda knew her mother worked extremely hard to raise her and her siblings as a single mother, and she was certain her mother's empathy for Fayetta hit home. Veola, too, had been in that exact situation, and she understood why her mother was going to do everything she could to help Fayetta—especially since Fayetta had no mother. Carneda knew her mother had many words of wisdom to share with Fayetta.

⚞⚟

As soon as she arrived home, Veola dropped her belongings in the living room and made her way to the kitchen, craving a glass of iced water. From her kitchen window, she saw the back of Ruben Earl heading in the opposite direction with his mule and tiller. By this weekend, she'd have rows for her squash, beans, onions, and greens. She hadn't planted collards in the winter like she wanted to, so she'd load more rows of mustard and turnip greens than usual. There was no such thing as too many greens.

After she downed her second full glass, she filled a Mason jar for Ruben Earl. Still clad in her uniform, she stood at the edge of her plot and waited for Ruben Earl. She was certain he'd be done this evening at the rate he was going. Now she had to live up to her promise of getting her plants in the ground by Saturday. She'd start tomorrow after she picked up her eyeglasses.

Ruben Earl made his turn just in time as the glass was getting cold in her hand. When the mule made a right angle, Veola and he made eye contact. "Hey, Ruben Earl, thought you could use this," she called out.

"I 'preciate it, Veola."

Ruben Earl drank his water faster than she had taken one complete breath. It scared Veola how fast he chugged it down. She watched his Adam's apple try to keep up with his gulps. "I have got to get out here and do my part since you're almost through with yours. I appreciate you doing this so quickly."

He handed her the glass then wiped his face with his shirttail.

Veola caught sight of sweat trickling through the shirt. It was obvious to her that Ruben Earl worked hard, and it paid off. He was her friend, but Lord, he needed to be taught a few manners. When it came to work like this, she guessed it didn't matter how he got the sweat off his forehead, but next time, she'd bring him a towel. Teaching him manners was not her job. The longstanding friendship was enough.

"Yeah, I'll get through with this tonight before I go home. I've got at least two to three hours of good daylight."

"Well, you gon' have to take a break in there somewhere."

"Naw, I'm all right. I know ol' Sugar here gon' hold up, 'cause she ain't did nothing all day long but eat and sleep."

"You call your mule, Sugar?"

"Yeah, you knew that."

"No, I didn't. In all the times you've been plowing my garden, I have never heard you call that mule by name."

"Well, this here ain't the same mule I had last year. I took Bess down to the country to my sister's house."

"Does your sister plow?"

"Do she plow?" Ruben Earl appeared startled. "Why sho she plow! My sister wanted to plant early this year, but her garden ain't near 'bout big as yours. She knew I was going to get me a new mule, so I let ol' Bess stay down there with her."

"We all had to know how to plow, too, but I gave it up the first chance I got. For years you've been doing this for me, and until you tell me otherwise, the job is yours." They laughed.

"More?" She held up the glass.

"Not yet, but thank you, though. I have to keep Sugar moving while she's hot."

Veola threw up her hand and waved Ruben Earl toward the garden. That was her cue to head for the back door.

Once inside, she dumped more ice in Ruben Earl's glass, grabbed more towels, including some for his sweat, and headed back outside. She placed everything on a wooden bench by the storage room. "Ruben Earl?" Veola pointed to the glass.

He nodded and waved.

"Hey there, Veola." Delphine hollered before Veola reached her back door. "Ruben Earl getting you all ready, huh?"

"Yeah."

"Seems like yesterday it was the New Year's, and here you are already planting yo garden."

Veola refused to let Delphine make idle conversation. She wasn't in the mood, especially with her work clothes still on. "Seems that way, don't it." Fayetta's pain surfaced in Veola's mind at the sight of Delphine. "Delphine, have you seen Leonard?"

"Naw, not today."

"Well, I just left the hospital, and I wonder if he knows that Fayetta Dewberry, you know her, Melda's daughter, had to be rushed to the emergency room late last night. If you see him, tell him he might want to check with me 'cause I may have heard from her just exactly how she's doing."

Veola went inside right after she'd done exactly what she wanted to do with Delphine—planted the seed to get Leonard to pay her a visit, with attitude, no less. If Fayetta did come over later, then Veola would have even more firsthand information. If Fayetta didn't make it, and Leonard still popped in, Veola could further her investigation. Besides, she wanted to give Leonard a piece of her mind.

With her door closed, Veola muttered, "Girl, you just tell Leonard what I said."

While she changed, Veola thought about the advice she had given Fayetta earlier. Veola listened to every word she'd said, for she was also speaking to herself. For a long time, she had suppressed certain feelings, and she wanted to keep them that way. She had tried to forget that it happened many, many years ago between her mother and father, but she couldn't. She had a secret, one she'd avoided telling.

Oh Lord, I want to ask you to come into the lives of some of your children and show them that this pain and sorrow and suffering won't last always. I know trouble don't last always. Their weeping may endure for a night, but keep them strong and in your faith so that they may realize and know that joy comes in the morning.

When she needed to talk to Him, she didn't announce it. She wanted this Esso man to hurry up, and when she got through with him, she had a few more choice words for her dear neighbor, Miss Loretta. She'd shout them through the closed door again if she had to.

Chapter Fourteen

Where was Mr. Etson? Veola guessed at the name of the oil and gas man without the letter in front of her. Edelson, that's it. While taking off her dress, the phone rang. She picked it up with a free hand. The other arm was buried in the dress, halfway over her head.

"Mrs. Cook?" the man voice asked.

Finally, she freed herself to talk. "Yes. Sorry about that."

"This is Dick Edelson, from the Esso Company. Is now a good time to come by and talk to you about your property and explain any questions you might have regarding the lease? I'm just leaving a client's home."

"Just as good a time as any. I'm at 116 West Jackson Street."

"I know how to get to Jackson Street, so expect me shortly."

Veola rushed to change into a spring dress that was better than the one she'd just climbed into. It wasn't lady-like for a woman of her stature and upbringing to have nothing on her legs. She grabbed the stockings and garters on the back of her closet door.

Her hair was presentable, but she rubbed a dab of petrolatum jelly in her hands and smoothed down the gray anyway. She wiped her face with a damp washcloth and Ivory soap. She was now groomed for accepting company.

She made iced tea with lemons, for she wanted her southern hospitality to be up to par by offering him something other than a Dr Pepper or water.

Usually, she'd open the front door, making sure the storm door was locked, in anticipation of guests, but the break-in had made her wary. What if someone was watching her right now? Where was Leonard anyway? She kept the door closed, plopped into her rocking chair, and watched the news.

A half an hour later, the doorbell rang. "Come on in," Veola said, shaking Mr. Edelson's hand.

"Thank you, Mrs. Cook. Richard Edelson, ma'am." He carried a file folder in the other hand.

Veola peered out at his white sedan, labeled with a decal on the passenger door. It looked official—a business car.

"You sound just like yourself on the telephone," Veola said.

"I should hope so." He chuckled.

"Sometimes people sound differently on the phone than they do in person. You know what I mean? Have a seat, Mr. Edelson." She directed him to her couch.

"Thank you, Mrs. Cook."

"Can I get you something? I made fresh iced tea."

"That would be fine."

While Veola was in the kitchen, she stole a glance into the living room. He appeared comfortable, yet he shole was looking around—like he was inspecting her place.

"Here you go, sir." Veola offered a tall glass of sweetened tea, full of ice cubes, and a napkin. She placed a coaster on the coffee table and sat on the opposite end of the couch. The manila file separated them.

"You have a very nice house, Mrs. Cook."

"Why thank you, sir."

Mr. Edelson filled her in on his job. On this particular assignment, a lot of the properties were owned by black people. He covered areas all over Texas, but primarily when it came to oil and gas leases, his area was concentrated in West and South Texas. Other representatives covered East Texas in the past. According to him, the amount of ownership for blacks in this part of Texas reached "astounding" numbers.

Veola listened but she couldn't figure out why he was taken aback by this fact.

"I brought you some additional information about your property." Mr. Edelson picked up the file. "These papers detail more than what you received in the mail. We have done extensive work on the land around your acreage, and there is a possibility that your area has natural gas. That's what our company is about. We search for resources to make fuel, and in turn, pay you for our exploration."

"Have you already been digging on my property?" Veola asked. She had not anticipated her own directness so quickly. *Don't let the iced tea fool you, Mister.*

"At this point, Mrs. Cook, we've only surveyed the property. We need your permission to go further."

"Now what's the timber?"

"In the process of getting to certain areas, some of the trees have to be sacrificed. This harvesting of timber will provide you additional income from the lumber company."

Veola understood. "The papers you have, Mr. Edelson, do they state how much the lumber company is going to pay and how much you're paying for the lease?"

"Yes, they do." He passed the file to Veola.

"Good. I'll study this and let my children read over it, too. I bet you've visited some of my relatives. A lot of that land was from my late husband's family, so I bet some of the people you've met have been my kinfolks."

"Probably so, Mrs. Cook. We're interested in much of that area."

Veola stood up. "Well, I want to thank you for coming by and giving me this. Were y'all going to send this to me if I hadn't called?"

"When you tell them you're interested in the lease, then the company sends you this information. This time you got it hand-delivered." Mr. Edelson smiled.

"Can I get you more tea before you go?"

"No, this is fine." He finished the remainder on his feet and passed the glass to Veola.

"After I check over these papers, I'll call you." Veola followed him to the door.

"We'll look forward to hearing from you." He trotted down Veola's steps.

Veola waved as he climbed into the car. Mr. Edelson drove to the end of the block and turned around. When he drove back by, Veola was still on her front porch. The company emblem was on the driver's side, too. He must be for real. Still, something felt strange, but exactly what it was eluded her. He waved again, and Veola watched him go to the corner and turn right. This time she only nodded.

Ruben Earl's truck pulled up as she walked through the storm door. With him arriving this quickly after Mr. Edelson left, she wondered if Ruben Earl had seen that company car up the street. Veola waited for Ruben Earl to get out of his truck.

"I saw your door open, and I came by to see if you liked your plowing."

"I didn't even know you were finished. I just left you a short while ago."

Ruben Earl made his way around back. Veola locked her door and followed.

"When you gon' get your stuff to plant?" he asked.

"That might depend on you."

"What do you mean?"

"Well, when you gonna take me so I can fill up your truck with what all I want. You know I think I can get more plants and supplies in your truck than I can get into the trunk of Carneda's car.

"When you want to go?"

"Maybe tomorrow or early Saturday morning. The market's big shipments come in late Friday afternoon and early on Saturday."

"Just let me know."

Now Ruben Earl and Veola surveyed the newly plowed soil. It even smelled ready, Veola thought. "You do such a good job for me every year. I depend on you."

"And I depend on your garden to keep me with a few vegetables throughout the year. This is the least I can do for my share."

"Now you know you're welcome to anything I grow. I'm just glad we get such a good crop every year."

"That's 'cause you know what you're doing."

Veola got quiet, then faced the direction of Delphine and Loretta's houses.

"Is everything all right?" he asked.

"What do you mean?"

"I drove by here on my way to the churchhouse a moment ago, and I saw a car out front. Company car?"

"Oh, everything's all right. That was a man from Esso, the gas company. They're interested in doing some drilling out on the family land."

"A lot of that's going on right now. My sister said these oil companies are drilling for everything, and sometimes they're doing stuff you don't even know about."

"What are you talking about?" He had Veola's full attention. "Make sure they put down on paper everything they're looking for."

"Like what?"

"Like oil, gas, coal, anything they can sell."

"I'll go over the papers he left me. There's no big rush, so I'll get around to it next week. But I was thinking 'bout something else, Ruben Earl."

"What is it?"

"I was looking up at Delphine and Loretta's houses, and mind you, I can't prove nothing yet, but I have a suspicion of who might have broken into my house."

"Who?"

Veola leaned close and whispered, "I don't know what it is, but I can't get Leonard out of my mind."

"What makes you think it's him?"

"Melda's daughter, Fayetta, is in town to get money for her kids from Leonard, and they've been in court. Last night, they went out to supposedly talk, and she ends up in the emergency room. Now what kind of talk is that?"

"I didn't know none of this."

"With him having to be in court right now and Fayetta getting man-handled, he just seems like he'd be up to no good. Now you know why I feel the way I do."

"I'll keep my eyes open. That Leonard wanders the streets so much, who's to say what all he's into?"

"That's exactly what I'm saying. If you look like you're up to no good, then you must be."

"Don't you go getting yourself in trouble, Veola, trying to make him be the one if he ain't."

"Oh, I ain't gon' do that. I'll get my answer in due time."

"And besides, don't you have enough on your plate already? You ain't the one to ever sit down for long?"

"You're a fine one to talk, somebody that don't ever get any rest. I worry about you working so much, and here I am asking you to take me to get my plants. I should be ashamed of myself."

"We both need more rest."

"Rest? What's that?" They both laughed.

"I'm gon' start right now and head on to the house. I'm glad you liked your plowing."

Veola followed him to this truck. "If I don't see you tomorrow, I'll call you and let you know about picking up some plants. I don't know what you got planned, but we'll work it out."

There was no other man in her life like him. He wasn't family, yet she cared about him just the same.

As Ruben Earl drove off, she had decided Loretta needed to be confronted one more time, but this time Veola knew she had to handle it differently. Loretta was set on being in that house, but Veola wanted to get her outside. She proceeded to ascend Loretta's front steps.

Veola knocked, waited a few seconds, and knocked again. "Loretta, I need to ask you if that was Leonard who was over here the other morning? Right now, a good friend of mine is laid up in the emergency room, and—"

Loretta cracked her door. "Meet me 'round back."

Veola darted off the porch to get around back as fast as she could. Veola thought she was making headway. At least Loretta agreed to listen to her this time, and hopefully, Loretta would come outside. Therefore she wouldn't be able to slam the door in Veola's face again.

Loretta opened her back door, but her screen door remained locked. "What about Leonard?"

"Loretta, the break-in has got me so unnerved, that when I'm asking you what you know, it's because I'm trying to get some answers. I don't know how safe I am over here. When I see you out here wrestling with some man, I have to think about whether or not that man could have been the one that broke into my house."

"What were you saying about Leonard?"

"Well, I know that Leonard is responsible for putting Fayetta Dewberry in the hospital. She's up in the emergency room right now because of him. Was that him you was scuffling with the other morning?"

"Miss Veola, I don't want no lecture on this right now, but yeah, that was him. Last weekend I found out he was selling dope out of my house."

"You and Leonard? Was he living here?"

"He wasn't living here, but he kept some clothes around. He had been putting the dope in my trash can, and folk would leave the money there for him. When I asked him about it, we got into it. He got mad, and that's what happened here." Loretta took off her glasses and pointed to her black eye.

"Lord, how mercy."

"He told me two guys were supposed to pick up their stash from the trash can, but I told him that somebody had stolen my trash can last week. So, he used yours instead. We fought, and I chunked all kinds of stuff at his ass. I'm mad already 'cause I found out all this stuff late Saturday night. My Easter Sunday was all jacked up because of him. In the process of us getting into it, he broke my glasses when he hit me in the eye. I had to find some tape to piece them back together so I could even see. He left out the back door, and I didn't care where he went. He walked 'round the side of your house, and then lights came from somewhere on that side. Probably shone on him, but I didn't give a damn—just as long as he was gone."

"Did you see anything else, anybody else?"

"I saw these young boys out back digging in your trash can. I followed them through the crack of my curtain and watched them come 'round to your front porch. Them ignant kids must not have had a flashlight and needed the street light to find what they was looking for. Your porch is closer to the light pole than mine, and I was too afraid to open my door."

"What happened to Leonard?"

"I don't know and didn't care. That's when he came traipsing back over here Monday morning, disturbing me, and I was through at that point. Look at my eye, Miss Veola. I can't go no where like this, even though it's better than it was."

"I knew about your glasses from Dr. Sweeney, 'cause he told me you had fallen."

"I fell all right, right in the hands of Leonard trying to whup my ass."

"Loretta, I didn't know about you and Leonard. That's your business. It gets to be my business when my house get broke into. Why didn't you say something when all that racket was going on at my house?"

"I wasn't even at home a couple of nights this week. Didn't want to be bothered with him or nobody else. I went to work and then stayed away for a while."

"That means you missed the police 'cause they been asking everybody have they noticed anyone acting unusual or with cuts on them."

"I knew they've been around, and I must have missed them. You think it was Leonard that broke into your house?"

"Why shole I think it was Leonard, and I'm about to prove it. I need a little more evidence that he did it, and once I get that, I'm going straight to the police. He's doing everything else 'round here, why wouldn't he be breaking in my house, too? Just look at what happened to Fayetta. I know you've heard about her."

"I did, and even though I don't know her that well, I still hated to hear that. But Miss Veola, Leonard ain't the type to be breaking in people's houses. That's not like him."

"How you know, Loretta?"

"It's just not him. I know him pretty well, and he ain't the type to steal. He just ain't no good when it comes to his personal stuff. Don't get me wrong, he got some bad habits, but he do more to hurt himself."

"How you gon' stand here with a black eye and tell me that he do more to hurt himself than other people. What do you think Fayetta in the emergency room for?"

Loretta said nothing.

Veola continued. "Why are you protecting him? You must be still sweet on him, Loretta, but I'm gon' find out for sho if he did it. Put a hot water bottle on your eye to make that black and blue go away quicker." She was through talking to Loretta, and Veola went back inside her house. It didn't make sense to Veola how Loretta could be so love struck and blind at the same time. Why did she need to cover for him?

Veola appreciated the wealth of information she had received, but her investigation was far from over.

Back in her kitchen, she rummaged through leftover ham, cabbage, and green beans from Sunday before sitting in her rocking chair. She wasn't ready for bed for she had far too much to do.

Oh, most mighty, most gracious One, you know my mind is concentrating on Leonard. That's where all my thoughts are, and I can't help it. He's got Fayetta in the hospital, gave Loretta a black eye, and Lord, she's still protecting him. How can someone you like do that and you still falling for them? Give us strength and let thy will be done. I just hope I can sleep tonight. Amen.

❦

Later that night, Veola realized it was time to get up from her chair and get the rest of her chores done. She had saved some pillowcases to be ironed, so she thought that now was as good of a time as any to get on them. She set up the ironing board in the dining room, and about the time she had four of her stack of ten ironed, someone knocked on her front door. She hollered out, "Just a minute."

The knock came again. "I'm coming." She didn't know if whoever it was could hear her through both of her doors, but she wanted to get there before whoever it was pounded on her door again. Five minutes after nine was not late, but visitation hours had long passed.

"Mrs. Veola?" A voice came through the door. "It's Fayetta."

Veola unlocked her latches in record time, anxious to get Fayetta off her front porch and into her house. "Come on in here, Chile," Veola instructed. She first examined Fayetta's face. Lord, she hoped she hadn't been beat up again.

"Miss Veola, I know it's late, but you were right. My kids are fast asleep, but I don't feel safe over there. Scared, I guess, and I can't sleep for worrying about tomorrow. I don't know what he's up to next."

"Say nothing else. You'll sleep here tonight. Ain't nobody gon' bother you here. You need your rest more than anybody for your big day ahead. You'll be fine, 'cause I have already prayed about it. I'm sure you have, too."

"That's harder to do than you'd think after last night."

"Well, come on. I'm back in here ironing some pillowcases. What can I get you? Did you eat? Want some tea or something?"

"No thank you," Fayetta said.

Veola commenced where she had stopped with her ironing.

Fayetta sat in Veola's dining room. "I was going crazy the longer I stayed in that house. Thank you, Miss Veola. I don't know what I'd do without you."

"That's why you're here, Chile. I've got to admit that you've been on my mind more then you know."

"How's that?"

"Well, I don't know if you realize it, but we have a lot in common. I didn't have any court to go to for getting help with my children. And up until now, neither have you."

"You have no idea how hard it's been on me."

"Yes, I do. That's what I'm saying. We both raised our kids on our own. We did it. We're the ones who taught them everything they know. They didn't have a daddy around to show them this, show them that. I had to be the mama and the daddy. You know what I'm talking about, huh?"

"Yeah, but I don't know how you did it with three kids. You're stronger than I could ever be."

"I didn't have a choice, Baby. My husband was dead, but I didn't have anybody I could go to for help. To pull in another husband would have been like having another child. Men get more helpless when they get a ready-made family."

"Is that what it is? I know exactly what you're talking about. I felt like I had to carry my ex-husband, too."

"That's why I never re-married. When it comes to dead weight, I can do bad all by myself."

"But you have some smart children, Miss Veola. I remember they were all smart."

"I bet yours are the same way. And that's what ought to make you feel good about doing what you're doing. Your kids gon' know you're doing the right thing for them. I'm sure you have told them that."

"I have, and they realize it's for their own good."

"You just be strong. Don't let anybody tell you otherwise."

"You're too much. I feel like I'm sitting here having this conversation with my mama."

"I told you that's what I'm here for, now didn't I?" They laughed. "Now that was my last pillowcase, and once I put these up, I'll show you where the bathroom is. Do you need something to sleep in? I have some big t-shirts 'cause I don't think I have a new gown to fit you."

"I'm covered up now with what I'd already laid down in, so I don't need a thing." Fayetta removed her sweater and pullover dress. Underneath, she wore a cotton nightgown.

"Well, the bathroom is here." Veola pointed the way. "Give me a minute, and I'll set you out a washcloth and towel."

"Before you do that, I'll just slip into the bathroom now. I tried to rest earlier, but I guess I got plenty laid up in the hospital today. I'm not quite as tired as I thought I was."

"I've got to get my clothes ready for tomorrow, so don't mind me."

Veola heard the water running in the bathroom, and while Fayetta was in there, Veola heard another knock. She was back at her front door. "Who is it?" She opened the deadbolts again.

"It's Leonard, Miss Veola, and I need to show you something. The word on the street is that you think I broke into your house, and I thought the best way to prove you wrong was to show up in person and tell you that."

"Get in here, Leonard, and quit creating all that racket." Veola didn't want to draw any more attention than he already had for it was obvious to Veola he was outraged. She knew exactly where her gun was in case she needed it to scare him once again.

"I don't want you to be going 'round spreading no more rumors 'bout me. So, I want you to see this." Leonard peeled off his windbreaker, and he was wearing a short-sleeved shirt. "I heard that you done beat up on somebody's arm and they got bruises to show for it. Look at my arm. Do you see any bruises? Huh, tell me what you see."

"I don't see nothing." Veola observed that there was not a single scratch on either of Leonard's arms. He held them out and even turned them over so she could see the underside.

"Now, you know it wasn't me," Leonard yelled.

"You ain't got to be yelling, for I can see it wasn't you."

"What would make you think I would go and do something that stupid when I'm already in court this week? The last thing I need is for the law to be after me more than they already is. You need to quit trying to make me something I'm not. I've done some bad stuff, but I ain't no thief. You need to quit telling folk that."

"Maybe you ain't no thief, but you ain't no saint neither."

"I didn't say I was. But you need to quit adding to my trouble. Don't you think I got enough of my own?"

"Now that you have, but it's your own fault. You're the one got yourself into all this mess. Messing with Loretta. Messing with Fayetta." Veola stood with her hands on her hips.

"And I'm gon' get myself out of it, too, and that's without your help. What choo know about Loretta?"

"I ain't blind, Leonard. I was up the other morning when you and her were out back. I saw you, yes I did. She even told me that you broke her glasses last weekend. Don't think that I haven't seen her black eye? What's got into you that you think you can just go around hitting on folk?"

"I'm dealing with that. And what's that got to do with you?"

"It's got everything to do with me, 'cause I'm the one that's looking out for Fayetta. You think you was gon' do the same thing to her and get away with it? Let me tell you something: I'm not having it. You need to put it in your mind that when you're raising your fist to her, you might as well be raising your fist at me, 'cause I'm her mama since her mama has gone on to glory."

"Don't you think I know that?" Leonard asked.

"Once you cross the line with her, you've crossed it with me, too. Why are you going around hitting women?" Veola wanted an answer.

"I don't be going around hitting women." Leonard said.

"Well, it sholе seem that way to me. You don't get to throw your hands and fists at everybody and not have to worry about where they land, because one of these days, somebody gon' get you back. And I just hope you're ready when that day comes."

"I ain't scared of you."

"And you shouldn't be as long as you keep your hands off of Fayetta, off of Loretta, and anybody else I know."

Fayetta entered the room, and Veola knew from the expression on her face, she was boiling mad. "Who else have you hit on this week, Leonard besides me and Loretta?"

"Fayetta?" Leonard's expression showed his surprise.

"Tell her what you're here for, Leonard. Gone on, tell her," Veola ordered. It was obvious to Veola that Fayetta had heard most of what they had said. "Sit down, Fayetta, I want you to hear all of this. Better yet, Leonard, why don't you answer her question? Who else have you hit this week?"

"I knew about the other women, Leonard, but I didn't know about Loretta. What were you doing over there so early in the morning?" Fayetta sat and Veola saw she was still fuming.

"Me and Loretta ain't like that," Leonard began.

"Not any more since she threw your clothes at you. Don't think I didn't see that either." Veola wanted every detail revealed. "Leonard, sit down. I got some things I need to tell you."

Leonard didn't move.

"Sit down, I said." Veola pointed to the couch.

Leonard sat and Veola continued. "You came here and proved one thing to me. That you didn't break into my house. But you got a lot of other things that go far beyond being a crook. You are a father to Fayetta's children, and you need to think about doing what's right."

"This ain't got nothing to do with being a father. It's all about money," Leonard said.

"Listen to me. I am not finished. The only reason you didn't have to go to court today was because of what you did last night. Don't you realize your foolishness can get you locked up? But tomorrow, you're back in court. When you're there, you need to behave as nice as you can because Fayetta's lawyer wants to put you behind bars and throw away the key."

Veola pointed to Fayetta. "This chile is just trying to make you be responsible for taking care of your own children. That's all she asks for. She doesn't want your stanky hand in marriage, and she doesn't want you for her boyfriend. All she wants is for you to own up to being responsible."

"I am doing the best I can," Leonard said.

"No, you are not," Fayetta disagreed.

"Leonard, if you were doing the best you could, then we wouldn't even be sitting here, and Fayetta would be in Dallas. Your children even know that. Part of being responsible also includes earning their respect. Do you think they are going to respect you after all of this? That's up to you."

"I've been telling you that, Leonard," Fayetta said.

"You ought to think about making it easy on yourself," Veola continued and Leonard finally appeared to be listening. "If you agree with what the court people offer, then at least you don't have to go to jail. And I don't care one way or the other. It don't mean a thing to me which way you choose 'cause I'm gon' rest easier when we put every one of you ignant fools behind bars who beat up on women. That's the way I feel."

Veola felt Fayetta's stare.

Leonard hung his head. "I just came over here to clear my name. That's all I wanted to do."

"And I didn't hear from you all day long. I laid in that hospital, and you didn't care if I was dead or alive," Fayetta said.

"I knew you wasn't dead, but I couldn't come down to the hospital. You know I didn't mean to hurt you. I was trying to keep you from wrecking my daddy's car."

"You didn't find a way to check on me. You don't care about nobody but yourself." Fayetta appeared thoroughly disgusted.

"You came here tonight, Leonard, to clear your name, but I hope you learned something else," Veola said.

"I got to get out of here," Leonard said and hurried to the door.

"Quit hurting people, Leonard. Stop it. It ain't good for you. For nobody."

Veola knew Fayetta was hurting, and Veola heard her sniffle. Veola saw tears well in her eyes.

"I'll see you in court," Fayetta said to Leonard.

"Yeah," Leonard said, facing the door.

Veola locked the door after Leonard left.

Fayetta closed her eyes and shook her head. "He's lucky, Miss Veola."

"He shole is. I knew a man like Leonard when I was growing up, and he went too far. His wife killed him one day with his own gun because that was the day she decided she was taking no more lickings. Yeah, he's lucky all right." Veola knew more, but she'd made her point. "You've got a big day ahead of you, and I know you didn't come over here for all of this. We have talked enough for the night, and we both need rest." Veola paused and shook her head. "I just knew Leonard was the one, but he's not. That just means I have to keep looking. He's still out there somewhere." Veola and Fayetta grabbed each other's hands.

Fayetta climbed into Veola's high bed. Veola retrieved one of her handmade quilts from the closet and tucked it around her in the crucial spots. Fayetta looked peaceful. Veola wondered what made Fayetta change her mind. Hopefully she realized she retreated to a place where there was peace. She knew she missed her mother terribly in times like these. She hoped Fayetta would feel the spirit of her mother here—safe, secure, and protected.

Veola went to her bathroom mirror and as she washed her face, she felt crushed. The evidence she was so sure about was imaginary; Leonard's arms bore no sign of injury. She felt like giving up, turning it over to the police and to the Lord. She felt tired, wondered if she could continue her pursuit.

She climbed into bed, and knowing Fayetta was in the next room gave her some sense of purpose. She'd accomplished something. Whether Leonard would take heed to what she had said, only God knew.

Lord, please help me. Help me find my perpetrator.

LIGHT BREAD

Chapter Fifteen

"Don't act like you asleep. Open the door."

Tyrone recognized Leonard's voice. He wanted to ignore him 'cause his buzz from the liquor and weed sholé was making his arm feel better. He'd started drinking as soon as he'd gotten home from work, so he was still in his work clothes.

"Open the door." Leonard banged on it hard.

Tyrone hustled toward the door before Leonard busted it down. "I'm coming, goddammit." Tyrone opened up, and Leonard barged past him.

"Did you know somebody broke into Miss Veola's house, and she thinks I did it?"

"You pushing all up in here this time of night to tell me that bullshit. What's that got to do with me?"

"You know something about it?"

"I don't know nothing."

"Well, Fayetta is down at her house right now, and Miss Veola spouting off at the mouth about why she thought I did it and for me to keep away from everybody she know. You ain't understood a word I've said with your high ass."

"I heard every goddam thing you said, and I still ain't figured out what this has to do with me. You're blowing my high, that's what you're doing." Tyrone fought to hold back his anger at that Cook bitch and her playing cop.

"I came up here 'cause I know for a fact that you've broken into some houses. Are you the one she's looking for?"

"Now you are just about as ignant as she is. That's my mama's good friend, fool. What would I look like trying to break up into Miss Veola's house, right up under my mama's nose. I'm smarter than that. You sure *you* ain't high, talking like that?"

"I ain't high, and Fayetta was there. She know about me now after Miss Veola rattled her goddam mouth about everything, and I have to see Fayetta in court tomorrow. Miss Veola even saw me coming from Loretta's the other morning."

"You in trouble, man."

"Hell, I know it. Fayetta can use everything she heard against me and she already gon' get her way."

"Then, you need to lay low and don't say shit about nothing."

"I didn't say no more than I had to. That's why I got my ass out from down there."

"Well, carry yo ass home. You don't need to be up in here worrying me to death. And naw, I ain't got no smokes for you."

"I didn't ask you for none. You just need to know that she's looking for anybody that's stupid enough to break up in her house. Miss Veola ain't playing, and she gon' find out who's been messing with her."

"I can take care of myself, and I'm even gon' help her by keeping my eyes and ears open. I run into a lot of cats out there, and they just may open their mouth at the wrong time."

"As soon as you find out, let her know, so she'll get off of my back."

"Later." Tyrone closed the door after Leonard left. His buzz was wearing off. He figured it was because his mind had to be sharp. Not only was he a good thief, but he was good at lying. It must have worked, since Leonard left him alone.

"Good morning, Miss Veola." Fayetta padded into the kitchen, clad in her sleepwear. "I got up and I thought I was in my mama's house. I didn't want to move, but I know you have to go to work, so I couldn't lie there too long. Your house is like protection. I slept like a baby, and I needed it."

"I know you did. I'm sorry you had to deal with Leonard again before today. But after a full night's sleep, you should feel better and have a clear mind."

"That sounds like mama, too."

"She probably did say that, and I'm here to remind you. That's my job—at least one of them." Veola smiled.

"I was on my way to the bathroom."

"Go right ahead, Baby. I set a new toothbrush out for you."

"I appreciate it." Fayetta made her way to the adjacent room. "You have no idea how much this means to me."

"Oh yes, I do." Veola knew Melda would be proud. "Coffee? I'm not a coffee drinker, so I don't perk it in the mornings. I have some instant, though."

"I don't need anything, coffee or tea. I'll get dressed and get back home and be out of your way."

"You're not bothering me. In the mornings, I piddle around, read my Bible and Daily Word before I get ready."

"Keep on then with what you were doing."

Veola got her Sunday school book, her Daily Word, and her Bible from her nightstand. She set a cup of tea on the dining room table. She heard Fayetta shuffling in the guest room. "Fayetta, don't you worry about making that bed. I was gon' pull the sheets anyway, unless you want me to leave them on for you tonight."

"Thanks, but I need to get back to Dallas tonight. I've been here long enough. No matter what happens today, I won't need to come back tonight. I'll be by on Sunday to say goodbye, though."

Veola had plenty of time to change the bed before the boys arrived tomorrow night, but she followed Fayetta into the guest room and pulled new sheets from the chest. "Let's just change these now while there are two of us."

"I'm glad I'm here to help. That's the least I can do for my stay."

"Chile, you don't have to earn your keep 'round here," Veola assured her.

Once the bed was done, Veola returned to the dining room table. She was anxious to read her private devotional.

When Fayetta came to bid Veola goodbye, Veola said, "Sit down for a minute. You got to hear this."

Fayetta sat down, her gaze fixed on Veola's cat-eyed glasses.

"This lesson is about peace when you're feeling anxious. This verse comes from Psalm 4, and you may have read it before, but I'm gon' share it with you since you seem to be feeling better today. Listen now.

'Be angry, and do not sin.
Meditate within your heart on your bed, and be still.
Offer the sacrifices of righteousness,
And put your trust in the LORD.' I just wanted you to hear that."

"Believe me, Miss Veola, I'm better today, and I know why."

"I'm still gon' pray everything's gon' be all right. When you believe it, it will. I got years of experience to know what I'm talking about."

"I know you do."

Veola gave Fayetta a hug for the road. Veola stood in the doorway and watched Fayetta's confident stride as she crossed the street. She appeared to have a better attitude on things. Veola thought Fayetta had Melda's strut. That was sho nuff Melda's daughter.

Hold her hand, Lord. Don't let her go.

☙❧

Mrs. Hall arrived a few minutes before eight to pick up Veola. Once at the Halls, Veola went straight to work, finishing the housework before she knew it. She barely saw either of them all day.

Afterward, Mrs. Hall dropped Veola at Dr. Sweeney's while she went to the drugstore. Veola noticed the same girl from Tuesday was up front sorting through frames.

Dr. Sweeney trailed the receptionist back to the counter carrying Veola's new glasses. "Here you go. Try them on her."

Veola put them on, a new version in silver with wood-grained ear handles of her old cat-eyed ones. She went straight to the mirror to assess them. The appearance was much more important than the function. "Oh, I do like my new glasses. Thank you, Dr. Sweeney. I promise not to sleep in these. I'll use my old ones for that."

"Now, thank you, Mrs. Cook. Glad we could help you. Now don't be a stranger." He extended his hand. "And if you see Miss Mayfield, let her know her glasses are ready, too."

"Why, I'll be sure to tell her." Veola retrieved her pocketbook, which was wrapped and tied in a handkerchief buried deep in her purse, and paid the $29.75 owed. She strutted to the drugstore, wanting the whole world to see her new glasses. She'd start with Mrs. Hall.

Sunday, she'd showcase them with Bobby and Cameron on her arm. All eyes would be on them. She wondered if Ruben Earl would notice.

Before she opened the door to the drugstore, Dr. Barton popped out.

"Veola, I'm glad I ran into you," Dr. Barton began. "Ann has a birthday next week, and you know she thinks I forgot. Tomorrow night when you have Bobby, I've planned a surprise dinner for her. Ann knows nothing about it, and I've worked on this for about two months."

"Two months? And you didn't tell me?"

"Exactly. I know how close you two are, and I didn't want to take any chances of her finding out. Jeremy knows nothing, and I couldn't dare tell Bobby either."

Veola nodded. She was pleasantly surprised that Dr. Barton would be this thoughtful.

"I'll tell Jeremy at the last minute. You know we've had some difficulty communicating these days, but I think it's only a matter of where his mind is this senior year. He seems totally oblivious and unconcerned about what he wants to do this next year. I get so frustrated that I sometimes have to walk away from him. You know how stubborn he can be."

"And I wonder where he got that from." Veola pursed her lips.

"What do you mean? His time is running short."

"Well, don't push him too fast. We just need to keep faith in him."

"I'm trying my best, Veola. Now, I've got to get back to the office. If I think of something at the last minute, I'll call you."

"We may be outside in the garden tomorrow afternoon. The boys are going to help me plant."

"Oh they'll love that. Okay, gotta go. Patients are waiting."

"You didn't say a word about my new glasses." Veola tried to get his attention as he walked to his car.

"I like them," he shouted over his shoulder. "They look like you."

"You get on back to work, 'cause you didn't even see them." Veola grinned and waved him off.

"All right. Talk to you later." Dr. Barton got into his car.

Veola did not like finding Dr. Barton back downtown at the drugstore. Could she have just missed that woman again? If he were having an affair, then maybe his taking some initiative and going out of his way for Mrs. Barton was a cover-up. The responsibility of keeping Mrs. Barton happy usually fell on Veola's shoulders. Her duties often extended beyond household chores, and she had no one to blame but herself. Veola knew an affair would kill Mrs. Barton. Veola desperately wanted to believe Dr. Barton was being faithful. She thought about Jeremy's comments of his daddy being gone a lot on Saturday. Unexplained absences were a sure sign of infidelity. *Please, Lord, don't let it be that.*

❧❧

When Veola got home, she left the front door open, but locked the storm door. Ruben Earl would be driving home close to four o'clock, and he may feel like hitting the farmer's market today.

Mr. Edelson's visit still bothered her. She picked up the Esso packet off the couch. She trusted her instincts. If she had these doubts, something was probably wrong.

She decided to change clothes and slowly go over the words and phrases in Mr. Edelson's papers. The lease part was different than a lease for renting a house. Those leases she understood. She read it four times, and with each time, more questions surfaced. Maybe she was overanalyzing it.

Eyeing the clock, she checked out front and spotted Ruben

Earl's truck pulling up. She met him on the porch. "Come on in here."

"You still want to go to the market?"

"I want to see their plants before they get picked over."

"Wait here then. I'll be back in about a half an hour after I get out of these clothes. Hey, I like your new glasses," he called back over his shoulder.

Veola was amazed that Ruben Earl noticed her new specs right off the bat.

҂Ӂ҃

At half past seven, Veola and Ruben Earl had unloaded all of her plants and seeds before he left. She was sitting in the swing thinking about how easily they'd worked together to get things done.

A car eased up in front that didn't look familiar.

Within seconds, Fayetta emerged. "Hi, Miss Veola." She walked with a spring in her step.

"Fayetta, Girl, I didn't know you had a car since you're always walking every time I see you. But how else would you have come from Dallas?"

"It was in the shop all week. It developed a knocking sound on our trip here, and the last thing I needed was to be stuck on the road somewhere."

"There's nothing worse than a woman stuck on the highway with car trouble. Fayetta, want to see the plants I bought for my garden?"

Veola descended the porch steps and Fayetta followed. She showed Fayetta the crates, packages, and bundles of plants.

"Miss Veola, I think I did the right thing. We were at the courthouse most of the day, and Leonard showed up, bringing all his papers. Afterwards, I had to do a lot of paperwork at my lawyer's office. The bottom line is that he _has_ to help me. Leonard didn't put up any kind of fight like he had been earlier. The judge approved everything I wanted, and he told Leonard he should have been doing this a long time ago. The judge acted surprised it had to come to this."

"How are you planning to get your money?"

"They'll take the money from his paycheck, and he has to report any changes in his job to the court. My lawyer said this was something new, so you know I'm hoping and praying it will work. If it does, all this trouble will be worth it."

"I can see the relief on your face."

"What do you mean?"

"When you left here this morning, your step had some pep. You were on a mission. You accomplished something for your children, so you should feel good."

"I thank you for that. You inspired my courage. I needed a shoulder to lift me up, and you played mama."

"Your mama and I had some things in common, particularly knowing who to turn to in times of trouble. Fayetta, I want to share something else with you. Listen closely.

When I was young, I saw my daddy hit my mama a couple of times, and that's just what I witnessed firsthand. My mama stayed with him for seven years. We saw some of her bruises; they kept getting worse and worse. She made excuses for him, saying it was the liquor. One night he came home in a rage and got mad about his food not being kept hot. He began to beat on me when I stood protecting her. Seeing me get hit by my daddy took my mama to her breaking point. She shot him right smack in the middle of his chest that very night.

My mama didn't do time 'cause the world knew she was defending herself and us. I will never forget how out of control he was. I thought I was gonna die! That's why I have a gun, Fayetta. I hope I don't ever have to use it, but you have to protect yourself. Don't ever forget that."

"I promise I won't."

"Your best protection is to stay away from men like that."

"I will, Miss Veola. Thank you for everything. One last hug for the road? I'll see you Sunday when I pick up my little girl who's in Henderson with her cousins." Fayetta hugged Veola.

"You take care of yourself." Veola wrapped her arm around Fayetta, and they made their way to the front. "Be careful, Baby, and stay in touch."

Fayetta drove off, and her news was too good to keep. Veola called Jessie and Eva Mae and asked them to meet her in the garden.

Veola showed Eva Mae and Jessie her plants and told them that she rewarded Ruben Earl with a meal for taking her to the market.

"You and your boyfriend. You is a mess, Girl." Jessie laughed the loudest at her own comment.

Veola knew her dear sweet cousin wasn't a bit of good, but she loved her anyway. Veola informed them of how the court was going to take money out of Leonard's check for his children. None of them had ever heard of that before, and they agreed that it was a good change in the court system.

"Is that what you called us down here for?" Eva Mae asked.

"Part of it. I got to show you what I found out." Veola led them to her back porch and went over every detail of what Loretta had told her about how her trash can had been used for the delivery of marijuana. Then she pointed to the open field behind Delphine's where Leonard and Loretta had tussled and described how she'd thrown his clothes at him. Away from Loretta's back window, just in case Loretta was snooping again, Veola performed every motion she could as she reenacted the scene, even picking up a stick to show how Loretta threatened Leonard. "And guess what?"

"What?" Eva Mae and Jessie spoke simultaneously.

"That wasn't the first time they'd got into it. Loretta told me that Leonard smacked her in the eye. That's how her glasses got broke, Jessie."

"He needs to be stopped," Eva Mae said.

"She said she had thrown every pot and pan in her house at him, and seeing how she was swinging and carrying on, that wasn't her first fight. I'm sure she got in a few licks. She ain't no pushover."

"I can't believe Loretta done stooped that low to be hanging out with Leonard. I'm shole gon' give her a look when she get back to prayer meeting, and then I'm gon' tell her what to do to his ass if he try that shit again," Eva Mae said.

"I'm not finished," Veola said. She walked them to the side of her house where her bushes had been trampled. Veola slung her hands against the side of her house and demonstrated how Leonard was hiding behind her bushes, avoiding lights coming on from somewhere down the street. "Jessie, that's it."

"What?" Jessie appeared confused.

"Remember Easter morning we saw a car at the end of the street and the headlights went out. I bet those lights shocked

Leonard, so he had to hide in my bushes. That was probably the noise I heard from this side. What I thought was those dogs was him right outside my window. That's got to be it."

"You done figured it out for sho, ain't you, Veola?" Eva Mae asked. "So that's why I ain't heard from you in two or three days. You been playing detective."

"If you haven't heard from me, you need to pick up the phone and find out if I'm alive or dead," Veola said.

"I'd have known if you was dead. Jessie would have told me," Eva Mae retorted. "Veola, you and I both know you've been busy. Now, getting back to Leonard. That no good bastard ain't been worth a quarter ever since he set foot on this earth, and I just knew that girl was gon' come down here and be sent home in the same position she was when she got here."

"Fayetta did it." Veola shook her head and rejoiced over Fayetta's accomplishment.

Eva Mae continued. "I just hope the fool can keep a job long enough for her to see some benefits. Better yet, I hope she get every damn penny he got."

"So that means you ain't gon' tell the police that Leonard broke in your house?" Jessie asked.

"Naw, Jessie, that's the other thing. Leonard been the one that's been doing all his stuff 'round here, but he ain't the one who broke into my house." Veola saw their amazed expressions. "That's right. He didn't do it."

"But he's the one—" Jessie began.

"Let me explain. I told y'all that I beat the poor chile to death, and the piece of glass came right down on his arm. Whoever it was got a cut from here to kingdom come. But Leonard came over here last night and showed me he didn't have no cuts, no scrapes, no nothing on his arms. Now, they were ashy, but clean as a whistle."

"So now, you back to playing detective," Eva Mae interrupted.

"And y'all got to help me. We got to find this person. Everywhere y'all go, y'all got to look for long-sleeved shirts covering a cut up arm. I have got to figure this out who would want to hurt me."

"All of this don't have to be about you, Veola. We all know some folk do this 'cause they ain't got nothing else to do," Eva Mae said.

202

"What choo got up in your house that they would want?" Jessie asked Veola.

"Nothing more than y'all got." Knowing Leonard was innocent of the break-in, Veola wanted to believe that she was not the target specifically. She wanted it to be a random act of violence.

"What else you got to show us, Veola?" Eva Mae asked.

"That's all. I wanted y'all to know everything I've been going through."

"Well, I'm gon' go make my grocery list out. Tyrone gon' take me to the store in the morning, early. I wants to be ready when he bam on my back door, hollering, 'Come on, Mama. Let's go.' Is you ready to go, Jessie?"

"Don't you go making that boy mad, Eva Mae, and he leave you somewhere stranded," Jessie warned Eva Mae.

"If a chile of mine ever do something like that to me, you just as well consider 'em dead, 'cause when I get back to the house, I'll shole kill 'em. You can count on that." Eva Mae shook her head. "But 'fo I go, I wanna know how many times you fed Ruben Earl this week?" Eva Mae walked in the direction of the street and the others followed.

"He helped me out. He took me to get my plants, so I fixed him food. So what?" Veola shot back.

"You got a way of making that man do anything you want, and he don't mind it one bit. You got yo door fixed, yo garden plowed, yo plants, and that's just this week."

"He's my good friend."

"She don't see it, Eva Mae. And most of the time Veola be smart," Jessie said.

"All I know is you ain't blind," Eva Mae said. "You have yourself a boyfriend." Eva Mae laughed out loud.

"You and Jessie just alike. One of these days, I ain't gon' talk to neither one of you 'bout nothing. Now, hush about Ruben Earl."

"We can't take no more news this evening," Jessie said. "You done gave us enough." With a wave, she headed home.

"See you later, Miss Veola Cook-Got-A-Boyfriend-Name-Ruben Earl Mosley," Eva Mae sang as she started home.

"I don't care what y'all say. Just be on the lookout for my robber."

Chapter Sixteen

Rest, ye children, of Israel, for otherwise ye shall become weary. They that wait on the Lord shall renew their strength (after they rest). They shall mount up on wings of an eagle (after they rest). Veola blended passages, but her recitations served a purpose. She needed to sit her behind down every once in a while before she fell out. *Ye shall not faint!* She translated scripture to fit her needs.

Veola had dozed in her rocking chair and was awakened by a quiet buzz from the television. The big white globe on the tube marked the end of a broadcasting day; obviously, it was after eleven o'clock. After she prepared herself for bed, she prayed quickly, promising God a longer session when she was in her right mind. In her well-worn, cotton nightgown, her body warmed instantly under two quilts, two blankets, and the bedspread.

It is well with my soul.

When a knock sounded, Veola was certain she was dreaming about last night. The knock intensified, and then she heard her name. Not again, Lord, not again. What was going on with folks these days, showing up at peoples' houses all times of the night.

In seconds, Veola had her slippers on her feet and her robe over her shoulders. She made her way to her front door.

"Veola, it's me, Jeremy."

Immediately, she became worried. "Jeremy?" She unlocked the deadbolt.

Veola led him into her living room. "What's going on with you this late? Is everything all right? Are you supposed to be home?" Jeremy stumbled onto the couch. She noticed his unsteadiness. "Jeremy, what's wrong?"

Jeremy laid his head back and stared at the ceiling. His eyes were fire engine red. Veola had never seen him this way.

"I, uh, didn't know where else to come."

"Tell me what's going on."

"I hung out with some friends, but I didn't want to go home."

"Didn't want to go home? Why?"

"It's Mom and Dad. They aren't getting along. I can feel it, and I think I know why."

"Are they fighting?"

"No. I think Dad is having an affair."

"An affair?" Veola stood in shock. Hearing Jeremy say it, she realized her suspicion may be on target.

"I think so. He's been acting so weird toward Mom. He says a few words to her every now and then. Something's strange, and I know she feels it. Mom feels pretty good about most things, but to me, she hadn't been herself lately. She might suspect something, too, but I'm afraid to bring it up. I saw Dad a few times out around town with a woman! And then he wonders why my mind isn't on college. It's difficult to be around him right now."

"You can't go home?" She didn't know if this was alcohol or dope talking. Nevertheless, she was grateful he finally revealed what had been troubling him, and she wouldn't dare stop him.

"I don't want to go home. I haven't told a single person, but I don't want to see my parents go through this."

His face flushed. Veola moved closer and sat beside him on the couch and grabbed his hand as he cried. "Oh, Baby, it's all right. I understand what you're going through."

He jerked his head up. "I don't know what to do."

"How long have you been thinking this about your daddy?"

"I don't know, maybe a month. I saw him with this woman the first part of March."

"You sound like your daddy is already guilty. You saw him with this woman a few weeks ago, and you've hung him out to dry. Maybe it's something we don't know."

"I know something's up because I saw him with her again two days ago coming out of the café downtown."

Veola was lost for words. Her mind flashbacked to the drugstore Tuesday. There was definitely a woman in that booth. "Oh, my Lord, naw," she blurted.

"My Lord what?" Jeremy asked. "What is it?"

"Nothing, I was thinking about the whole thing," Veola explained. She did not have the courage to tell him she'd witnessed the same thing. "Let me get you something to drink. Want some iced tea?" She proposed iced tea to overcome her own heat and get out of the room.

"No, just water." Jeremy followed her to the kitchen.

Veola realized Jeremy hadn't been in her house in over a year. She poured the water. "Jeremy, I have to admit I've been worried about y'all's entire household. Everybody."

"Everybody? Why?"

"Let's go back in the living room. Then, I'll tell you."

Jeremy drank two glasses in the kitchen and poured more.

Veola wondered what the extreme thirst was a sign of. Liquor or dope? She led the way back to the front of the house. "Wait a minute. Does your mama or daddy know where you are?"

"I told them that I was going out, so they probably think I'm out with my friends."

"After what happened last Friday night, I'm gon' call and tell them you're over here with me and you're spending the night. They don't need to go through that again."

"Spending the night?"

"I want to talk to you about some things, and if I'm the reason you're out late, I'll be responsible for where you are. They're light-sleeping now until you come home. Their deep sleep won't start until you set foot in that house."

"What makes you say that?"

"Sometimes, Jeremy, you have to ease your parents' minds when you get the chance. Remember, I got kids of my own." Veola placed the call to the Bartons and returned to the living room. "They said they were glad you were here and not out in the streets."

Veola noticed Jeremy had taken off his shoes. She sat next to him and took his hand again. "Now, when you showed up tonight, the first thing I saw was your eyes. Where were you tonight before you got here?"

"Just driving around, hanging out."

"Have you been drinking?"

"No, I'm not drunk." He blinked at Veola.

"I wanna know," she caught her breath, "because when I was at your house this week, I was going through your clothes for the laundry. I found matches. I didn't know you smoked."

"Matches? They're probably from somewhere I ate, Veola."

She felt his stare intensify. "Jeremy, this is me, not your mama or daddy, but I know you, too. You carrying matches is strange to me."

"Veola, I'm not—"

"Wait a minute. I have more to say," she interrupted. "The other day, Jessie and I were on our way to our friend, Eva Mae's house, and I thought I recognized your truck going around the corner. Sure enough, it was your truck parked right next door to where we were going. Eva Mae's son, Tyrone, lives there, and he's got a good friend named Leonard. How do you know them?"

Jeremy averted his eyes.

"Is Tyrone a friend of yours?" Veola could feel him want to pull his hand away.

"I know him. I wouldn't call him a friend, though."

"Tyrone has a reputation, Jeremy. Some folks say he sell dope. I don't know for sure since I ain't ever bought none from him and don't plan to either."

Jeremy's face turned beet-red, and Veola felt she had gotten her answer. She wouldn't dare let go of his hand. Tears welled in his eyes, and he laid his head back on Veola's couch.

"I'm sorry, Veola. I am."

"How long have you been knowing Tyrone?" Veola knew when she asked this question, she'd know how long Jeremy had been smoking dope.

"Not long, a couple of months." He sat back up.

"Are you smoking because you think your daddy's been

courting this other woman?"

"No, Veola. It's just a lot of other stuff I have to think about."

"Does this have anything to do with why you haven't put much thought into school next year?"

"Is that what he told you? I've been thinking about Texas, but mainly to play baseball. The season isn't over, so I'm hoping it goes well. Dad has pressured me about being a doctor, and after all of this with that woman, I don't want to talk to him about it."

"You're mad at him, Jeremy, but that's not going to solve anything. What does the dope do for you?"

"Why do you call it dope? It's just marijuana."

"No matter what you call it, it's not something I want to see you do. You're too good of a boy to get mixed up with it. Even I know smart ball players stay away from that stuff. I'm glad you're having this conversation with me and not with your mama and daddy."

"I don't go out and drink a lot. You know that."

"And you're not the type of person to get yourself in trouble either. You finding Tyrone tells me this is more than what you want to admit."

"It's only every couple of weeks. The day you saw me, I bought a small bag. Dad had gotten to me last weekend."

"That's what I'm talking about. You sound like your daddy is pushing you to this because you're mad at him. Leonard and Tyrone are nothing but trouble. They've both been to jail, got police records, and you don't need to be at his house for nothing—marywanna or nothing else. You have too much to risk by hanging out with them. Don't do that to yourself." She wondered what was in his pockets right now.

Sensing his guilt, she knew he needed time to think about what she had said. "Come on, let's turn down your bed."

Jeremy helped remove the dolls and pillows.

"Do you know this woman you're talking about?" Veola asked.

"Yeah. That's what makes it worse. It's Mrs. Simpson, someone Mom and Dad know, and she's pretty. Mom just mentioned her name the other day about her house being broken into."

"I know who you're talking about, and she's a good-looking woman." Veola not only remembered Mrs. Simpson but also tried to connect Mrs. Simpson's burglary to her own. Could the same burglar be in both the white and black parts of town? Quickly, she refocused on Jeremy's problems. "I want answers to some of what's been on my mind, too, so we both can put some notions to rest. Now, let's get some sleep." She retrieved Jeremy's glass from the living room. "Do you need anything else while I'm in the kitchen?"

"No, but I might be starving in the morning," Jeremy shouted back.

"I knew that already. And I might get you to take me to the grocery store after breakfast. That is, if your folks don't mind."

"They'd make me take you anyway."

Veola knew he'd spoken the truth. "I'll lay out a toothbrush for you in the bathroom." That was her last new one. She prayed for no more visitors this week.

Making her way out of the bathroom, she called back to him. "Oh, Jeremy, one more thing...you decent?"

"Yes, ma'am. Come on in."

Veola put a hand on his shoulder as he sat on the bed. "I just wanted to tell you that you're like one of mine, and I love you—always will. Everything's gon' be all right, including you. School. That dope. We'll work through this." She hugged him. "Goodnight. Sleep tight, Baby."

Jeremy kept his firm grip. "Goodnight. God, I haven't heard that since I stayed over here last."

"Well, don't let the bedbugs bite either."

They laughed, and Veola trudged back to her bedroom, turning off the lights on the way.

116 West Jackson Street was far away from the cruel environment of racial stirrings in East Texas. What was going on in Veola's house was a far cry from what black people were experiencing in Alabama, Mississippi, even Georgia. Veola wished everybody everywhere could see what living was supposed to be like—all God's children together, under one roof. But she knew she was one of the lucky ones. There were places where Jeremy sleeping at her house could not happen.

Veola assumed Jeremy was far away from his usual escape with Leonard and Tyrone. She felt hers was better, his refuge away from home.

I woke up this morning with my mind, Stayed on Jesus.
I woke up this morning with my mind, Stayed on Jesus.
I woke up this morning with my mind, Stayed on Jesus.
Hal-le-lu, Hal-le-lu, Hal-le-lu-jah.

Veola vacillated between singing and humming this Saturday morning, even while brushing her teeth. The song stuck—not only in her mind, but in her heart.

She awoke at seven, later than usual, which she blamed on all these night visitors this week. Everyone had interrupted her sleep. She figured Jeremy needed his rest, so she wouldn't wake him now. Later, she'd let the smell of frying bacon do it for her.

Veola got a notion. Her plan for the day had not included Jeremy, until now. She wasn't ready to send him home. Her grocery list was finished, so Veola threw on a house dress over her nightgown, some socks, then donned a spring coat.

She made her way to the back door without even a stir from Jeremy and retrieved her gardening tools from the storage room. She glanced over the crates of plants and bags of seeds she and Ruben Earl had purchased, strategizing her garden placement. The greens and onions needed to be closest to the house for easy-picking. Bobby and Cameron could start with the onions, sure to enjoy the smell of them on their fingers.

Next, she headed back in the house, for her plans for Jeremy would require him to have energy, be alert. She'd start by filling him up. A full breakfast, like the one she made for Dr. Barton, would be a treat for Jeremy since he had missed the one she'd cooked earlier in the week.

Two minutes after she'd filled her frying pan, the smell of bacon permeated the house. She cracked eggs and buttered bread. She was ready to get the morning paper.

"I smell bacon," Jeremy shouted through the strain of a yawn.

The paper could wait. It was time to put her plan into motion. She went to her bedroom to get the Esso letter.

"Good morning, Mister Sleepy Head," Veola called back across the cozy house.

"Morning," Jeremy answered clearly, still in bed.

"This breakfast is not for you. I have to take it next door."

"What?"

"April Fool." She laughed. "I got you already. You've got to get up early around here."

"That wasn't fair."

"I can't believe it's already April. March got on up and marched itself right on out of here. Are you moving?"

"Barely. Can I stay here all day?"

"You cannot, Mister. Breakfast in ten minutes."

"That means I have nine more minutes to lie here." He began counting. "Eight and a half."

"Boy, you are a mess." Veola amused herself with her conversation with her guest across the house.

After his bathroom run, he was in Veola's kitchen within five minutes. "What do you need me to do?"

"I'm ready. Time for you to eat. You want orange juice? Jelly?"

"Both."

"Here you go." Veola passed Jeremy his plate, laden with eggs, bacon, and toast.

Jeremy took his plate and smiled. "I'll bless the food."

"Go right ahead." Veola had witnessed it twice already this week.

"Dear God, thank you for all you do to keep us healthy, and continue to watch over us. Bless the cook for she keeps us well fed. Amen."

"Now that was a blessing from the heart." She noticed Jeremy trying to keep from laughing while he layered his toast with jelly.

About the time she felt Jeremy was getting full, she put her plan into play. Maybe they could help each other today. She needed transportation, and most importantly, she wanted Jeremy to do it— not Ruben Earl, not Carneda. "Jeremy, I need to ask a favor."

"What is it?" The smacking of eggs and bacon continued.

"I know we talked about the grocery store, but I want you to take me to my property near New Winterfield. It's about fifteen minutes away and to and fro would take about an hour of your time.

I'll be ready 'fo you know it, so I won't mess with your plans for the rest of the day."

Jeremy agreed without hesitation. "I'm ready now. Take your time."

"How can you be ready when you keep grabbing more toast?" She watched him pile jelly on his third piece.

Veola had inherent magical powers through her food. Nothing she flaunted, just something she knew.

✂❧

Veola had ridden in Jeremy's truck before, but today felt different—like she was the one driving. She had one goal in mind—to see what Mr. Edelson and the Esso Company were up to.

"Did you grow up out this way?" Jeremy asked.

"I didn't, but my husband did. I still grew up in the country, though."

"You inherited the land?"

"Some of it. One plot of land I got from Ervin, but the other plot I bought long after he'd died and we were living in Parkerville.

"Is someone trying to buy your land?"

"That's not what this is about. They want to lease it and buy the timber on it."

Jeremy was a teenager with good sense, Veola thought, at least most of the time. He was responsible and mature, and good at heart didn't hurt. She was certain their conversation last night lingered in his head. So, she was ready to discuss his dope experience and his connections with Tyrone and Leonard if he brought it up.

As they turned off the main highway onto the county road, she saw a hint of smoke percolating from the distant trees in the direction of her property. She didn't think twice about it, assuming someone in the distance was burning debris. The smoke became thicker as they neared the property, and it appeared to be the end of a grass fire. The blaze had died to a minimum, but the smoke was thick and black. Someone was burning more than just grass.

A company car and two lumber trucks were parked right off the fenced plot. Perhaps they were on the adjacent land, Veola hoped, though feeling apprehensive. Veola noticed it was the same car Mr. Edelson drove the day he visited her. The emblems on the car doors matched.

"Oh, Lord, what's happening? That fire, Jeremy, is coming from my land." Veola grew frantic, her heart began to pound.

"Are you sure?"

"We're gon' see firsthand." She jumped out of the truck before Jeremy turned off the ignition and began to sprint. She'd hoped her footsteps would keep up with her racing heartbeat. "Oh, Lord, Oh, Lord, Oh, Lord."

"Wait for me," Jeremy said, close behind.

Veola's stride was purposeful, and in the distance, she saw Mr. Edelson waving his arms as if he was disgusted or down right mad with the man he was talking to. A big log truck was parked nearby, and she was certain the fire was on her land. "Mr. Edelson! Mr. Edelson!" She yelled at him.

The man Mr. Edelson was talking to went to see the driver of the logging truck, and they occupied themselves with papers.

Mr. Edelson ran to meet her. "Mrs. Cook, there has been a huge misunderstanding."

"What are y'all doing? You've cut down my trees, and I haven't signed a single paper." It was difficult for her to catch her breath.

"That's what I'm telling the lumber people. They said they had the paperwork for this particular property, but I told them it couldn't be. The lumber that was approved was from your neighbor, not yours. You have no idea how sorry I am about this, Mrs. Cook."

"Something told me to get out here, and I can't believe y'all are burning my trees. Oh, my word, my big tree."

"You're right, Mrs. Cook. They cut the branches that can't be used for timber, and they burn them over the area they want to excavate," Mr. Edelson explained.

"You're burning my land, Mr. Edelson, my land." Veola was so distraught, that she had not bothered to introduce Jeremy to Mr. Edelson.

"I just happened to come out here this morning, myself, and I thought the area was marked off where they were to have started. This was not an area they were to touch until after you had agreed. I've already been to the other plot that is marked off where they were to have started. Obviously, they got mixed up."

"Well, tell them to stop. Can't they put out this fire? Y'all don't even have permission to be on my land. You told me y'all were just looking at the properties." Furious, Veola struggled to maintain her demeanor.

"The fire is contained. They have placed a chemical around the border, so it won't go out any further."

Once Veola got over her shock, she realized exactly where she was standing. "Oh my Lord, what about my tree. My special tree!" Veola saw that the single tree that bore her name was right on the side of the dying flame. The branches had been cut, and the top of the tree had been singed. She hadn't seen the tree in years, and she went to look for the spot where their names had been carved. It wasn't the same. There was no more Ervin. The only part of Ervin and Veola that remained was the lower half, so the "V" of Veola had been lost, too. She rubbed her hand over "eola". Her long-time memory she had held on to for so many years was gone. Even though it had been etched in her heart, the tree was special in its own right.

Mr. Edelson continued. "Mrs. Cook, I know you're upset, and I want to apologize for this break down in communication. This should never have happened, and I'm sure something will be done to compensate for your loss and damage.

"I just can't believe it. Jeremy, look at this. Look at what they've done."

Jeremy said nothing.

"Richard Edelson here."

"Jeremy Barton." The men folk greeted one another with a handshake.

Veola cared nothing about their introductions at this point. She realized her world had changed. She thought about the pocket-knife in her dresser drawer. "This tree here, Mr. Edelson, meant something to me."

"Whatever damage that's been done, I'm sure we'll get it taken care of for you, Mrs. Cook. We'll have to get with the lumber company to sort this out. Obviously, there has been a big mistake."

"What else have y'all done out here that you're not supposed to?"

"Nothing, Mrs. Cook. Absolutely nothing."

"Y'all are trespassing, you've destroyed my property, and I was just telling myself the other day if I were to let your company do something with the timber, this particular tree was not to be touched." Veola felt Jeremy listening and watching her every move.

"We deeply regret what we've done, and I can assure you, Mrs. Cook, we're going to correct it. To get our trucks and rigs in here, it is always customary to remove the timber first, and this was to have been worthwhile for both of us."

"How are you going to correct your mistake, Mr. Edelson? You cannot bring my tree back. You could have had any other tree out here except this one." She grew further upset as she listened to Mr. Edelson ramble. It was always somebody else's fault. She hated Jeremy having to see this side of her. Throughout all of this, he hadn't moved.

"Mr. Edelson, maybe you aren't the bad guy here, but right now, that doesn't matter to me. I just want everyone off of my property before I get back to town and come back out here with the police. It seems like everybody wants to take something from me lately, and I'm not having it. My lawyer was to look at my papers before I was gon' do anything, and now I'm gon' have to let him see them for another reason. You set foot on my land and you never, ever had permission."

"Mrs. Cook, that's not the way it was supposed to have been. I assure you we'll be out of here when the last of these ashes die down. I wouldn't want to leave it until I know it's safe. The problem here is a matter of miscommunication with the timber company, and I'm apologizing once again. We're going to get this worked out. I promise you we will."

"I should hope so, Mr. Edelson. I should hope so. This is not the way we do business around here. This property here is owned by cousins of mine who live out of town. They trust me to take a look at things for them, too, and I find it strange that I haven't heard a word from them. Jeremy, it's time for us to go." Veola walked toward the tree once again.

"Mrs. Cook, I'm sorry, your neighbors did give us permission. We have the paperwork." Mr. Edelson turned to Jeremy. "Jeremy, you might explain to her that—"

Jeremy cut him off. "This is between you or your company and

Mrs. Cook, sir, and I'm not in it at all. I'm with her, and she is our dear friend, but I can tell I've never seen her like this. She's mad, and I bet you'll have to prove to her how all of this got screwed up."

The men stood face to face, Jeremy edging Mr. Edelson in height.

"Hell, we did what we were supposed to do to get the lease signed, but now the lumber company has gone and made us look bad. We'll never get these goddam people to sign now, and paying them for the right to drill and for the timber is not nearly going to be enough for them to be happy. I can only imagine how much more they're going to ask for."

"Sir, even I know you have to have permission to do what you're doing," Jeremy said.

"These goddamn people want this, they want that, they want everything," Mr. Edelson screamed.

"What people? Exactly who are you taking the Lord's name in vain about?" Veola turned around and headed straight for Mr. Edelson.

At the same time, Jeremy edged closer to Mr. Edelson himself.

Veola was furious. "What people are you referring to, Mr. Edelson? Black people? Colored people? Or do you have another word you might want to use?" Veola stared at Mr. Edelson.

Jeremy balled up his fists.

"Son, don't even think about it," Mr. Edelson warned.

"Jeremy, don't you do it," Veola shouted. She turned toward Mr. Edelson. "So now Mr. Edelson, are we really finding out what's going on?"

Jeremy pointed his finger directly at Mr. Edelson. "Don't you ever think you can disrespect Miss Cook in front of me, Mr. Edelson. You don't have any idea what that woman means to me and my family, and we don't allow her to be insulted. Especially not in front of us."

"I'm sorry, Mrs. Cook." Mr. Edelson began. "I didn't mean to imply—"

"Leave that alone, Mr. Edelson. I'm not going to make this about anything other than my property," Veola said.

Mr. Edelson rambled. "Today has been more than frustrating for me. I can just smell trouble, but I'm going to keep my word and get this matter resolved so that it benefits everyone. I'm going to start by getting rid of this incompetent lumber company."

"Mr. Edelson, this might not be your fault, but you're the one I'm counting on to fix it. That tree was my only connection to the man I married forty plus years ago, and now it's gone. Sometimes mistakes happen for a reason, but you crossed the line with me." Veola made her point. "Jeremy, let's go before I say something I'm going to regret."

"Are you all right, Veola?" Jeremy asked.

"Yeah, I'm fine." Veola turned back toward the truck.

Jeremy stood still. "Mr. Edelson, do what's right by her. She knows a lot of people who will make sure that will happen."

"She'll hear from me next week," Mr. Edelson said.

Jeremy began to follow Veola. When he caught up with her, Jeremy put an arm around her shoulder.

In Veola's eyes, Mr. Edelson did his best to reassure her for what was unexpectedly found. She had given him the benefit of the doubt, but his true feelings surfaced about how he felt about her people. Somehow, though, she wasn't mad at him, or surprised, just disappointed. Maybe he thought he was doing *us* a favor by getting *us* money, simply because it was more than *we* had to begin with. Veola believed that sooner or later, a person's true feelings always surface. Just sit back and wait, she'd tell herself.

"Let's get out of here, Veola," Jeremy said after they got into the truck.

"Thank you, Jeremy," Veola said. "And you know what for."

"I didn't do anything I shouldn't have done. You're one of ours, Veola."

Veola knew balling up his fists to a grown man was not necessarily classified as nothing, but she didn't press the issue. "Something told me to get out here and see what was going on." She was convinced she'd done right to follow her instincts. "I have too much to do today to be worried about this, so I'll send some of my kinfolk out here to make sure Mr. Edelson and the trucks have left."

"Does that mean we're heading home?"

"Yeah, let's go." Realizing she hadn't been the only one rattled by what she saw, Veola detected Jeremy's frustration with the situation.

Jeremy broke the silence. "You're not *like* family to us, Veola, you *are* family, and you know it. He picked the wrong lady to take advantage of. If you need some help, like legal stuff, I'm sure Mr. Holcomb can help you. Don't forget to ask Dad for whatever you need, too."

"I'm going to wait and see what Mr. Edelson does."

"He said he'd be by to see you next week."

"I'll be waiting for him, and this time, I might not be so nice."

"You'll call Dad or Mr. Holcomb if you need them?"

"I can take care of myself, Jeremy. I always have."

"I know you can. Go easy on him, though. I think he wants to make up for this."

"Listen to you telling me what to do, sounding all grown-up. Now that's the Jeremy I miss, so that Jeremy who arrived at my house last night with fire engine red eyes is the one we're going to have to get rid of. He's the one who gets into stuff we don't like." Veola reached over and slapped his arm. She heard him chuckle underneath his faint smile. "Now you know I want you to stop at Piggly Wiggly on the way in. I need to pick up a few groceries before that brother of yours and my grandson arrive."

"You're making me pay for sleeping and eating at your house, aren't you?"

"Why, yeah. You have to earn your keep when you hang out with me." They laughed again.

On the return drive, Veola made Jeremy talk about college, and she suspected he longed for a conversation like this with his dad. Time flew until he pulled into the parking lot of Piggly Wiggly.

"I'll just be in here a minute," Veola said, getting out of the truck.

"Do you need help?"

"No, the list is short."

"I'll wait, then."

When she returned with her one paper sack of groceries, Jeremy jumped out to help, putting the grocery bag between them. "Thanks, Veola."

"For what?" She shrugged her shoulders.

"I took it personally when I thought about how you were being disrespected on your own land. To get to the point that I wanted to fight was not like me. For me to get that angry means something has to change. A lot is going on right now, school and all, and maybe I'm bringing some of this on myself."

"Remember, Jeremy, everything that's going on will eventually work itself out. You have to handle what you're supposed to do, but with everything else, there is a saying. *This too shall pass.* What else are you worried about?"

"I thought smoking would help me to relax. Maybe it's doing the opposite."

"What are you going to do about it?"

"I'm not dependent on it, but I still feel guilty. I've got to cut my ties with Tyrone and Leonard. They've never done anything to me, but hearing what you said last night, I don't want to get to the point that something worse could happen."

"You're doing the right thing, Jeremy."

"I've got to start somewhere, and maybe spending time with you was just what I needed, getting me to act like I'm supposed to do. You know you're known for that. The thing with Mom and Dad bugs me, too, so I'm going to talk to Dad tomorrow when we're home. Maybe Sunday when we're all in a good mood."

Veola reached over and grabbed his hand. "I didn't have nothing to do with that, just so you know it. Did you do all this growing up while I was in the grocery store? You have too much going for you to throw it away on that stuff. Now, we could sit here all day, but after what we've been through this morning, take me to 116 West Jackson, please."

Veola knew this conversation had been difficult for Jeremy. She recalled their conversation when he'd come home for lunch, and she praised God he was now acting like the Jeremy she knew.

❧❧

Jeremy returned home to find only his dad. His mother was out on her usual Saturday morning pit stops with Bobby. He shared his journey with Veola, everything from Mr. Edelson being on the property without permission to Veola's expectation of the company to make good on their promise to rectify their mistake.

"I'll ask her what happened, and I won't get involved unless she asks me to help," Dr. Barton said.

Jeremy knew Veola deserved to be protected, and he knew his dad would do whatever he could to insure that. While his mind was set to tackle these demons that had plagued him, he knew he first had to address the ones with him directly.

"Now what about you?" Dr. Barton asked.

"What do you mean?"

"Jeremy, I don't want a shouting match like last weekend, but this is two Fridays in a row you weren't home."

"Dad, I'm sorry. Is there something you want to tell me? Am I missing something?"

"No, you're not missing anything. Last Friday it was all about being with the guys at the lake, but last night was more about me."

"And you end up over at Veola's?"

"Yes, sir. I should have come home, but I told myself if I wasn't ready to sit up here at home for the night, I figured Veola's was the next best place."

"I'm glad you feel that way, for you know she'll take care of you. But son, I don't ever want you to feel that we can't talk about what's happening with you. You hear?"

"I know that, Dad, and I'm working through some stuff. I'm okay, though, seriously." Jeremy wished he could talk about what was happening with his dad.

"All right. Don't come at us with any surprises."

"No surprises. I promise." Jeremy hoped his dad didn't have any surprises for him as well. To talk about college right now would bring about the same heated discussion they got into last weekend, and he wanted to avoid that, too. Besides, he'd promised Veola he'd do that tomorrow. So there was no time like the present to head over to Tyrone's. "Dad, I've got a run to make. I'll be back."

"Before you go, do you have plans tonight?"

"No, not really. Why?"

"We're going over to the Simpsons for dinner. Drop by if you can. They live on Hillman, 408 Hillman Drive. Your mother doesn't know it, but it's her birthday party."

Jeremy was relieved by the fact that his dad remembered his mom's special day. So, his dad is not going to be in trouble after all. At least not for this. But now, he was going to see his dad and Mrs.

Simpson together in front of his mom, so he felt he had to be there. "What time?"

"About eight or so. I bet your mother would really like to see you. She deserves something special."

"I'll be there for Mom." Jeremy left.

As he drove, he thought about the evening. Jeremy figured that an unexpected appearance from him would top off the surprise. He doubted if any other teenagers would be there, but he didn't care. It was all about his mother's happiness.

He'd eventually approach his father about what he had been feeling, but not tonight. He knew every time he thought about the possibility of his dad having an affair, he felt disdain toward him. Maybe the party would help in working through his pent-up anger. As upset as he was, he knew that he had to address his own issues before attacking his dad.

Spending the night at Veola's resulted in a positive effect on him. He noticed Veola faced her problems head-on. She resolved her matters by getting whomever involved. For him, observing and listening to Veola had been therapy. Now he had to do what he had to do.

Within minutes, he pulled up to Tyrone's place.

Tyrone answered the door on the first knock. "What's going on, Mr. Jeremy? Come on in."

"I'll come in, but I won't need anything. I came by to tell you that I won't be needing any more bags for a while."

"What's up with you?"

"I just don't need the stuff right now."

"Are you changing your wicked ways? Did you get caught?"

"No, it had nothing to do with getting caught. I just think I've had a lot on my mind, and I'm trying to make some of that right. The weed messes with my mind. I was using it as an escape, but it may be causing me more trouble than it's worth."

"You've been thinking too much. Let that shit go. I bet you'll be back up here next week. Watch and see."

"Well, if I do, that just meant I didn't work hard enough. Don't knock me for trying, though."

As Jeremy figured, Tyrone didn't lend his support. Jeremy knew Tyrone would have to find a new buyer.

"I'm still betting you got caught, could have been trying to sell it yourself. No teenage white boy could be smoking all that stash. Hell, three or four joints a day is a lot of smoke for even you."

At that moment, Jeremy was convinced he'd made the right decision. It was time to go, refusing to respond to Tyrone's comment. Jeremy also realized that he hadn't told Veola the whole truth as to how much and how often he indulged in his bad habit.

But Tyrone continued. "All right, then. Good luck to you, man. See you soon."

Jeremy nodded and walked to his truck, eager to get away from Tyrone and the stuff.

The pride Jeremy felt as he drove away was exhilarating. It took a lot of courage to confront the man partially responsible for his habit. Jeremy knew he could blame no one but himself, but it was cool to have shared his secret with Veola. He was on such a mental high and there were more emotions involved than he dared to realize. Today was about him—his life, his direction, and his family. He made that commitment to himself. Bucking up to a grown man at Veola's property, a man he didn't even know, made him think about what was important.

Leonard was next, his source when Tyrone wasn't available. But he had no idea where to start. He was always picking up and dropping Leonard off at different houses.

He bypassed his turn toward home and headed for the lake house. He frowned when he encountered a strange car parked outside, a faded green '62 Ford.

The door was locked. "Hello?" No one answered. Using his key, he found no one inside. From a distance, he saw a couple sitting on the pier.

Once outside, Jeremy could see that they were engaged in what appeared to be a deep conversation. As he approached them, he recognized Leonard. Just the man he needed to see, but not like this.

"Leonard?" Jeremy asked. "What are you doing here?"

"I hope you don't mind us out here enjoying the peace and quiet of the water. This is Fayetta."

"Hello, ma'am." Jeremy was not interested in talking to her.

"Leonard, this is my parents' place. What are you doing here?"

"Hoping nobody was out here. Fayetta came back in town

this morning to pick up our daughter. We got together this morning, and afterward, she and I wanted to go somewhere to talk. We went through a lot this week, and we took a chance on coming out here where we didn't have to worry about people looking for us. I remembered how to get here from the couple of times me, you, and Tyrone came to the lake. If somebody would have been here, we wouldn't have stopped."

"But what if my dad or somebody had come out here now? You and I would both be in trouble. You can't just come out here like this."

Fayetta took her feet out of the water and put on her sandals. "I told you, Leonard, that we shouldn't be on these people's property. Come on, let's go. We're not through talking, and you're still not through apologizing." She walked toward her car. "We're sorry for being on your property. Come on, Leonard. I need to go by Miss Veola's later on anyway," Fayetta said.

"Miss Veola?" Jeremy's light bulb flashed.

Fayetta stopped walking with Leonard close by. "Yes, Miss Veola Cook. Do you know her?"

"She takes care of my family. She's been with me since I was born almost." Jeremy's tension eased. "I just left her a little while ago."

Jeremy now felt comfortable enough to bring other matters to light. "Leonard, I saw Tyrone earlier. I won't be making my usual stops. You should know, too."

"Getting to you, huh? Hey, it's cool," Leonard responded.

"Got to change some things, if you know what I mean." Jeremy was being informative, not looking for approval.

"I understand man," Leonard said. "I have my own issues. And no thanks to that Miss Veola. She shamed me into trying to make a few things right myself. I'm working on it, and I'm starting with Fayetta and our kids."

Instantly, Jeremy saw Leonard look at Fayetta as he made his statement and approached the passenger seat of Fayetta's car. She was already behind the wheel. Leonard rolled down his window facing Jeremy. "Later," Leonard called out.

"Yeah, later," Jeremy said.

Jeremy watched them drive away. Still feeling good for conquering his demons, he went and sat on the edge of the pier. A fisherman glided by in his canoe. They exchanged waves. One of these days, Jeremy decided he wanted to be just like that fisherman, appearing not to have a care in the world on a Saturday afternoon. Then, he realized, grown-ups had their own worries. Veola and his parents could vouch for that. He dreaded confronting his dad, getting over his desire to grab a joint, and deciding on where to go to school, but he knew he must.

⚜

Thirty minutes later, Jeremy sprung up off the pier and decided he'd clean up the yard a bit. He piddled around disposing of empty cans and bottles, moving branches that had fallen, and when he tried to gather all the branches in one big pile, it reminded him of something. An idea popped into his head, and he wanted to act upon it quickly. He jumped into his truck and headed east, toward New Winterfield. Veola's property had been on his mind, so he might as well make sure a task was completed.

When he drove up, the land was devoid of all vehicles, no company cars, no logging trucks, no one. He had to see for himself that Mr. Edelson was living up to his word. Maybe Veola had already heard from her family that everyone had gone, so he knew he didn't have to tell her.

All that remained from the burning earlier was the charred area where he assumed the company planned to start drilling, and now that he was out here, he had to see this tree. He found the tree where her name remained. Amazingly, he spotted a large branch that appeared to be connected to the exact part of the bark that was missing. That was it. He found the "Ervin" part, even though the "V" from Veola's name was broken off. This is what Veola was looking for. He didn't know what good it would do her now, but at least he had located it. No one could put it back together, but he decided to break off the part that read "Ervin" and take it back to town. The least he could do was to try to take away some of Veola's hurt.

Chapter Seventeen

Veola gave specific orders for Cameron and Bobby to arrive at two o'clock. Remembering what Cameron asked about Bobby being allowed to call her by her first name, she wanted to avoid any remote chance of jealousy—possibly still fresh on Cameron's mind.

The mothers arrived less than one minute apart and found Veola in her garden.

"Hey, Mama," Cameron screamed, running toward Veola.

"We're here, Veola," Bobby exclaimed and followed him.

Veola stopped planting squash and zucchini. "Hey, there." Veola removed her gloves and hugged her tykes. The mothers waved back from the edge of the garden.

"I want to help," the boys proclaimed in unison.

Exactly what she wanted to hear, for at least now she had willing participants. "Are you boys hungry?" she asked, getting this out of the way first so she didn't have to stop gardening to satisfy their appetites.

"Yes ma'am."

"Bobby, you just had lunch," Mrs. Barton interrupted.

"You, too, Cameron," Carneda interjected.

"Veola will have something good," Bobby stated.

"Now, y'all know they always want something from my kitchen," Veola told the mothers. "I don't know why you two are surprised. You both used to be the same way about what was on your grandmother's stove." She then turned to the boys. "Well, I am hungry, too. I know I have hot dogs, and I can use one myself."

The boys greeted the notion of hot dogs with unanimous approval.

Making her way through her rows, Veola dumped some containers in her outside trash can. She figured Loretta's slugfest with Leonard the other morning had taken care of the matter of Veola's trash can being used as a dope-smoking transit. Her trash now reverted to its rightful purpose.

While Veola went inside to prepare lunch, the boys retrieved their overnight bundles, placed them in the guest room, then said goodbye to their mothers.

Veola listened to their lively lunch conversation. With mustard smeared on their mouths, Veola insisted they wash up before getting dirty again in the garden. She figured she'd get at least an hour and a half's worth of work from them before they'd complain of being tired or bored.

The boys were fast learners in helping Veola create her garden masterpiece. They kept within the rows and their spacing was closely supervised by Veola. Just as he'd promised, Veola glanced around and saw Ruben Earl striding toward them.

In no time, she watched Ruben Earl share his wisdom and tidbits about planting with the boys. They seemed to soak up all the knowledge they could. Ruben Earl said he couldn't stay long.

"Bye, Mr. Ruben Earl. You coming back?" The boys' good manners reflected their Southern gentlemen upbringing.

Ruben Earl said he'd try, but Veola doubted he'd return today. He'd been at Veola's house almost every day this week.

Veola realized that they'd accomplished more in two hours than she had expected. With three crates emptied, she suggested a break. "Okay, now. I think you two are finished." She was impressed with what they'd done.

"Yeah, yeah," they cheered, clapping for themselves.

"You've really helped me, so let's think of something fun for you."

"I know, I know," Cameron exclaimed emphatically. "Can I take Bobby to the store? Please, please, please?"

Helping Veola didn't normally constitute a reward process for Cameron, but since he'd brought it up, she had to comply.

"Can he take me?" Bobby asked.

"Well, I need you to be extra careful," Veola cautioned, "and you have to look both ways when you cross the street. You promise?"

"Yes, ma'am," Cameron obliged, and Bobby mimicked him jumping for joy.

Veola had always known Cameron considered visiting Veola's favorite store as a high point. She remembered when he was three years old, he walked to the store with her, and he always held her hand. At age six, he'd matured and she permitted him to go to the store by himself. But only after he begged and pleaded did she finally relent.

"Let's wash your hands outside with the hose, and we'll shake them dry." Veola didn't want them tracking dirt inside.

The "yeah, yeahs" and the jumping up and down commenced.

Veola had her money on her. All the time she talked, she unbuttoned the top button of her dress. She reached underneath her brassiere and pulled out her coin purse, wrapped and tied in a handkerchief. The knot was removed from the handkerchief, and she retrieved a quarter for each. One quarter bought a twenty-cent soda and five Jack cookies for a penny a piece. No change was expected.

The boys began their walk toward Guthrie's Corner Store after Veola instructed them to come straight back. She wasn't worried as she watched them turn down Jessie's street. After they rounded the corner, she planted her last row of peppers.

Right after she'd planted the row, she glanced around at her neighbors' houses and wondered about her robber. Could it be someone physically close to her? Surely not since she knew all of her neighbors. It had to be a stranger, just had to be. What bothered her most was that if he was someone she didn't know, she may never meet up with him again before he was off doing his criminal work somewhere else.

Veola's curiosity settled on Loretta's house. What if Loretta had another man besides Leonard in her life? Was Loretta spending the night with him when she said she was gone two days this week, which included the night of Veola's break-in? But why would she go running into the arms of another man when she had a beat-up face?

Surely this other man was not the answer, but why is Loretta keeping her whereabouts a secret? Loretta admitted to her everything that happened last Sunday, so why would she keep this information about where she was?

Maybe Veola had gotten it wrong? Loretta may have wanted to get Leonard out of the way because she was sweet on this other man. Or maybe Loretta may not have wanted to incriminate the new man for fear of losing him, too, since Leonard and she had split. The bottom line was that possibly none of this had anything to do with her robber. They could both be innocent, and even though Veola wanted desperately to weave this all together, the web became more twisted the more she thought about it.

⚞⚟

"Cameron, does Veola always keep money in her dress?" Bobby asked.

"I think so. Every time she gives me money she gets it from there."

"Why doesn't she keep her money in her purse?"

"I don't know."

"Look," Cameron said, pointing to the honeysuckle plants. They scampered over and pulled the strings from the flowers and tasted Mother Nature's sweet nectar inside.

Cameron and Bobby obeyed the rules for crossing the street. Mr. Guthrie greeted them, and Cameron was glad to see the man his grandmother had known for so long.

After Cameron had introduced Bobby, Cameron and Bobby took it upon themselves to tell Mr. Guthrie how they'd made their fifty cents and what all they'd planted in Veola's garden. Next, they shopped and picked out RC colas and set them on the counter. Finally, they asked for the exact same items—two Jack cookies each, a cherry and a grape-flavored Jolly rancher, and one plain Bubble gum. The entire treasury was spent.

"Thank you, boys. I appreciate your business," Mr. Guthrie said, as he opened each of the sodas. He reached over the counter to give the boys their purchases, and after they'd put their gum and candy in their pockets, he gave each a handshake.

"Thank you, Mr. Guthrie," the boys sang in chorus.

"Y'all come back to see me, you hear?"

"We will." Bobby opened the big door and the announcing cowbell over it rang.

"Tell your grandmother hello," Mr. Guthrie added.

"I will," Cameron shouted, looking back.

Going back, they drank and walked at the same time. Cameron had an idea. His eyes gleamed with excitement. "I want to show you something, come on." He walked in front of Bobby.

"What?" Bobby skipped along beside him.

"Just come on. Watch your soda."

The boys carried the sodas in front of them, careful not to spill a single drop. Cameron knew where he was going. This was not the usual path he and his grandmother took when they walked to the store, for Veola wouldn't cut through a field. The fear of snakes, sticker burrs, grasshoppers, and other creepy crawlers kept her on the street at all times. Close to the bridge, a second path veered off and Cameron headed in that direction. The path took a sharp turn downward. They climbed into a huge cement pipe with the bridge now above them. It was believed to be an overflow area, but Cameron had never seen any water in it ever.

"Look!" Cameron pointed down the waterway to the other side of the street. The boys walked through the dry pipeway, which made a good hiding place.

Bobby followed closely behind Cameron. They sat in the middle of the underground water drain, anchored their sodas between their legs, and opened their cookie sack.

"Look what I found." Cameron spotted a cigarette on the ground.

"Somebody must have dropped it."

The boys played make-believe grown-ups, pretending to smoke the dirty, unlit cigarette.

"So, did you go to work today?" Cameron faked a puff and passed the cigarette.

"Yeah, after I dropped my kids off at school." Bobby passed the cigarette back to Cameron.

"I worked today, too. At the hospital." The cigarette went back and forth, and fake smoke was blown into the air.

"I work at the car shop, but I only fix trucks." Between his smoke puffs, Bobby took a drink of his real soda.

"How many kids do you have?"

"Two. How about you?"

"I've got three. How many cars do you have? I have a truck and my wife has a car."

"I have two cars and a truck. My wife drives one, and I drive my Mustang. I use my truck when I have to haul stuff," Bobby said.

The smoking went on long enough for the sodas to be finished. If one had two of anything, the other had three, and vice versa. They had it all—kids, cars, jobs, and houses.

They made their way to the top of the incline to get back on the main street when Cameron realized Veola may be wondering where they were. "Let's go." The remaining two cookies were saved for later, and with their empty bottles in their hands, they high-tailed it back to Veola's garden.

❧ ❧

Veola saw the boys approaching as she washed at the outside hydrant. "I see you two made it to the store all right," she said.

"Yes, ma'am, and Mr. Guthrie said hello," Bobby said.

"And we saved a cookie for later." Cameron showed Veola the sack.

"Well, let me get cleaned up, and we'll see what's next for you two. We might hang around here for a while and walk to the park later on."

The boys did the jumping-for-excitement routine again.

"What toys did you bring?" Cameron asked Bobby.

Veola watched them run inside to check out each other's stash. "Hey, you two," she shouted at them. "Help me pick up the seed packages and the other containers and put them behind the storage house."

They raced into the garden once again and gathered all they could.

"Thank you," Veola told them. "Now you can go check out what each other brought. Wash your hands first."

They used the water faucet again, drying their hands on their clothes. They weren't quite as dirty as they'd been when they were in the soil. Veola heard them inside debating over what they would play with first, Hot Wheels or the Old Maid card game.

Even though her work outside was accomplished, Veola's Saturday was far from over. She read the Parkerville Daily Progress at the dining room table while the boys amused themselves playing cards.

When Veola got to the Memorial and Obituary section of her paper, she read everybody's name and examined every picture, searching for anyone she knew. Finally, the very last memorial was for Luberdia Marie Walters, one of her acquaintances. "That's her," she said out loud.

Veola knew Luberdia passed this week, and she read her entire obituary. Afterward, she went to the guest room and had to trample over the boys' belongings to get to her chair. As she was about to sit down to pick up the phone, the doorbell rang. Jessie was standing outside.

"Hey, Girl," Veola greeted her. "I was fixin' to call you. Come on in here. Did you read the paper yet?"

"Yeah, I read it. Saw Luberdia in there, too," Jessie said.

"That's what I'm talkin' 'bout. You see how old that picture was?" Veola opened the paper and laid it on the dining room table in front of them.

"I saw her. She ain't looked like that in twenty years."

"Why did her family use such an old picture?"

"Eva Mae saw it, too. She said Luberdia got kids older than when that picture was took. That's a shame," Jessie added.

"Sparkling Funeral Home got the body. Maybe Monday we can go see her."

"Fine by me, and Eva Mae ain't got nothing to do. We'll meet over here before we go down there."

"The wake start at seven, so we'll go down there after I get off of work, be in and out before everybody else get there. I'll call you when I get home."

"I'm telling y'all now. When I check out of here, keep me out of Sparkling, otherwise, I'm gon' come back and haunt y'all."

"Girl, don't nobody want to be down there."

"If you ask me, their embalming fluid make you look too dark."

"Eva Mae swears up and down that too much embalming fluid gives folks too many wrinkles if they don't get you into the ground quick enough. She thinks like that, anyhow, but she might have a point."

"Just get me six feet under, quick, fast, and in a hurry. That's all I got to say."

"I remember hearing one of them morticians down there dropped a body once. I can't think of who it was, but you remember, don't you?"

"Why sho, I remember. I'm the one told you."

"We'll see what she look like on Monday—that is, if her body ready."

On Monday, the sistahs would have a full report on the way Sparkling had handled Luberdia. They'd see if she looked too dark, had too many wrinkles, and determine if her body had been dropped. Luberdia had no idea one of her judgment days would come sooner than she thought. First by her sistahs, then she'd get to God.

"I'm gon' get out of here. I stopped by since I saw yo door open. On my way to Shawty's. Where your boys at?"

"Can't you hear them in there?"

"Chile, I thought that was the TV," Jessie said. "You gon' have all yo family with you at church in the morning, Girl."

"We'll be there, bright and early. Come to think of it, I don't think Bobby has been to church with me without his mama, and that was a couple of years ago. Now you know he won't have no problem fitting in anywhere."

"Probably not, but we gon' see."

"See what?"

"Come here." Jessie walked to the front porch and Veola followed her. Veola figured Jessie wanted to be out of earshot of Bobby.

"That little boy ain't gon' know what to think trying to go to church with a whole bunch of us, Veola. You gon' ruin that boy for life," Jessie proclaimed.

"You 'bout crazy as Eva Mae. Why you say that?"

"'Cause he been used to his kind of church downtown. You

know how white people praise God. The only noise you got going on in their churches is the sound of an organ and the bell waking up everybody across town on Sunday morning. Ain't no hallelujahs, and the amens don't come often enough. Don't act like you don't know that I'm talking about."

"Jessie, you're as crazy as they come, but I ain't gon' hold that against you. That boy can fit in anywhere he wants to, and he ain't scared of nothing having to do with black people. See what I tell you in the morning. Now you go on to the store, 'cause I'm gon' finish reading the paper."

"Okay, then. I'm gon' watch him tomorrow and if he start crying, I'm shole gon' tell you I told you so. You know I will. Oh yeah, I forgot to tell you. I ain't seen nobody with a cut-up arm. You done ran him out of town."

Veola waved Jessie off and went back inside. She listened to the boys laughing in the next room. Bobby will be just fine tomorrow, and she knew it.

By the time Veola felt the boys had become bored with their inside activities, they were on their way to the park. Of course, they talked Jessie into joining them.

Veola hoped every house she passed on the way to the park had someone out front or on the side of the house so she could speak and get them all to wave. She was on a mission: broke-up arm hunting. She spoke to everyone she could. She saw many arms a-waving, but none fit the bill for providing her evidence.

At the park, the boys ran and played. They raced their cars on the slide. They turned upside down, inside out, and every other way they could on the monkey bars. Veola hollered, "be careful" and "quit scaring me."

She and Jessie sat on the swing. They sat in different directions according to where the boys were. The boys consumed a full hour, and Veola didn't realize it. "Jessie, I might not ever know who did it."

"Don't go saying that, Veola. You got to be patient."

"I am not the patient kind. You know that."

"Well, you can't line up every man in Parkerville and inspect arms. You still might not find him."

"You know that's what I want to do, don't you?"

"See, and you call me crazy."

The boys' energy was still at full momentum on the walk home; they jumped over potholes and cracks in the cement. Veola assumed they never tired, and from the look on Jessie's face, she was worn out from watching them, so she went home. They had already had a full day, and it wasn't even dark.

Dinner was without question the boys' favorite meal. Veola made spaghetti—simple for her, heaven for the boys. Nosey Eva Mae stopped by on her way from Guthrie's. She got a plate, too.

The boys talked in between bites, and even at this hour, all subjects had yet to be explored, Veola and Eva Mae eyed one another, but listened to them at the opposite end of the table. Veola saw Eva Mae was amused, laughing when the boys talked about the mystery meat they were served Tuesday at school.

"Chile, them boys is a mess," Eva Mae said to Veola. "They would keep me laughing all day long."

When the boys finished, they took their plates to the kitchen. Then they were off to the bathroom to wash up. Veola watched Eva Mae eye them peripherally with at least one eye on her own plate.

"I'm not far behind them, but I'm gon' eat this one last bit," Eva Mae said. "You know I don't ever leave nothing on my plate when I eat over here. That little boy can eat up some food, can't he?"

"Both of them can, Eva Mae. What do you expect?"

"Why he don't seem shy 'round you at all. He acts like he's at home over here. Like he was one of yours."

"And that's the way it should be. I have determined there is no hope for you. Every day I think you gon' get a little more sense, but you keep proving me wrong. That boy been in my keeps ever since he was born, and not only that, he and Cameron are friends from school. Bobby don't even see what you see when it comes to color. We have our talks about differences and what we all have in common. Sometimes he bring up stuff. Other times, it's me educating him. I'm gon' make sure of that."

"Girl, I give you credit, 'cause see, I don't think no white man has ever been inside my house except the insurance man, or folk trying to sell me a vacuum cleaner or some 'cyclopedias. I don't need none of them thangs, but I listen to them just the same."

Veola turned the attention back to the meal. "Are you

finished?"

"Wait a minute." Eva Mae whisked her fork around the last morsel on her plate. "Girl, you know that was good."

"I'm glad you enjoyed yourself. That's twice you done set your behind over here this week and got full. I can't wait to next week to eat at your house," Veola joked.

"You is more than welcome at anytime to break bread with me, and next week sound good for that. I got a taste for some good cabbage myself. I'd better make enough for Tyrone 'cause he loves 'em."

"I was joking with you, but I need to get that jar of preserves you been meaning to bring me for over a month. I didn't make any last year, and I'm about to run out 'cause I done gave so much away."

"I'mmo bring yo preserves to church in the morning. You can put it underneath the pew, but don't you forget it."

"As long as I've been waiting on those preserves, I ain't gon' dare forget it. Speaking of Tyrone, how's he doing?"

"Ain't nothing wrong with him. Still sorry as hell, kind of quiet lately. With all that's been going on at his house this week, I ain't surprised."

For a brief instance, Tyrone flashed across Veola's mind and wondered since he and Leonard were such good friends, could Tyrone know about the dope-planting going on with Leonard and Loretta? Tyrone might even know about Loretta and Leonard's little cavorting with each other. Why was she the last to know anything going on right outside her door, Veola thought. She quickly dismissed Tyrone and all that foolishness and blamed herself for asking about Tyrone in the first place.

Soon afterward, Eva Mae announced her need to depart after she got hugs from Cameron and Bobby.

Veola watched all of this transpire. Maybe Eva Mae's ignorance was from lack of exposure. Veola loved the idea that Bobby played a part in changing some of Eva Mae's stereotypes, and Veola basked as she took credit for it.

"Good night, Eva Mae. We'll see you in the morning," Veola said as Eva Mae descended the steps. "We might have some more hugs for you in the morning. Be ready."

"All right now. I don't know if I can handle all this love," Eva

Mae said, waving back.

Outside on the porch, Veola could see a faint light coming from Loretta's bedroom window. The light flickered, so she figured Loretta was watching TV, hopefully in her recently repaired glasses. Veola thought that she'd see Loretta at church, too, since she missed last Sunday. Missing two Sundays in a row was grounds for needing a good talking-to.

For a second, Veola realized she had slipped to an all-time low. When she thought about church, she wished all the men in church would take off their suits and shirts so she could see every one of their arms. Now, why, Veola, she asked herself, would she think that one of the men at church did it? Church men would not do something like that. No, they wouldn't, but then again, we are all sinners. We all have to have a reason to be there.

"Okay now, where are y'alls clothes for in the morning?" Veola asked the boys once she was back inside. "It's about bath time, and let's get everything ready for tomorrow."

Veola had made her announcement, and she went into the guest room to help them. Their shoes were shined, and the short-sleeved cotton shirts didn't require ironing, but Veola had to put her touch on them, a little extra starch.

After their bath, they needed help drying off. Veola didn't let them out of the bathroom without their teeth brushed. She informed them that bath time didn't necessarily mean bedtime. TV was okay, just as long as it was quiet.

Veola pulled another treat out of her hat. "I'll tell you what. I'm not quite ready for bed, so I'm going to let you lie in my bed to watch TV while I get myself ready for tomorrow. How's that?" She asked as if she didn't know their answer.

"Oooh, yeah," Cameron immediately responded with a smile. "I like your bed, Mama. It's always warm."

"Well, I don't know how warm it will be now that there is no one in there. It's warm when we are both there," Veola explained.

As Cameron and Bobby climbed into Veola's heavily covered bed, Veola read their pajamas. "Bobby, you're sleeping in Superman, and Cameron, you're in Batman."

"Batman and Robin," Cameron corrected Veola.

"Okay, I hope I don't have to call on Superman, Batman, or

Robin to make you go to sleep tonight," Veola warned with a wink.

They crawled into bed and giggled as Veola watched them maneuver around among her covers.

"I can't move," Bobby stated.

"Me either. These covers are heavy." Cameron chuckled.

After Veola found something for them to watch, they laid with their feet toward the headboard, heads propped up by their elbows to be closer to the TV.

"I don't want you guys going to sleep without saying your prayers," Veola ordered. "Let's go. Out of bed and on your knees."

Bobby crawled out first and it didn't take long for him to assume the praying position. With the height of Veola's bed, his hands were at the level of his forehead, and Cameron soon joined him. Veola purposely bowed on the side of them so they could be next to each other.

"Are we ready?" Veola asked.

"Yes," they said simultaneously.

They recited in unison:

"Now I lay me down to sleep, I pray the Lord my soul to keep. If I should die before I wake, I pray the Lord my soul to take. Amen."

Cameron continued. "And God bless Dear, Daddy, Kenny, and—"

"And God bless my Mom and Dad and Jeremy, too," Bobby interrupted. "And Veola," Bobby added.

"Lord, listen to the prayers of these children and know that we need you to bless all of our families. We don't know the needs of all of your children, but hear our prayer and know that we thank you for letting us see another day. Touch our garden that we planted, Lord. Thank you for the love you show us all the time, for that is what keeps us together. Keep us in your care and may we continue to receive your ever-flowing and abundant blessings. In your name we pray, Amen."

"Amen," the boys said, seconds apart. They were back in their positions at the foot of the bed in no time flat, once again eyes glued to the TV. Veola knew they wondered what they'd missed.

It didn't take Veola long to get her Sunday clothes together, and luckily, tomorrow was not her day to usher. She compared the boys' prayers. Bobby blessed his *mom* and *dad*, while Cameron said *mama* and *daddy*. The differences between her white and black grandchildren didn't go unnoticed.

Veola was already thinking about being at church with them. They'd sit with her, not by themselves. Otherwise, race cars may appear out of nowhere. Cameron had been taught to respect God's house, but she didn't want him tempted for mischief.

By the time Veola finished her bath, she watched the eyes close for her two rug rats were sleeping. She lugged them one at a time to the next room. They uttered not a peep when placed under the clean sheets and heavy covers. Exhaustion had finally taken its toll.

Veola crawled into her bed, now warm from the body heat of the boys. No Bible passage for the night. Since she'd prayed with the boys, the next thing was lights out.

She talked to herself as she turned to the side, re-adjusting her pillow. "And Lord, bless all my families. You know I got more than one set."

Once again, it is well with my soul, but my heart is troubled. A burglar is out there, and he still lurks outside these walls.

❦

Jeremy loved his parents, both of them, but tonight, he wanted nothing but the best for his mother. *Come through for her, Dad, please come through.*

He left the house Saturday morning, to avoid running into his mother. She'd try to find out what he was doing tonight, and he was not good at lying to her. Luckily, she had the day to herself with Bobby gone. Jeremy thought Veola saved the day for his family in more ways than she knew.

After a full day of running around, Jeremy came home in the early evening to an empty house and a note from his mom:

> *Honey, your father and I have gone out for the evening. We're at the Simpsons. You're on your own for dinner, but there's sandwich meat in the fridge. Be careful if you go out tonight, but can you at least sleep in your own bed one night this weekend? (smile). Love, Mom*

Jeremy didn't want to wait all night before going over to the

Simpsons because he thought he'd leave by ten o'clock or so if the party for his mom was boring with too many adults. At that point he'd have plenty of time to hook up with his friends on the Safeway parking lot. So he dressed for both events—a clean pair of jeans, a nice sport shirt, with a white T-shirt underneath.

The Simpsons had quite a few cars parked on the street. All of this for his mom, he thought, now wondering if his dad had anything to do with this event. He reminded himself to give his dad the benefit of the doubt and deal with his frustration, confusion, and doubts later.

Mr. Simpson greeted him at the front door and directed him to where his mom and dad were. The first thing he noticed was his father standing next to his mother with a big smile on his face. His mother was blinking back tears. The woman must be Mrs. Simpson, and she smiled as she carried the birthday cake to the table.

Jeremy looked directly at Mrs. Simpson, and the wires connected. She was the lady, the mystery person he'd seen with his dad over the past two months. He was sure of it.

"Look everybody, Jeremy's here," Mr. Simpson announced.

Everyone clapped, and Jeremy knew to make a bee-line for his mother. She met him halfway around the table, darting in and out of guests. When they reached each other, they exchanged hugs and pecks on the cheek. The guests clapped more.

"Honey, your dad surprised me tonight. I walked into this party not knowing a thing." Mrs. Barton took Jeremy by the hand and led him back over to her original place between Mrs. Simpson and his dad. "You remember Mrs. Simpson, don't you?"

"Hello, Jeremy," Mrs. Simpson said. "You know I haven't seen you in such a long time, but I've been keeping up with you."

"The Simpsons travel a lot visiting their family," Mrs. Barton added.

"That's right. We've been blessed with three grandchildren this year. While we were in Houston this week, our house was broken into. Luckily, I can't find anything missing. Just had to get one window replaced."

"Hi, Mrs. Simpson," Jeremy said, hoping he didn't cut Mrs. Simpson off explaining her robbery.

"Hey, Son. Glad you could make it." Dr. Barton spoke through the cackling of the women.

"Hey, Dad." Jeremy smiled at his dad, this time with heart. He was glad to see them both in a good mood, particularly his mom.

"Can you believe your dad and Mrs. Simpson kept all of this a secret from me?" his mom asked. His parents exchanged glances and even lifted their glasses.

"He was quite sneaky," Mrs. Simpson added. "I don't think he told anyone."

"Absolutely nobody," Dr. Barton said.

"I know he didn't," Mrs. Barton said. "Otherwise, I would have known about it."

"The few times we met to discuss the birthday party, it was over lunch when I was in town. He didn't dare risk calling me long distance, thinking you would see it on the telephone bill," Mrs. Simpson explained.

The grown-ups laughed and Jeremy excused himself to the bathroom, not knowing where it was. So he went around the corner and peaked back at his parents with Mrs. Simpson. She was definitely the woman—the right height, the brunette hair. His suspicions had been dead wrong, and all of his sightings now made sense. He felt enormous relief.

Watching his dad's plans unfold for his mom, Jeremy was now more convinced than ever to get his own plans in order. He felt his attendance was no longer required, and he chose to let the grown-ups play, enjoy the evening. On the way to rejoin his mom and dad, he grabbed a small plate of roast beef and potatoes. It wasn't Veola's.

"I'm getting out of here," Jeremy announced, interrupting them.

"So soon?" his mother asked. "You just got here. Want some cake?"

"Grab some for Bobby and me if there's any left."

"You're right," she agreed. "I wonder how he's doing with Cameron and Veola tonight."

"That's the least of my worries," his dad interjected, laughing.

Jeremy saw a sense of accomplishment written all over his dad's face.

"Honey, I'm so glad you came by," his mom said as she hugged him. "We'll see you later at home."

"Right. I may head downtown for a while. If no one's out, I'll be home early."

"Be careful, Son," his dad warned.

"You did good tonight, Dad. Just like you've been worried about me, I was kind of worried about you, too. Maybe tomorrow we'll talk about school next year," Jeremy said, reaching for his dad's hand. The two embraced as if Jeremy had just won his first little league baseball game. He spotted his mother's eyes tearing up.

"Love y'all," Jeremy said, heading for the door.

"Love you, too. Say goodbye to the Simpsons, Honey," she instructed.

"I will." He thanked the Simpsons for making the night special. Because of the way he felt and seeing his mother so ecstatic, Mrs. Simpson even got a hug—well worth it since his dad's mystery had turned better than he'd expected.

Not that he was desperately seeking the company of his friends, he drove down the strip out of habit, then went home. As he pulled into his driveway, he thought about that close call a month ago. He had had a few beers and a couple of joints with his buddies. On the way home, a police car sped past them, lights flashing, in the opposite direction. At the sound of the siren, Jeremy had slowed down. Had he not, they would have hit a sharp curve ahead far too fast. He was too high and not in his right mind. They all could have been killed!

Jeremy went inside knowing the sobering fact that he'd taken too many risks with his habits and gotten away with them. He knew damn well he'd done the right thing with Tyrone and Leonard today, but the hardest part was yet to come. He hoped he'd find the strength to get back into control again, yet he wasn't quite sure how.

Chapter Eighteen

This Sunday morning, Veola had no use for her alarm. The Sunday after Easter was usually without commotion, but Veola found herself with the same amount of hustle and bustle she'd experienced one week ago with breakfast underway for three. Since it would be close to one o'clock by the time they made it home from church, she didn't want to be blamed for growling stomachs.

Preparing the entire Sunday meal was on her, not simply the extras for dinner on the ground. In spite of all she did yesterday, she'd found the time to season a roast while she made spaghetti. Now, once she'd cut up the potatoes, carrots, and celery, the roast would be in the oven before the bacon hit the frying pan.

Batman and Superman were perched at the dining room table, and from the looks of their hair, they'd been flying through the sky trying to save the world. Veola didn't crave the scrambled eggs and rice the boys dug into, so she settled for her favorite, her fresh tomato half-sandwich.

Time was of the essence, so while the boys ate, she cleaned. After they finished, they got dressed, and Veola gave them specific instructions to sit still in the living room while she finished the kitchen and dressed herself.

Teeth were brushed, faces weren't ashy, shoes were tied, and no toys protruded from their pockets. The combing of the hair was easy, and that was the last touch Veola administered before they walked out.

Veola realized for the first time she had to do something different for Bobby than for Cameron. Bobby's hair had to go from oily to dry—add water and air dry. Cameron's, from dry to oily—add Royal Crown hair grease and let it shine.

Luckily, Vaseline was universal, used for all elbows. One jar fits all races.

She sent up a private thank you under her breath to God. In spite of all of the differences in His people, there were far too many similarities. She hoped Eva Mae would discover it, too, this morning at church. One God, one faith. *Get on board all ye peoples.*

"Everybody ready?" Veola asked.

"Yes, ma'am," they said in unison.

"Well, let's go." Before Veola closed the door, she realized she was doing something that was almost sinful for her, leaving her house with an unmade bed. This past week, Veola had entertained overnight guests three times. She deserved a break, and the bed needed to air out.

The boys waited on the front porch while Veola placed her belongings in the swing and locked the door.

"Cameron, I need you to carry my Bible. Bobby, you get my Sunday school books."

A sense of pride ran rampant over her on her short walk to the churchhouse. Anyone passing by noticed a black woman walking to church with a couple of boys. Not just any boys, but ones she called her *own*—one white, one black.

People with televisions and radios had seen and heard about issues regarding civil and equal rights. She didn't even think that this particular morning, the Reverend Dr. Martin Luther King, Jr., would take notice of her doing what she does best. He needed to concentrate on changing other people, not her. She was equally moved, vitalized, nourished, and motivated by his words, but her spirit had been planted and formulated by the love of God and His people long before Dr. King came along.

As they neared the church, her thought process continued to

wander. There was a lot to be said about the man, this Dr. King, for he got to the core of some of the problems that faced America. Bringing people together was what she loved to hear most in his speeches, and she admired his bravery through all the confrontations he'd encountered. That gave her something to pray about and something to pray for.

Photos of her family members were commonplace for her, but she had hung the photos of John F. Kennedy, Jr., and Dr. King in her guest room. She loved President Kennedy, and the world knew he loved everybody—Jews, Gentiles, black and white. She had heard his brother, Robert, was the same way. She never understood President Kennedy's assassination, and she remembered that day in '63 like it just happened. Because of that, she feared for Dr. King. There was no doubt that the evildoers and haters were out there. _Some of them right in her own backyard._ If they can kill a president, then they can surely kill a black preacher from Georgia. _Watch over him, Lord, please watch over him._

Everyone greeted one another as Veola, Cameron, and Bobby entered the church, and Veola watched Bobby smile from all the attention he received. Finally, Cameron broke away from Veola, with Bobby close behind, and went to where his Sunday school class was being held. Carneda taught the Sunday school class for the elementary school children. Cameron and Bobby both got hugs from Carneda, and Bobby was introduced to Cameron's friends from church.

Veola searched for the boys before class began, for she had forgotten to give them money. "Now here, Bobby, this is for Sunday school and morning worship. And Cameron, this is for you." Veola gave them each two quarters. "Now put that in your pocket so you won't lose it." When the offering plates circulated, she wanted them ready.

"Yes, ma'am," each said and scurried back to class.

After Sunday school, Veola watched Cameron get his hug from big brother Kenny and Bobby got a fairly stiff handshake.

Before worship service began, Cameron and Bobby approached Veola. "Mama, remember I told you I had something for you when I came by your house this week?" Cameron asked.

"Yes, but you never gave it to me," Veola said.

"We drew a picture of you one day after school, and I gave it to

Dear to keep. After I found out we were spending the night with you, we decided to finish it in Sunday school this morning," Cameron said.

"Cameron had finished his part, but I didn't get the chance to finish mine, so Cameron's mom brought it for me this morning. Here, Veola," Bobby said, and handed her a drawing.

Veola took the picture and saw that it was a lady, colored tan with a crayola, in a white dress. On the top of the drawing were these words: YOUR NAMES IN OUR FAMILY. Across the bottom was printed: MAMA AND VEOLA.

Veola knew exactly what this meant. Cameron and Bobby had worked on their interpretation of what she had meant to both of them. In spite of the different names, she was still the same person. Maybe the white dress was Bobby's idea since he often saw her in uniform, but the flower on the dress and the hat tilted to one side added spunk.

"I don't know what to say, other than I love it, and thank you for thinking of me. You know I'm going to show everybody. Cameron, this sure beats that ant farm you gave me last time." They laughed and Veola got two more hugs.

During worship service, Veola sat in her usual spot when she wasn't ushering: second pew, right side. Bobby sat next to her and Cameron sat on her other side. Veola thought maybe Cameron preferred to sit with Carneda this morning since he had spent the night away from home, but he'd chosen to be with Bobby and her. Veola heard him tell his mother he'd be with her all day after church, but he'd sit with Mama so Bobby wouldn't be the only kid with his grandmother.

Eva Mae sat caddy-cornered to Veola's left on the back pew of the rows at the front of the church that faced each other. Veola knew Eva Mae sat where she didn't miss a thing. Veola saw Eva Mae watching Bobby from the moment he entered the churchhouse.

As an elder, Ruben Earl was way up in the front, almost on the pulpit stage, sharing a row with the other governing men of the church who faced Eva Mae. As a deacon, church duties kept him occupied, so he didn't greet Veola and her gang before Sunday school. Once worship service began, he nodded in Veola's direction.

She smiled back.

Suddenly, Veola felt a tap on her shoulder.

"Good morning, stranger. I thought maybe you could use some

help with these two," Jeremy said.

"Lord, have mercy, Jeremy," Veola said. "Oh, my Lord."

Veola extended a hand over her shoulder. He grabbed her hand, but also hugged her from behind, putting his cheek directly against hers. Veola patted his face and whispered, "I'm glad you're here, Baby."

"Me, too," he replied.

"Jeremy," Bobby exclaimed.

"Hey, you guys," Jeremy whispered and touched the top of Bobby's head.

During the congregation song, "I Surrender All," latecomers continued to enter the doors of worship. Again, Veola turned to see who was still arriving and saw Fayetta make her way to a pew behind Jessie. Fayetta pulled out a hymnal and started to sing. Immediately, Veola wondered where Leonard could be.

Fayetta nodded at Veola, and Veola returned the gesture. Veola couldn't figure out why Fayetta had returned so soon or if she had even left. Veola was sure Fayetta would explain later. Then, perhaps the song's refrain was fitting for the way Veola felt. *I Surrender All.*

With all the previous nodding and head bobbing, the three sistahs gave their own winks and head tilts which all seem to say, "take all of this in, 'cause you know we gon' talk about it later."

Veola turned back around to face the front of the church, and with no warning, she got caught up in the moment. God does that to his believers. He won't tell them anything, but He'll show up in spirit. Veola stopped singing and hummed. Tears welled in her eyes as she had reason to rejoice. Her immediate family and many of her extended family were here.

When the words of the chorus, "All to Jesus, I surrender, I surrender all," were sang again, Veola sat down. She had her eyes closed and said softly to herself, "yes, Lord, yes, Lord." She repeated the words over and over again. This was her time to thank God for what He meant to her and no one interfered.

Veola was unaware of the others then. It didn't matter, for the Lord was at work. She let Him do what He does best.

✺

Tyrone grinned as he thought that Miss Veola ain't gon' know what hit her. Since she didn't act right and play by his rulebook the first time, then he would change his plan around a bit. She gave him hell when he tried to get into her house, so he'd get in this time when she's away. Certain she was at church, nothing stood in his way. Nobody expects nothing to be going on while they're at church. His high was feeling good.

He made his way to Miss Veola's side window and easily removed one of the screens. His mother never missed church as it was her richest source of gossip. Loretta should be sanging in the church choir right about now, and Mr. Eli and Miss Delphine, two houses over, couldn't see nothing he was doing. He was assured he'd get in with ease. He concentrated on being quiet. If someone walked by, he'd hide in the bushes.

He used his screwdriver to pry open the window latches, and he climbed in. Once inside, he went straight for her chest of drawers and dresser. A bunch of jewelry was all he saw. Where was her money? It had to be hidden. He'd start with her shoeboxes.

In her closet, he threw shoes around. Nothing. He pulled down some hatboxes. Still nothing. Okay, old purses. There were papers galore, and even old coin purses. Empty, empty. He saw that she was better at his game than he was. He was even more frustrated because this was his second attempt. And dammit, she was winning. He folded back the edges of her floor rugs for any hiding places she might like. Miss Veola wasn't giving him a goddam thing.

✺

After church, Veola was a magnet. Everyone made their way to her to either meet her guests or assess her spiritual encounter. Jeremy was the first to get his proper hug.

"Were you surprised to see me?" he asked.

"Why, of course I was, but I'm so glad you came."

"Me, too," he said.

Bobby wrapped his arms around his brother's waist. "Hey,

Jeremy."

"Hey, you," Jeremy replied. "You guys have fun?"

"You know we did," Bobby responded.

"Hey, Cameron, how are you?" Jeremy extended his hand to shake Cameron's.

"I'm fine," Cameron replied and smiled at Veola.

Veola knew Cameron was glad that Jeremy had remembered his name. "You're coming to the house and eat, right?" Veola asked.

"Well, I thought I would take Bobby home for Mom," Jeremy said.

"That's all well and good, but you know he's not going anywhere until he feeds his face one more time."

"All right, then," Jeremy consented. "We'll wait for you at the house." He turned away and spoke to Fayetta as she was next in line to see Veola. "Where's Leonard?"

"Since the kids didn't want to come to church this morning, he went by the house to be with them. That's two days in a row. We'll see what happens." Fayetta then directed her attention to Veola. "Miss Veola, thank you again." The two embraced.

"For what, Chile?" Veola asked.

"For your support, your advice. It's much too early to tell what Leonard is going to do for his children, Miss Veola, outside of the money, but maybe they'll spend some time with him on a more regular basis. We'll see."

"Let me tell you something, Baby," Veola began. "Leonard has a lot of growing up to do. You just don't want to be the one who has to raise him. There is no harm in letting your children see for themselves just what their daddy is all about. Do you trust Leonard?"

"Not really, but I'm tired of being mad. I've got to do something different. I know he won't hurt our children. Him wanting to do right by them might even help me take care of myself. I'll keep you posted."

"You don't have to explain a thing to me. You have to do what's best for the kids, but don't forget about you. And don't forget about what I said," Veola continued. She held up an index finger. "It only took one time for my daddy to go too far."

Fayetta nodded as she walked away.

Veola saw Jeremy engaged in conversation with Eva Mae at the back of the churchhouse. Veola suspected people were watching all of this hugging of white folks and strangers, so she knew her phone would ring off the hook later on. Then she made her way to Carneda, and reminded her that Cameron and Bobby needed to get their clothes and toys.

Still inside, Veola scanned the crowd to find Ruben Earl.

Ruben Earl waved and strided toward her. "Got to ask you something. With all this company you got, are you going to be home later?"

"Why, shole I am. This evening, say around seven o'clock, why don't you drop by?" Veola sensed he'd rather come over rather than be on the phone.

"That's fine. I'll be back from my sister's by then easy."

"See you later."

Veola went through the front doors of the church and Cameron and Bobby were waiting for her. Carneda promised to pick Cameron up later, so he could spend more time with Bobby.

"I've got to drive my truck, Veola, so I'll meet you at your house," Jeremy said.

Clusters of people stood on the doorsteps of the church or out front engaged in their conversations. A siren grew louder, and a police car sped by and turned quickly down Veola's street.

❦

Tyrone heard the police siren. It sounded far away, but he knew he'd been in this house too long. No one had seen him, but he didn't want to risk them coming somewhere nearby. The siren grew louder; they must be heading somewhere in his vicinity. His time here was done. Dammit.

As he made his way to Miss Veola's dining room window, he moved the blinds to crawl out. As soon as he straddled the window frame exiting, he heard a voice and froze.

"Don't you dare move, or you're a dead son of a bitch," a female voice ordered.

Tyrone turned and saw Loretta Mayfield standing right outside the window with a gun pointed at him.

"Tyrone Walker. I don't believe it. Ain't this something? What are you doing breaking into Miss Veola's house? Lord, have mercy."

"Loretta, put the gun down." He tried to hoist the other leg over.

"Dammit, I said, don't move. Tyrone Walker. Don't try me, you hear?"

"Come on, Loretta, it's me. Go on, put the gun down."

"Don't move! Don't say a word, and keep your ass still. You crawl back inside, I'm gon' shoot. You crawl out, I'm gon' shoot. You keep your ass right where you are until the police get here."

"Don't do this, Loretta." Tyrone did not move. He had never been caught and here he was being held at gunpoint by a neighbor. And to make matters worse, he was robbing his mama's friend's house. He became flushed and he started sweating profusely. The siren seemed to roar as the police approached Miss Veola's house, and he could do nothing. What was his mama going to say? Would Miss Veola put him in jail? If he moved, would this ignant bitch, Loretta, put a cap in his ass?

Tyrone heard the police car stop in front. He could see the reflection on the outside of Loretta's house that the police car lights still flashed even though the siren went off. He heard two car doors open and close.

"Back here, officers. Over here." Loretta hollered.

"Ma'am, put the gun down," one policeman ordered.

"I will as soon as you lock him up," Loretta said.

"We've got him, ma'am."

Tyrone realized one officer had taken the gun Loretta gave him, but he saw through the window that the other one had drawn his gun, pointing it directly at him.

"Sir, bring your hands through the window. Let me see them at all times. Come back through the window, Sir, and don't do anything stupid."

Now both policemen pointed their weapons at him, and he realized he was cornered. There was no way out. He made his way through the window, and an officer handcuffed him.

"Ma'am, let's get him in custody before we get any information from you," one officer stated as they led Tyrone to the front yard.

The conversations ceased and those on the sidewalk moved closer to the street to see that the police car stopped right in front of Miss Veola's house. The police cruiser's siren stopped.

From near the street, someone shouted, "Miss Veola, Miss Veola. The police are at your house."

Several people began running across the street. Veola kept trying to get in front to see. By the time she made it to her house, the crowd had cleared the way for her to break through to the front and witness everything. The police were bringing a man in handcuffs through the bushes on the side of Miss Veola's house. Once the policeman got out of the way, the crowd gasped. Veola cried, "Oh, no!" when she saw it was Tyrone. Loretta walked behind the two policemen with Tyrone. Someone shouted, "Loretta, Loretta."

"Jeremy, find Carneda," Veola whispered, "and make sure she's got the boys." Her heart raced as she stared at Tyrone.

Tyrone didn't say a word. His head was bowed.

As the policemen turned Tyrone around to put him in the squad car, Veola noticed he was wearing a short-sleeved shirt. She saw the wound, bandaged big as day. Veola gasped and covered her mouth in the same motion. There was the cut, the broke-up arm. She could barely catch her breath.

Veola continued to stare at Tyrone through the squad car window. Then, she realized that she had to talk to Loretta. Loretta was right in front of her, but Veola had been too busy getting over the shock of Tyrone that she'd forgotten her. Then, Veola heard the piercing scream.

"Oh, my Lord," Eva Mae kept screaming. Jessie fanned her with a cardboard church fan, and the deacons tried to hold her up. Eva Mae had been pushed up to the front of the crowd as soon as the folk saw Tyrone.

"What happened, Loretta?" Veola asked. "Tell me everything." She realized that Eva Mae would never hear this right now for she was jumping up and down, crying, and trying to get to the squad car.

The policemen had surrounded Loretta and Veola and one policeman was prepared to take notes. Veola saw Jessie, Fayetta, and Carneda push up close by Loretta.

"Miss Veola, I'm sorry," Loretta began.

"Don't worry about me, Loretta." Veola desperately wanted her to get on with it.

"I didn't feel like going to church, since this eye ain't quite right, so I was at home reading my Bible. About twenty minutes ago, I looked out my window and saw your window was open with the screen on the ground. I called the police right away and told them to get here as fast as they could 'cause someone must be in your house. I told them they should make a lot of noise, because I wanted whoever was in your house to get out of there. In case whoever was in there got out before the police got here, I got my pistol and came to your front yard so I could get a view of your front door, your side window, and your back door. I figured they was gon' have to come through one of them to get out."

Eva Mae screamed again. Veola was certain Eva Mae couldn't hear a word of what Loretta had said for she was too distraught over her son handcuffed in a police car for the whole world to see.

"Eva Mae, Eva Mae, calm down," Jessie said.

Loretta continued. "I heard the siren getting louder and louder, and I hoped whoever this was would hurry and make a move, and sure 'nough, he set foot out your window. I was ready for him. You should have seen the look on his face, Miss Veola. I still can't believe it was Tyrone. Even Leonard is smart enough not to do some shit like this."

"Lord, have mercy. Tyrone Walker," Veola said. "Not in my wildest dreams would I have ever thought that he would do something this dumb—and to me! Look at what it's doing to his mama."

Then Veola figured the police realized what effect this was having on the people, so they said they were going to go down to the station and book him. Afterward, they would return to get any additional information.

"For now, Mrs. Cook, don't touch anything," the officer ordered.

"I'm not going to touch a thing, but I have to go inside my house," Veola said.

"Ma'am, we'd appreciate it if you'd wait until we take him downtown and we'd like to go in with you to assess any damages."

"That's fine, officer, but I can't just stand out here." Veola felt surely the police understood that.

Veola watched Eva Mae as the police car drove off. Finally, the crowd began to disperse, and Veola knew she had to say something to Eva Mae. "Eva Mae, try to calm down. When everybody leaves, we'll talk."

Eva Mae dried her tears, but more came. "Lord, what I am going to do?"

"Don't say nothing," Veola warned.

Carneda found Jeremy and told him that she'd go inside with him to get the boys' belongings.

"Tell your mother, I'll call her later, Jeremy," Veola told him. "You know I don't feel much like cooking now."

"I know that, Veola. Are you going to be all right?" Jeremy asked.

"I'm better now that I know who did it."

"I'm going to take Bobby home, and I'll be back to check on you."

"You don't have to come back. I'm all right, really." Veola hugged Jeremy and Bobby.

The crowd ambled back toward the churchhouse once the police car left. Veola thought all the excitement had left once the squad car headed downtown.

"Mama, I'm going to get the car. Kenny and Cameron are with me. We'll be right back," Carneda said. She left with her boys at her side.

Veola heard Carneda and nodded, yet she had to find Loretta again. "Loretta, I don't know how to thank you for what you've done. I have been so wrapped up trying to figure this out, that it was getting the best of me. Here I am thinking you've been hiding something from me, and you're the one who has to solve it for the rest of us. I'm so glad you didn't come to church."

"Miss Veola, are you ready for this? Tyrone wanted me to let him go because I knew him."

"No, he didn't?" Veola asked, stunned.

"Yes, he did."

Veola shook her head. She knew Tyrone was where he needed to be for now, but that didn't stop the fact that she still had to talk to her good sistah, Eva Mae. Veola noticed Jessie was talking to Eva Mae now, assuming Jessie was trying to ease her obvious hurting.

Veola found Fayetta.

"Maybe I can rest easier, now, Fayetta."

"I bet you can," Fayetta said. "I'm going to get on to my mama's house and pick up the kids. I know you're going to do what's best for you, but I have to tell you how badly I felt when I saw it was Tyrone. Wait 'til I see Leonard."

"Oh, Lord, tell Leonard I'm sorry."

"I'm sure he'll understand. I'll find him later, but right now, Tyrone's on my mind."

"Me, too, and that's why I have to go talk to Eva Mae."

"I know you do." Fayetta walked toward her mother's house.

Veola saw her yard was empty except for Eva Mae, Jessie, and Loretta.

"Loretta, I have to go inside and talk to Eva Mae right now. I'll come and get you in a minute."

"I'm not going anywhere, Miss Veola. I have to wait for the police to bring me back my pistol anyway."

"I didn't even know you had a gun."

"You either. You told me the other day when you told me about the break-in."

"Guess we learned a lot about each other, huh? I'll come and get you when the police come back."

Veola made her way to Eva Mae and Jessie. They were sitting in Veola's swing, still clad in their Sunday best. "Let's go inside."

"No, I don't want to," Eva Mae said.

"Come on, where we can talk," Veola suggested.

"Veola, I don't want to see what my child could have done to your house. Some things I just don't need right now," Eva Mae said.

"Eva Mae, this is not your fault. Tyrone breaking into my house ain't got nothing to do with you," Veola said. She leaned against her front porch column.

"He's back in trouble again. But this time he's gone too far. In your house, Veola. How ignant can you be?"

Jessie said nothing.

"Eva Mae," Veola began, "you've been through this before with Tyrone, and you know he gets himself in trouble on his own. You're the one that's got to be strong. You can love him no matter what, but you can't save him. He's gon' have to do that himself."

"Veola, I'm sitting here at your house, and here I am thinking about how this looks to me. I should be worried about you, what would have happened to you, how you could have been hurt, and I'm thinking about that boy of mine embarrassed me beyond belief by trying to steal from you."

Finally, Jessie chimed in. "He's grown, Eva Mae. You've done your part. He knows right from wrong."

"I know, but why you, Veola? Of all people."

"Sometimes you can get so caught up in mess like this, that you don't care who's connected to whom. That boy has a problem, his head ain't on straight, and you ain't got nothing to do with it."

"I just wish I could do something with him," Eva Mae said.

"You can't keep bailing him out, Eva Mae. That's what you have to quit doing," Veola said.

"Veola's right, Eva Mae," Jessie said.

"I'm not gon' do it, y'all. I can't. This time he's on his own. I've done all I can."

"Eva Mae, go home. Let's just be grateful that I didn't pull the trigger the other night. What in the world would that have done to us?"

Eva Mae clamped a hand over her mouth, her eyes filled with tears.

Veola continued. "The police will be back over here in a minute, and I'm going to have to go through my house. You're probably right. You don't need to be here when I do. We're going to get through this, but I need to handle my house and what has happened to me on my own. Jessie, can you help her?"

"I'm okay. I can make it home," Eva Mae said. She turned to Veola. "I'd better quit wanting to shoot everybody, huh?"

No one said a word.

"I'll walk with you if you want me to, Eva Mae," Jessie offered.

"No, I can make it home." Eva Mae reached down in her purse. "Here, Veola. These are yours. I didn't forget."

Veola took the preserves from Eva Mae, then watched her sistahs head to their houses. She noticed that Delphine was nowhere to be found. She must still be at her own church service, Veola thought. She assumed Eli's probably in that back bedroom with the TV blaring with no idea of what's happened.

Carneda and the boys drove up. "Mama," she began, "since the police are coming back, we're going to go get out of these clothes. We'll come back later."

Veola waved and the police car rolled up as Carneda pulled away. They went next door first and Veola saw them give back Loretta's gun.

Once inside, Veola waded carefully through everything and found only that she had been ransacked. Her shoes were everywhere, but nothing appeared to be missing. Her baubles were tossed around in her drawers, and she inspected her old jewelry box in her dresser. The hidden compartment had not been discovered. The old knife and the hundred-dollar bill, untouched. The gun was hidden under the bed, locked in a metal box of letters in anticipation of the boys' visit.

The police didn't have much to take or report since nothing appeared to have been stolen. They went to the outside window with Veola and put her screen back in place. They made sure the window could be re-locked. They told her to go through everything and make sure nothing was missing, and if she found something later, she could always report it. The police said that there had been other robberies that Tyrone was being questioned about, so it was most likely he would be there at least through the night.

Veola did not want to talk anymore about Tyrone. What she knew could put Tyrone behind bars for a while, and she knew what that would do to Eva Mae. Now her nerves were rattled, so she had to get out of the house. She went outside to check the security of all of her windows. She noticed Ruben Earl's truck coming down the street, and she waved him down.

"Ruben Earl, Loretta caught Tyrone breaking into my house."
"When?"
"Right when church service was ending."
"I drove to the farm right afterward and missed all that?"
"I'm glad you did. But Tyrone is in jail right now as we speak."
"Maybe now you can rest. Eva Mae know?"
"Yeah, she knows. She'll be all right. Give her time."
"I'm going to the house and come back a little more presentable. Every time you see me I'm always looking a mess, unless it's at church. I'm trying to change that."
"Well, when you want to be seen, you'll come back," Veola

joked. "Ruben Earl, I forgot to eat. There's dinner in there in case you want to eat later."

"You always feeding me. I'll come by and for a change, I won't be in your pots and pans begging for a meal."

"Don't you worry about that. If you weren't welcome at my table, you'd know it."

Ruben Earl left.

Veola had no appetite for her roast, but she managed to throw something down. Here she was relieved of finding out her burglar had been caught, but it almost made her feel worse that it was Tyrone.

Jeremy returned. "I had no idea Tyrone was up to robbery, Veola."

"Me either.

"You were right about him. I'm through with him and that stuff, too."

"Praise God, Jeremy. Seems like everybody has had something they're trying to hide."

"Speaking of hiding, last night, Dad threw Mom a surprise birthday dinner at the Simpsons, and Mrs. Simpson is the one who I thought he was sneaking around with. She and Dad were planning the surprise."

"I'm so glad Dr. Barton is doing some good these days. Have y'all talked?"

"Last night and today. I brought you something." Jeremy passed Veola a sack.

"What's this?" Veola asked.

"I went back out to your property, and this might interest you."

Veola pulled out the tree bark and held it. She saw Ervin's name. "Lord, Lord, Lord. I don't know what to say."

"I don't know what you would need it for, but I wanted to find the missing part."

"This had been out there for years, Jeremy, and only upon occasion did I ever think about it. Just when I thought it could be gone, I wanted it. Maybe I've tried to hold onto something much too long." Veola's voice cracked, tears welled in her eyes.

"At least you have it back to do whatever you want with it. I'm sure Mom and Dad will pick your brain tomorrow about everything that's happened."

"You know they will. Thanks, Jeremy. This time, you've helped me." She hugged Jeremy, drying her eyes in the process.

They said goodbye and Veola decided to freshen up a bit—not necessarily for Ruben Earl, but for her. She returned outside to her swing.

In a few minutes, Ruben Earl drove up, and Veola moved from the center of her swing to one end. He was neatly dressed, and his shirt had no wasted oil, dirt, grease, or food on it. He even had on some good smell-good—Brut or English Leather. She recognized it from the bottles in Dr. Barton's bathroom.

"Ruben Earl, you almost look like you're going back to church. You dressed up twice today. Sit down," Veola directed, patting her cushioned seat. She'd left him plenty of room.

He sat in the swing, starting a slight sway. "Veola, we've been knowing each other for almost forty years." He looked straight ahead.

"Has it been that long? I guess it has," Veola said, facing the same direction, her hands clasped in her lap.

"I think you know more about me than anyone else in this town."

"Don't say that."

"Well, it's true. I don't let a whole lot of people in my business, Veola, including the pastor."

"What are you trying to say?" She met his eyes.

"This is hard for me, because I'm not used to this kind of talk. I want to be able to spend a little more time with you. That's all." He placed his right hand over hers.

She stared at him and he stared back.

At that moment, Veola knew what he felt. She saw it in his eyes. She felt it with the weight of his hand covering hers. "Come inside." She knew someone could be watching and sharing this special moment; she wanted privacy.

They moved into the living room, and she locked the storm door.

"Come over here and sit down," Veola said, leading the way to the couch.

He followed and obliged.

"Ruben Earl, I can't think of anyone else I'd rather spend time with outside of Jessie and Eva Mae. And you know I can't get rid of them. I realize you're talking 'bout something different, for I see it in your eyes. I never thought I would get involved with someone again. Sometimes I think I'm too old to spend time with a man. I've kept something in my heart for a long time, maybe too long, and I think I may have a reason to get over that."

"I'm not asking for your heart, Veola. I just want a little of your time."

"But you're making me realize something. I got a whiff of you 'fo you hit my porch, and I like giving you a reason to get cleaned up. I can't do anything too fast, because this is new for me at my age. Let's take this slow.

"I didn't say nothing about taking anything fast." He chuckled.

"Some people told me you might be feeling this way, and I refused to believe it. I didn't think much about it, because I wouldn't want anything to affect you being my good friend. And besides, how you know I can start courting at this age?"

"We're not gon' plan this like that, Veola. That would be too hard to do, and neither one of us wants to upset our friendship. It's just that every now and then, I would rather be somewhere sitting and talking with you than with someone else."

"Oh Lord, Ruben Earl, you're scaring me."

"There's no reason to be scared. Like right now on a Sunday evening, I want to go get me an ice cream sandwich down at the corner store. If it was a weeknight, then I'd go to the Dairy Queen for an ice cream cone. The point is, I'd be going down there by myself, and I'm getting kind of tired of doing that. I want to take you with me. Buy you one, too."

She realized he was trying his best to ease through this most serious conversation. "Ruben Earl, I don't know what I'm going to do with you, but while you are in the mood for an ice cream sandwich, I'll get my purse."

"You don't have to get your purse." Ruben Earl pulled Veola close, grabbing both of her hands. "Veola, I want to be more than just a friend."

She lightly tapped Ruben Earl on his chest. "You know you ain't quite right, but I knew that already." She smiled at him. "Do I look all right?" Veola asked as she ran a hand over her hair and dress.

"Trust me, you look fine. We're just going to the store."

"To you, we're just going to the store, but to me, somebody special's gon' buy me an ice cream sandwich. I'll get my keys."

Veola passed by the shoes and hats Tyrone threw all over the place and realized all of that could wait. Someone in her living room was waiting to take her to a place where she had not been in a long time—not the convenience store, but somewhere in her heart.

When they got to the passenger side of the truck, he opened the door for her like he always did.

Veola climbed up into his truck and after he got in and started down the road, he glanced over at her.

She stared ahead feeling his eyes upon her. As many times as she'd ridden in his truck, only now did she worry about him driving too fast. She questioned herself on what she really meant by that.

Don't you take me too fast, Ruben Earl.

Hallelujah, what a week!

Questions for Discussion

1. What character did you most identify with and why?

2. Does the Barton family remind you of families you have known? How did that family's lack of communication contribute to difficulty between family members?

3. Did you have a grandmother with traits like Veola? What role did she play in your life?

4. Did you have a family member who acted as a surrogate mother or grandmother? How did their comfort and guidance shape your decision-making?

5. Do the men in the story remind you of men you know or have known in the past? Do you have empathy for Tyrone? For Dr. Barton? For Ruben Earl?

6. How do each of the women in Veola's neighborhood (Eva Mae, Jessie, Delphine, and Loretta) benefit from the friendships they share? In what ways do your friendships provide similar benefits to you?

7. Did you expect Veola to shoot the intruder? Why or why not?

8. Do you think Fayetta will stay away from Leonard in the future? Why or why not? What plights do single mothers of today share with Fayetta?

9. Describe the relationship between Veola and Ruben Earl. What specific events happened to change or strengthen their bond?

The following questions address significant social issues that arise
in
LIGHT BREAD:

10. Why do you think the author chose to set this story in 1967? What took place in the United States that year that contributes to the conflict in the story?

11. Jeremy experiments with the recreational drugs of his time. How has recreational drug use and society's attitude toward the use of recreational drugs changed since 1967? Why do you think these changes have occurred?

12. Recall your first friendship with a person of another race. Describe the person and your feeling for them. What is your response to Veola and her close relationship with the Bartons? What is your response to the friendship that developed between Cameron and Bobby?

13. Which characters were uncomfortable interacting with other racial groups? Why do you think they felt that way? Which characters in the story held more positive views of other racial groups? Why do you think they felt that way?

14. When Mr. Edelson loses his temper with Veola, Jeremy defends her. Did Jeremy's action surprise you? Have you ever experienced prejudice? What type was it: racial, religious, social class, gender, other? How did it make you feel? How did you react?

15. In the late 1960s, laws were passed to open schools, jobs, and other institutions to people of all races and ethnicities without restriction. These laws, often collectively referred to as "integration," are now a common part of life in America. How has integration affected you?

LIGHT BREAD

266